middlewest

IMAGE COMICS, INC. ROBERT KIRKMAN: Chief Operating Officer • ERIK LARSEN: Chief Financial Officer • TODD McFARLANE: President • MARC SILVESTRI: Chief Executive Officer • JIM VALENTINO: Vice President • ERIC STEPHENSON: Publisher/Chief Creative Officer • COREY HART: Director of Sales • JEFF BOISON: Director of Publishing Planning & Book Trade Sales • CHRIS ROSS: Director of Digital Sales • JEFF STANG: Director of Specialty Sales • KAT SALAZAR: Director of PR & Marketing • DREW GILL: Art Director • HEATHER DOORNINK: Production Director • NICOLE LAPALME: Controller **IMAGECOMICS.COM**

MIDDLEWEST, BOOK 1. First printing. May 2019. Published by Image Comics, Inc. Office of publication: 2701 NW Vaughn St., Suite 780, Portland, OR 97210. Copyright © 2019 Skottie Young & Jorge Corona. All rights reserved. Contains material originally published in single magazine form as MIDDLEWEST #1-6. "MIDDLEWEST," its logos, and the likenesses of all characters herein are trademarks of Skottie Young & Jorge Corona, unless otherwise noted. "Image" and the Image Comics logos are registered trademarks of Image Comics, Inc. No part of this publication may be reproduced or transmitted, in any form or by any means (except for short excerpts for journalistic or review purposes), without the express written permission of Skottie Young & Jorge Corona, or Image Comics, Inc. All names, characters, events, and locales in this publication are entirely fictional. Any resemblance to actual persons (living or dead), events, or places, without satirical intent, is coincidental. Printed in the USA. For information regarding the CPSIA on this printed material call: 203-595-3636. For international rights, contact: foreignlicensing@imagecomics.com. ISBN: 978-1-5343-1217-3 THIRD EYE EXCLUSIVE COVER ISBN: 978-1-5343-1448-1

SKOTTIE YOUNG

ART

JORGE CORONA

COLORS

JEAN-FRANCOIS BEAULIEU

LETTERING

NATE PIEKOS OF BLAMBOT

COVER ART

JORGE CORONA &
JEAN-FRANCOIS BEAULIEU

EDITOR

KENT WAGENSCHUTZ

DESIGN

CAREY HALL

CHAPTER
ONE

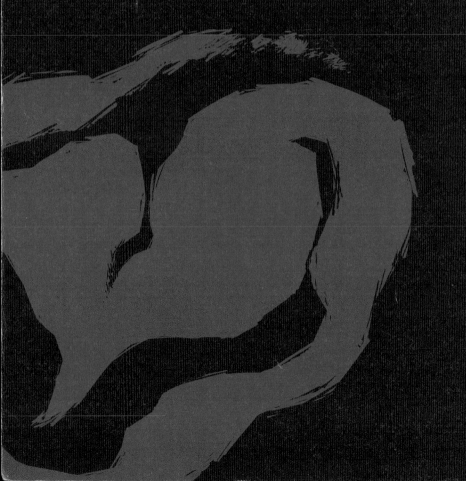

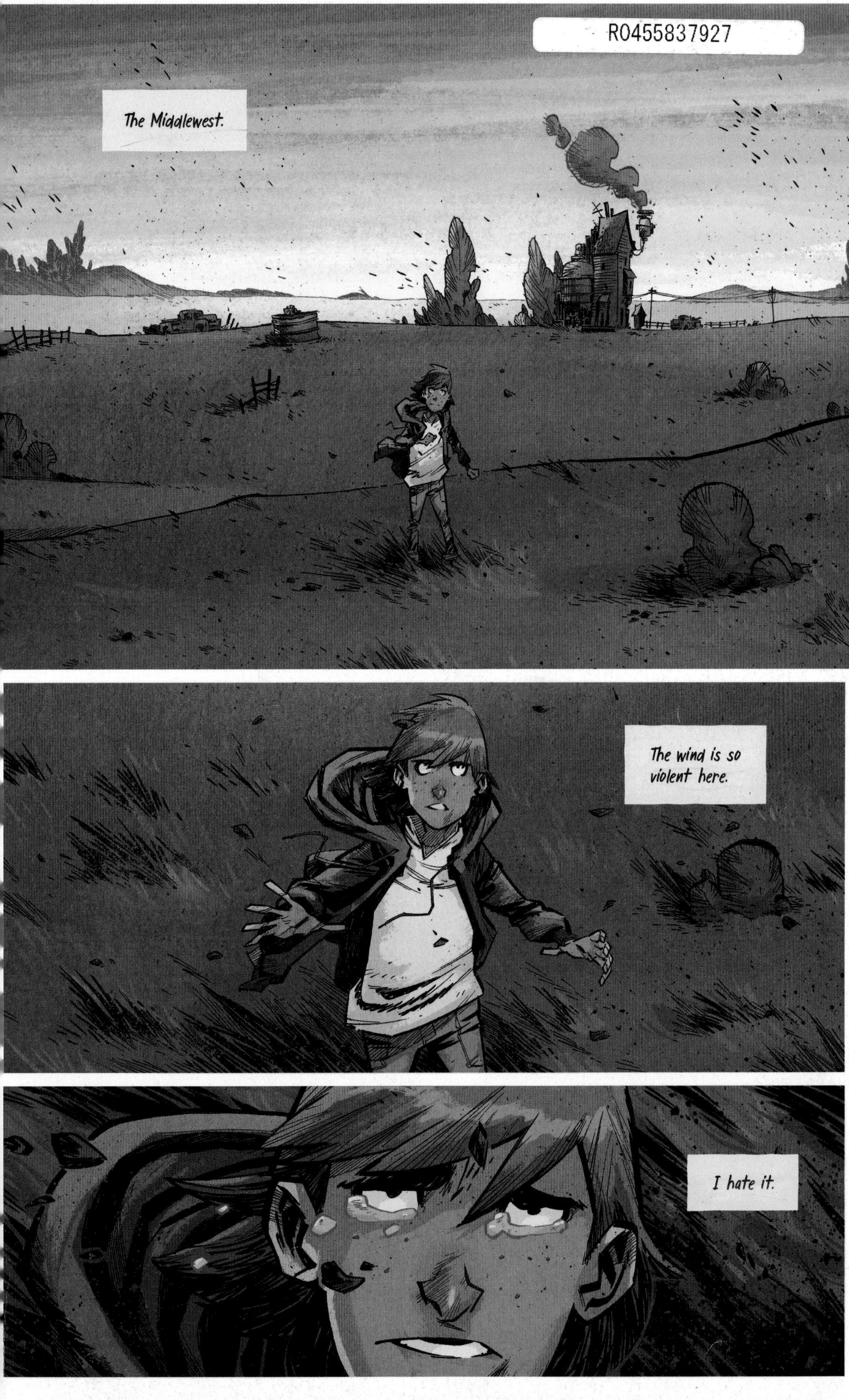
The Middlewest.
The wind is so violent here.
I hate it.

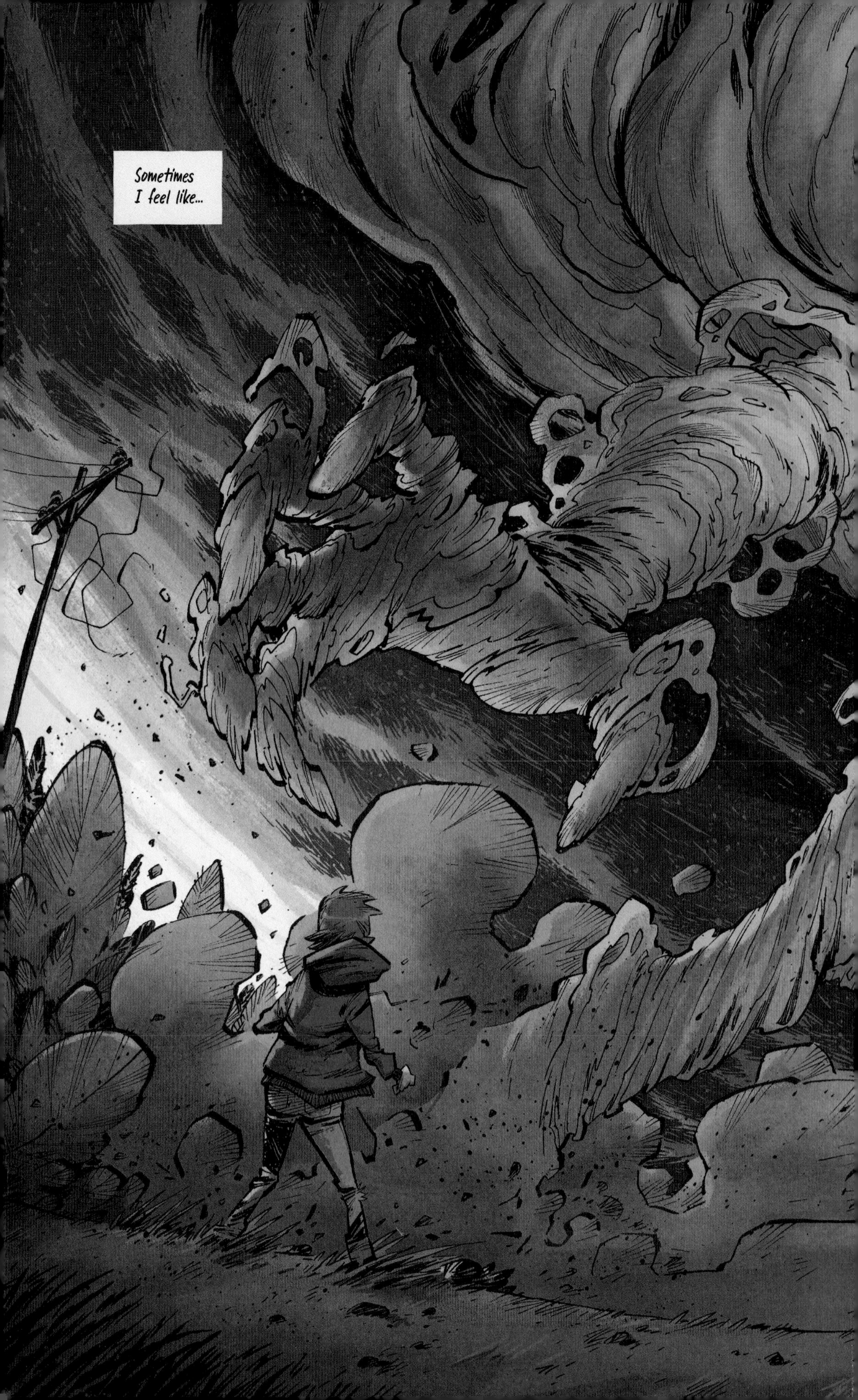
Sometimes
I feel like...

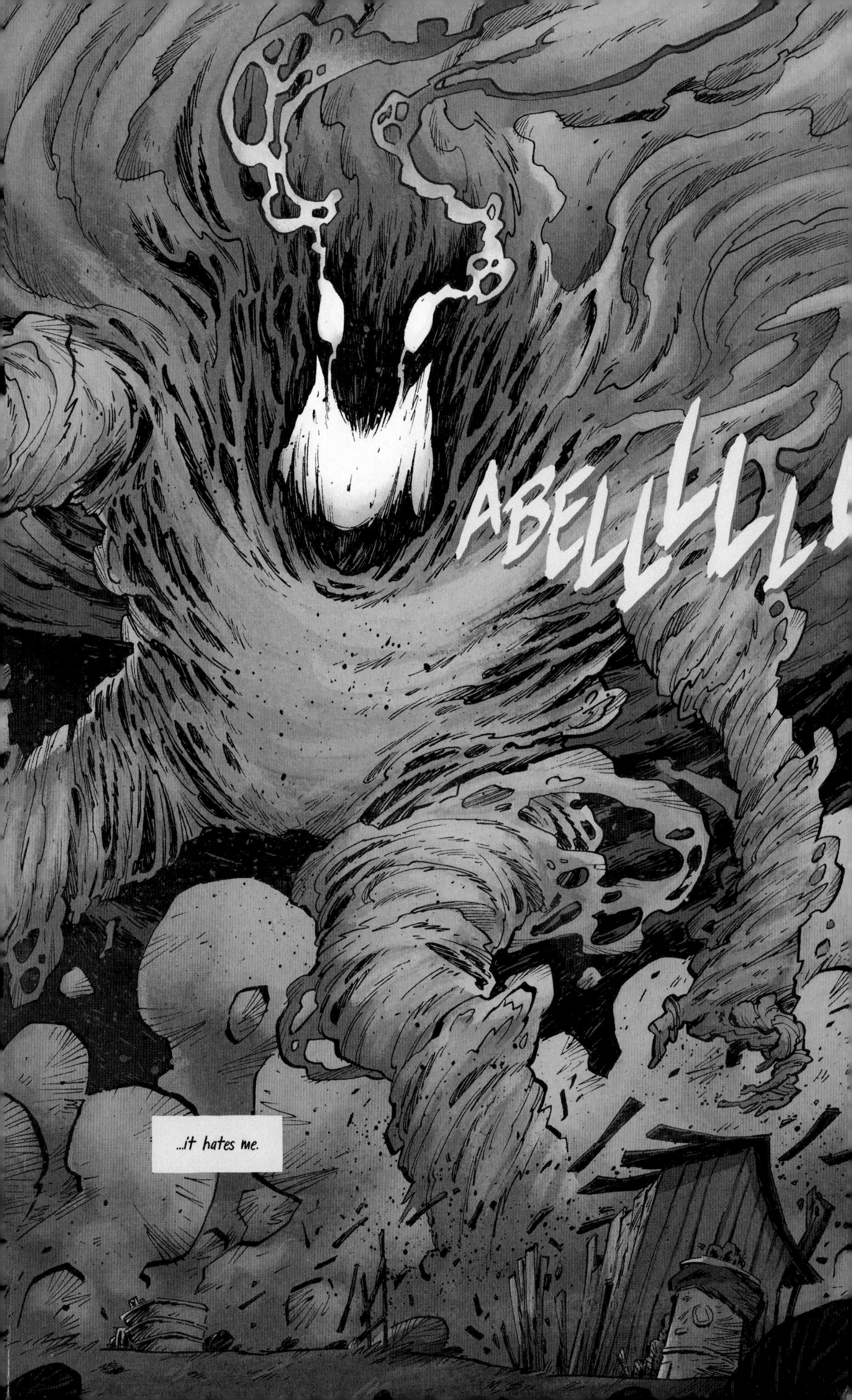
ABELLLLLL
...it hates me.

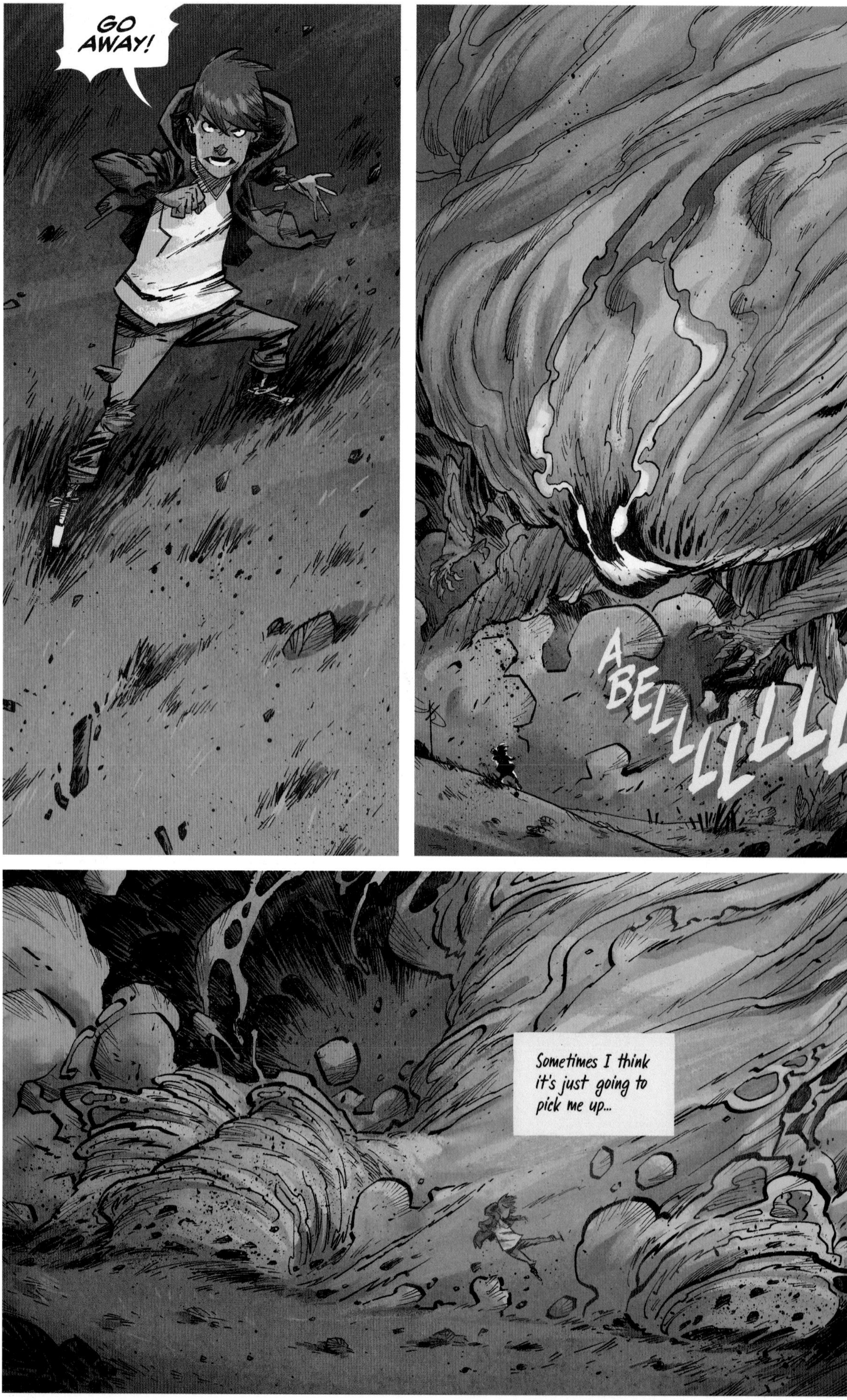
GO AWAY!
ABELLLLLLLL
Sometimes I think it's just going to pick me up...

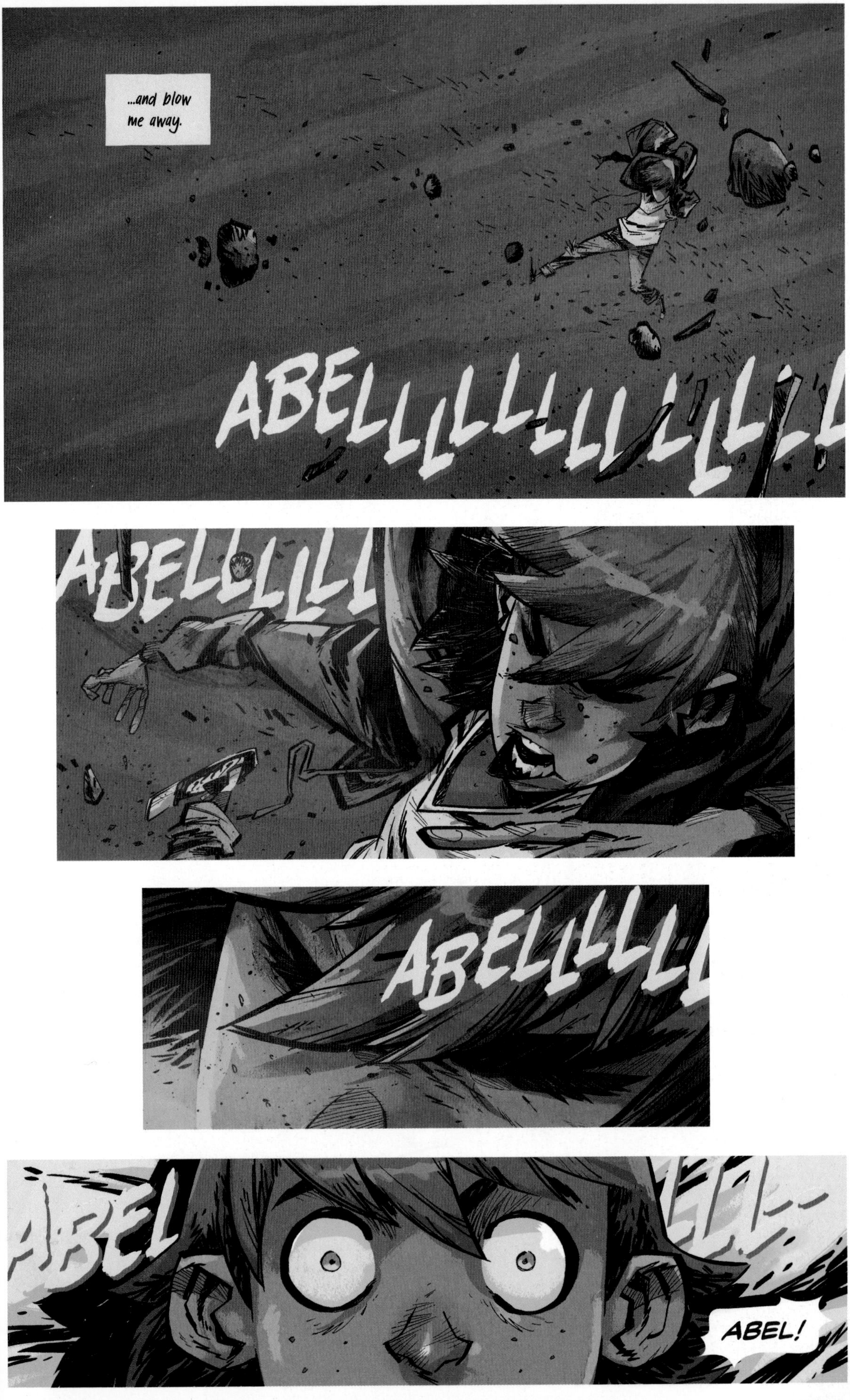
...and blow me away.
ABELLLLLLLLLLLL
ABELLLLLL
ABELLLLLL
ABEL
LLL
ABEL!

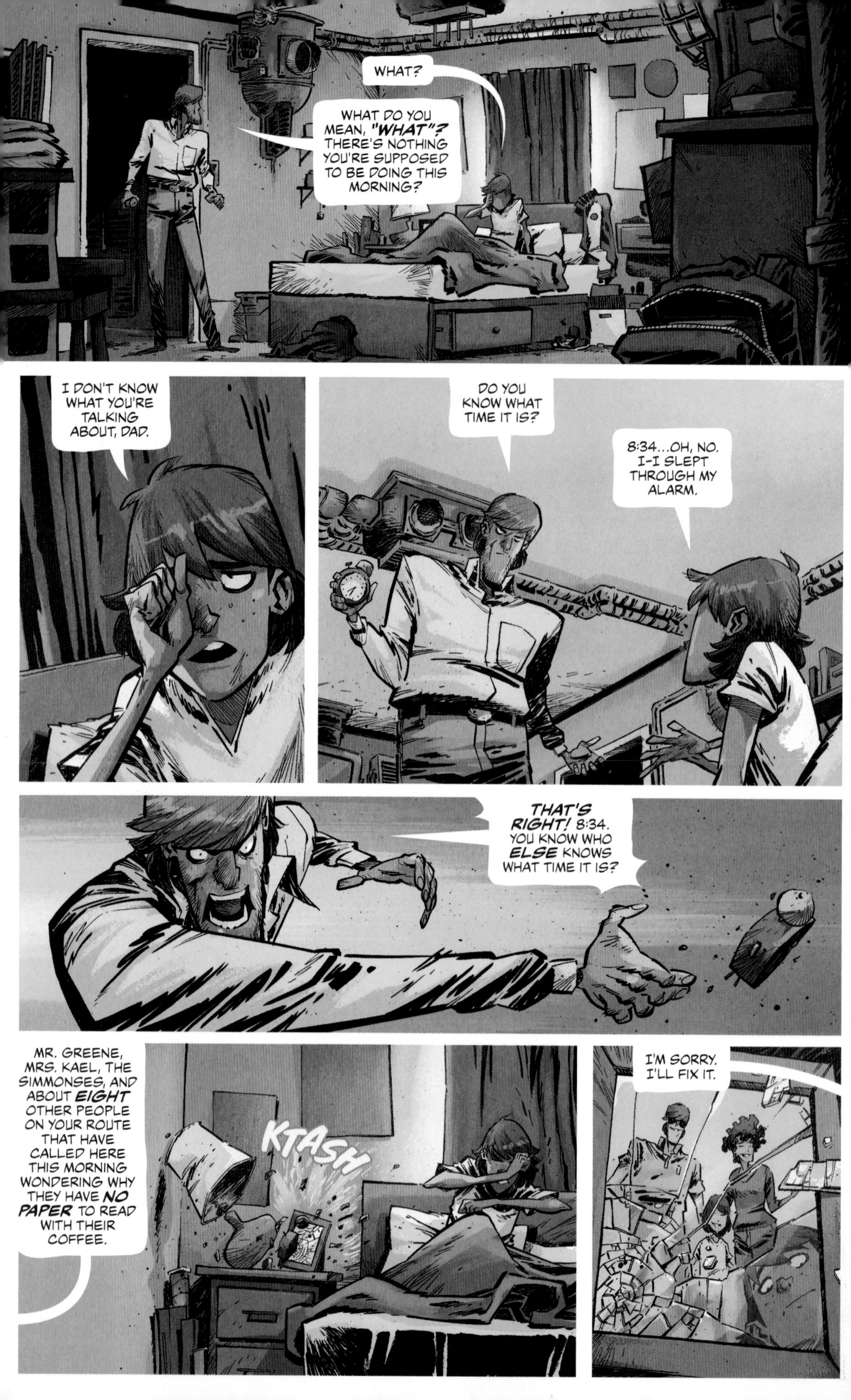
WHAT?
WHAT DO YOU MEAN, "WHAT"? THERE'S NOTHING YOU'RE SUPPOSED TO BE DOING THIS MORNING?
I DON'T KNOW WHAT YOU'RE TALKING ABOUT, DAD.
DO YOU KNOW WHAT TIME IT IS?
8:34...OH, NO. I-I SLEPT THROUGH MY ALARM.
THAT'S RIGHT! 8:34. YOU KNOW WHO ELSE KNOWS WHAT TIME IT IS?
MR. GREENE, MRS. KAEL, THE SIMMONSES, AND ABOUT EIGHT OTHER PEOPLE ON YOUR ROUTE THAT HAVE CALLED HERE THIS MORNING WONDERING WHY THEY HAVE NO PAPER TO READ WITH THEIR COFFEE.
KTASH
I'M SORRY. I'LL FIX IT.

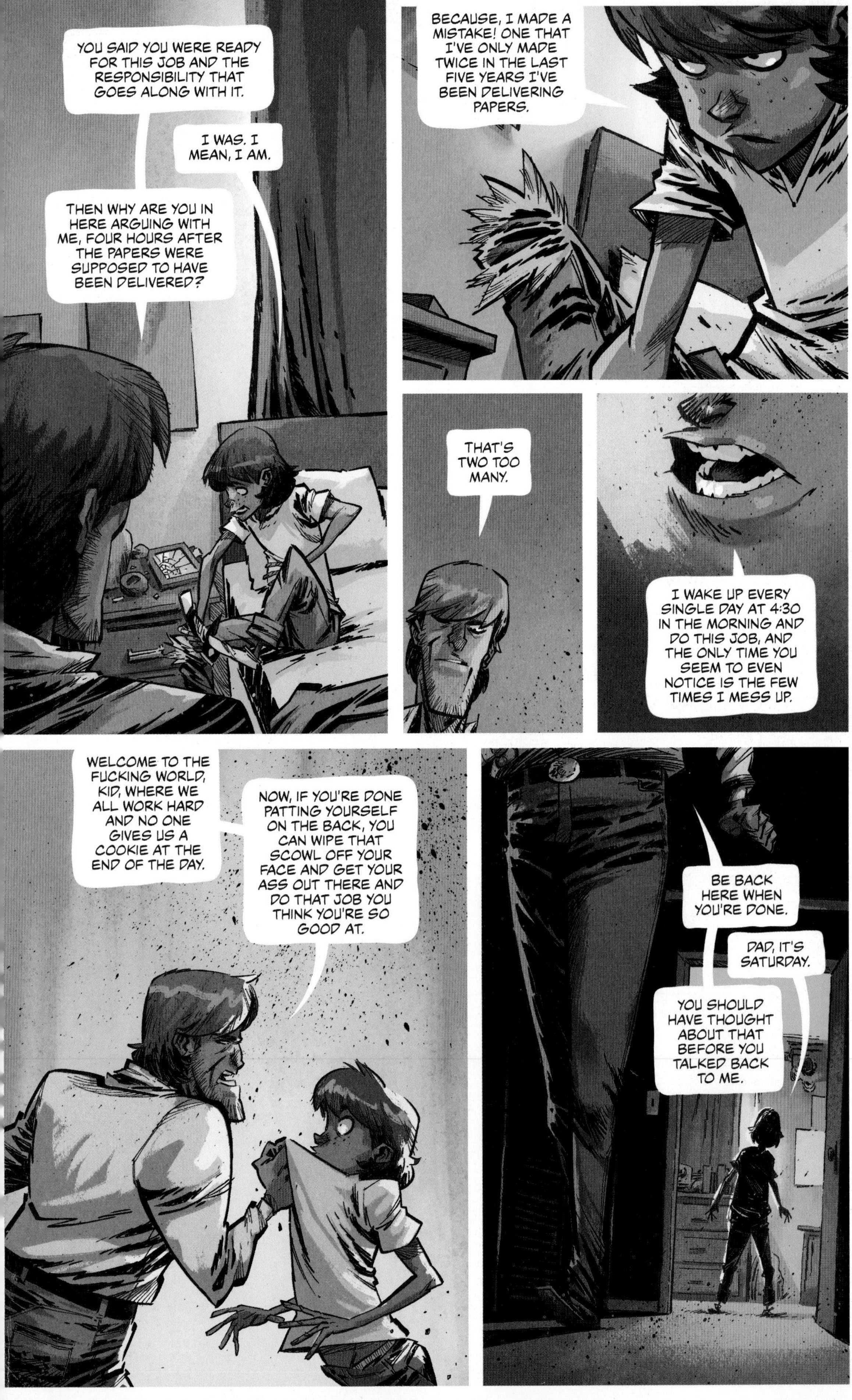

YOU SAID YOU WERE READY FOR THIS JOB AND THE RESPONSIBILITY THAT GOES ALONG WITH IT.
I WAS. I MEAN, I AM.
THEN WHY ARE YOU IN HERE ARGUING WITH ME, FOUR HOURS AFTER THE PAPERS WERE SUPPOSED TO HAVE BEEN DELIVERED?
BECAUSE, I MADE A MISTAKE! ONE THAT I'VE ONLY MADE TWICE IN THE LAST FIVE YEARS I'VE BEEN DELIVERING PAPERS.
THAT'S TWO TOO MANY.
I WAKE UP EVERY SINGLE DAY AT 4:30 IN THE MORNING AND DO THIS JOB, AND THE ONLY TIME YOU SEEM TO EVEN NOTICE IS THE FEW TIMES I MESS UP.
WELCOME TO THE FUCKING WORLD, KID, WHERE WE ALL WORK HARD AND NO ONE GIVES US A COOKIE AT THE END OF THE DAY.
NOW, IF YOU'RE DONE PATTING YOURSELF ON THE BACK, YOU CAN WIPE THAT SCOWL OFF YOUR FACE AND GET YOUR ASS OUT THERE AND DO THAT JOB YOU THINK YOU'RE SO GOOD AT.
BE BACK HERE WHEN YOU'RE DONE.
DAD, IT'S SATURDAY.
YOU SHOULD HAVE THOUGHT ABOUT THAT BEFORE YOU TALKED BACK TO ME.

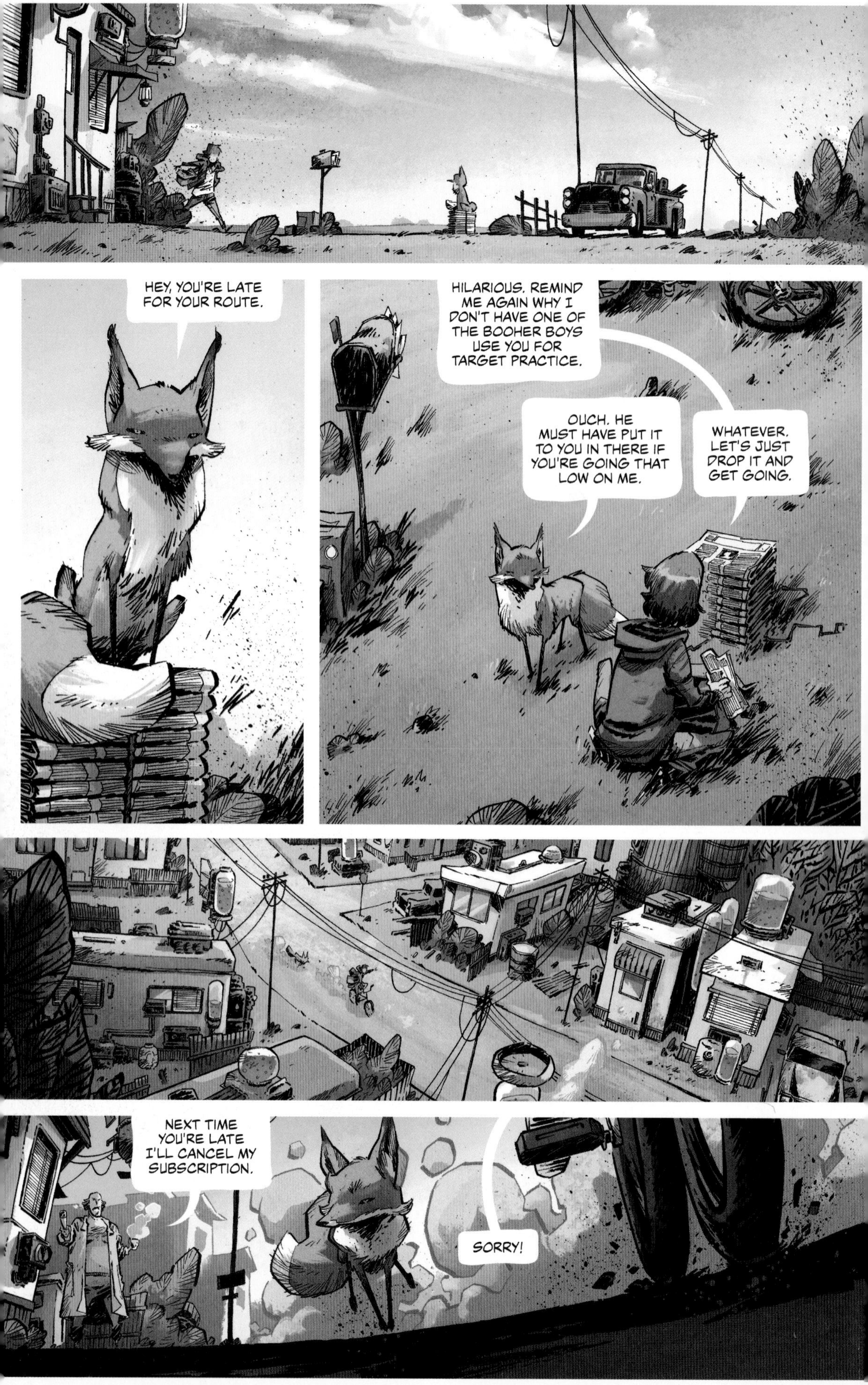
HEY, YOU'RE LATE FOR YOUR ROUTE.
HILARIOUS. REMIND ME AGAIN WHY I DON'T HAVE ONE OF THE BOOHER BOYS USE YOU FOR TARGET PRACTICE.
OUCH. HE MUST HAVE PUT IT TO YOU IN THERE IF YOU'RE GOING THAT LOW ON ME.
WHATEVER. LET'S JUST DROP IT AND GET GOING.
NEXT TIME YOU'RE LATE I'LL CANCEL MY SUBSCRIPTION.
SORRY!

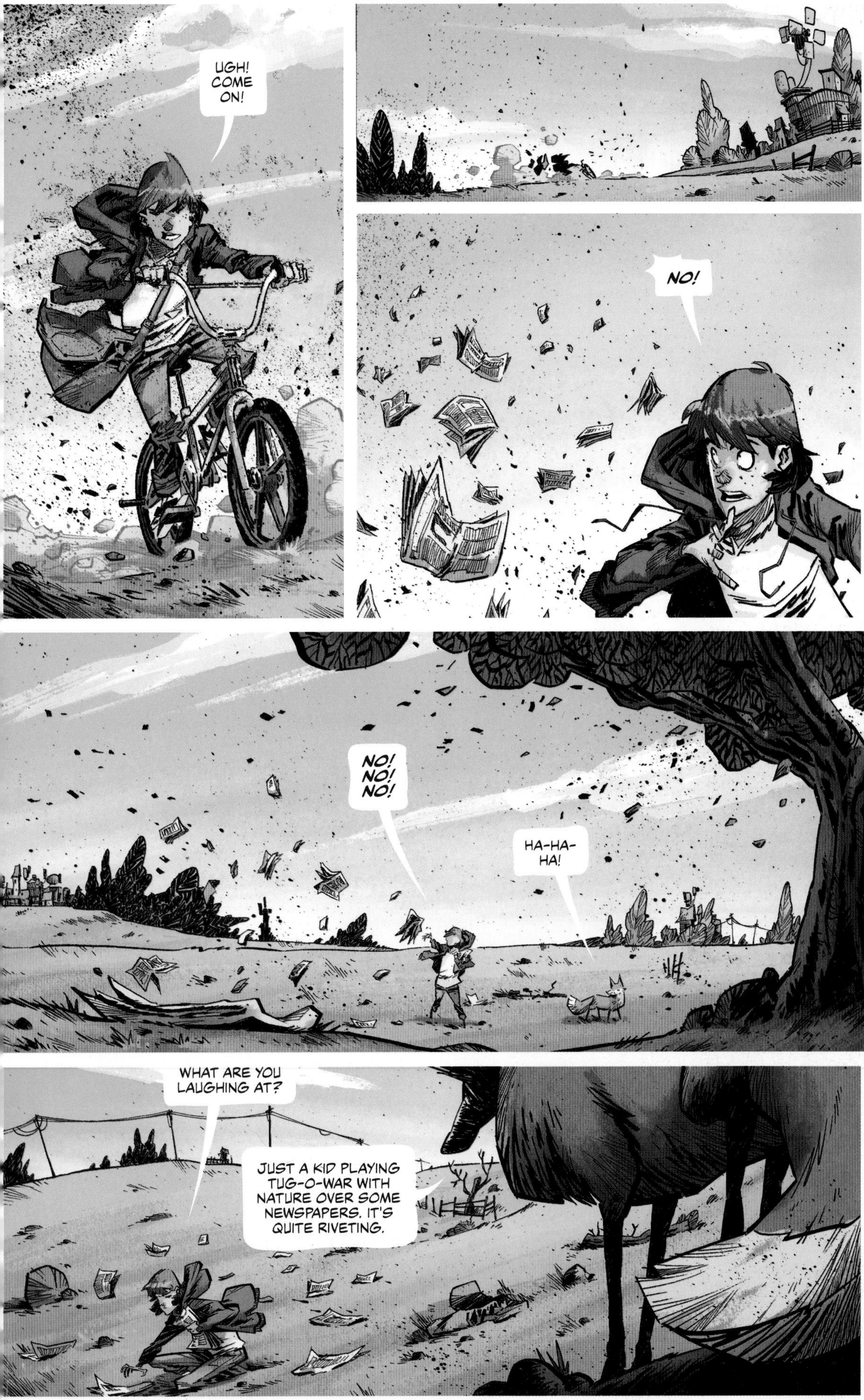
UGH! COME ON!
NO!
NO! NO! NO!
HA-HA-HA!
WHAT ARE YOU LAUGHING AT?
JUST A KID PLAYING TUG-O-WAR WITH NATURE OVER SOME NEWSPAPERS. IT'S QUITE RIVETING.

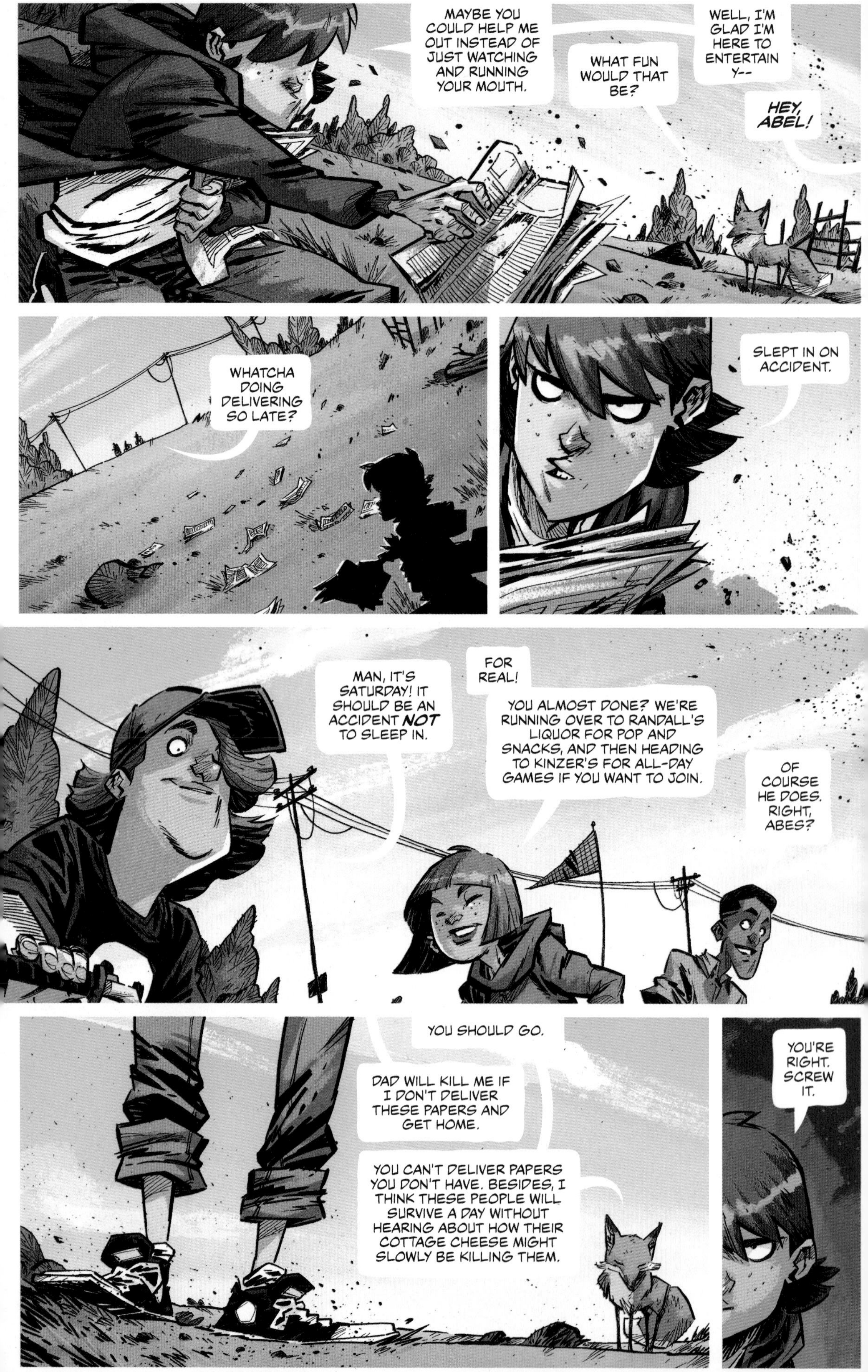
MAYBE YOU COULD HELP ME OUT INSTEAD OF JUST WATCHING AND RUNNING YOUR MOUTH.
WHAT FUN WOULD THAT BE?
WELL, I'M GLAD I'M HERE TO ENTERTAIN Y--
HEY, ABEL!
WHATCHA DOING DELIVERING SO LATE?
SLEPT IN ON ACCIDENT.
MAN, IT'S SATURDAY! IT SHOULD BE AN ACCIDENT NOT TO SLEEP IN.
FOR REAL!
YOU ALMOST DONE? WE'RE RUNNING OVER TO RANDALL'S LIQUOR FOR POP AND SNACKS, AND THEN HEADING TO KINZER'S FOR ALL-DAY GAMES IF YOU WANT TO JOIN.
OF COURSE HE DOES. RIGHT, ABES?
YOU SHOULD GO.
DAD WILL KILL ME IF I DON'T DELIVER THESE PAPERS AND GET HOME.
YOU CAN'T DELIVER PAPERS YOU DON'T HAVE. BESIDES, I THINK THESE PEOPLE WILL SURVIVE A DAY WITHOUT HEARING ABOUT HOW THEIR COTTAGE CHEESE MIGHT SLOWLY BE KILLING THEM.
YOU'RE RIGHT. SCREW IT.

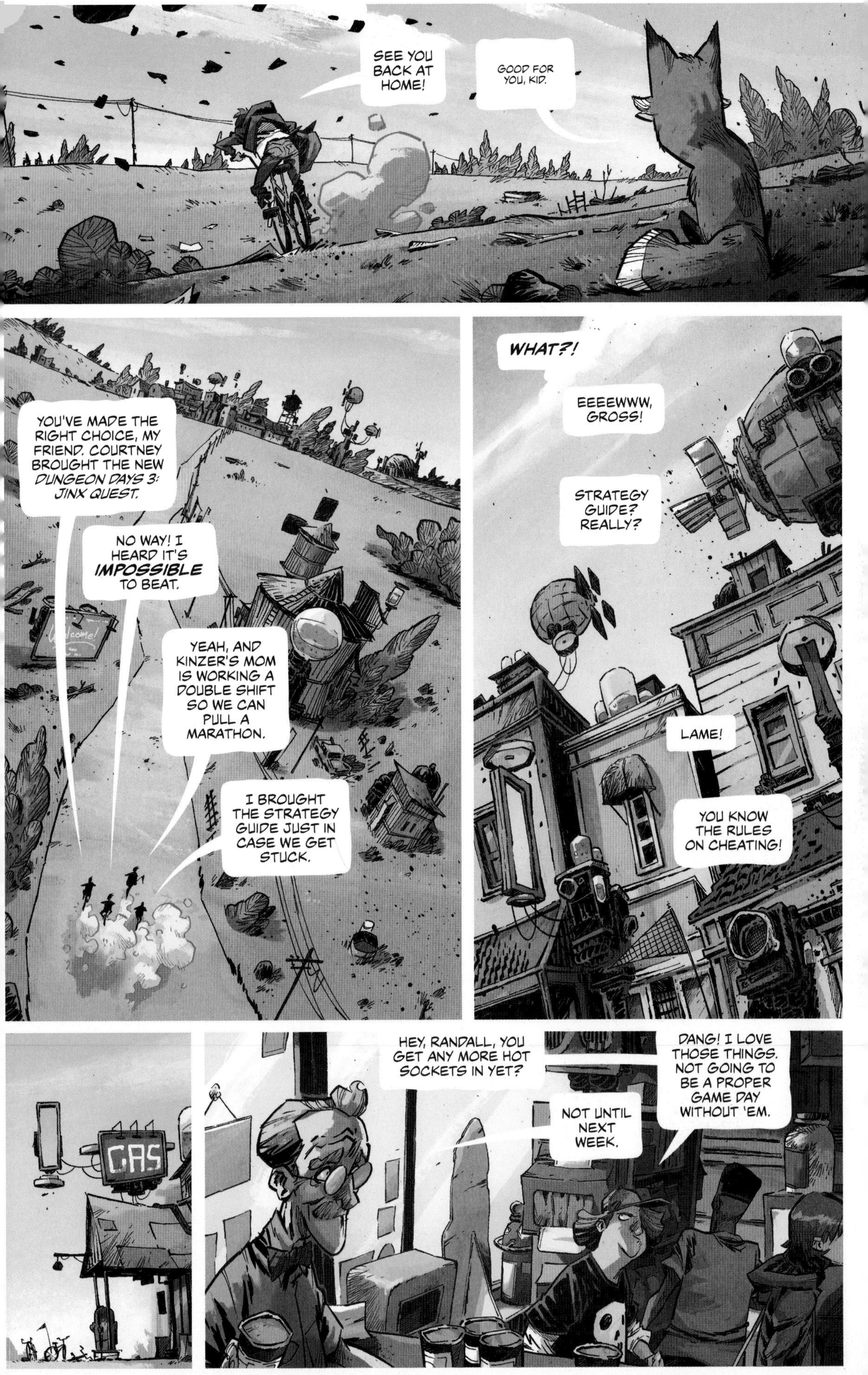

SEE YOU BACK AT HOME!
GOOD FOR YOU, KID.
YOU'VE MADE THE RIGHT CHOICE, MY FRIEND. COURTNEY BROUGHT THE NEW *DUNGEON DAYS 3: JINX QUEST.*
NO WAY! I HEARD IT'S ***IMPOSSIBLE*** TO BEAT.
YEAH, AND KINZER'S MOM IS WORKING A DOUBLE SHIFT SO WE CAN PULL A MARATHON.
I BROUGHT THE STRATEGY GUIDE JUST IN CASE WE GET STUCK.
WHAT?!
EEEEWWW, GROSS!
STRATEGY GUIDE? REALLY?
LAME!
YOU KNOW THE RULES ON CHEATING!
GAS
HEY, RANDALL, YOU GET ANY MORE HOT SOCKETS IN YET?
NOT UNTIL NEXT WEEK.
DANG! I LOVE THOSE THINGS. NOT GOING TO BE A PROPER GAME DAY WITHOUT 'EM.

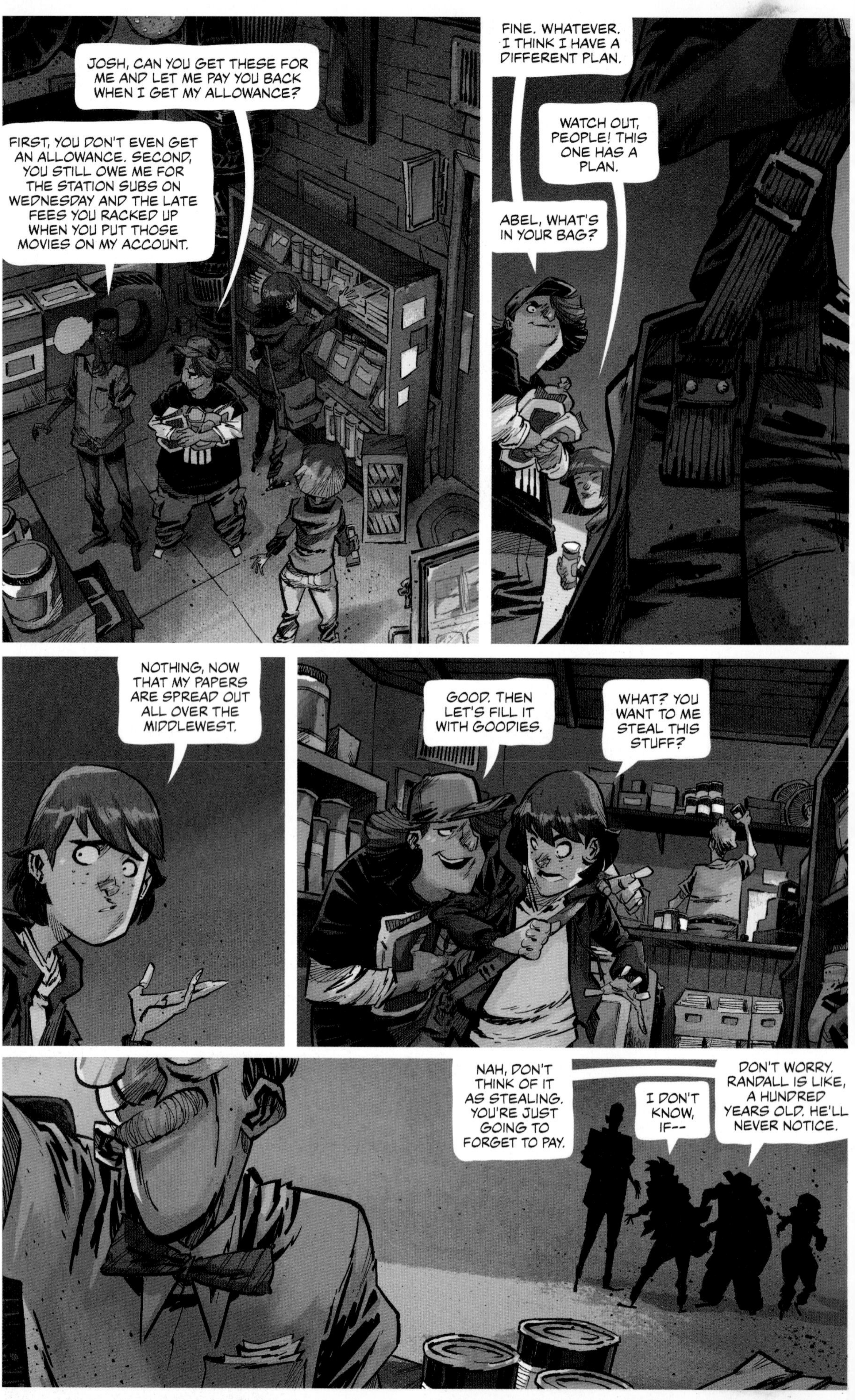
JOSH, CAN YOU GET THESE FOR ME AND LET ME PAY YOU BACK WHEN I GET MY ALLOWANCE?
FIRST, YOU DON'T EVEN GET AN ALLOWANCE. SECOND, YOU STILL OWE ME FOR THE STATION SUBS ON WEDNESDAY AND THE LATE FEES YOU RACKED UP WHEN YOU PUT THOSE MOVIES ON MY ACCOUNT.
FINE. WHATEVER. I THINK I HAVE A DIFFERENT PLAN.
WATCH OUT, PEOPLE! THIS ONE HAS A PLAN.
ABEL, WHAT'S IN YOUR BAG?
NOTHING, NOW THAT MY PAPERS ARE SPREAD OUT ALL OVER THE MIDDLEWEST.
GOOD. THEN LET'S FILL IT WITH GOODIES.
WHAT? YOU WANT TO ME STEAL THIS STUFF?
NAH, DON'T THINK OF IT AS STEALING. YOU'RE JUST GOING TO FORGET TO PAY.
I DON'T KNOW, IF--
DON'T WORRY. RANDALL IS LIKE, A HUNDRED YEARS OLD. HE'LL NEVER NOTICE.

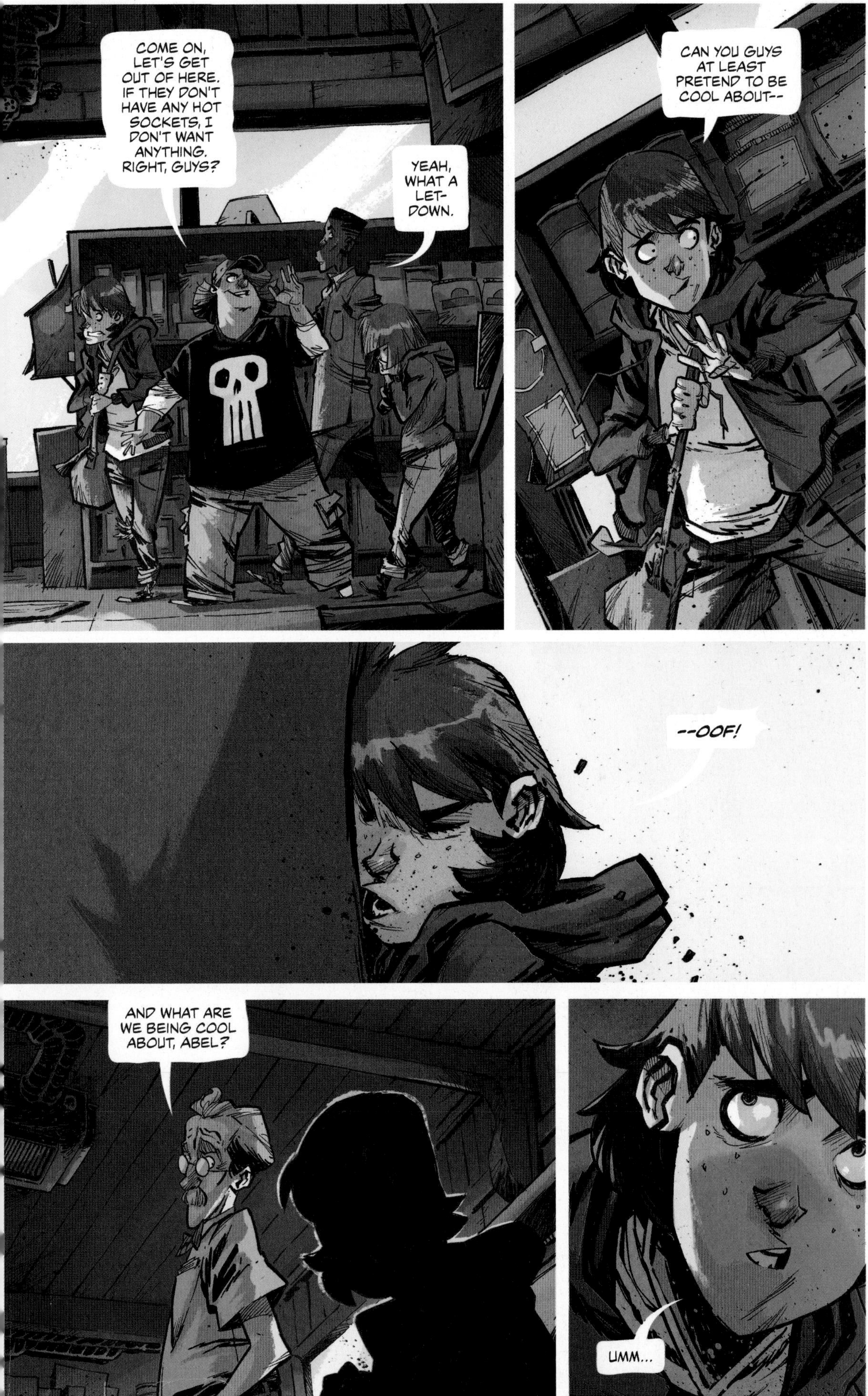
COME ON, LET'S GET OUT OF HERE. IF THEY DON'T HAVE ANY HOT SOCKETS, I DON'T WANT ANYTHING. RIGHT, GUYS?
YEAH, WHAT A LET-DOWN.
CAN YOU GUYS AT LEAST PRETEND TO BE COOL ABOUT--
--OOF!
AND WHAT ARE WE BEING COOL ABOUT, ABEL?
UMM...

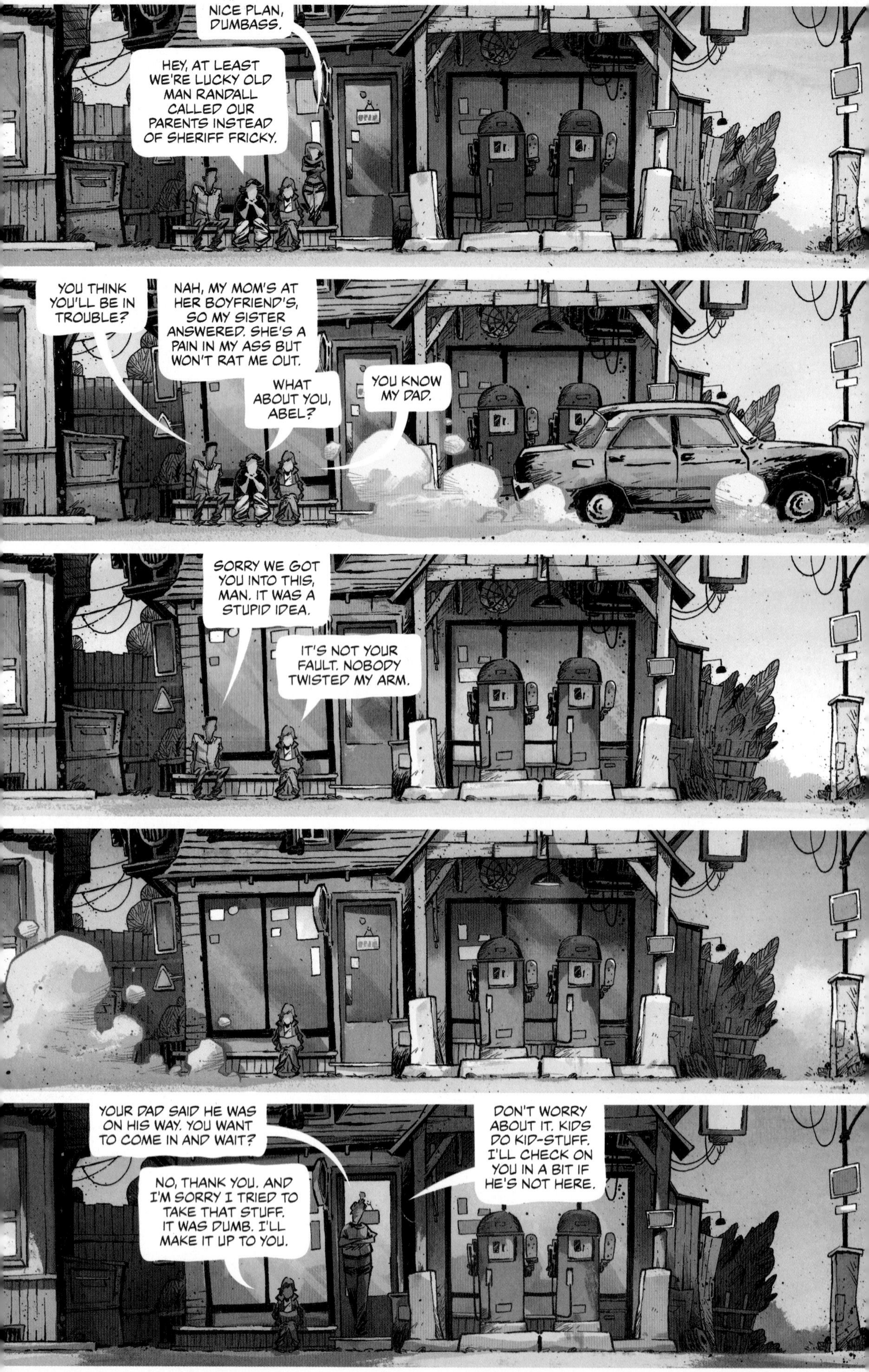
NICE PLAN, DUMBASS.
HEY, AT LEAST WE'RE LUCKY OLD MAN RANDALL CALLED OUR PARENTS INSTEAD OF SHERIFF FRICKY.
YOU THINK YOU'LL BE IN TROUBLE?
NAH, MY MOM'S AT HER BOYFRIEND'S, SO MY SISTER ANSWERED. SHE'S A PAIN IN MY ASS BUT WON'T RAT ME OUT.
WHAT ABOUT YOU, ABEL?
YOU KNOW MY DAD.
SORRY WE GOT YOU INTO THIS, MAN. IT WAS A STUPID IDEA.
IT'S NOT YOUR FAULT. NOBODY TWISTED MY ARM.
YOUR DAD SAID HE WAS ON HIS WAY. YOU WANT TO COME IN AND WAIT?
NO, THANK YOU. AND I'M SORRY I TRIED TO TAKE THAT STUFF. IT WAS DUMB. I'LL MAKE IT UP TO YOU.
DON'T WORRY ABOUT IT. KIDS DO KID-STUFF. I'LL CHECK ON YOU IN A BIT IF HE'S NOT HERE.

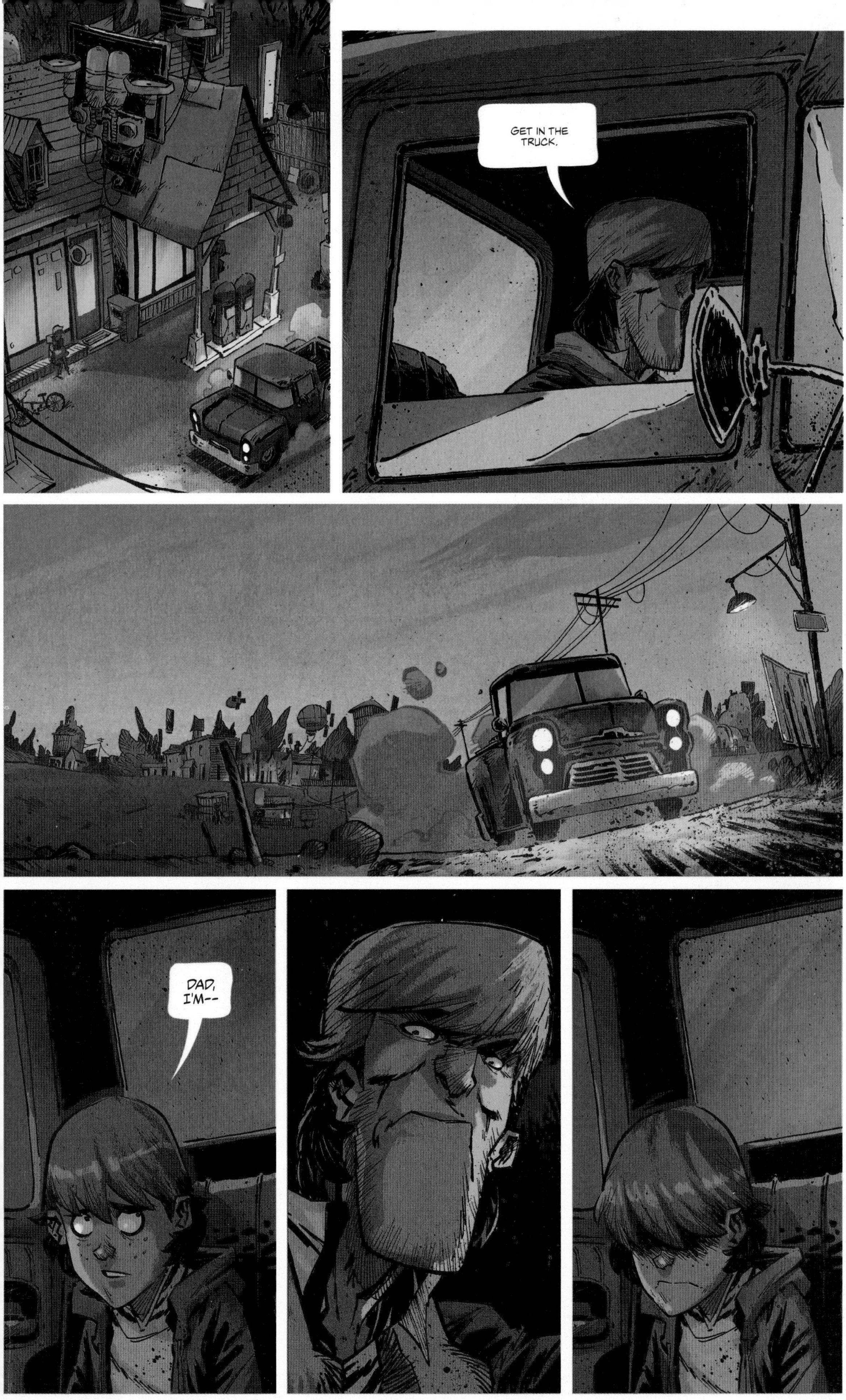
GET IN THE TRUCK.
DAD, I'M--

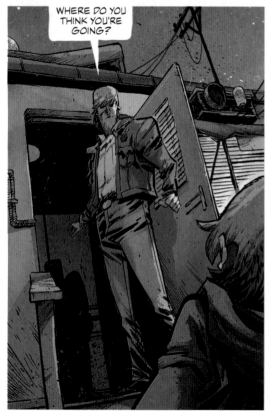

WHERE DO YOU THINK YOU'RE GOING?

INSIDE? TO GO TO BED.

NO, YOU'RE NOT. YOU'RE SLEEPING OUT HERE.

WHAT DO YOU MEAN?

I MEAN, IF YOU THINK YOU'RE A BIG MAN THAT CAN DO WHAT HE WANTS, WHEN HE WANTS, A BIG MAN THAT CAN TAKE CARE OF HIMSELF...

DAD, I--

YOU JUST SHRUG OFF YOUR RESPONSIBILITIES. THEN WHEN I TELL YOU TO COME HOME, YOU DECIDE TO DO YOUR OWN THING--RUN AROUND TOWN WITH YOUR LOSER FRIENDS, AND THEN...*AND THEN...*

...GET CAUGHT *SHOPLIFTING.*

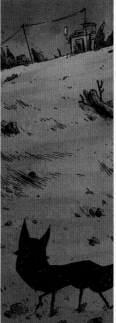

YOU'RE TELLING ME YOU'RE A BIG MAN NOW. YOU CLEARLY DON'T NEED ME, OR THE ROOF I PUT OVER YOUR HEAD.

SO YOU CAN STAY OUT HERE, *BIG MAN.*

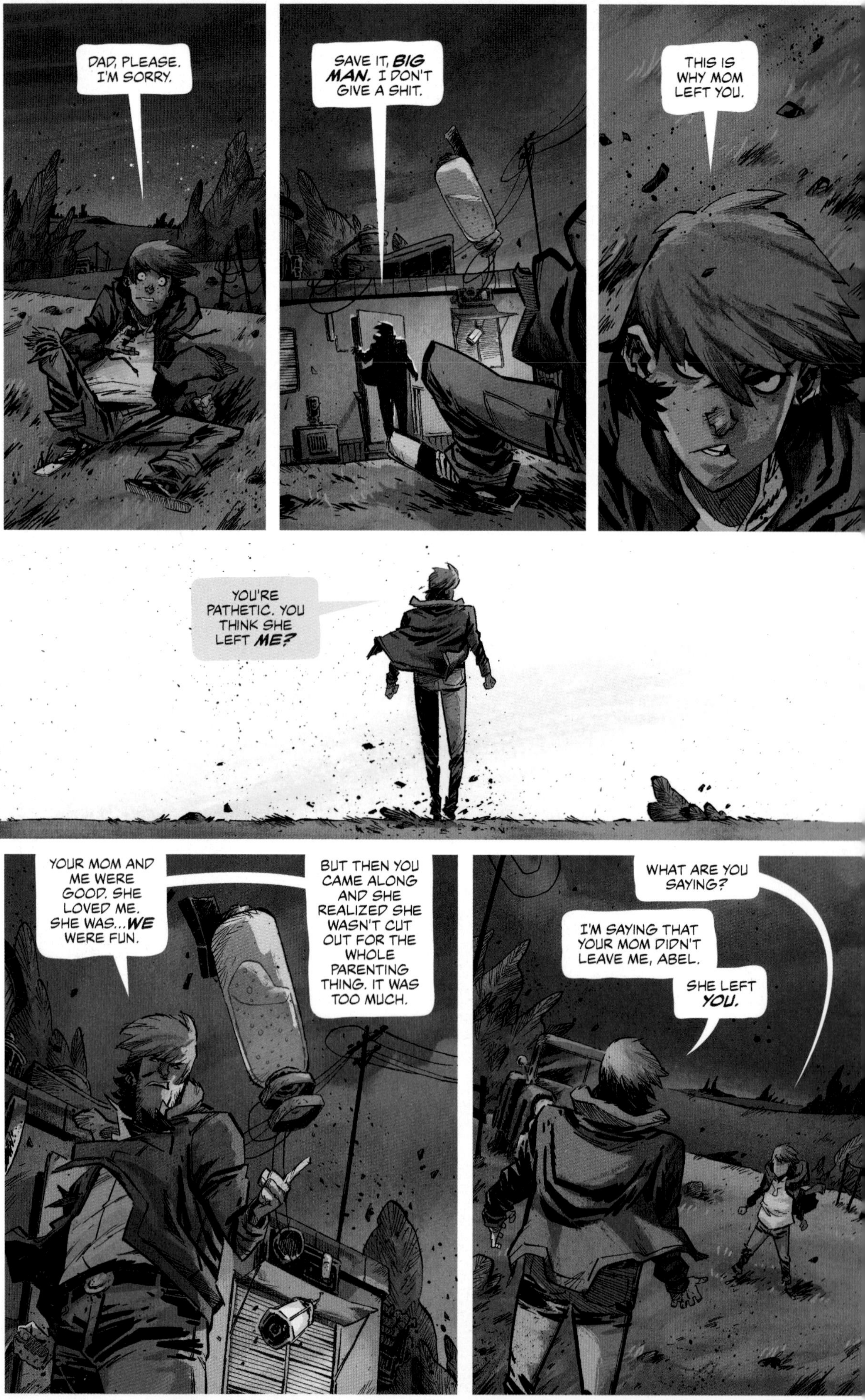
DAD, PLEASE. I'M SORRY.
SAVE IT, **BIG MAN.** I DON'T GIVE A SHIT.
THIS IS WHY MOM LEFT YOU.
YOU'RE PATHETIC. YOU THINK SHE LEFT **ME?**
YOUR MOM AND ME WERE GOOD. SHE LOVED ME. SHE WAS... **WE** WERE FUN.
BUT THEN YOU CAME ALONG AND SHE REALIZED SHE WASN'T CUT OUT FOR THE WHOLE PARENTING THING. IT WAS TOO MUCH.
WHAT ARE YOU SAYING?
I'M SAYING THAT YOUR MOM DIDN'T LEAVE ME, ABEL.
SHE LEFT **YOU.**

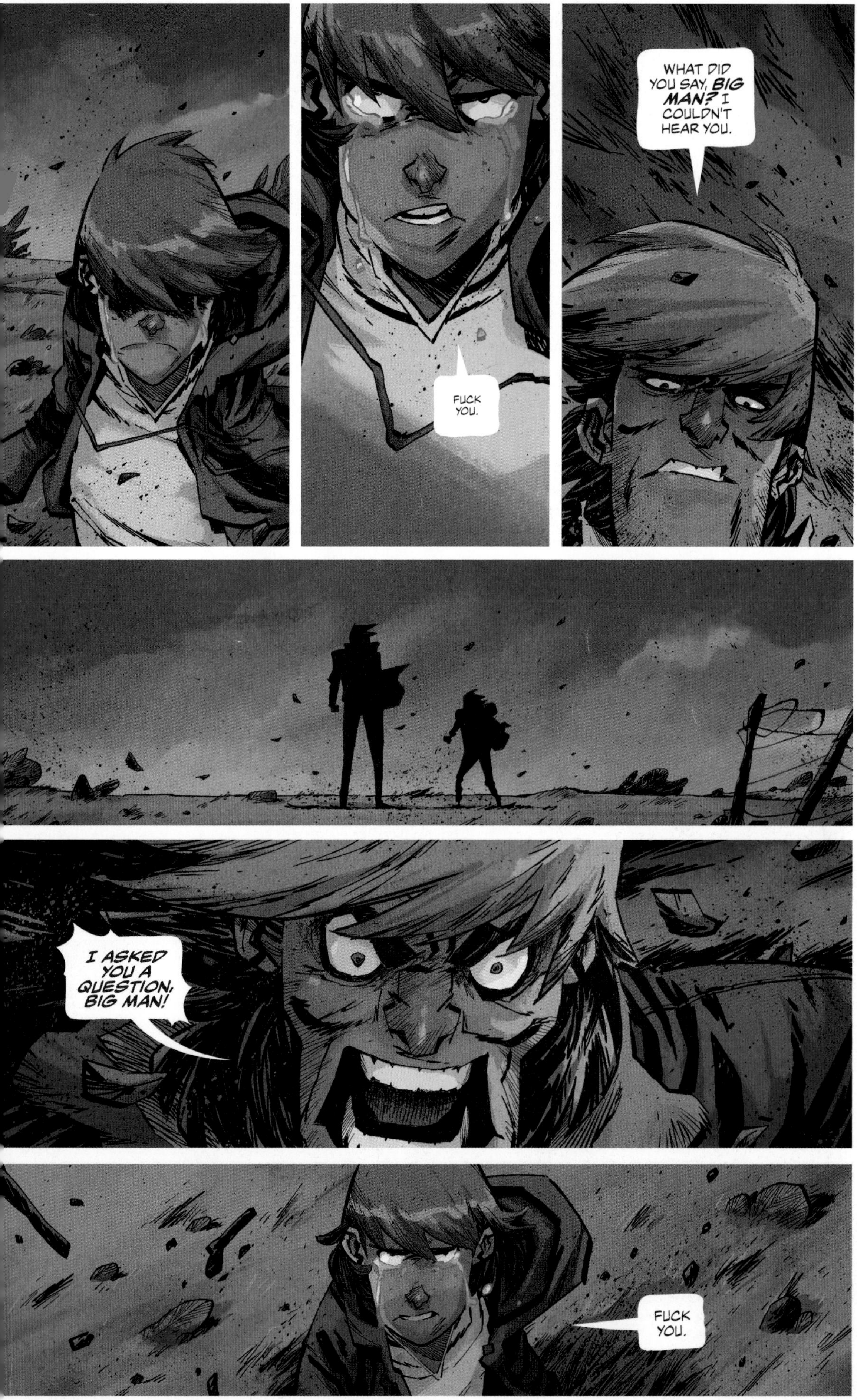
FUCK YOU.
WHAT DID YOU SAY, BIG MAN? I COULDN'T HEAR YOU.
I ASKED YOU A QUESTION, BIG MAN!
FUCK YOU.

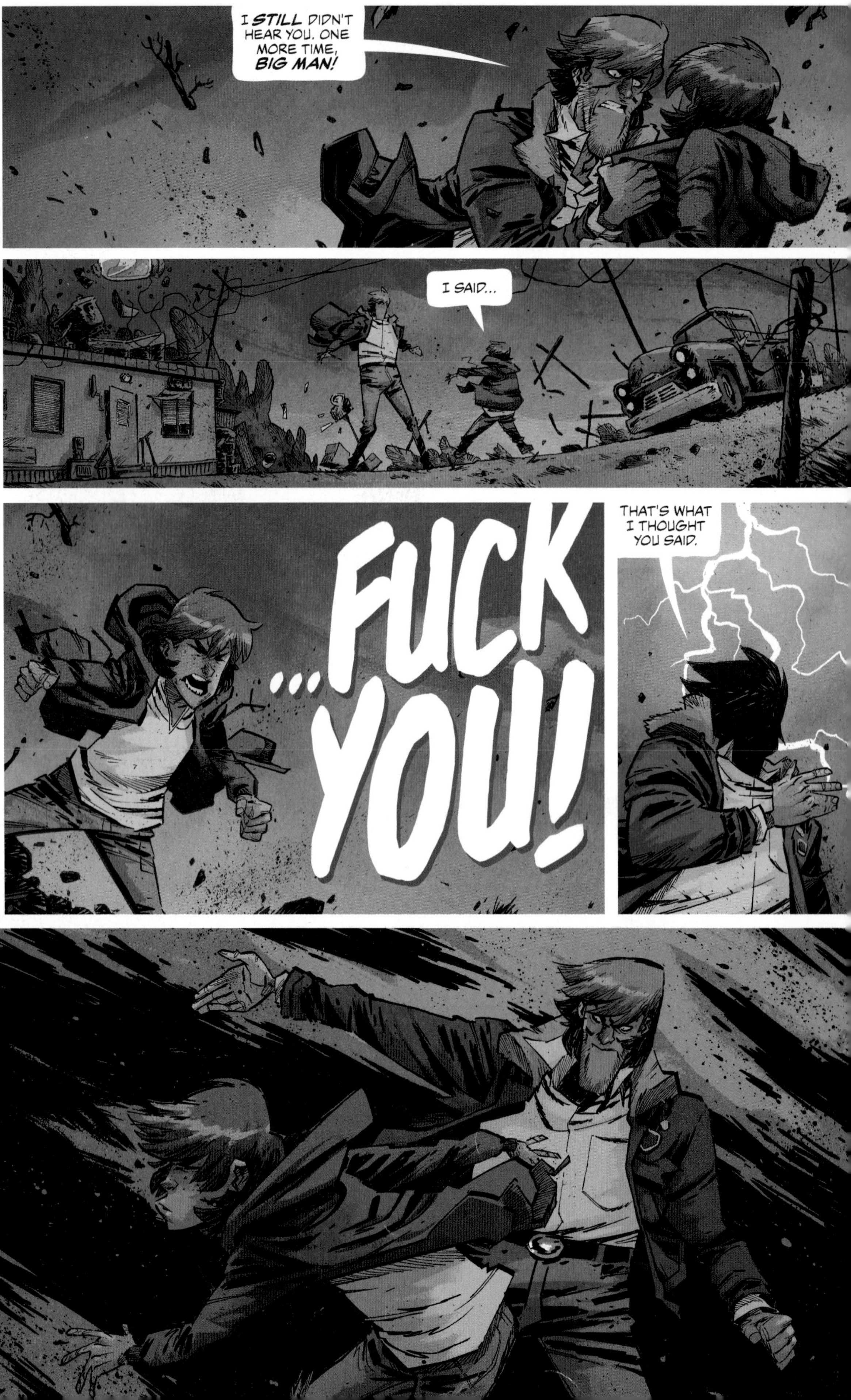
I STILL DIDN'T HEAR YOU. ONE MORE TIME, BIG MAN!
I SAID...
...FUCK YOU!
THAT'S WHAT I THOUGHT YOU SAID.

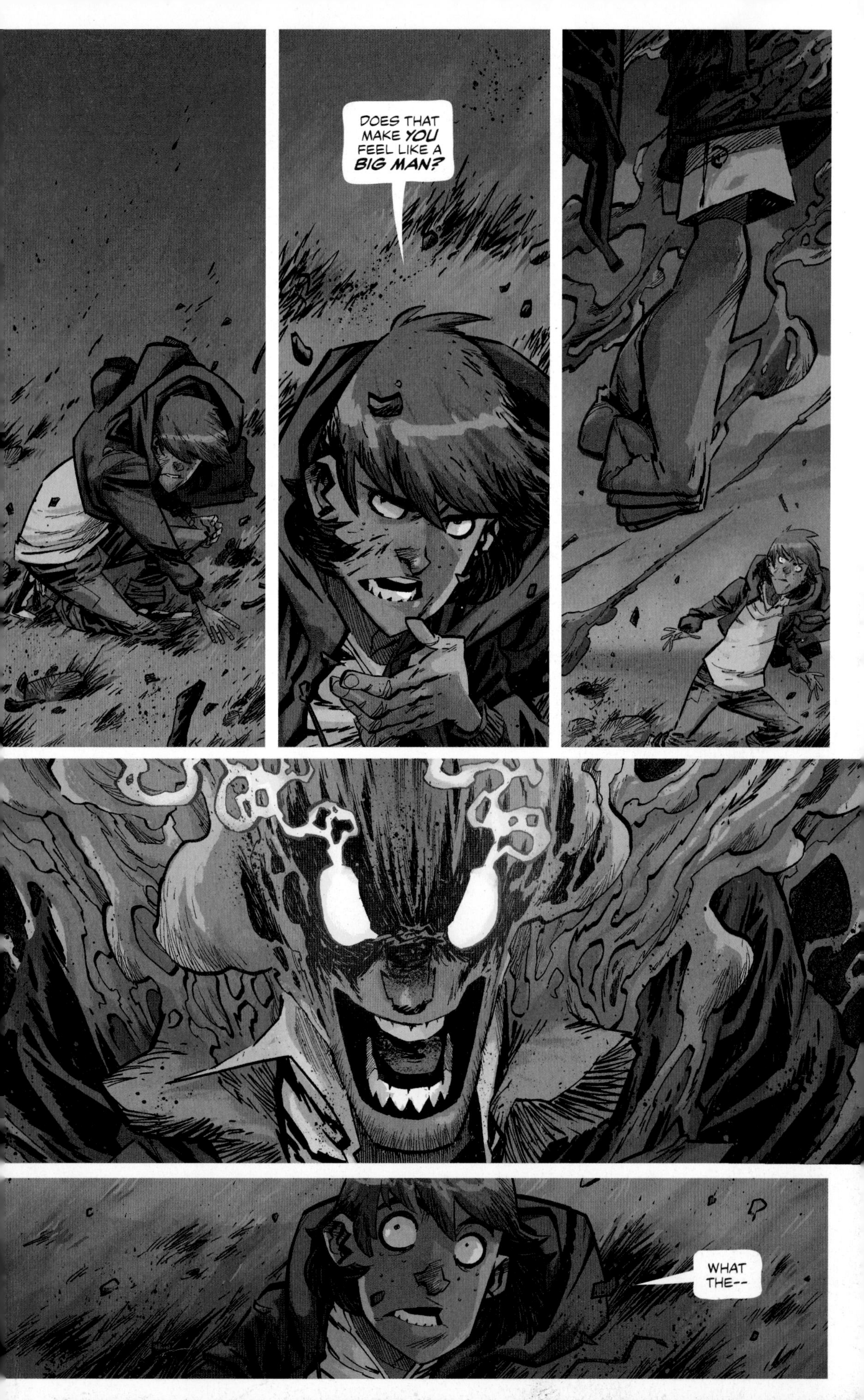
DOES THAT MAKE *YOU* FEEL LIKE A ***BIG MAN?***
WHAT THE--

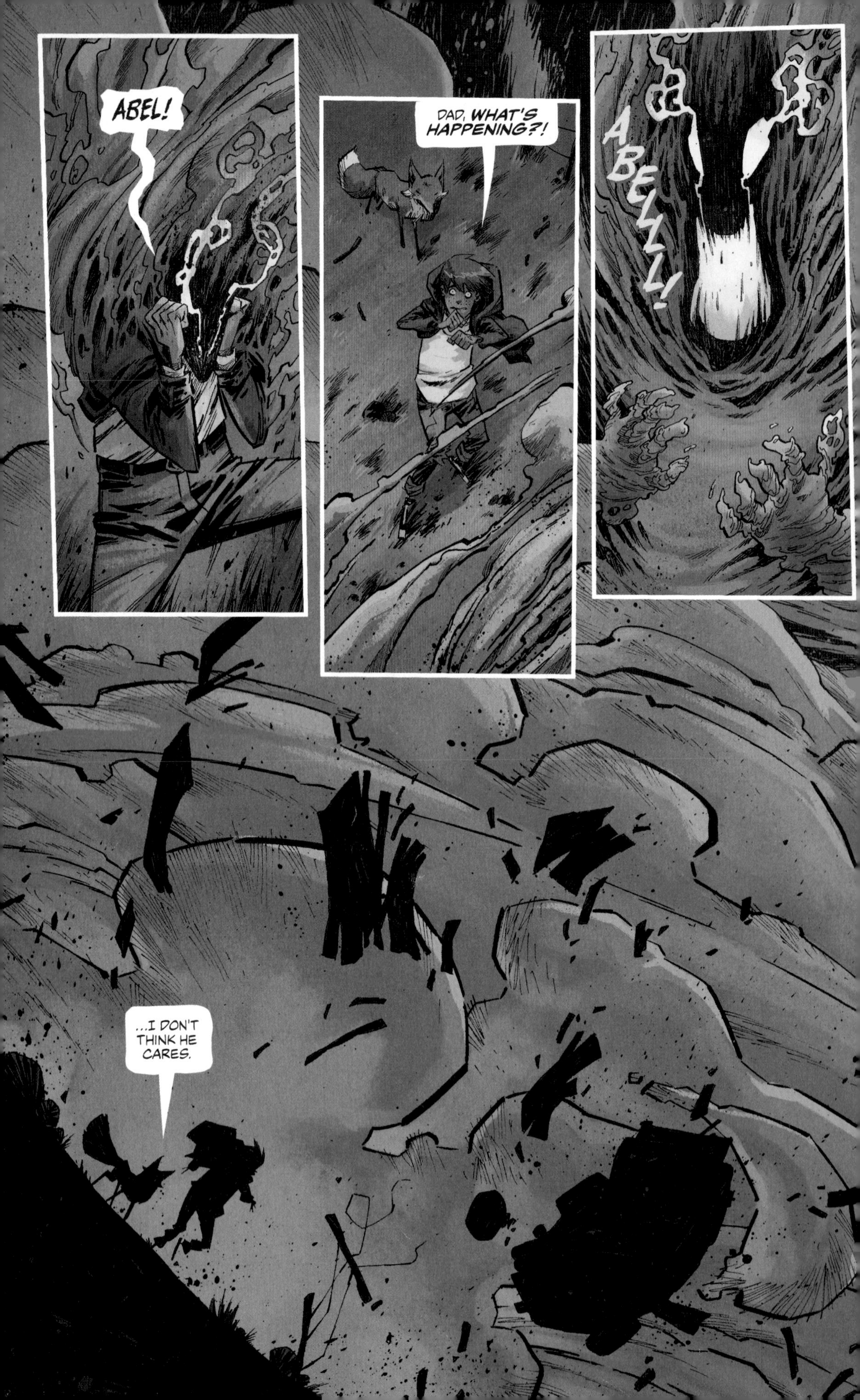
ABEL!
DAD, WHAT'S HAPPENING?!
ABELLL!
...I DON'T THINK HE CARES.

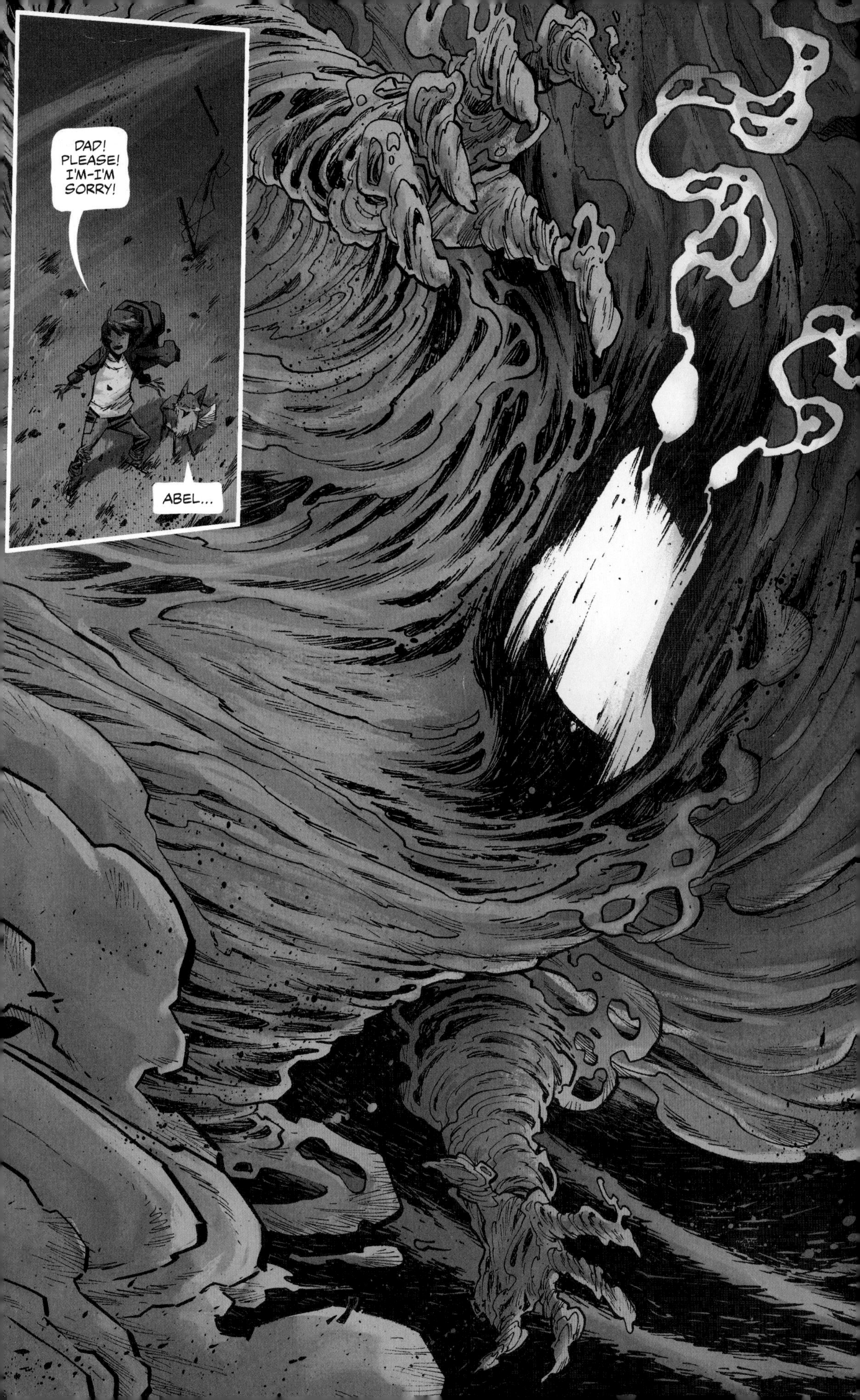
DAD! PLEASE! I'M-I'M SORRY!
ABEL...

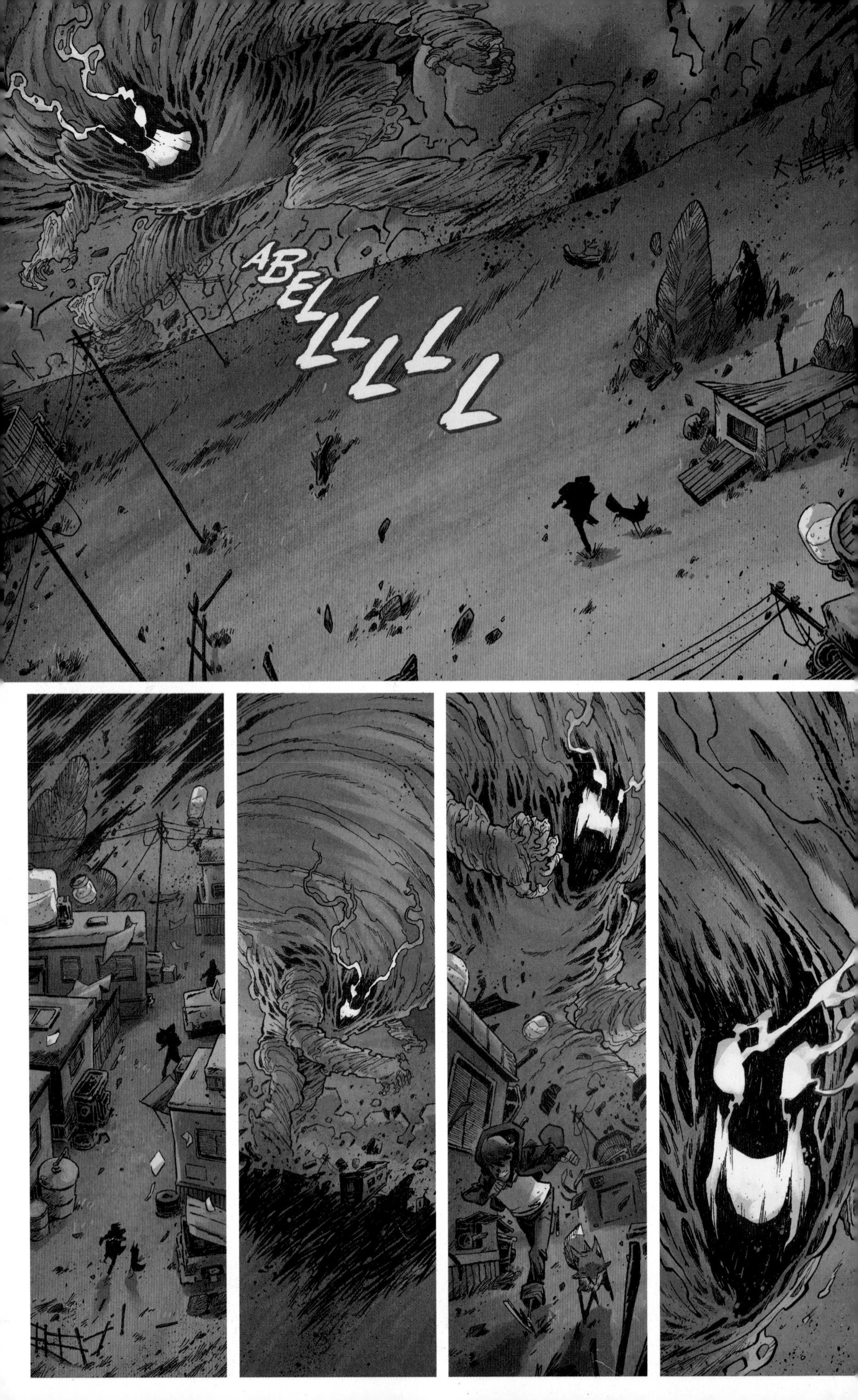
ABELLLLLL

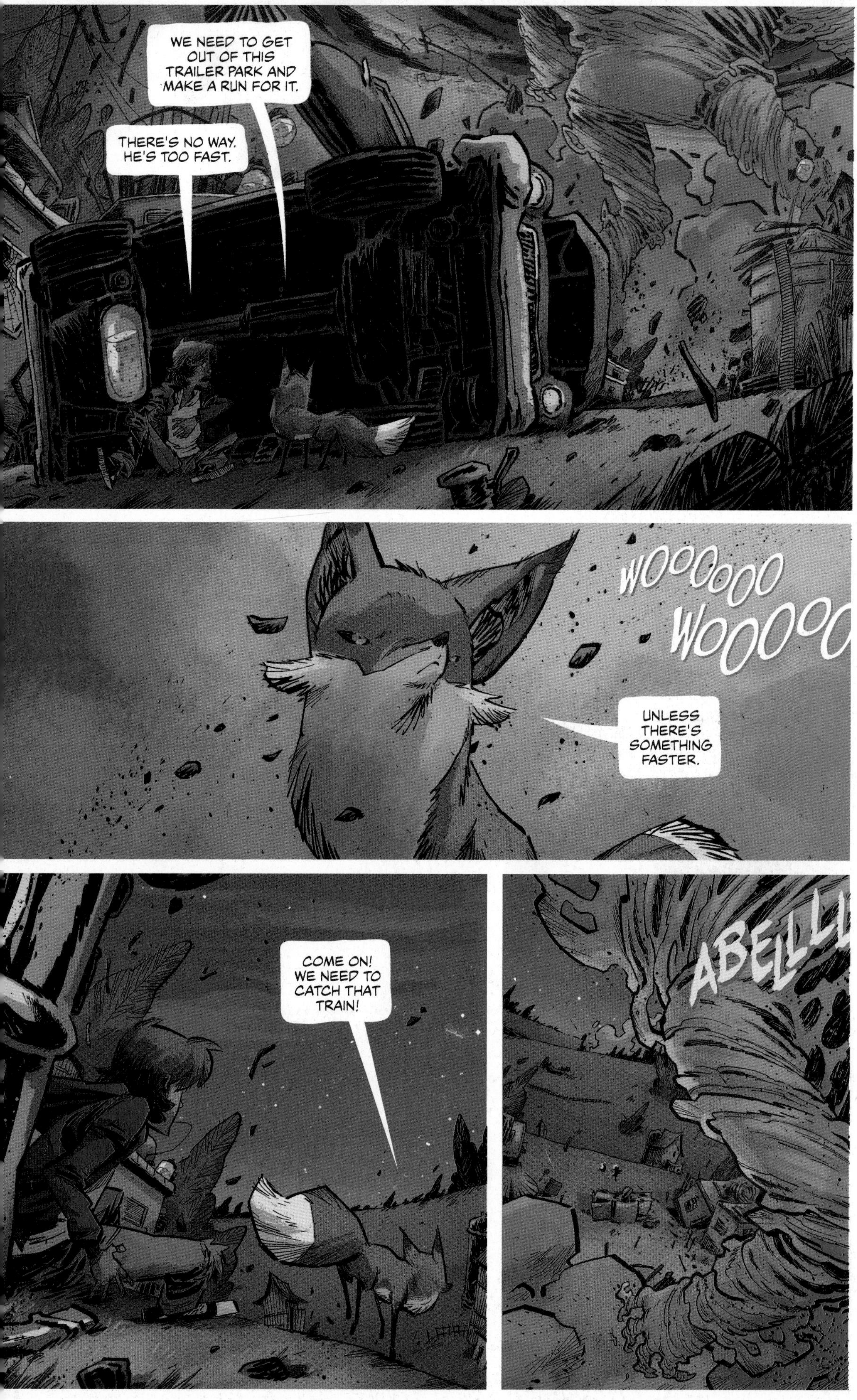
WE NEED TO GET OUT OF THIS TRAILER PARK AND MAKE A RUN FOR IT.
THERE'S NO WAY. HE'S TOO FAST.
WOOOOOO WOOOOO
UNLESS THERE'S SOMETHING FASTER.
COME ON! WE NEED TO CATCH THAT TRAIN!
ABELLL

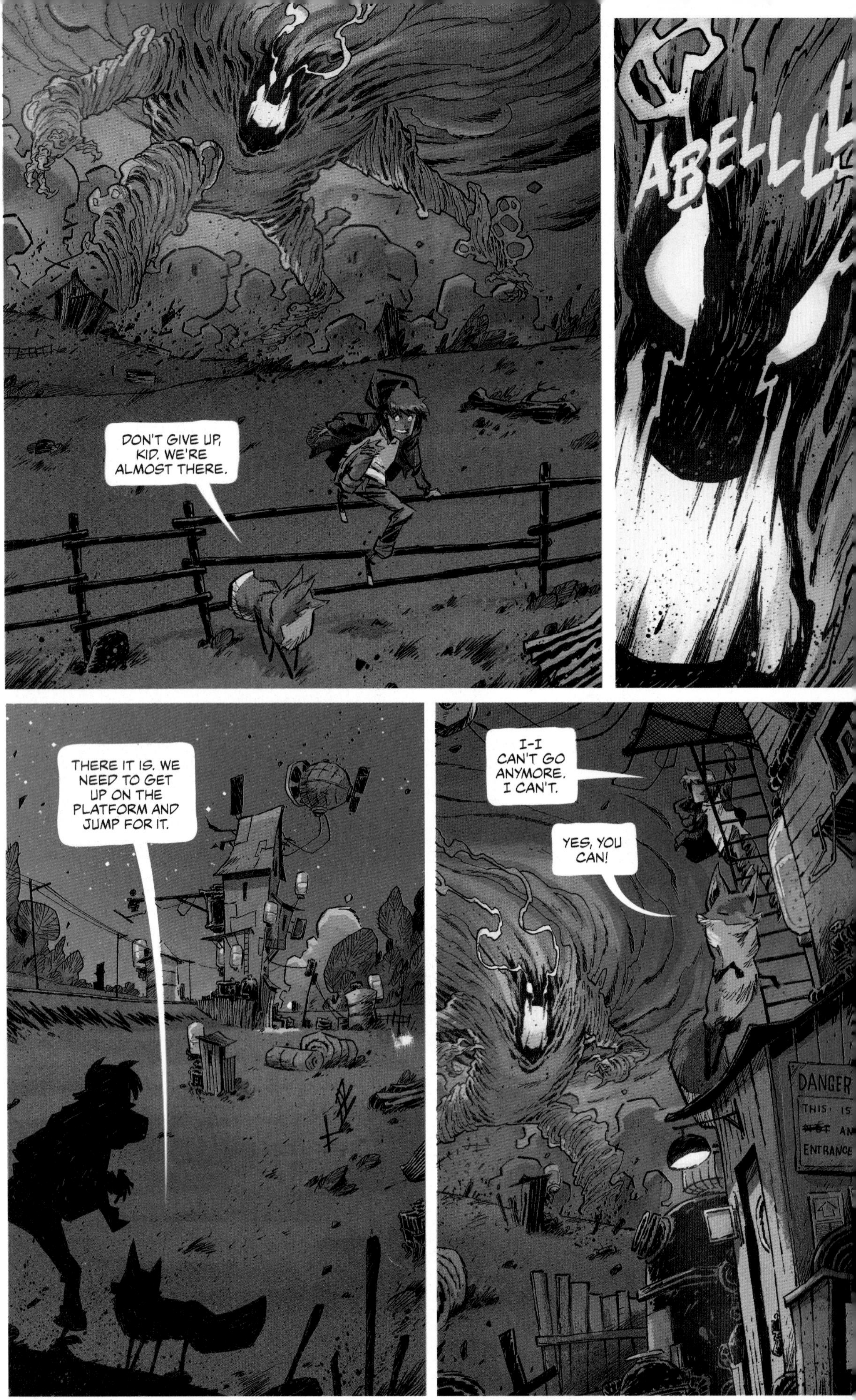
DON'T GIVE UP, KID. WE'RE ALMOST THERE.
ABELLL
THERE IT IS. WE NEED TO GET UP ON THE PLATFORM AND JUMP FOR IT.
I-I CAN'T GO ANYMORE. I CAN'T.
YES, YOU CAN!
DANGER
THIS IS
NOT AN
ENTRANCE

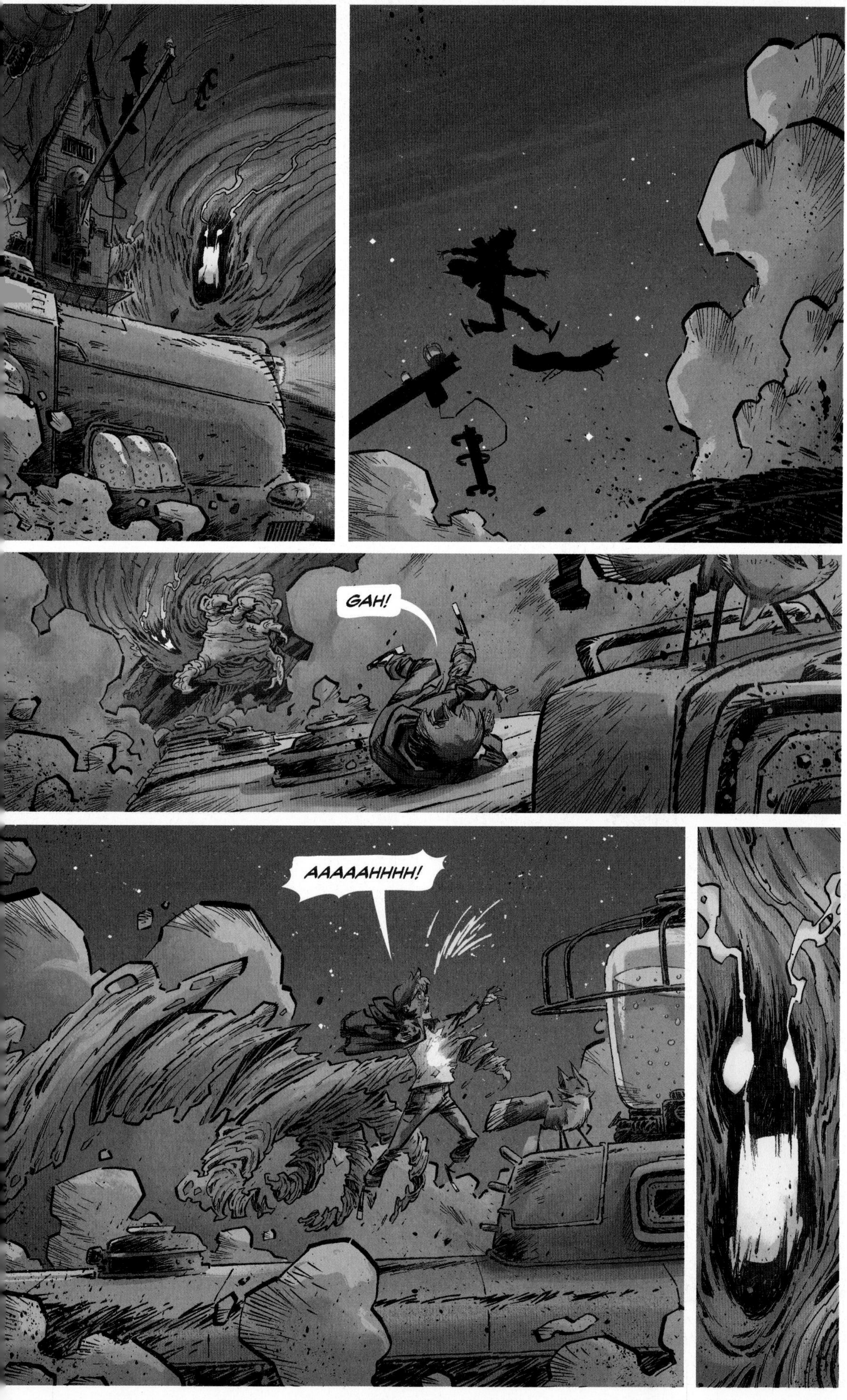
GAH!
AAAAAHHHH!

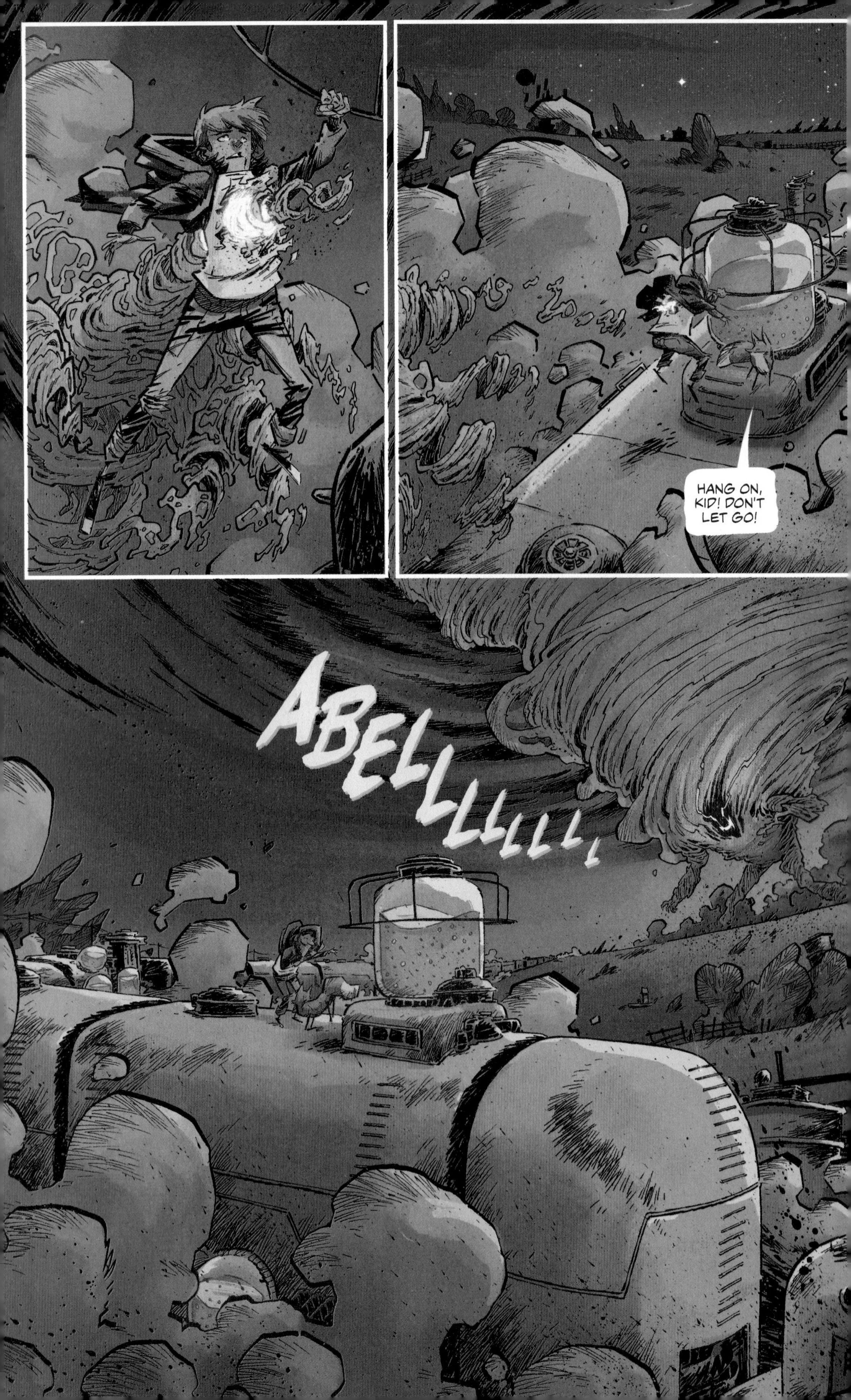
HANG ON, KID! DON'T LET GO!
ABELLLLLLLL

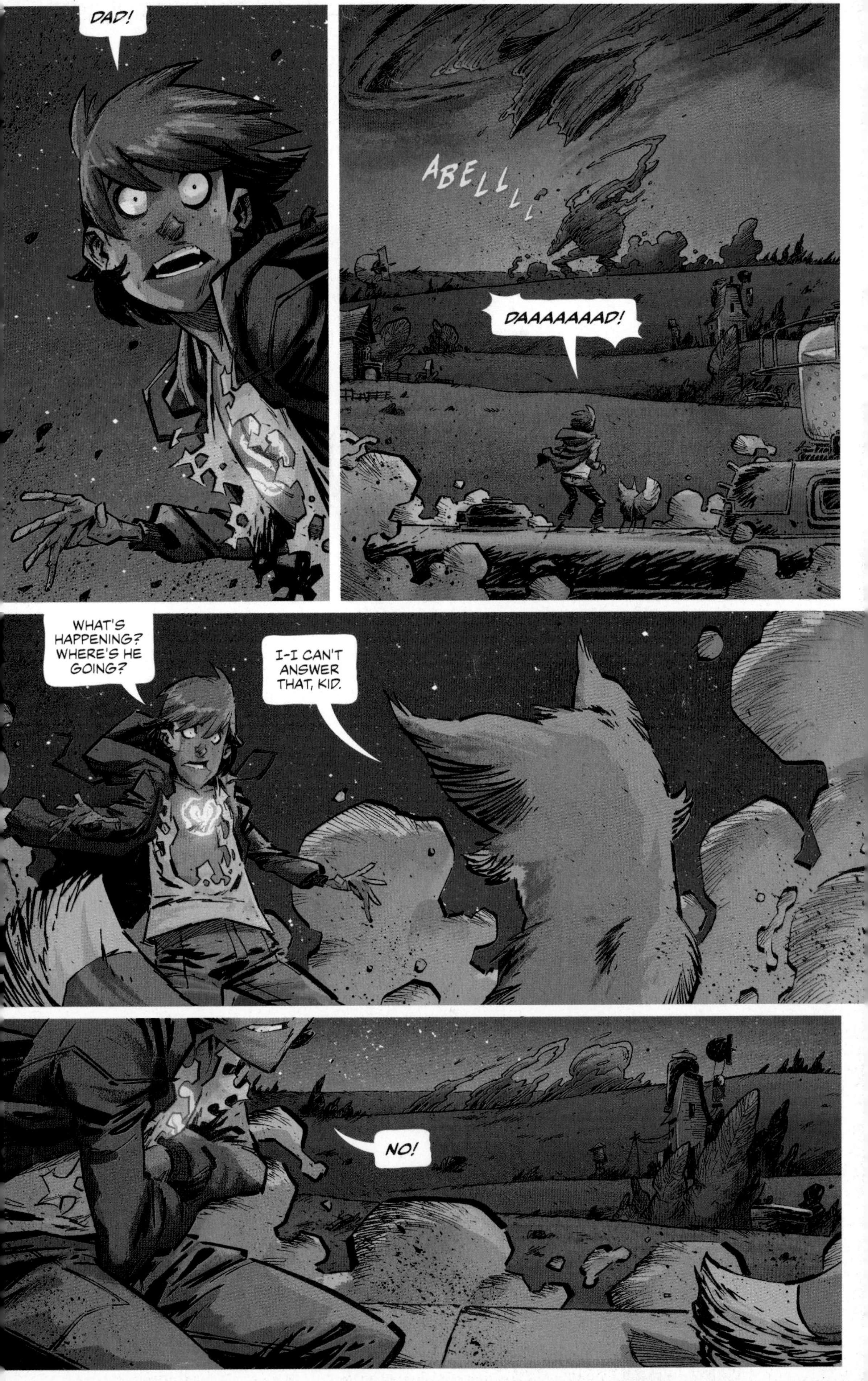
DAD!
ABELLLL
DAAAAAAAD!
WHAT'S HAPPENING? WHERE'S HE GOING?
I-I CAN'T ANSWER THAT, KID.
NO!

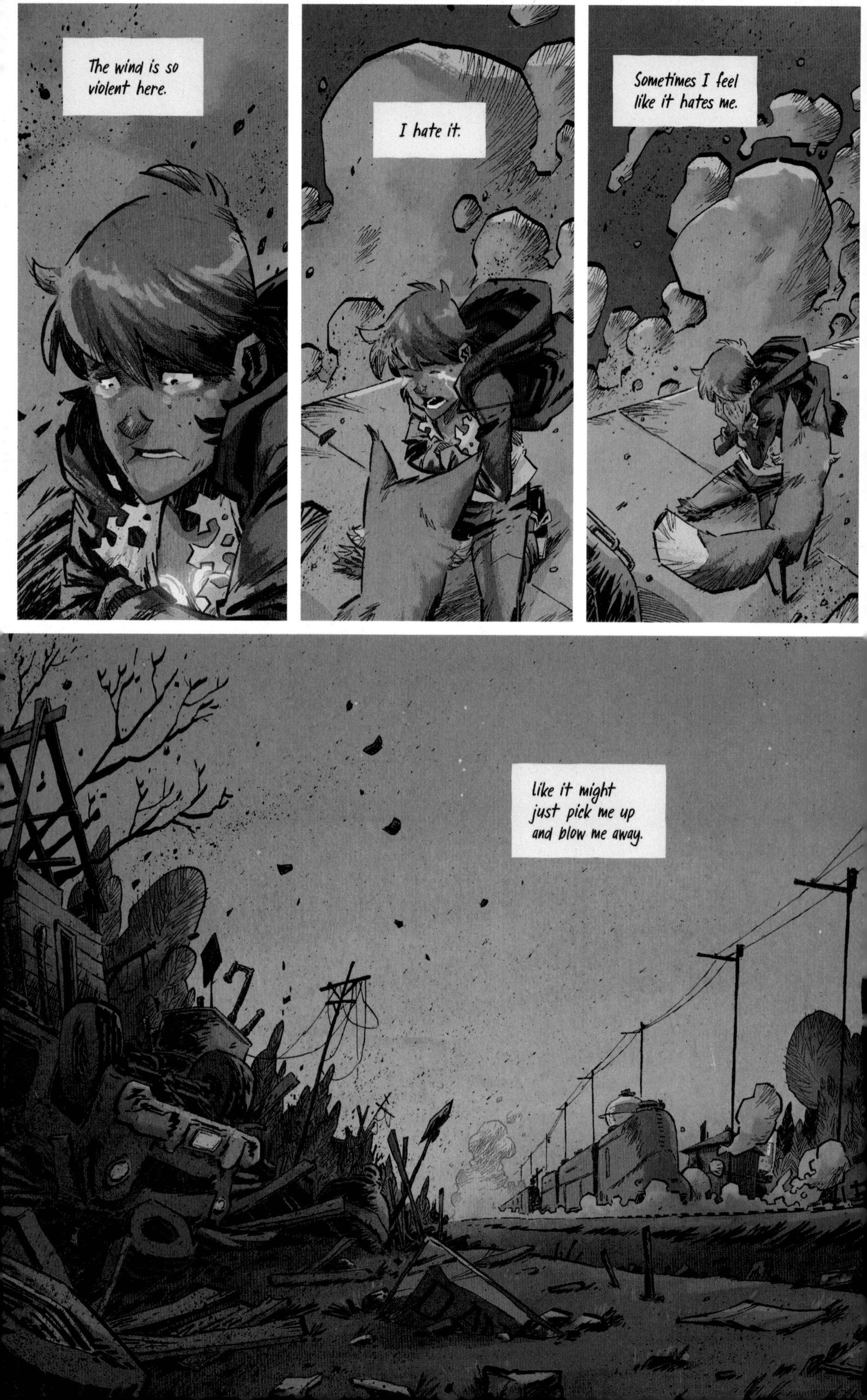
The wind is so violent here.
I hate it.
Sometimes I feel like it hates me.
like it might just pick me up and blow me away.

CHAPTER
TWO

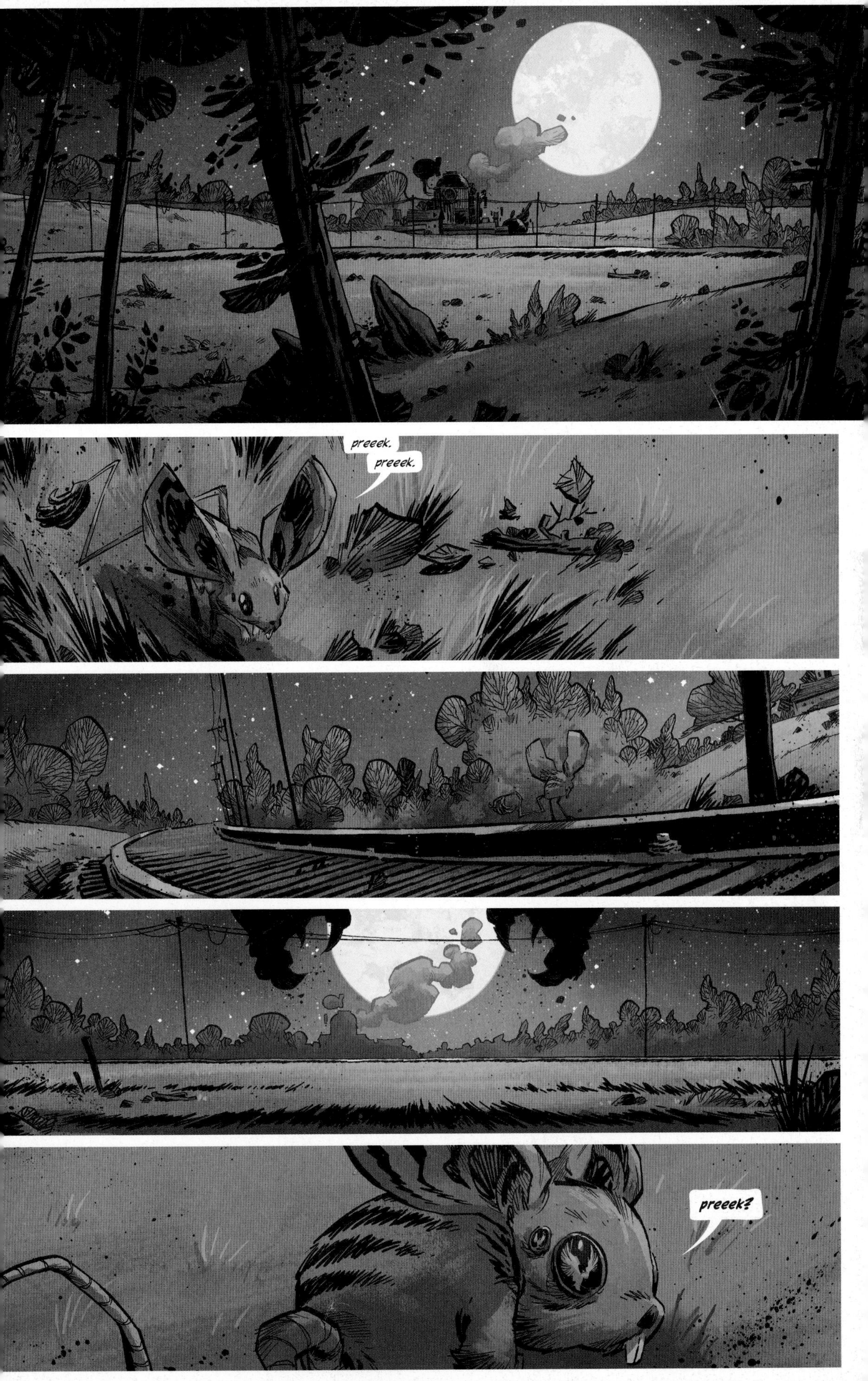
preeek.
preeek.
preeek?

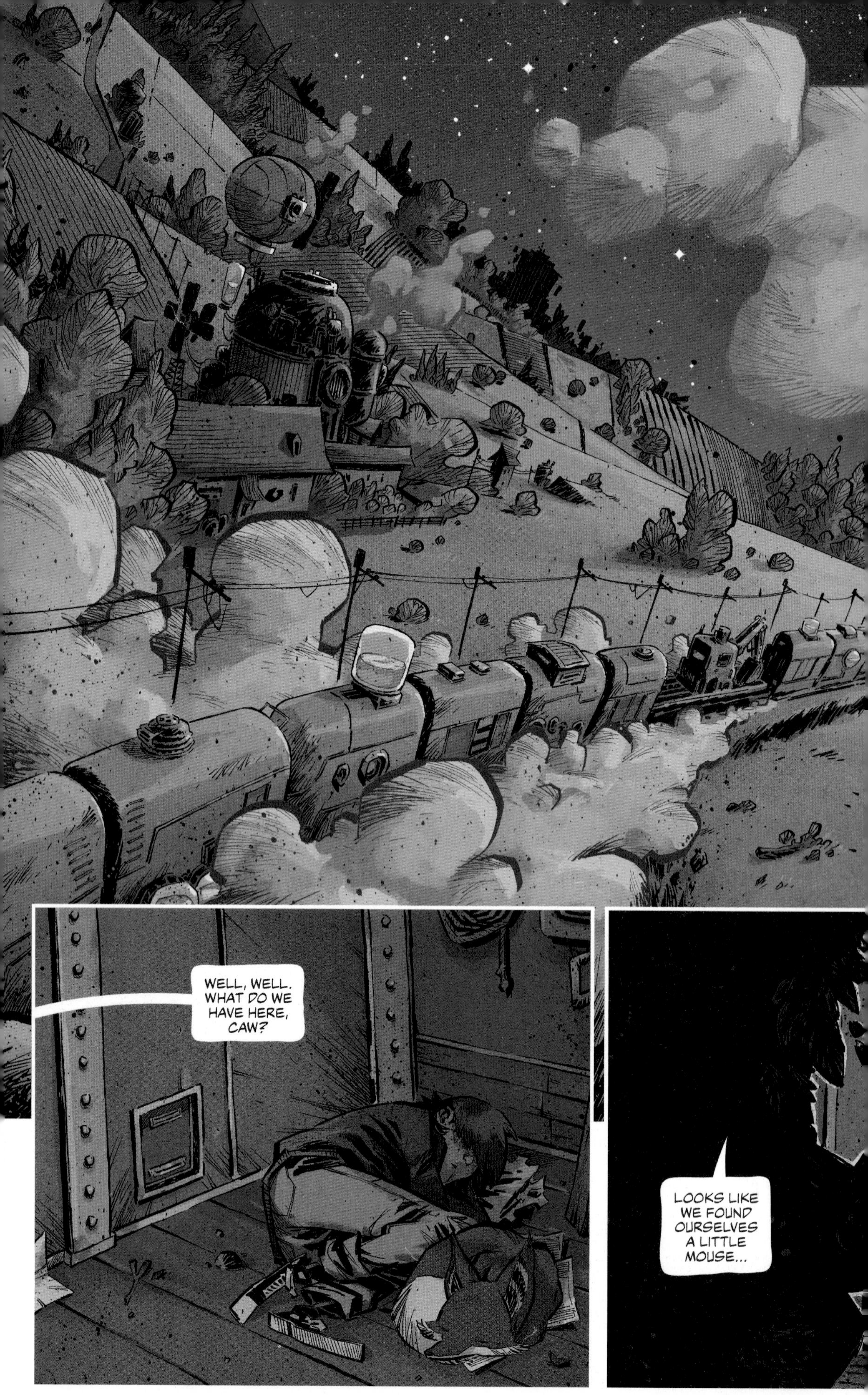
WELL, WELL. WHAT DO WE HAVE HERE, CAW?
LOOKS LIKE WE FOUND OURSELVES A LITTLE MOUSE...

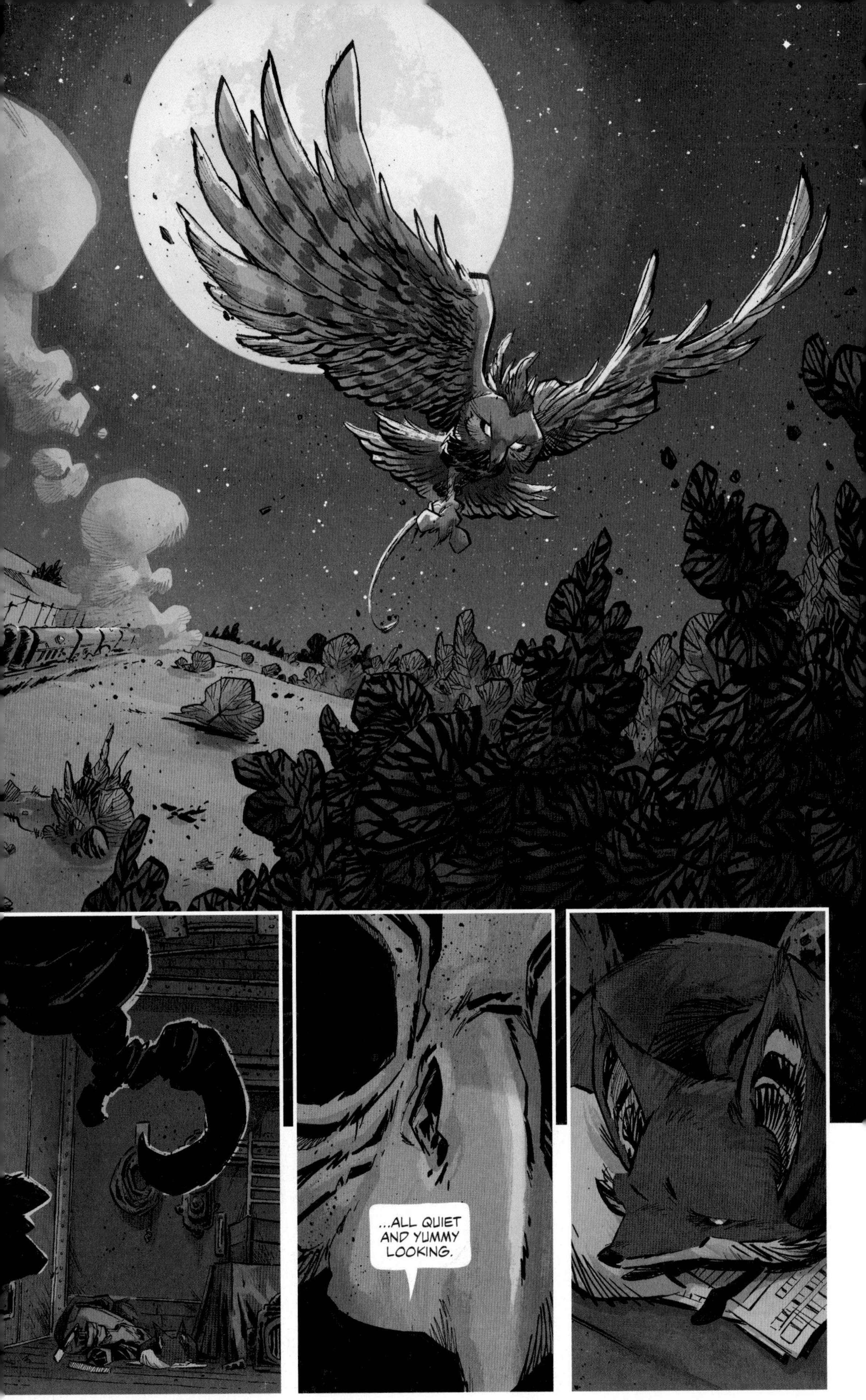
...ALL QUIET AND YUMMY LOOKING.

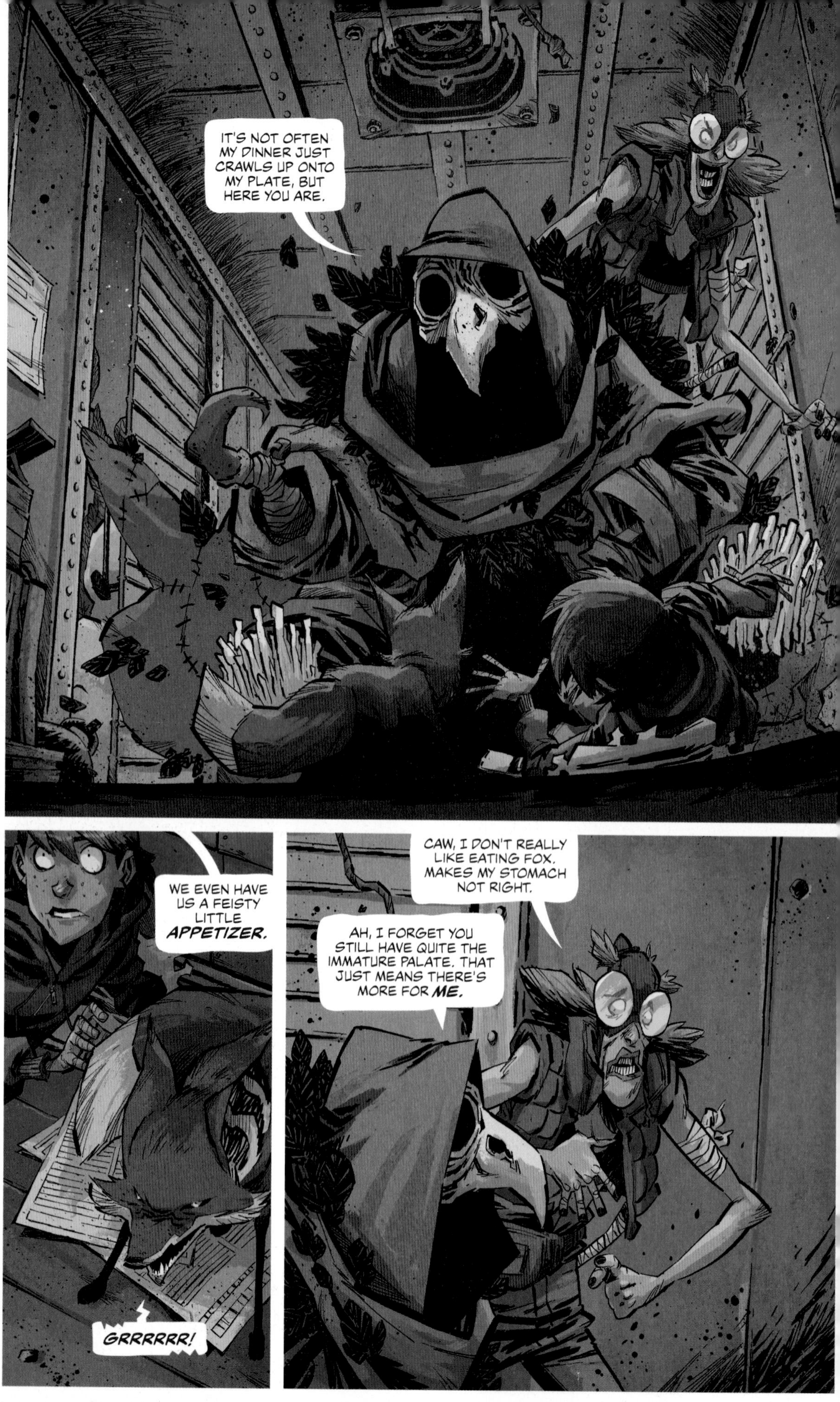
IT'S NOT OFTEN MY DINNER JUST CRAWLS UP ONTO MY PLATE, BUT HERE YOU ARE.
WE EVEN HAVE US A FEISTY LITTLE APPETIZER.
GRRRRRR!
CAW, I DON'T REALLY LIKE EATING FOX. MAKES MY STOMACH NOT RIGHT.
AH, I FORGET YOU STILL HAVE QUITE THE IMMATURE PALATE. THAT JUST MEANS THERE'S MORE FOR ME.

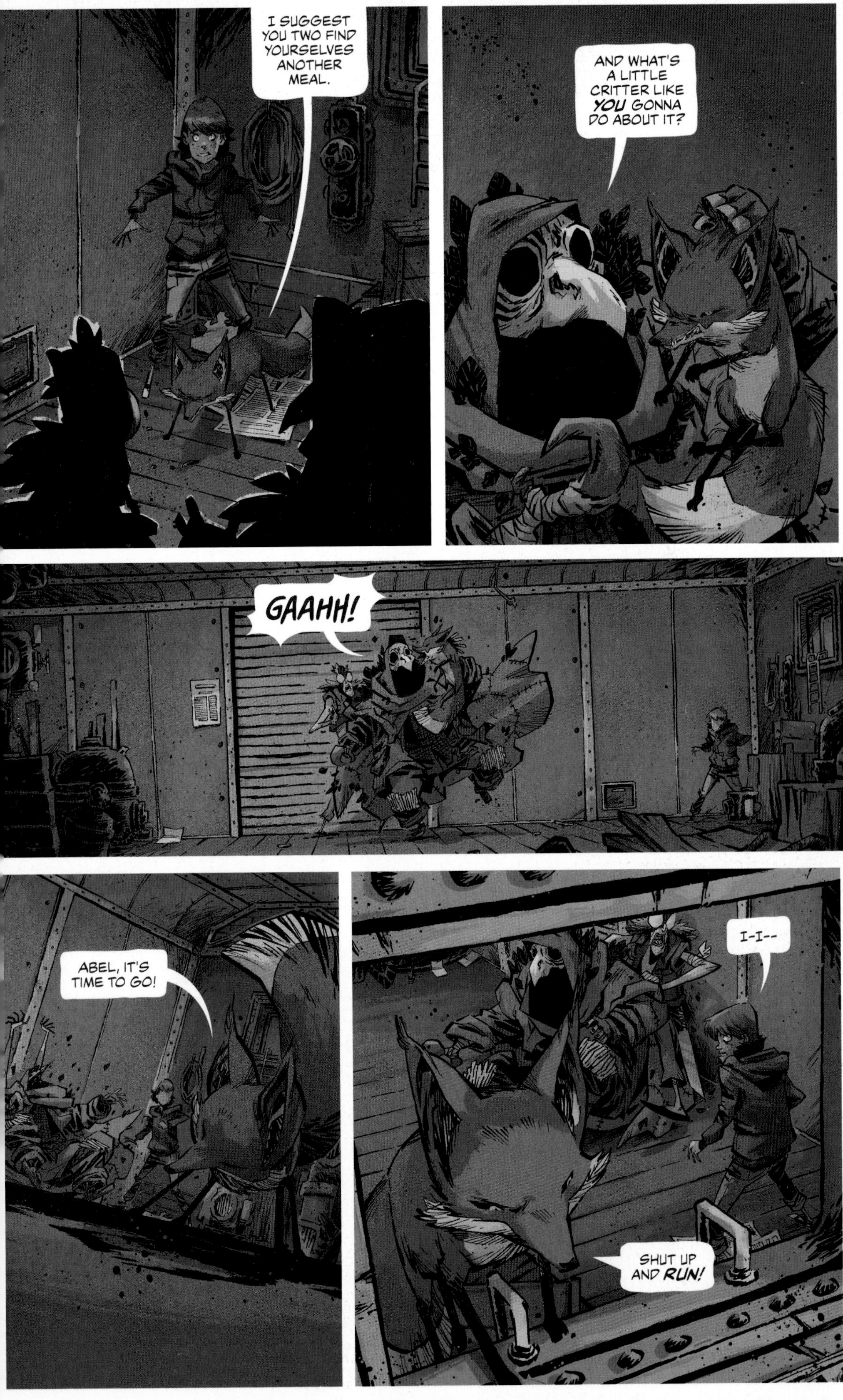
I SUGGEST YOU TWO FIND YOURSELVES ANOTHER MEAL.
AND WHAT'S A LITTLE CRITTER LIKE YOU GONNA DO ABOUT IT?
GAAHH!
ABEL, IT'S TIME TO GO!
I-I--
SHUT UP AND RUN!

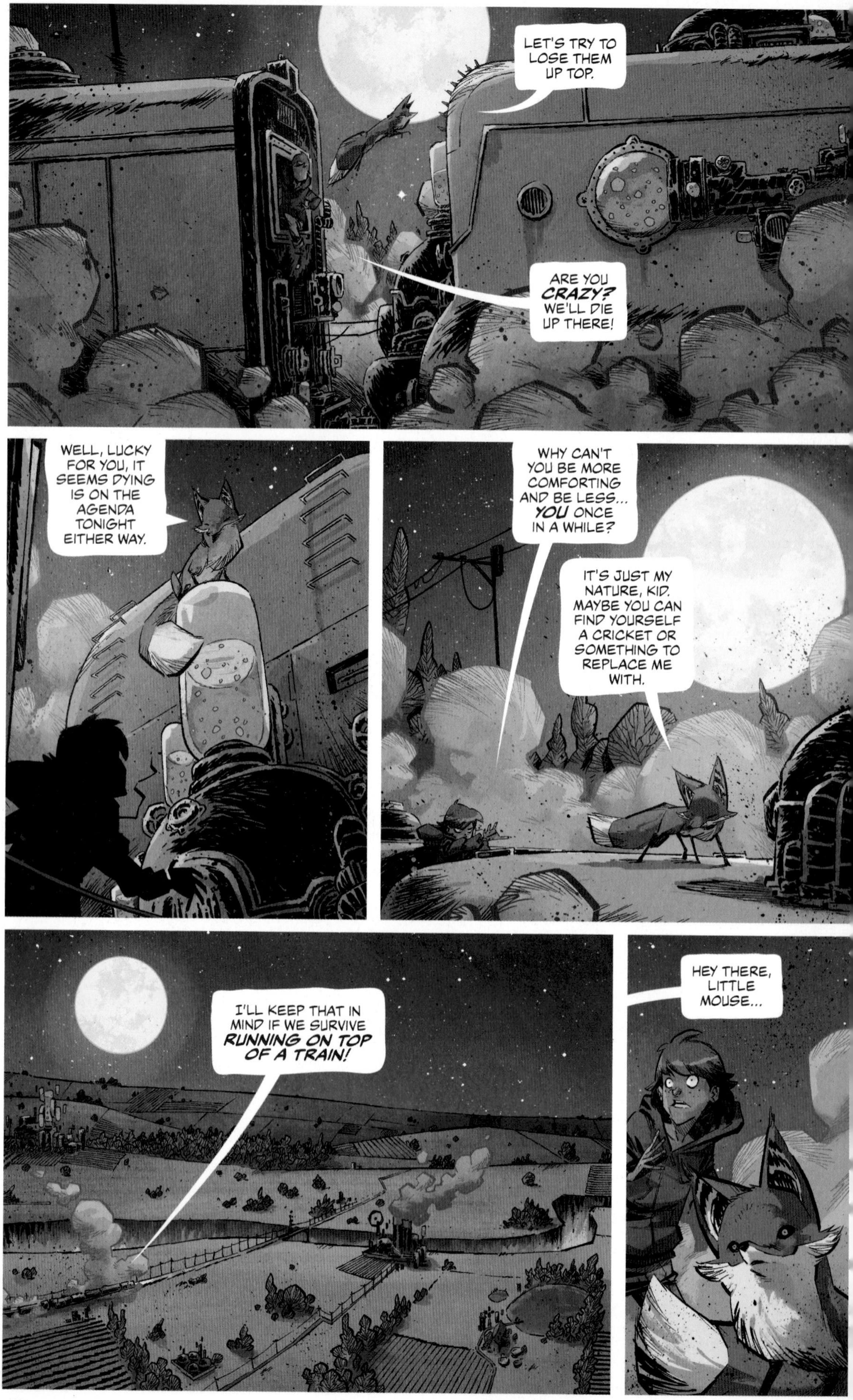
LET'S TRY TO LOSE THEM UP TOP.
ARE YOU CRAZY? WE'LL DIE UP THERE!
WELL, LUCKY FOR YOU, IT SEEMS DYING IS ON THE AGENDA TONIGHT EITHER WAY.
WHY CAN'T YOU BE MORE COMFORTING AND BE LESS... YOU ONCE IN A WHILE?
IT'S JUST MY NATURE, KID. MAYBE YOU CAN FIND YOURSELF A CRICKET OR SOMETHING TO REPLACE ME WITH.
I'LL KEEP THAT IN MIND IF WE SURVIVE RUNNING ON TOP OF A TRAIN!
HEY THERE, LITTLE MOUSE...

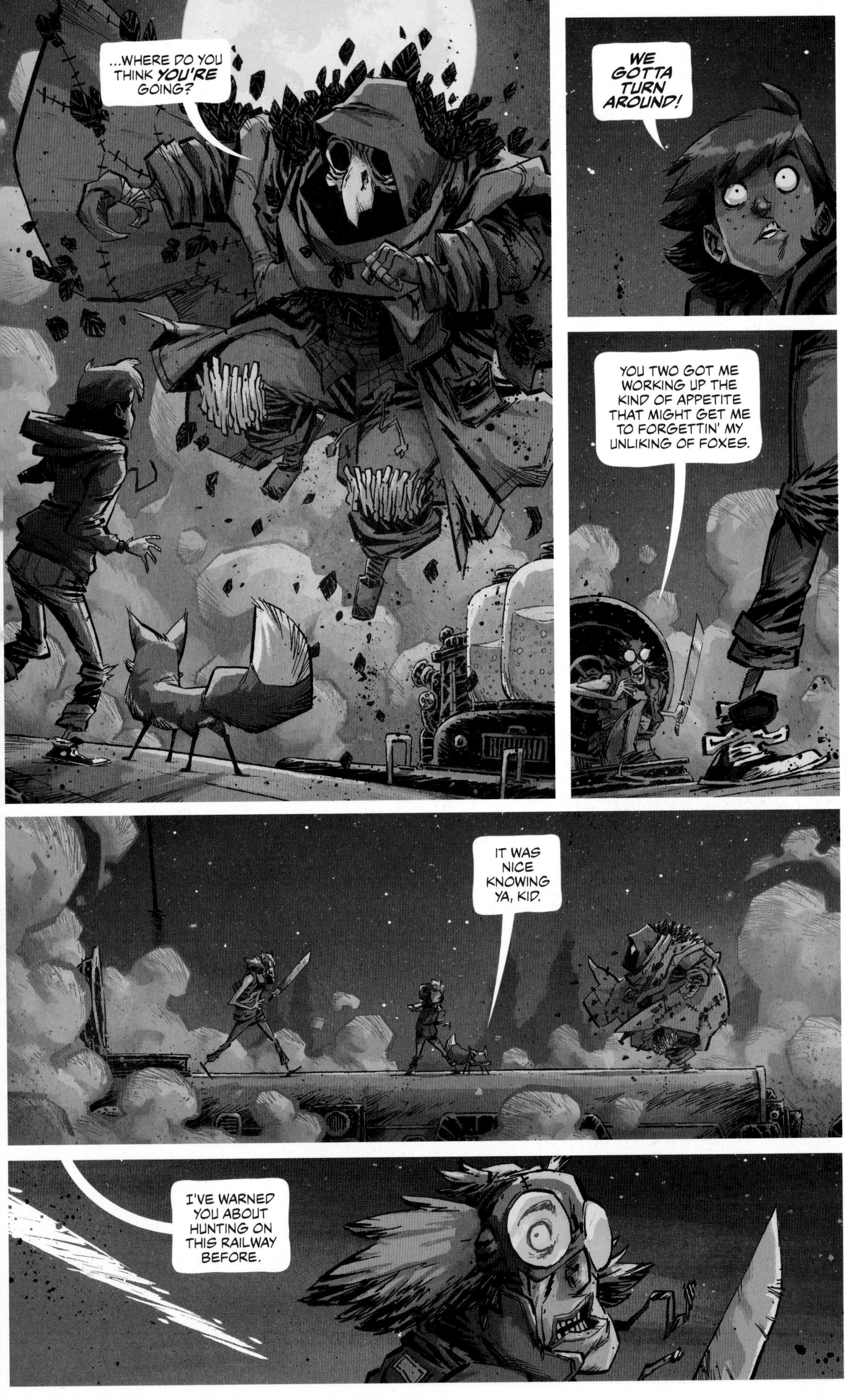
...WHERE DO YOU THINK YOU'RE GOING?
WE GOTTA TURN AROUND!
YOU TWO GOT ME WORKING UP THE KIND OF APPETITE THAT MIGHT GET ME TO FORGETTIN' MY UNLIKING OF FOXES.
IT WAS NICE KNOWING YA, KID.
I'VE WARNED YOU ABOUT HUNTING ON THIS RAILWAY BEFORE.

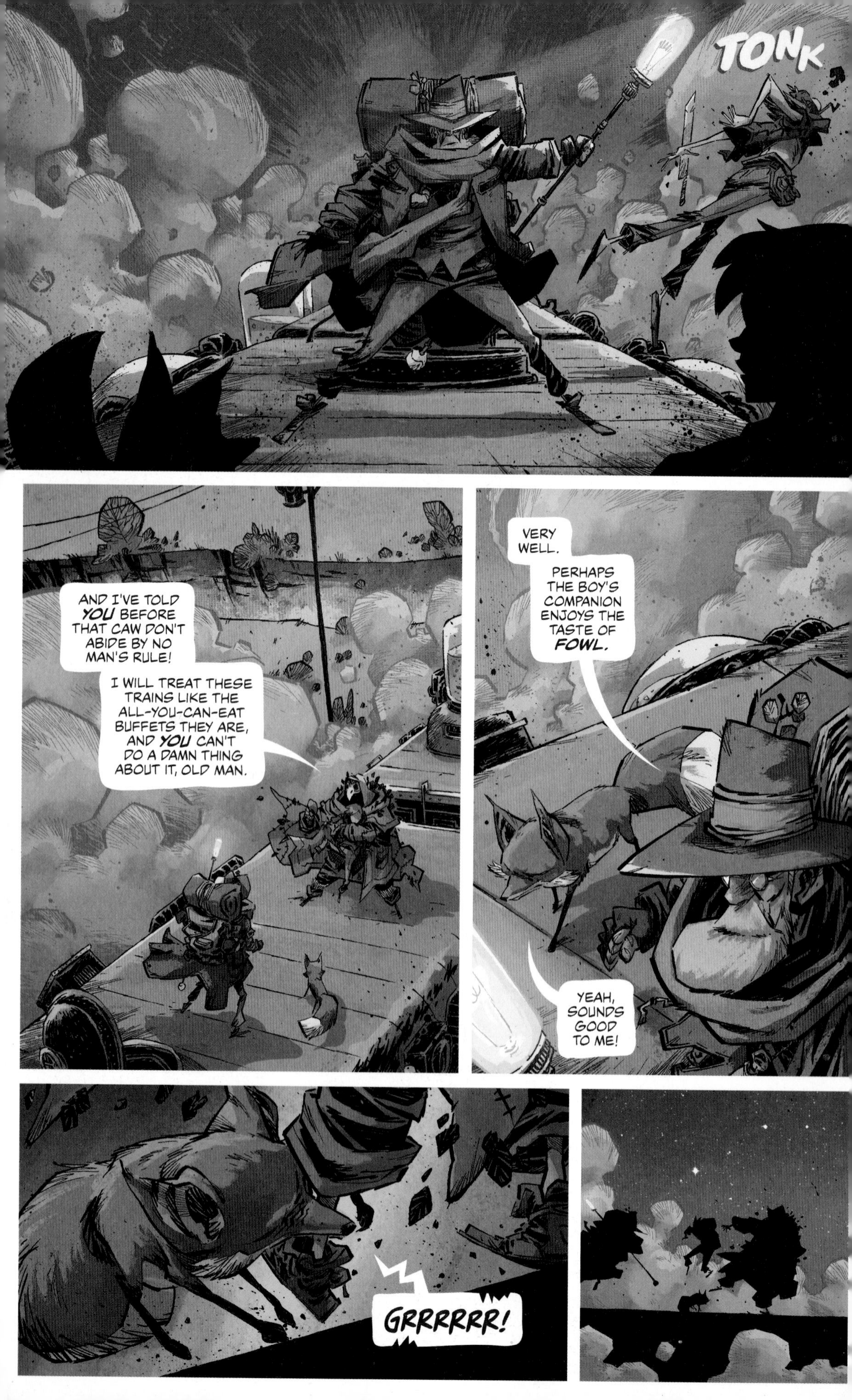
TONK
AND I'VE TOLD YOU BEFORE THAT CAW DON'T ABIDE BY NO MAN'S RULE!
I WILL TREAT THESE TRAINS LIKE THE ALL-YOU-CAN-EAT BUFFETS THEY ARE, AND YOU CAN'T DO A DAMN THING ABOUT IT, OLD MAN.
VERY WELL.
PERHAPS THE BOY'S COMPANION ENJOYS THE TASTE OF FOWL.
YEAH, SOUNDS GOOD TO ME!
GRRRRRR!

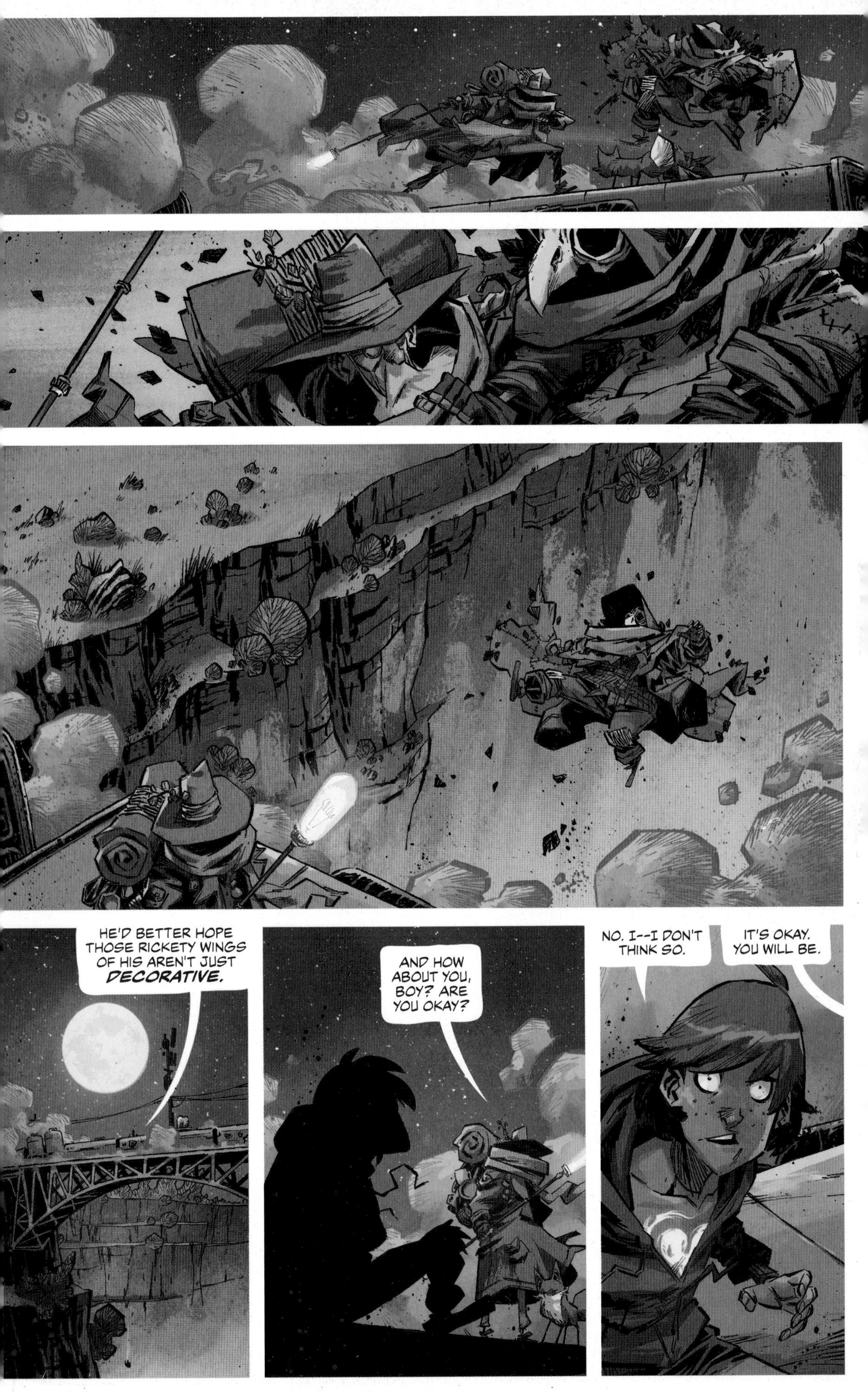

HE'D BETTER HOPE THOSE RICKETY WINGS OF HIS AREN'T JUST *DECORATIVE.*
AND HOW ABOUT YOU, BOY? ARE YOU OKAY?
NO. I--I DON'T THINK SO.
IT'S OKAY. YOU WILL BE.

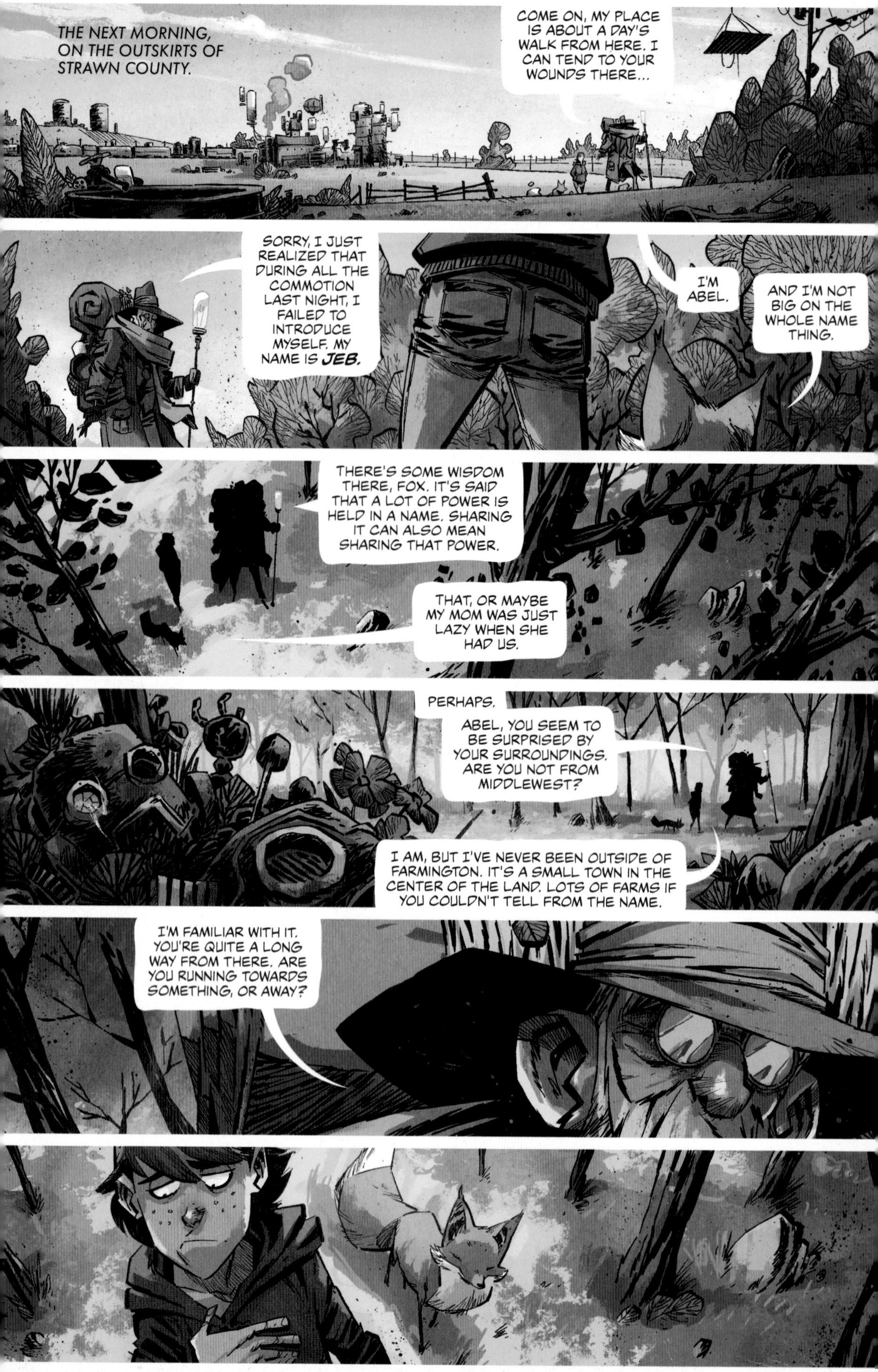
THE NEXT MORNING, ON THE OUTSKIRTS OF STRAWN COUNTY.
COME ON, MY PLACE IS ABOUT A DAY'S WALK FROM HERE. I CAN TEND TO YOUR WOUNDS THERE...
SORRY, I JUST REALIZED THAT DURING ALL THE COMMOTION LAST NIGHT, I FAILED TO INTRODUCE MYSELF. MY NAME IS JEB.
I'M ABEL.
AND I'M NOT BIG ON THE WHOLE NAME THING.
THERE'S SOME WISDOM THERE, FOX. IT'S SAID THAT A LOT OF POWER IS HELD IN A NAME. SHARING IT CAN ALSO MEAN SHARING THAT POWER.
THAT, OR MAYBE MY MOM WAS JUST LAZY WHEN SHE HAD US.
PERHAPS.
ABEL, YOU SEEM TO BE SURPRISED BY YOUR SURROUNDINGS. ARE YOU NOT FROM MIDDLEWEST?
I AM, BUT I'VE NEVER BEEN OUTSIDE OF FARMINGTON. IT'S A SMALL TOWN IN THE CENTER OF THE LAND. LOTS OF FARMS IF YOU COULDN'T TELL FROM THE NAME.
I'M FAMILIAR WITH IT. YOU'RE QUITE A LONG WAY FROM THERE. ARE YOU RUNNING TOWARDS SOMETHING, OR AWAY?

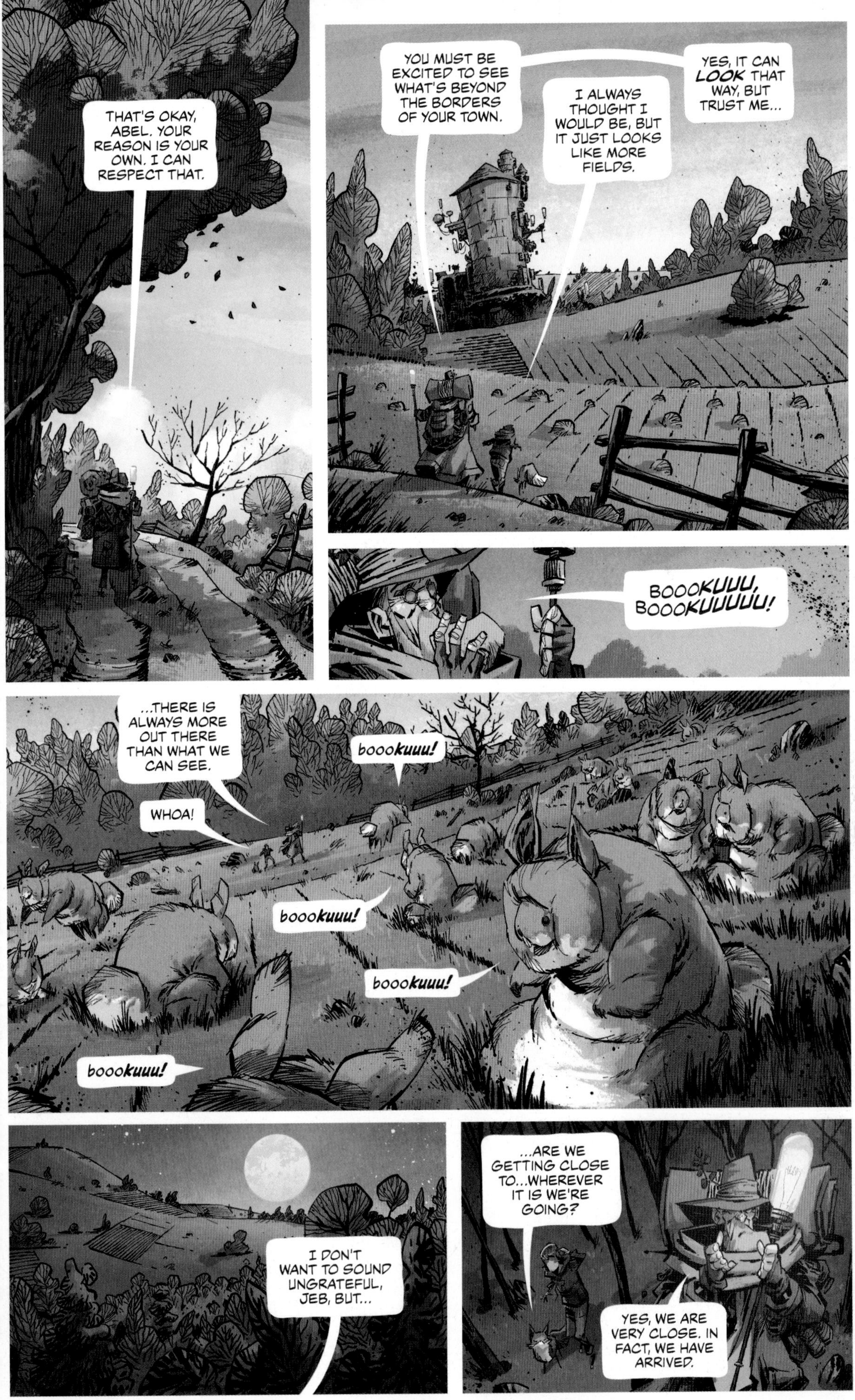
THAT'S OKAY, ABEL. YOUR REASON IS YOUR OWN. I CAN RESPECT THAT.
YOU MUST BE EXCITED TO SEE WHAT'S BEYOND THE BORDERS OF YOUR TOWN.
I ALWAYS THOUGHT I WOULD BE, BUT IT JUST LOOKS LIKE MORE FIELDS.
YES, IT CAN LOOK THAT WAY, BUT TRUST ME...
BOOOKUUU, BOOOKUUUUU!
...THERE IS ALWAYS MORE OUT THERE THAN WHAT WE CAN SEE.
boookuuu!
WHOA!
boookuuu!
boookuuu!
boookuuu!
I DON'T WANT TO SOUND UNGRATEFUL, JEB, BUT...
...ARE WE GETTING CLOSE TO...WHEREVER IT IS WE'RE GOING?
YES, WE ARE VERY CLOSE. IN FACT, WE HAVE ARRIVED.

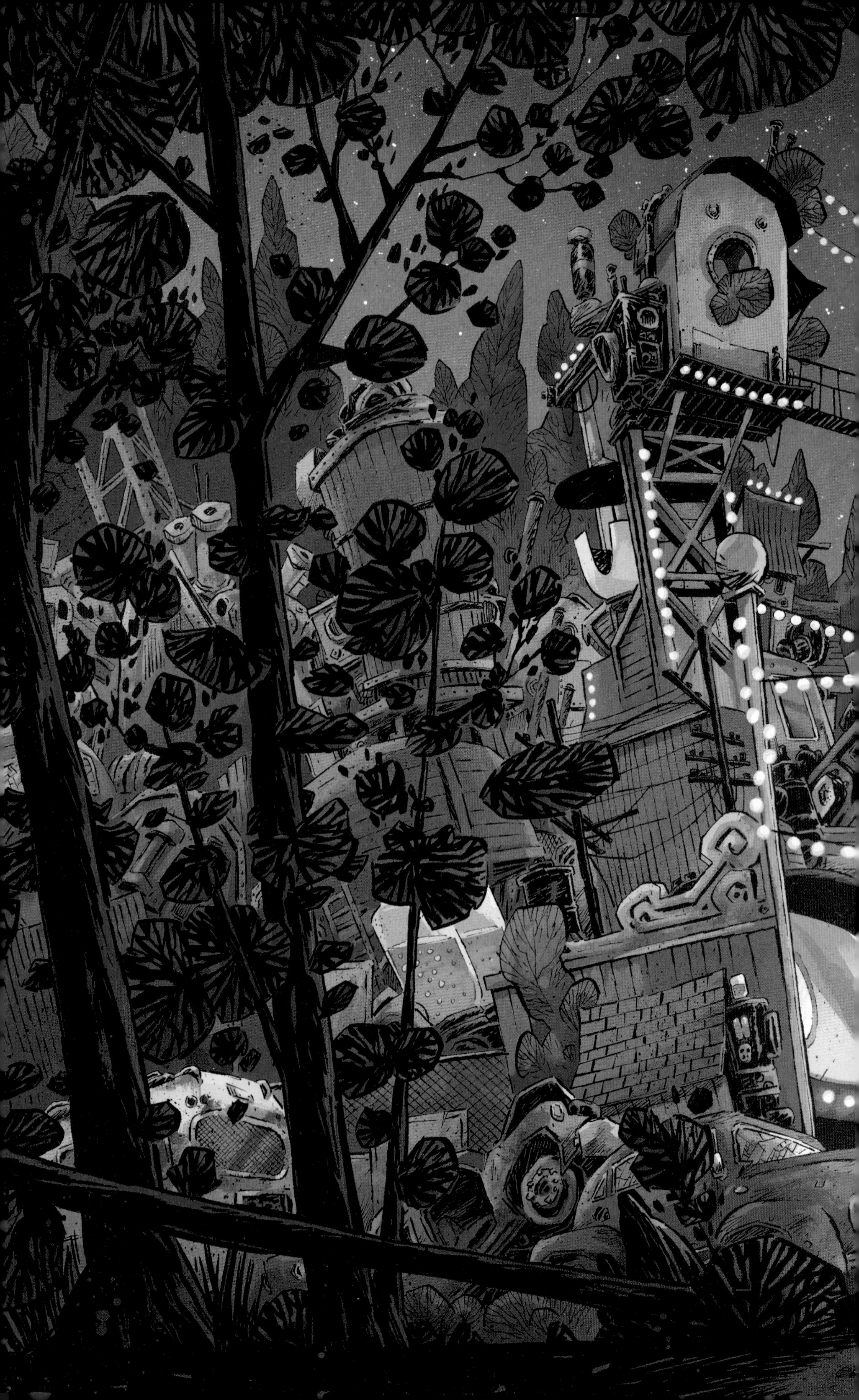

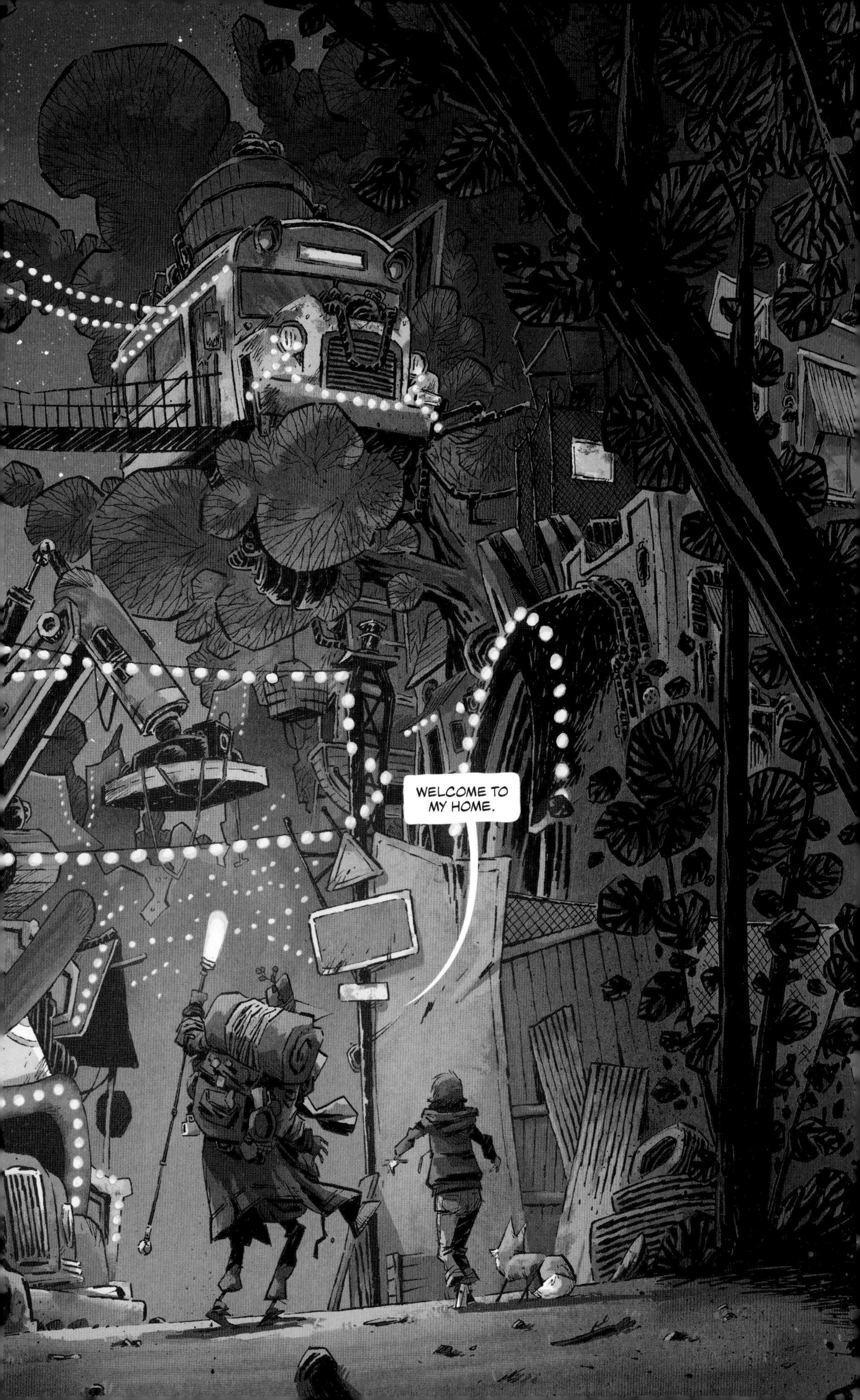
WELCOME TO MY HOME.

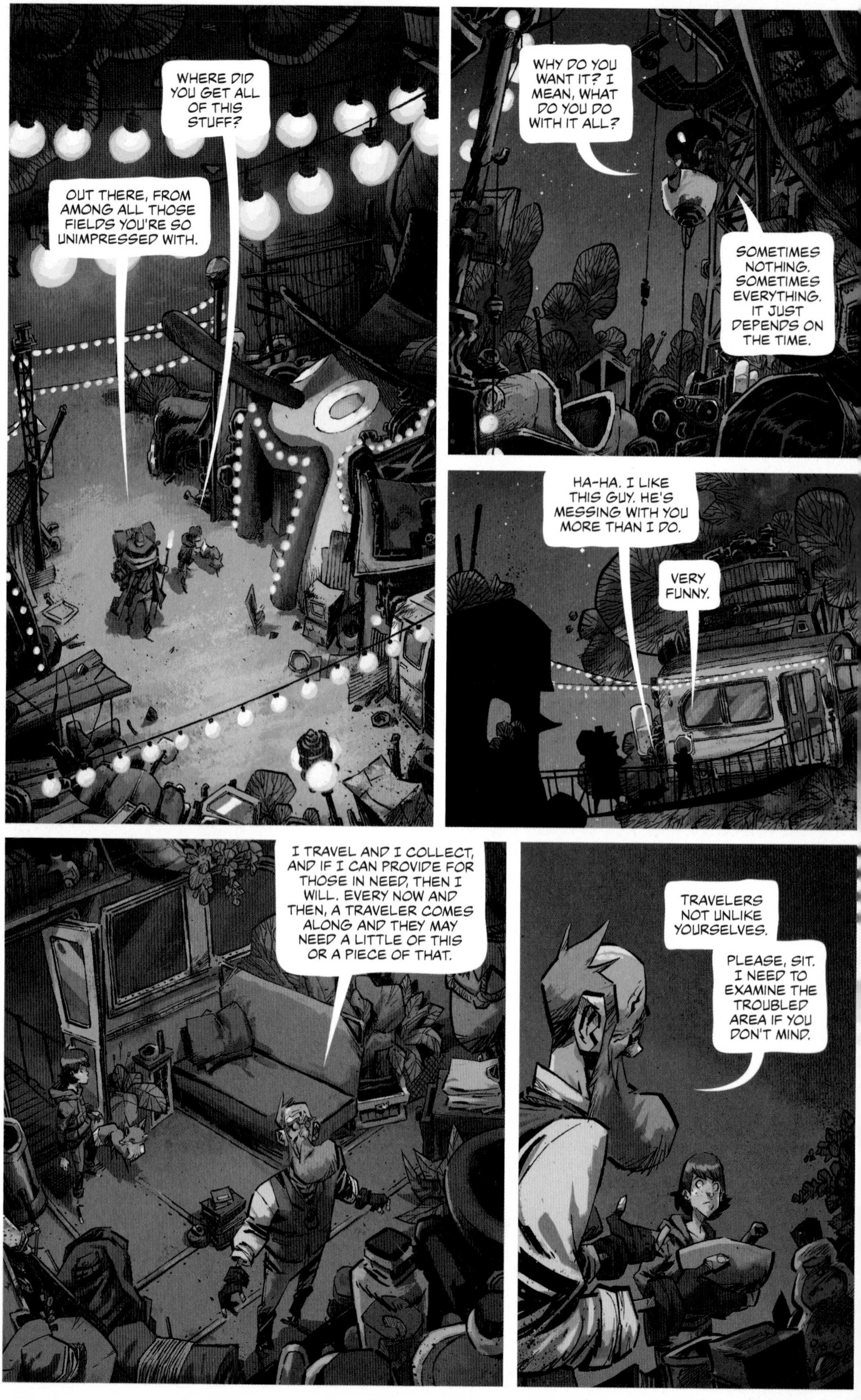
WHERE DID YOU GET ALL OF THIS STUFF?
OUT THERE, FROM AMONG ALL THOSE FIELDS YOU'RE SO UNIMPRESSED WITH.
WHY DO YOU WANT IT? I MEAN, WHAT DO YOU DO WITH IT ALL?
SOMETIMES NOTHING. SOMETIMES EVERYTHING. IT JUST DEPENDS ON THE TIME.
HA-HA. I LIKE THIS GUY. HE'S MESSING WITH YOU MORE THAN I DO.
VERY FUNNY.
I TRAVEL AND I COLLECT, AND IF I CAN PROVIDE FOR THOSE IN NEED, THEN I WILL. EVERY NOW AND THEN, A TRAVELER COMES ALONG AND THEY MAY NEED A LITTLE OF THIS OR A PIECE OF THAT.
TRAVELERS NOT UNLIKE YOURSELVES.
PLEASE, SIT. I NEED TO EXAMINE THE TROUBLED AREA IF YOU DON'T MIND.

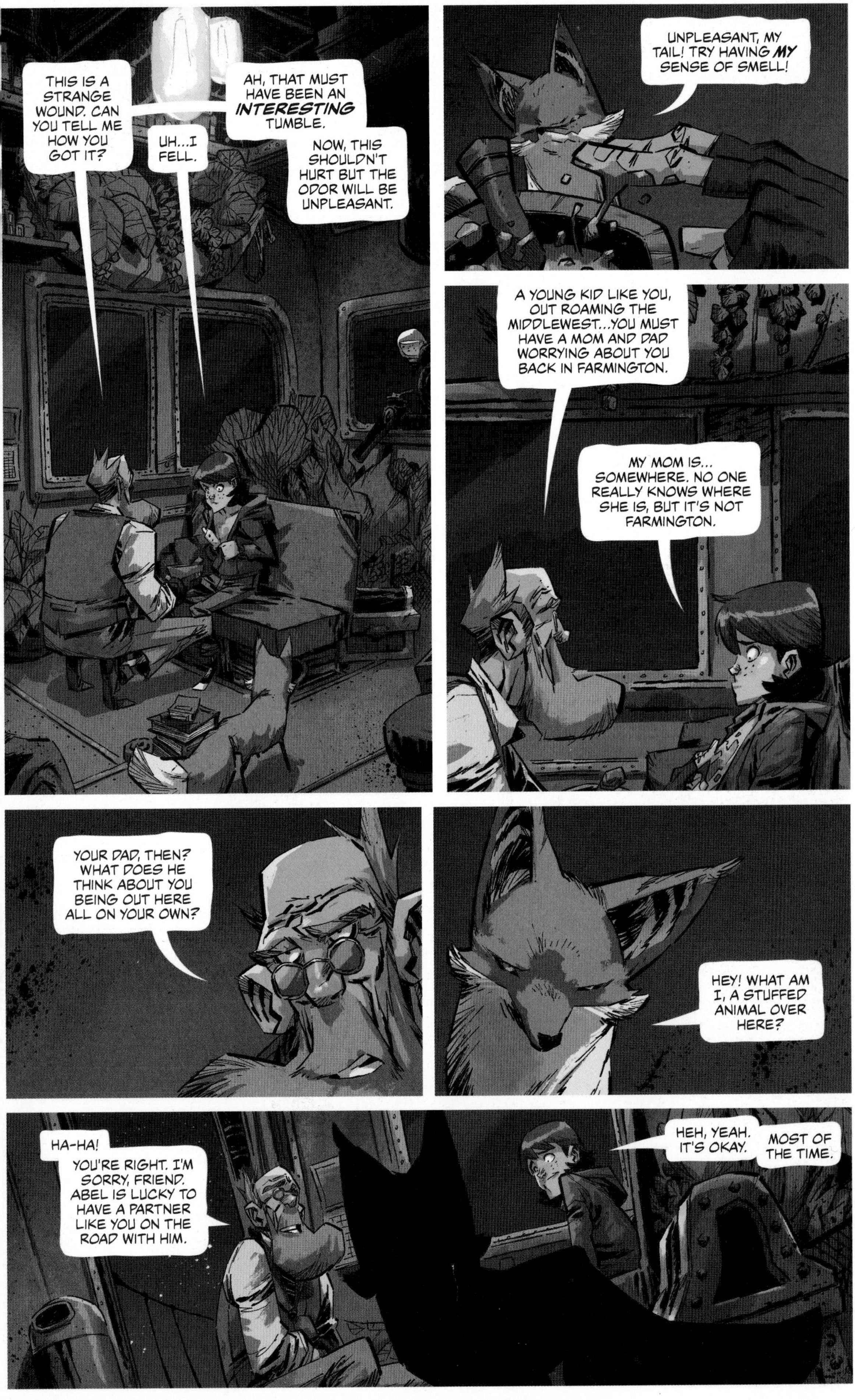
THIS IS A STRANGE WOUND. CAN YOU TELL ME HOW YOU GOT IT?
UH...I FELL.
AH, THAT MUST HAVE BEEN AN INTERESTING TUMBLE.
NOW, THIS SHOULDN'T HURT BUT THE ODOR WILL BE UNPLEASANT.
UNPLEASANT, MY TAIL! TRY HAVING MY SENSE OF SMELL!
A YOUNG KID LIKE YOU, OUT ROAMING THE MIDDLEWEST...YOU MUST HAVE A MOM AND DAD WORRYING ABOUT YOU BACK IN FARMINGTON.
MY MOM IS... SOMEWHERE. NO ONE REALLY KNOWS WHERE SHE IS, BUT IT'S NOT FARMINGTON.
YOUR DAD, THEN? WHAT DOES HE THINK ABOUT YOU BEING OUT HERE ALL ON YOUR OWN?
HEY! WHAT AM I, A STUFFED ANIMAL OVER HERE?
HA-HA!
YOU'RE RIGHT. I'M SORRY, FRIEND. ABEL IS LUCKY TO HAVE A PARTNER LIKE YOU ON THE ROAD WITH HIM.
HEH, YEAH. IT'S OKAY.
MOST OF THE TIME.

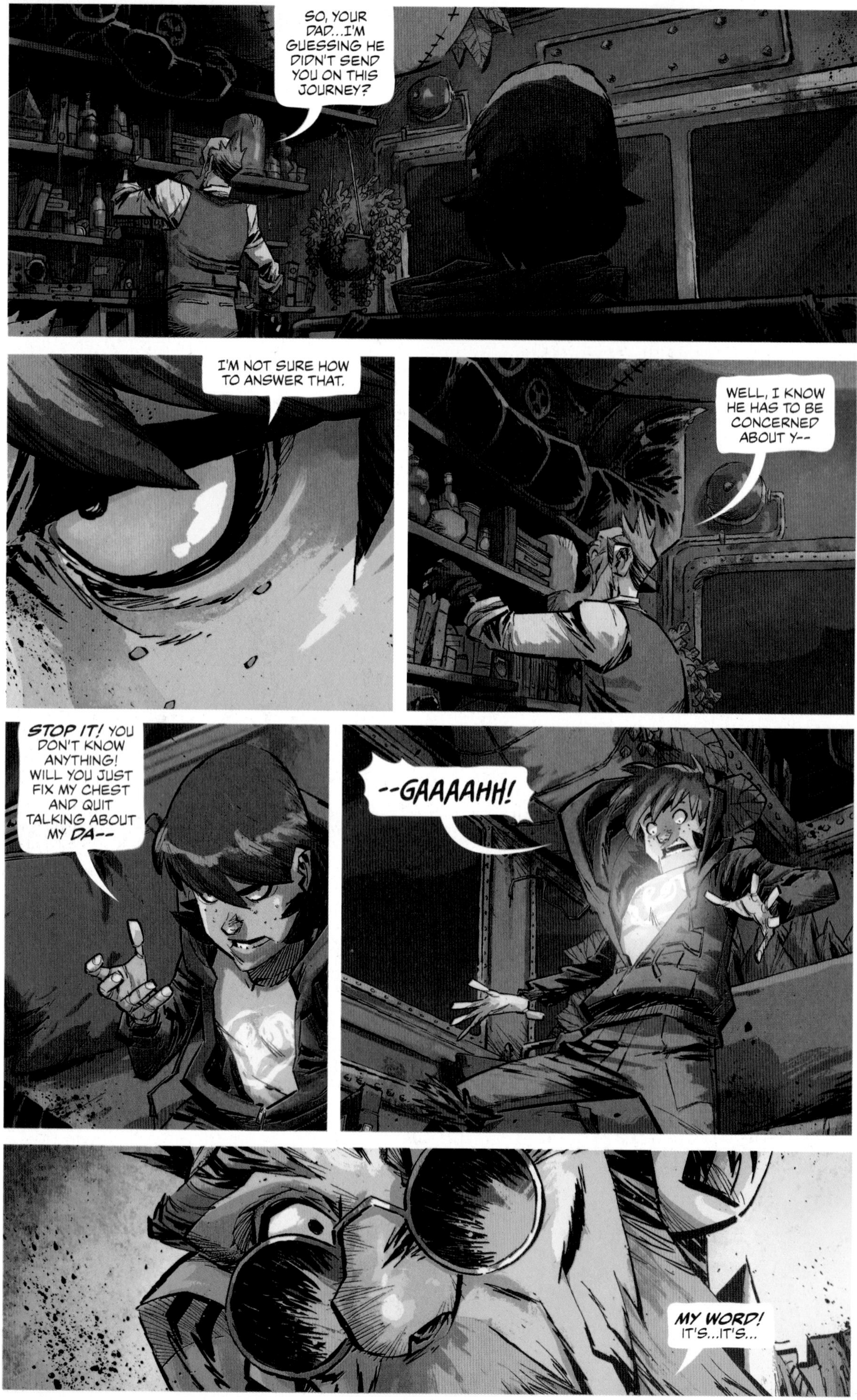
SO, YOUR DAD...I'M GUESSING HE DIDN'T SEND YOU ON THIS JOURNEY?
I'M NOT SURE HOW TO ANSWER THAT.
WELL, I KNOW HE HAS TO BE CONCERNED ABOUT Y--
STOP IT! YOU DON'T KNOW ANYTHING! WILL YOU JUST FIX MY CHEST AND QUIT TALKING ABOUT MY DA--
--GAAAAHH!
MY WORD! IT'S...IT'S...

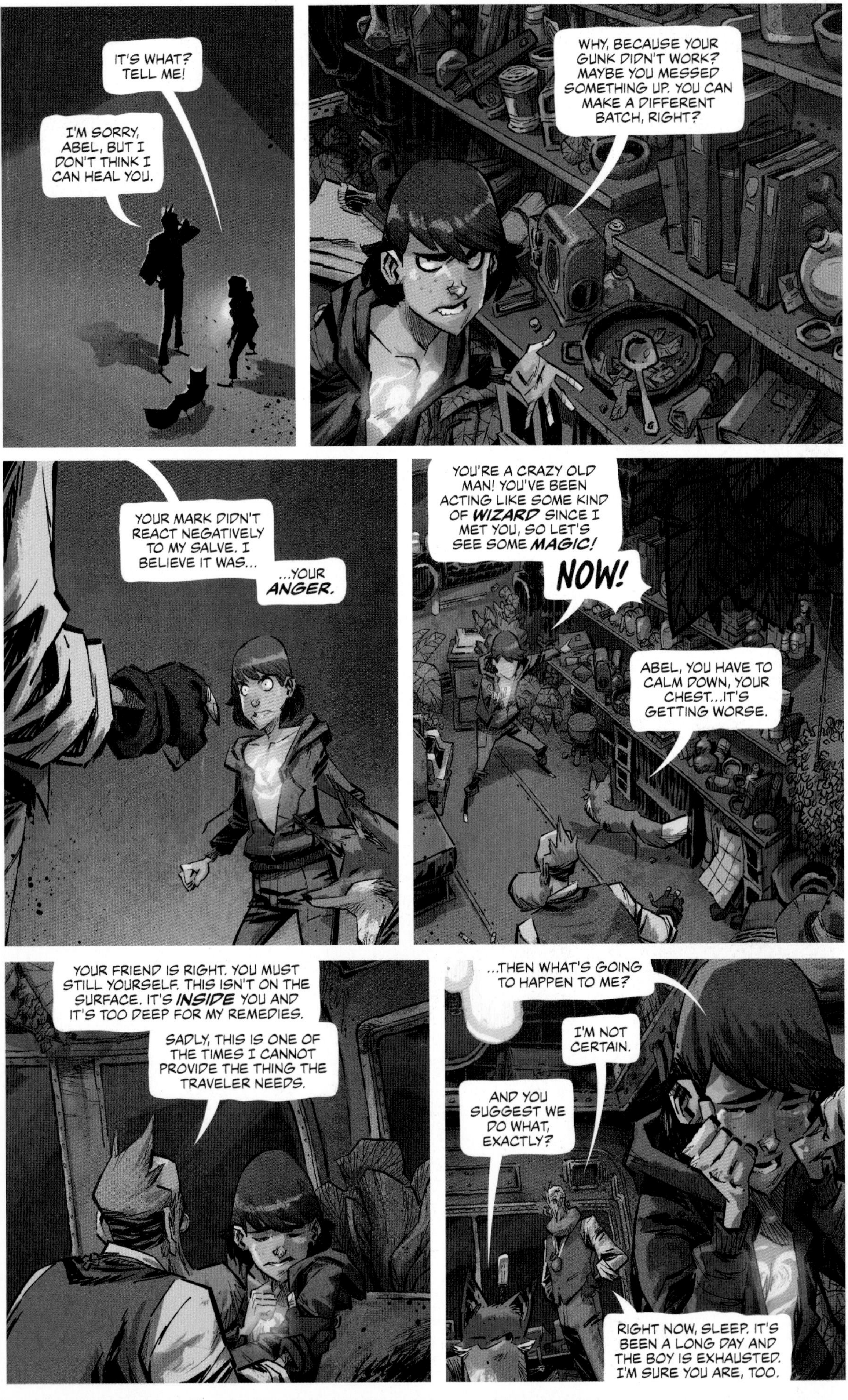
IT'S WHAT? TELL ME!
I'M SORRY, ABEL, BUT I DON'T THINK I CAN HEAL YOU.
WHY, BECAUSE YOUR GUNK DIDN'T WORK? MAYBE YOU MESSED SOMETHING UP. YOU CAN MAKE A DIFFERENT BATCH, RIGHT?
YOUR MARK DIDN'T REACT NEGATIVELY TO MY SALVE. I BELIEVE IT WAS...
...YOUR ANGER.
YOU'RE A CRAZY OLD MAN! YOU'VE BEEN ACTING LIKE SOME KIND OF WIZARD SINCE I MET YOU, SO LET'S SEE SOME MAGIC!
NOW!
ABEL, YOU HAVE TO CALM DOWN, YOUR CHEST...IT'S GETTING WORSE.
YOUR FRIEND IS RIGHT. YOU MUST STILL YOURSELF. THIS ISN'T ON THE SURFACE. IT'S INSIDE YOU AND IT'S TOO DEEP FOR MY REMEDIES.
SADLY, THIS IS ONE OF THE TIMES I CANNOT PROVIDE THE THING THE TRAVELER NEEDS.
...THEN WHAT'S GOING TO HAPPEN TO ME?
I'M NOT CERTAIN.
AND YOU SUGGEST WE DO WHAT, EXACTLY?
RIGHT NOW, SLEEP. IT'S BEEN A LONG DAY AND THE BOY IS EXHAUSTED. I'M SURE YOU ARE, TOO.

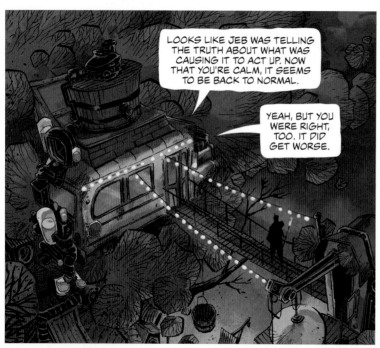

LOOKS LIKE JEB WAS TELLING THE TRUTH ABOUT WHAT WAS CAUSING IT TO ACT UP. NOW THAT YOU'RE CALM, IT SEEMS TO BE BACK TO NORMAL.

YEAH, BUT YOU WERE RIGHT, TOO. IT DID GET WORSE.

IT'S GROWING, SPREADING OUT MORE THAN IT WAS BEFORE.

HOPEFULLY OL' JEB WILL HAVE MORE ANSWERS FOR US IN THE MORNING.

WE'RE NOT WAITING.

YOU NEED SOME SLEEP, ABEL.

NO WAY. IF THIS THING IS SPREADING, THEN I NEED TO FIGURE OUT HOW TO GET RID OF IT *NOW.*

OH, SO WHAT? YOU'RE A WIZARD NOW, TOO?

NO, BUT JEB KNOWS MORE THAN HE'S TELLING ME.

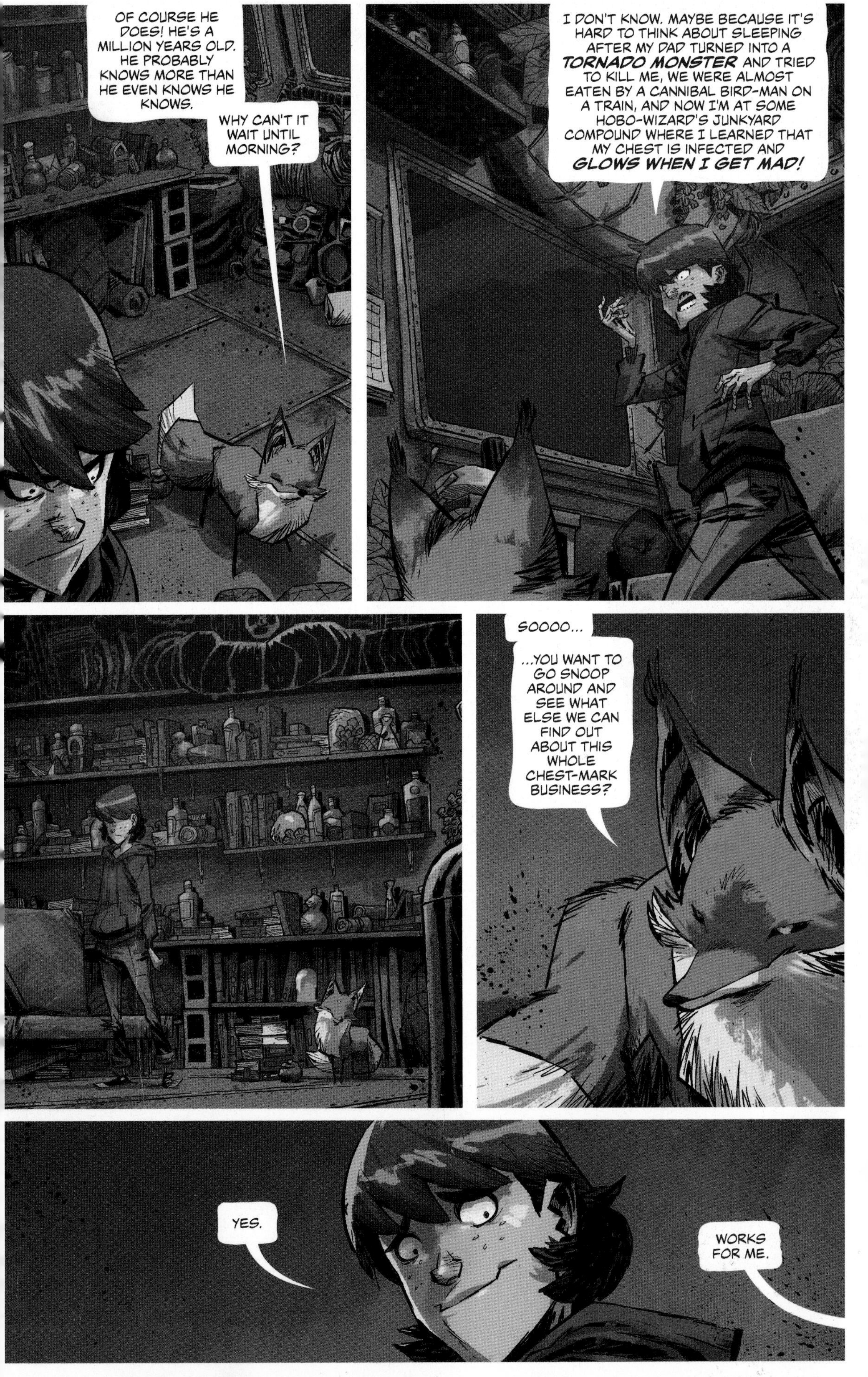

OF COURSE HE DOES! HE'S A MILLION YEARS OLD. HE PROBABLY KNOWS MORE THAN HE EVEN KNOWS HE KNOWS.
WHY CAN'T IT WAIT UNTIL MORNING?
I DON'T KNOW. MAYBE BECAUSE IT'S HARD TO THINK ABOUT SLEEPING AFTER MY DAD TURNED INTO A **TORNADO MONSTER** AND TRIED TO KILL ME, WE WERE ALMOST EATEN BY A CANNIBAL BIRD-MAN ON A TRAIN, AND NOW I'M AT SOME HOBO-WIZARD'S JUNKYARD COMPOUND WHERE I LEARNED THAT MY CHEST IS INFECTED AND **GLOWS WHEN I GET MAD!**
SOOOO...
...YOU WANT TO GO SNOOP AROUND AND SEE WHAT ELSE WE CAN FIND OUT ABOUT THIS WHOLE CHEST-MARK BUSINESS?
YES.
WORKS FOR ME.

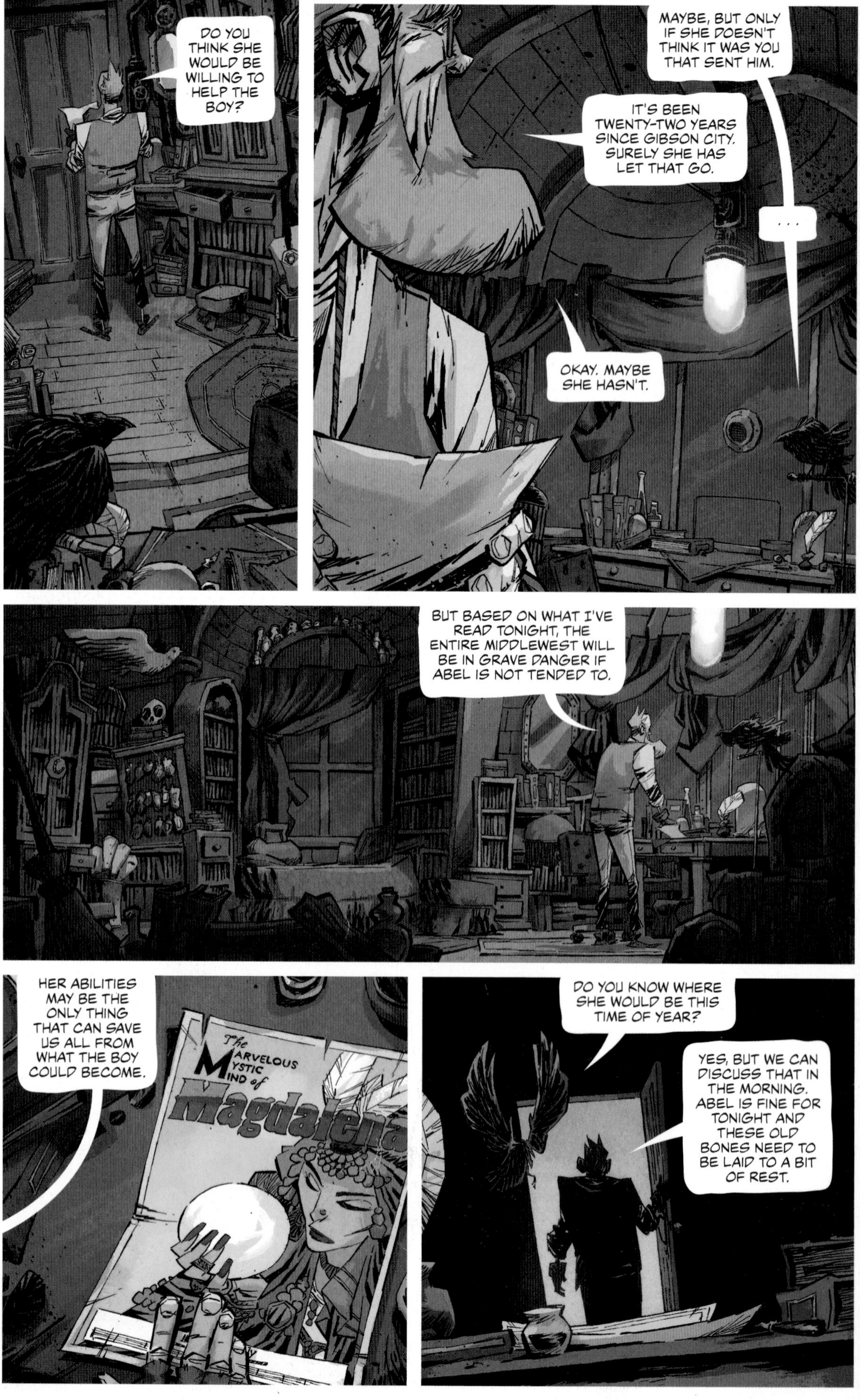
DO YOU THINK SHE WOULD BE WILLING TO HELP THE BOY?
MAYBE, BUT ONLY IF SHE DOESN'T THINK IT WAS YOU THAT SENT HIM.
IT'S BEEN TWENTY-TWO YEARS SINCE GIBSON CITY. SURELY SHE HAS LET THAT GO.
. . .
OKAY. MAYBE SHE HASN'T.
BUT BASED ON WHAT I'VE READ TONIGHT, THE ENTIRE MIDDLEWEST WILL BE IN GRAVE DANGER IF ABEL IS NOT TENDED TO.
HER ABILITIES MAY BE THE ONLY THING THAT CAN SAVE US ALL FROM WHAT THE BOY COULD BECOME.
The Marvelous Mystic Mind of Magdalena
DO YOU KNOW WHERE SHE WOULD BE THIS TIME OF YEAR?
YES, BUT WE CAN DISCUSS THAT IN THE MORNING. ABEL IS FINE FOR TONIGHT AND THESE OLD BONES NEED TO BE LAID TO A BIT OF REST.

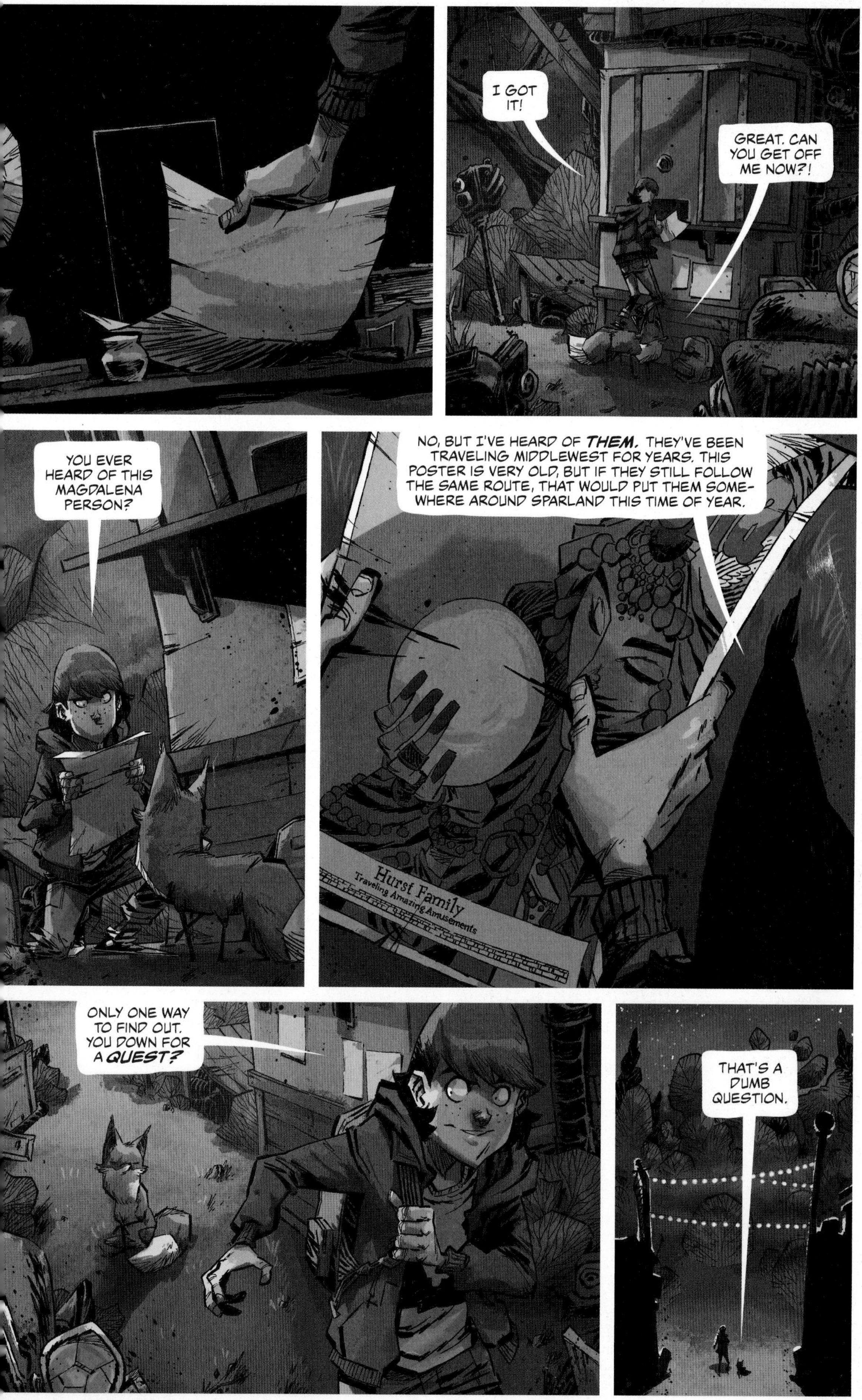
I GOT IT!
GREAT. CAN YOU GET OFF ME NOW?!
YOU EVER HEARD OF THIS MAGDALENA PERSON?
NO, BUT I'VE HEARD OF **THEM.** THEY'VE BEEN TRAVELING MIDDLEWEST FOR YEARS. THIS POSTER IS VERY OLD, BUT IF THEY STILL FOLLOW THE SAME ROUTE, THAT WOULD PUT THEM SOMEWHERE AROUND SPARLAND THIS TIME OF YEAR.
Hurst Family
Traveling Amazing Amusements
ONLY ONE WAY TO FIND OUT. YOU DOWN FOR A **QUEST?**
THAT'S A DUMB QUESTION.

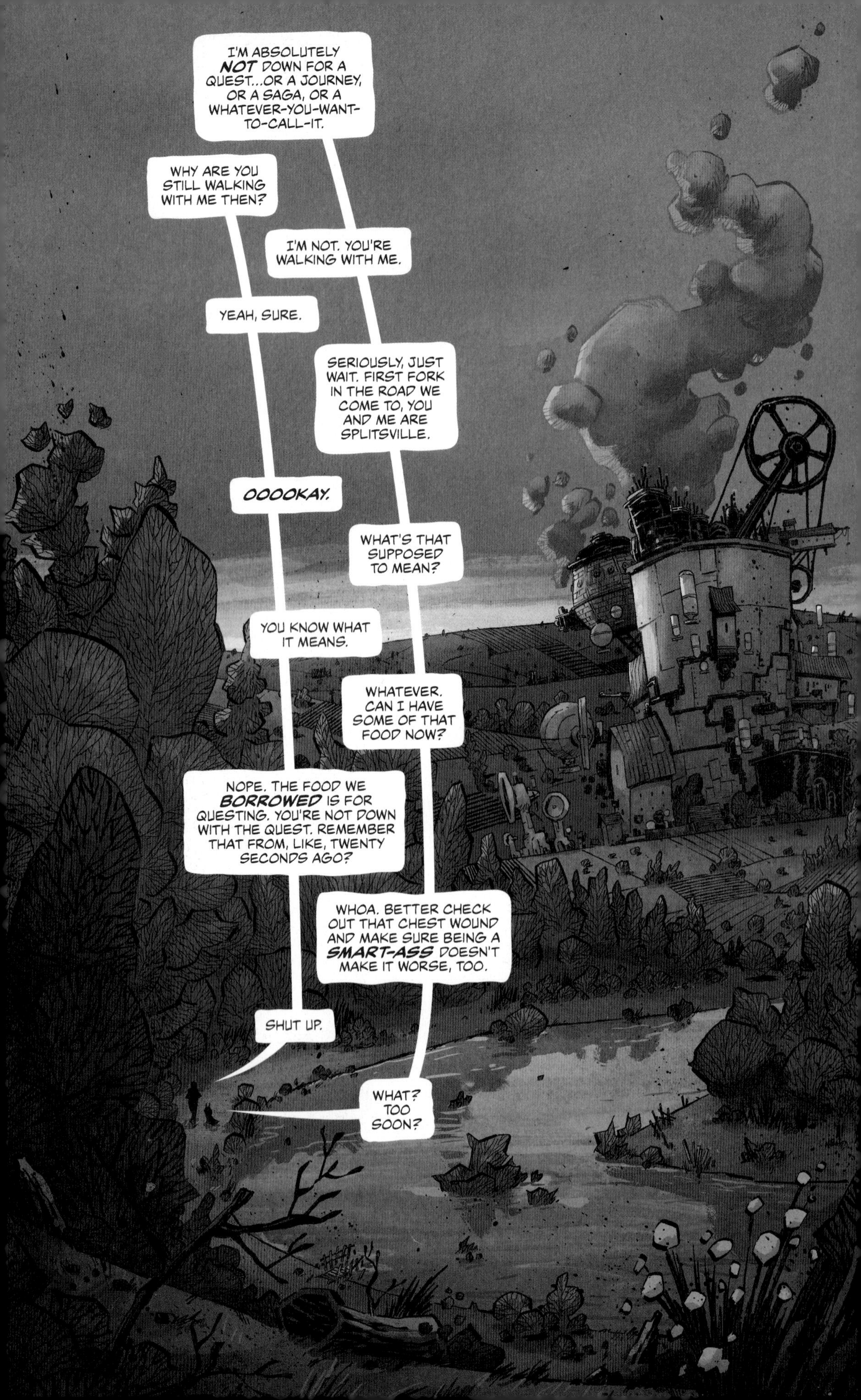
I'M ABSOLUTELY NOT DOWN FOR A QUEST...OR A JOURNEY, OR A SAGA, OR A WHATEVER-YOU-WANT-TO-CALL-IT.
WHY ARE YOU STILL WALKING WITH ME THEN?
I'M NOT. YOU'RE WALKING WITH ME.
YEAH, SURE.
SERIOUSLY, JUST WAIT. FIRST FORK IN THE ROAD WE COME TO, YOU AND ME ARE SPLITSVILLE.
OOOOKAY.
WHAT'S THAT SUPPOSED TO MEAN?
YOU KNOW WHAT IT MEANS.
WHATEVER. CAN I HAVE SOME OF THAT FOOD NOW?
NOPE. THE FOOD WE BORROWED IS FOR QUESTING. YOU'RE NOT DOWN WITH THE QUEST. REMEMBER THAT FROM, LIKE, TWENTY SECONDS AGO?
WHOA. BETTER CHECK OUT THAT CHEST WOUND AND MAKE SURE BEING A SMART-ASS DOESN'T MAKE IT WORSE, TOO.
SHUT UP.
WHAT? TOO SOON?

CHAPTER
THREE

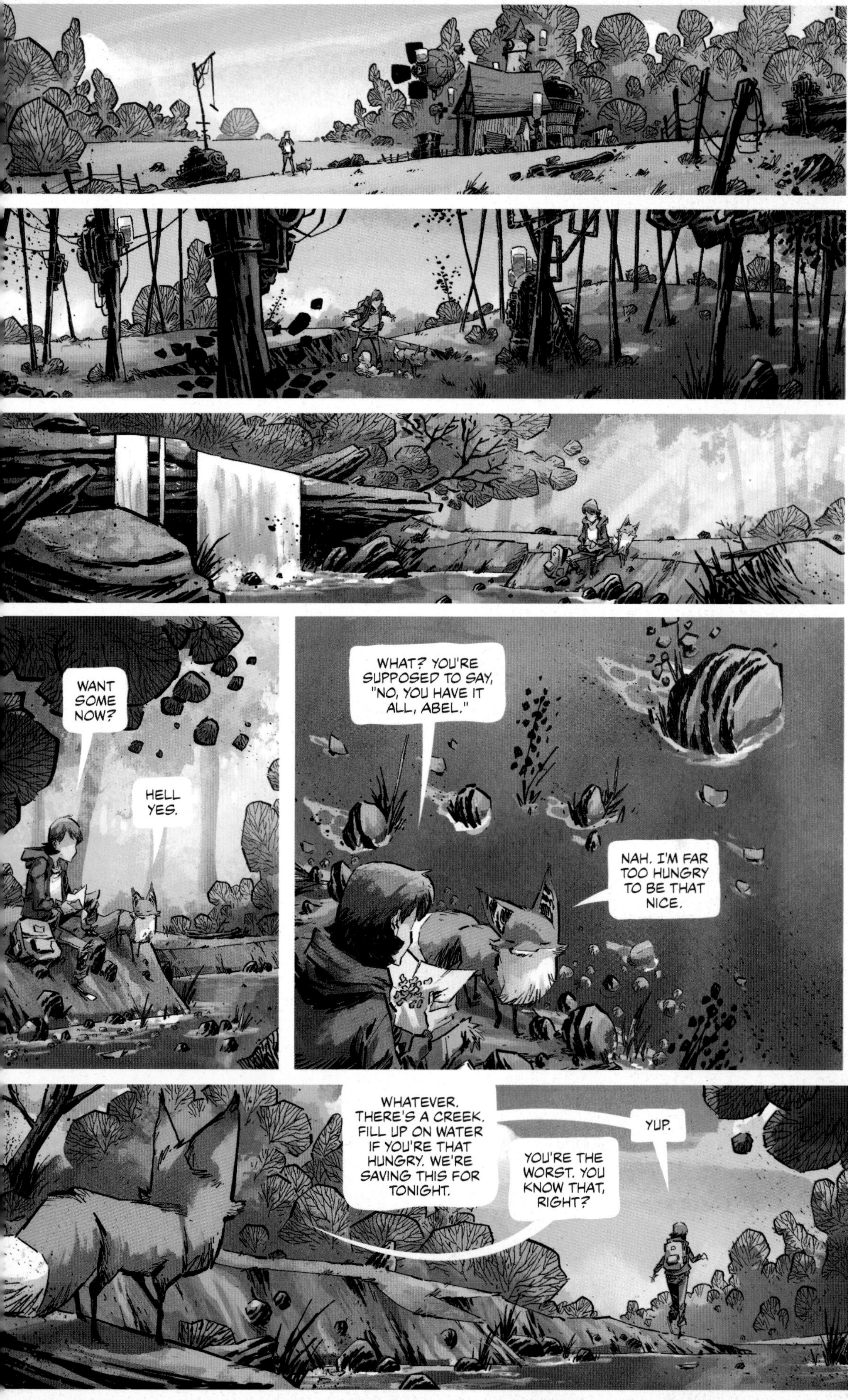
WANT SOME NOW?
HELL YES.
WHAT? YOU'RE SUPPOSED TO SAY, "NO, YOU HAVE IT ALL, ABEL."
NAH. I'M FAR TOO HUNGRY TO BE THAT NICE.
WHATEVER. THERE'S A CREEK. FILL UP ON WATER IF YOU'RE THAT HUNGRY. WE'RE SAVING THIS FOR TONIGHT.
YOU'RE THE WORST. YOU KNOW THAT, RIGHT?
YUP.

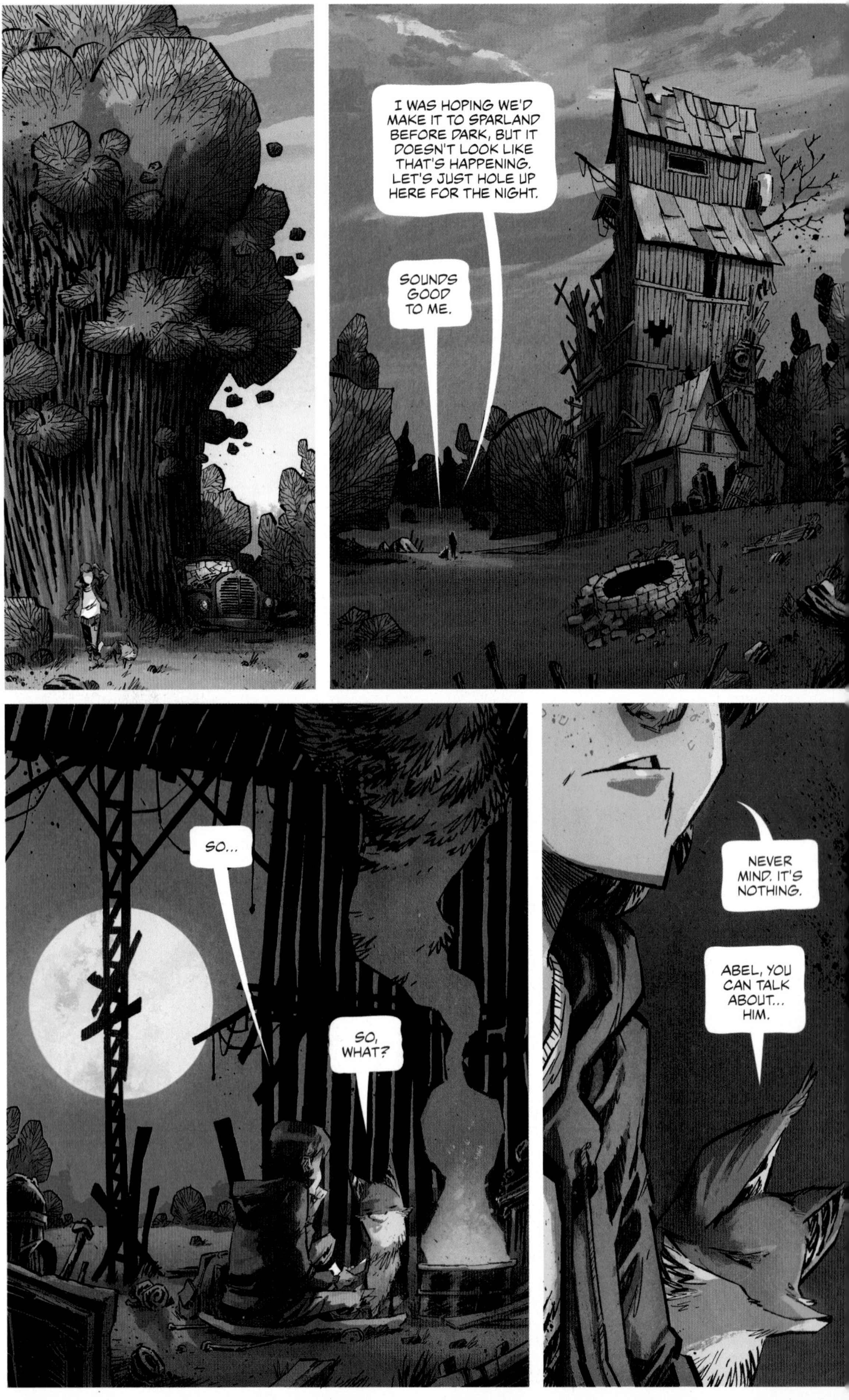
I WAS HOPING WE'D MAKE IT TO SPARLAND BEFORE DARK, BUT IT DOESN'T LOOK LIKE THAT'S HAPPENING. LET'S JUST HOLE UP HERE FOR THE NIGHT.
SOUNDS GOOD TO ME.
SO...
SO, WHAT?
NEVER MIND. IT'S NOTHING.
ABEL, YOU CAN TALK ABOUT... HIM.

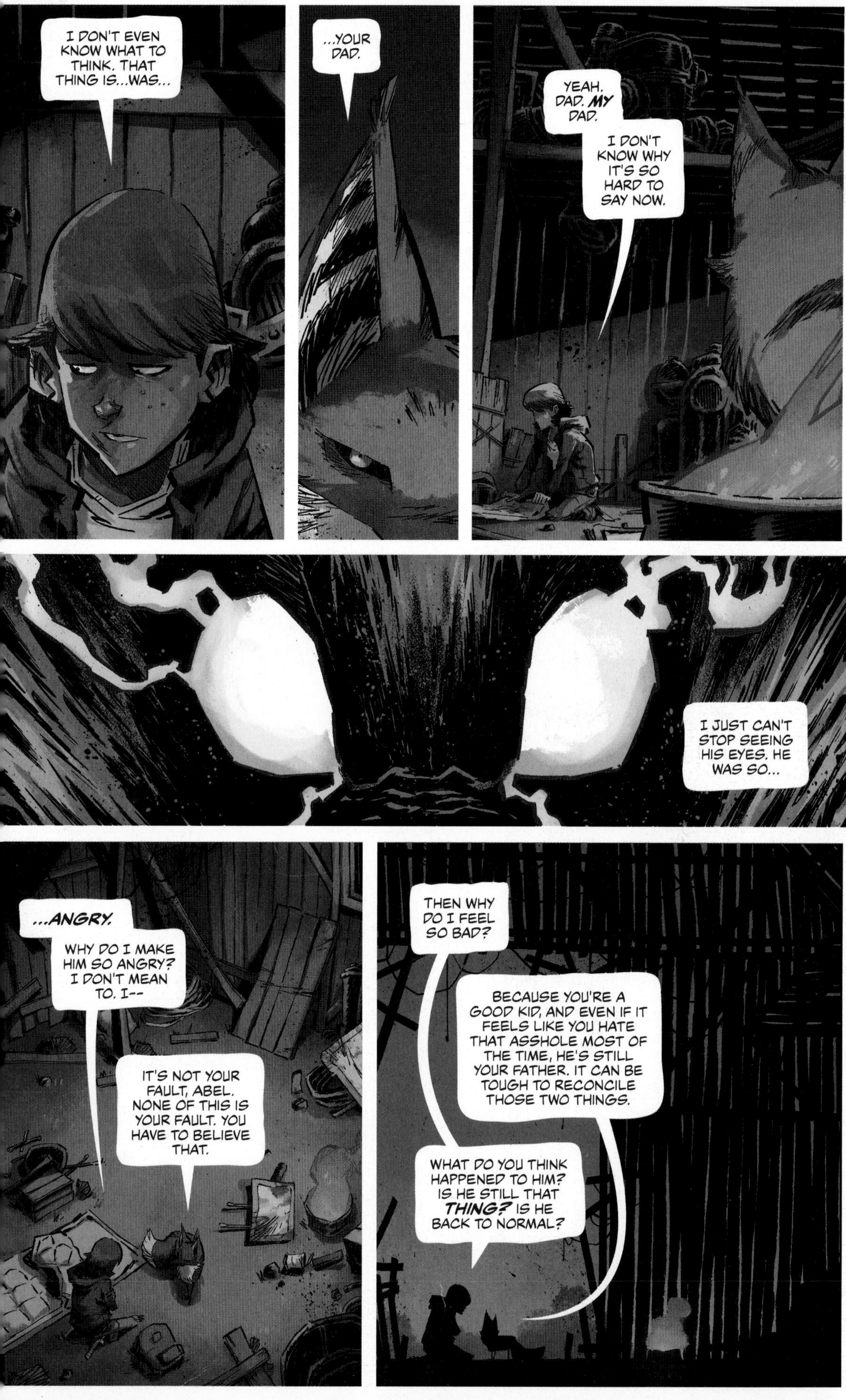
I DON'T EVEN KNOW WHAT TO THINK. THAT THING IS...WAS...
...YOUR DAD.
YEAH. DAD. MY DAD.
I DON'T KNOW WHY IT'S SO HARD TO SAY NOW.
I JUST CAN'T STOP SEEING HIS EYES. HE WAS SO...
...ANGRY.
WHY DO I MAKE HIM SO ANGRY? I DON'T MEAN TO. I--
IT'S NOT YOUR FAULT, ABEL. NONE OF THIS IS YOUR FAULT. YOU HAVE TO BELIEVE THAT.
THEN WHY DO I FEEL SO BAD?
BECAUSE YOU'RE A GOOD KID, AND EVEN IF IT FEELS LIKE YOU HATE THAT ASSHOLE MOST OF THE TIME, HE'S STILL YOUR FATHER. IT CAN BE TOUGH TO RECONCILE THOSE TWO THINGS.
WHAT DO YOU THINK HAPPENED TO HIM? IS HE STILL THAT THING? IS HE BACK TO NORMAL?

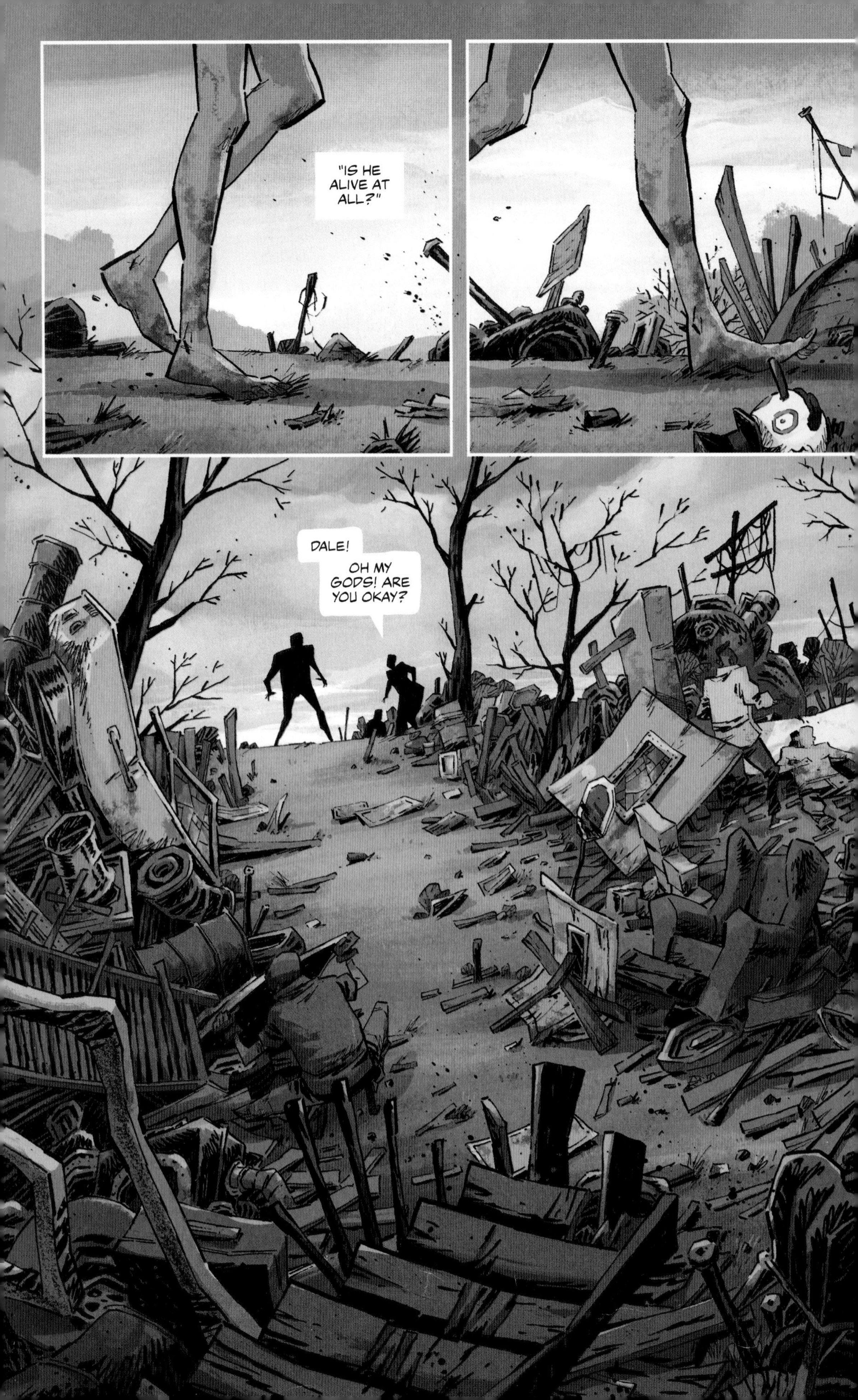
"IS HE ALIVE AT ALL?"
DALE!
OH MY GODS! ARE YOU OKAY?

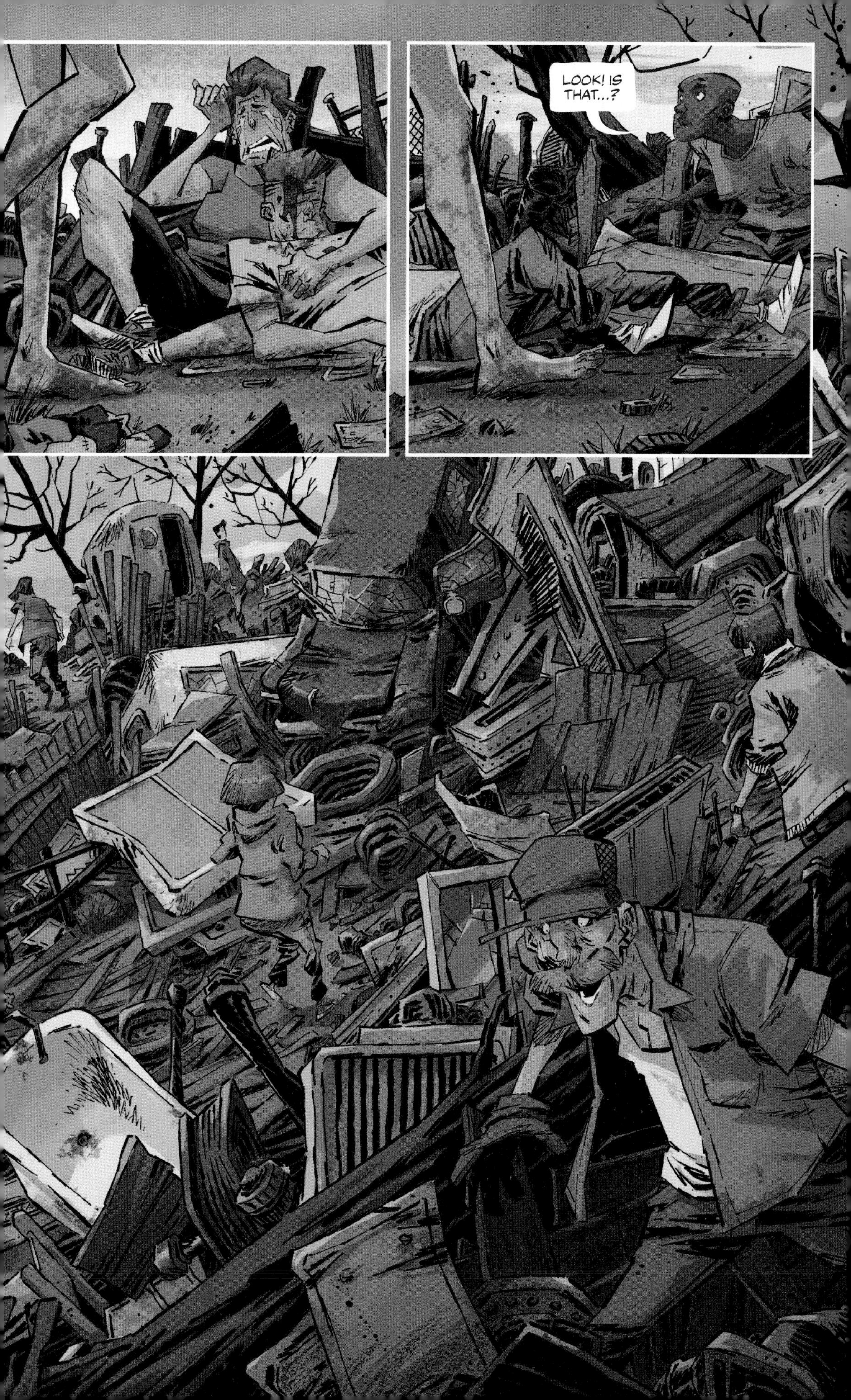
LOOK! IS THAT...?

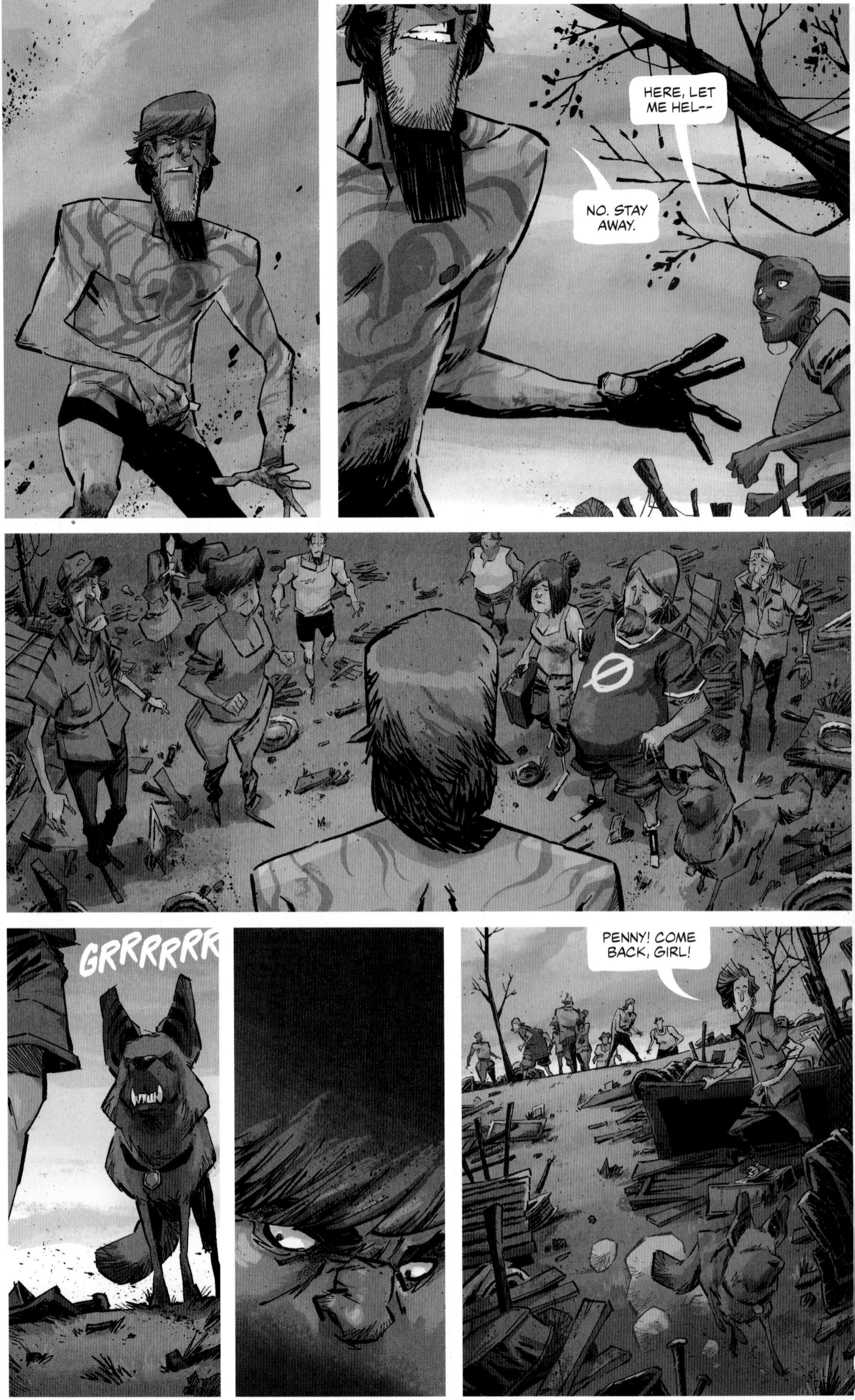
HERE, LET ME HEL--
NO. STAY AWAY.
GRRRRRR
PENNY! COME BACK, GIRL!

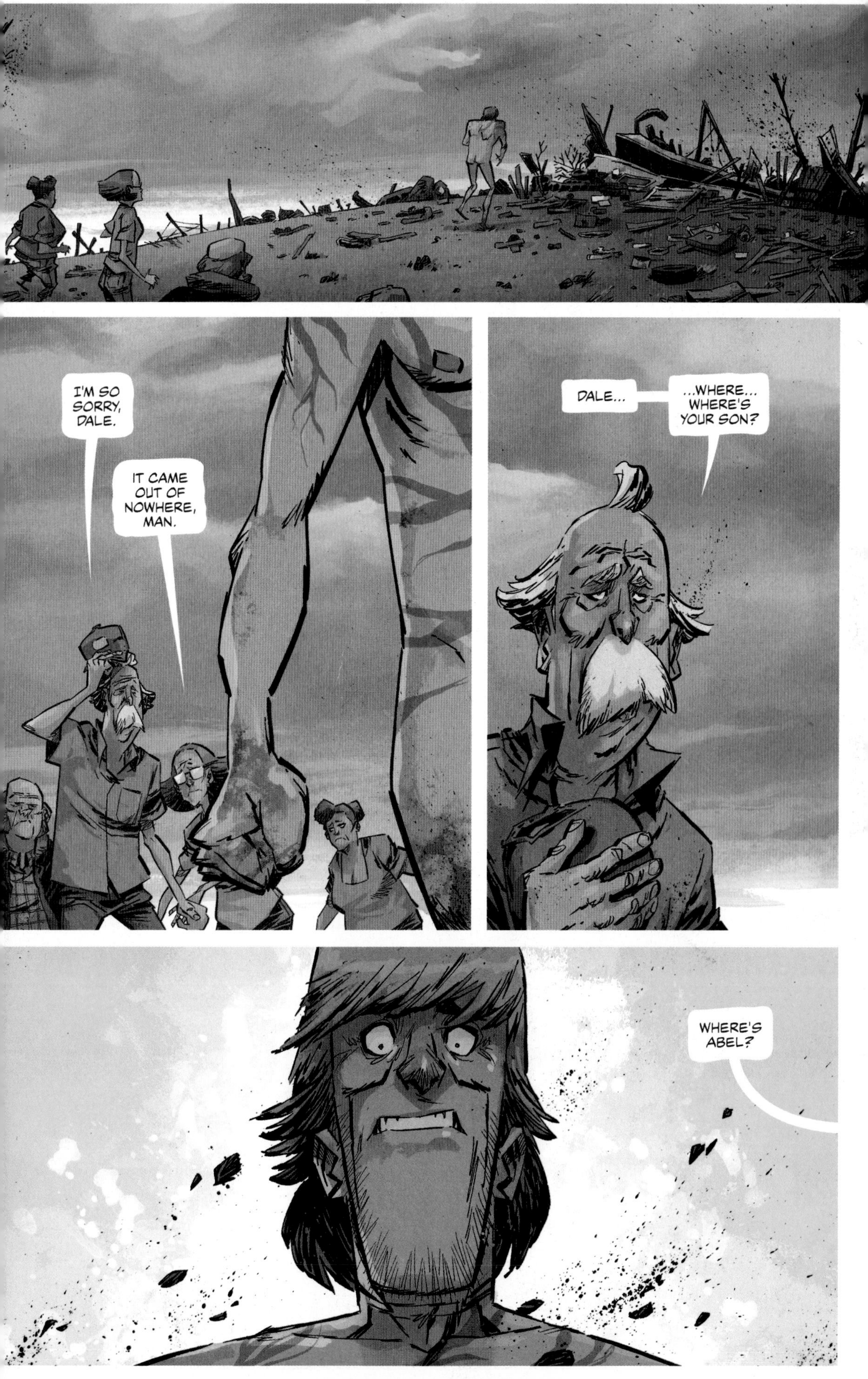
I'M SO SORRY, DALE.
IT CAME OUT OF NOWHERE, MAN.
DALE...
...WHERE... WHERE'S YOUR SON?
WHERE'S ABEL?

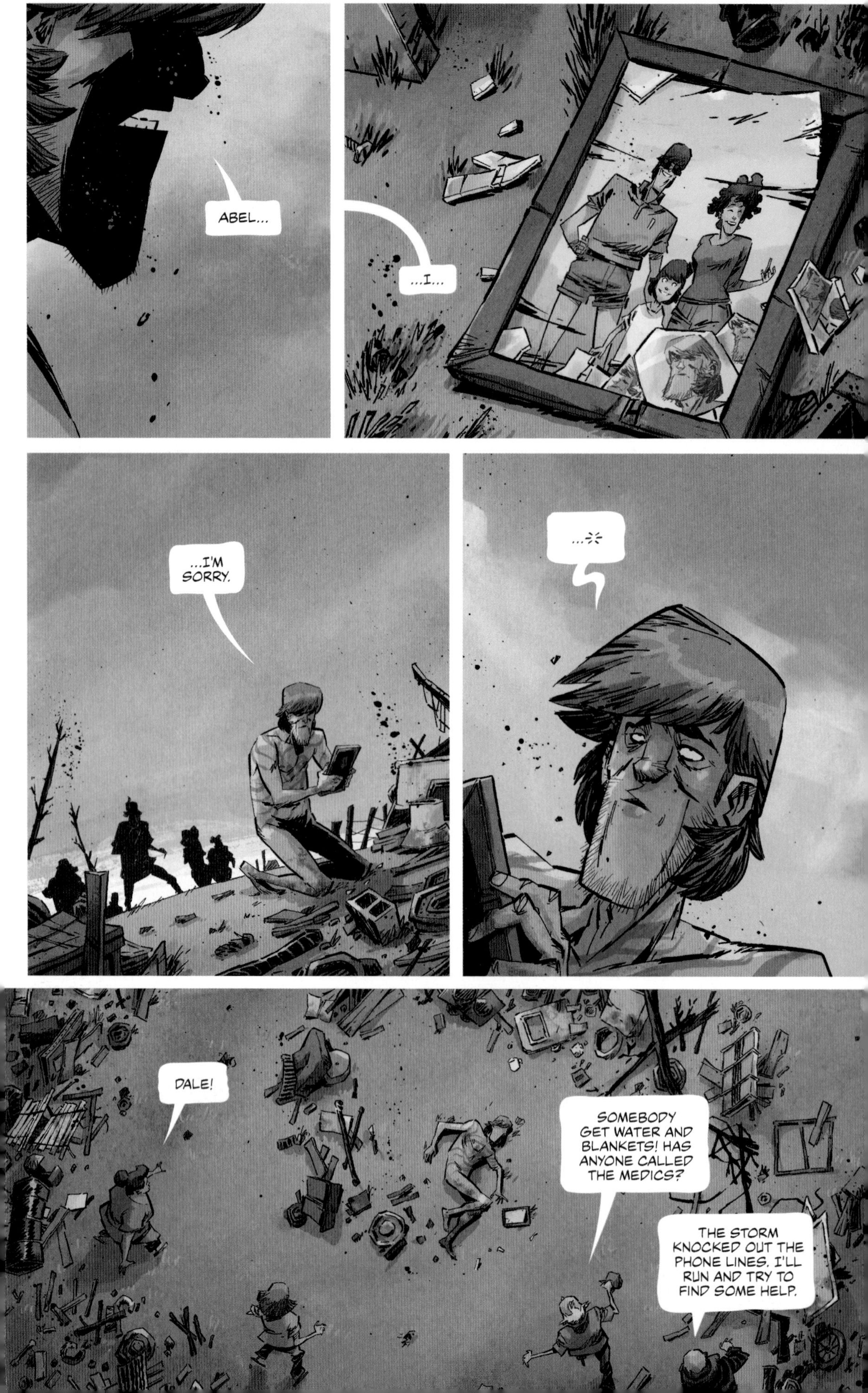
ABEL...
...I...
...I'M SORRY.
...
DALE!
SOMEBODY GET WATER AND BLANKETS! HAS ANYONE CALLED THE MEDICS?
THE STORM KNOCKED OUT THE PHONE LINES. I'LL RUN AND TRY TO FIND SOME HELP.

TWO DAYS LATER.

HE'S STILL UNCONSCIOUS, BUT ALL OF HIS VITALS ARE NORMAL.

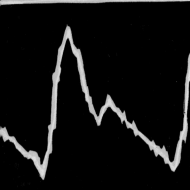

DID THE BLOOD PANEL COME BACK YET?

YES, ALL CLEAR AS WELL.

NONE OF THIS MAKES ANY SENSE. IF NOTHING IS WRONG WITH HIM...

...THEN HOW DO WE EXPLAIN *THAT?*

AN INFECTION OF THIS KIND SHOULD HAVE RAVAGED HIS BLOOD-STREAM BY NOW--OR WORSE, KILLED HIM. BUT--

DOCTOR, LOOK. HE'S WAKING UP.

M-M-MY... SON.

ABEL...

...W-WHERE'S... MY...SON?

KORI, CAN YOU SEE IF THE SHERIFF IS STILL DOWN THE HALL AND ASK HER TO COME IN HERE?

DALE, YOU WERE CAUGHT IN A STORM A FEW DAYS AGO, BUT YOU'RE OKAY NOW. WE'RE TAKING GOOD CARE OF YOU.

I HAVE TO GO.

I UNDERSTAND, BUT RIGHT NOW I NEED YOU TO LIE DOWN AND STAY CALM.

YOU JUST SAID I WAS OKAY, RIGHT?

YES, BUT--

GOOD. THEN I NEED TO GO FIND MY BOY.

WE NEED TO TALK ABOUT THAT.

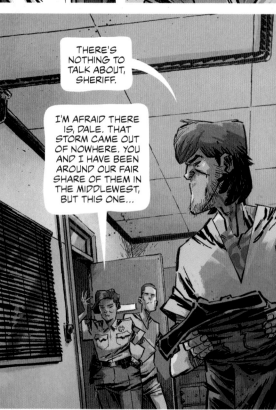

THERE'S NOTHING TO TALK ABOUT, SHERIFF.

I'M AFRAID THERE IS, DALE. THAT STORM CAME OUT OF NOWHERE. YOU AND I HAVE BEEN AROUND OUR FAIR SHARE OF THEM IN THE MIDDLEWEST, BUT THIS ONE...

...IT WAS DIFFERENT. SOMETHING MUCH WORSE THAN WE'VE EVER SEEN. AS IF IT WAS, I DON'T KNOW...

...ANGRY?

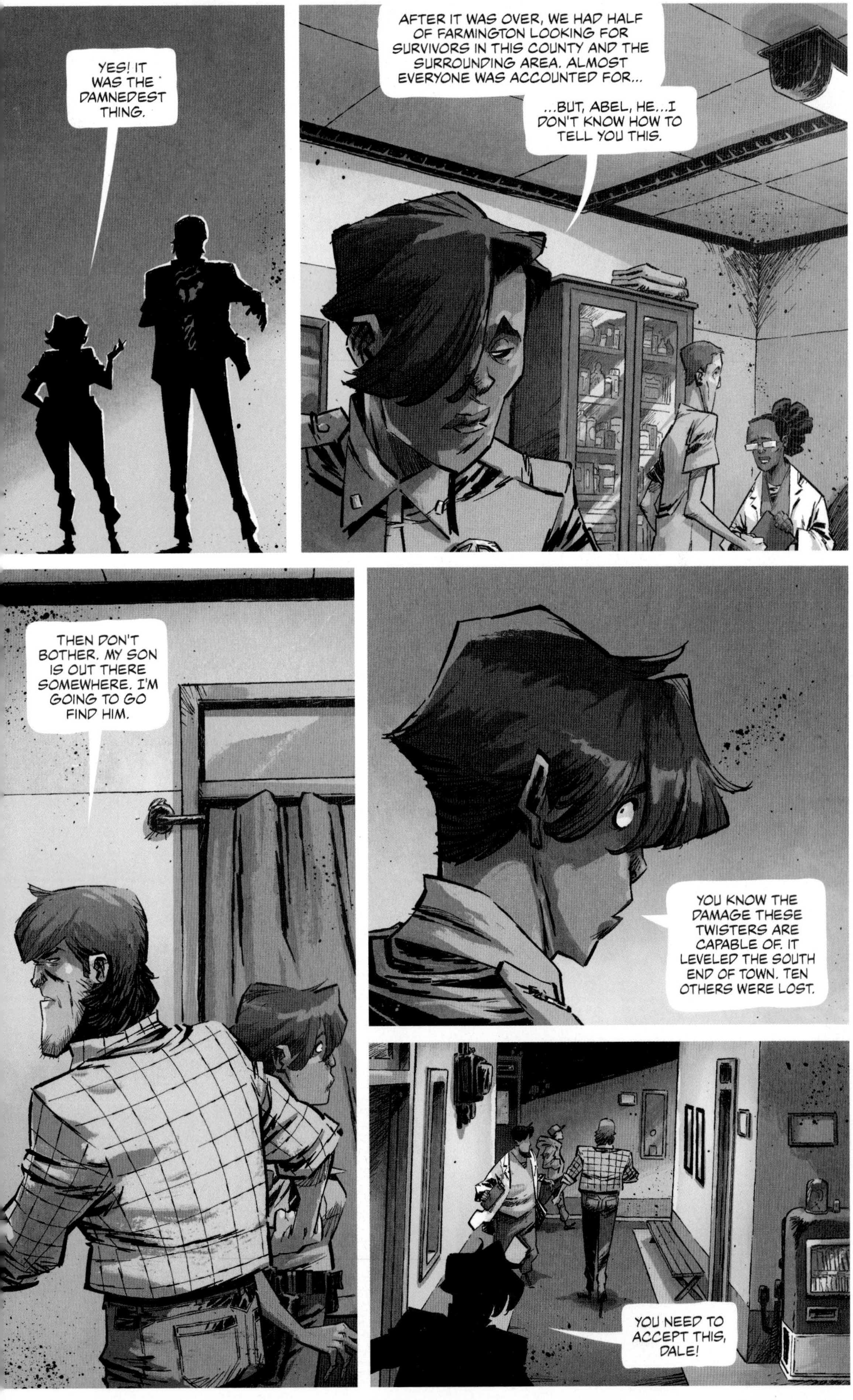
YES! IT WAS THE DAMNEDEST THING.
AFTER IT WAS OVER, WE HAD HALF OF FARMINGTON LOOKING FOR SURVIVORS IN THIS COUNTY AND THE SURROUNDING AREA. ALMOST EVERYONE WAS ACCOUNTED FOR...
...BUT, ABEL, HE...I DON'T KNOW HOW TO TELL YOU THIS.
THEN DON'T BOTHER. MY SON IS OUT THERE SOMEWHERE. I'M GOING TO GO FIND HIM.
YOU KNOW THE DAMAGE THESE TWISTERS ARE CAPABLE OF. IT LEVELED THE SOUTH END OF TOWN. TEN OTHERS WERE LOST.
YOU NEED TO ACCEPT THIS, DALE!

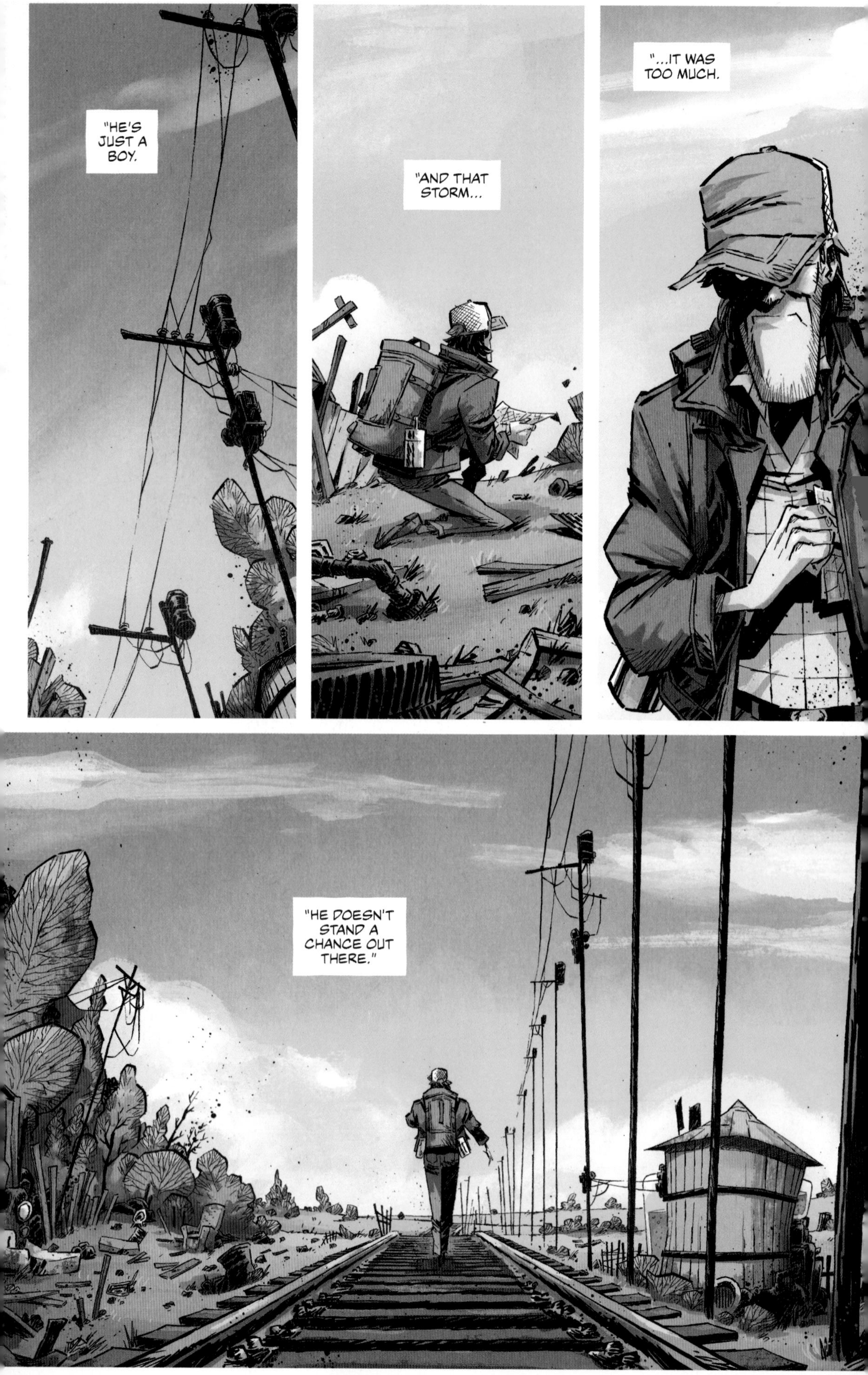
"HE'S JUST A BOY.
"AND THAT STORM...
"...IT WAS TOO MUCH.
"HE DOESN'T STAND A CHANCE OUT THERE."

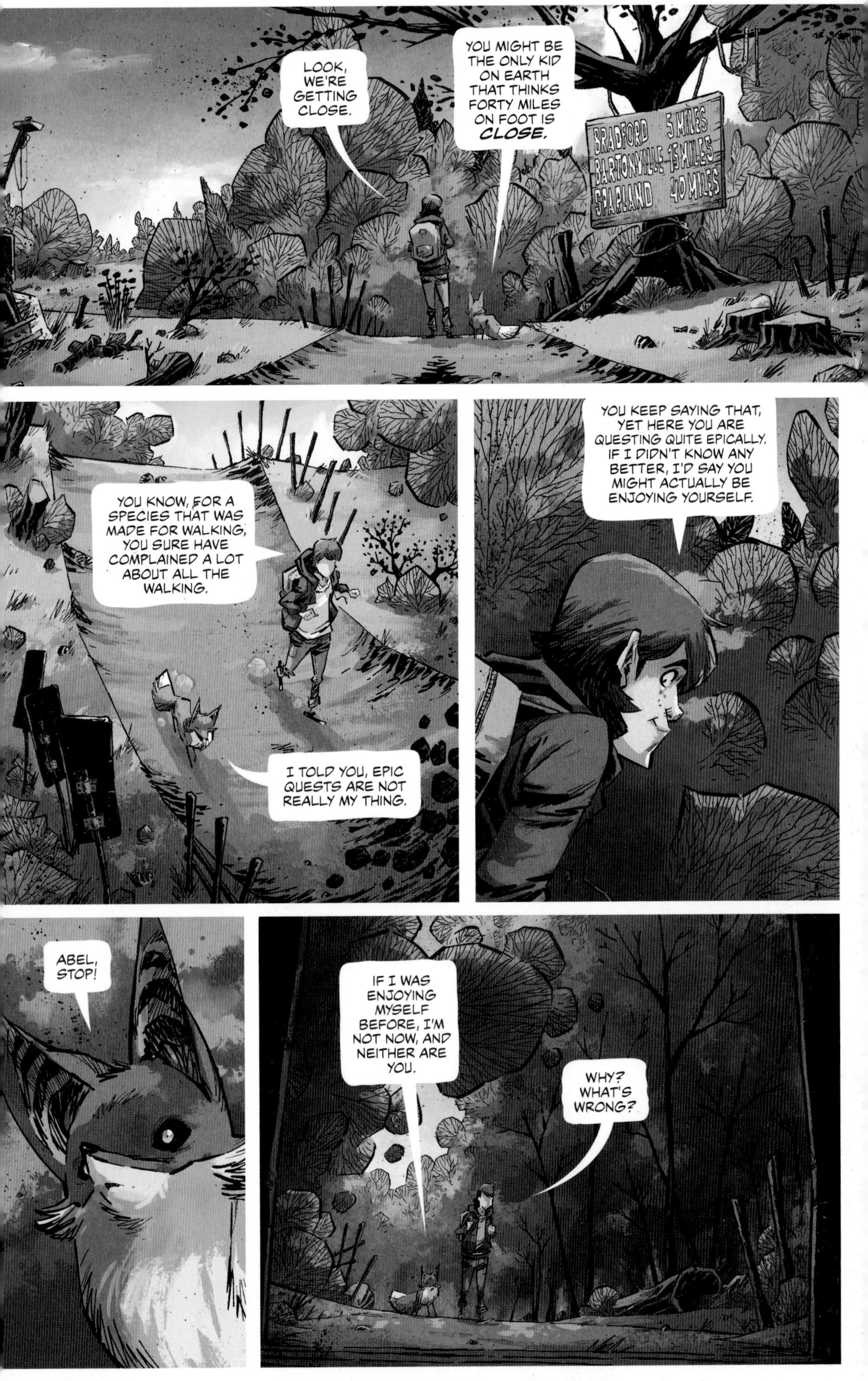
LOOK, WE'RE GETTING CLOSE.
YOU MIGHT BE THE ONLY KID ON EARTH THAT THINKS FORTY MILES ON FOOT IS *CLOSE.*
BRADFORD 5 MILES
BARTONVILLE 15 MILES
SPARLAND 40 MILES
YOU KNOW, FOR A SPECIES THAT WAS MADE FOR WALKING, YOU SURE HAVE COMPLAINED A LOT ABOUT ALL THE WALKING.
I TOLD YOU, EPIC QUESTS ARE NOT REALLY MY THING.
YOU KEEP SAYING THAT, YET HERE YOU ARE QUESTING QUITE EPICALLY. IF I DIDN'T KNOW ANY BETTER, I'D SAY YOU MIGHT ACTUALLY BE ENJOYING YOURSELF.
ABEL, STOP!
IF I WAS ENJOYING MYSELF BEFORE, I'M NOT NOW, AND NEITHER ARE YOU.
WHY? WHAT'S WRONG?

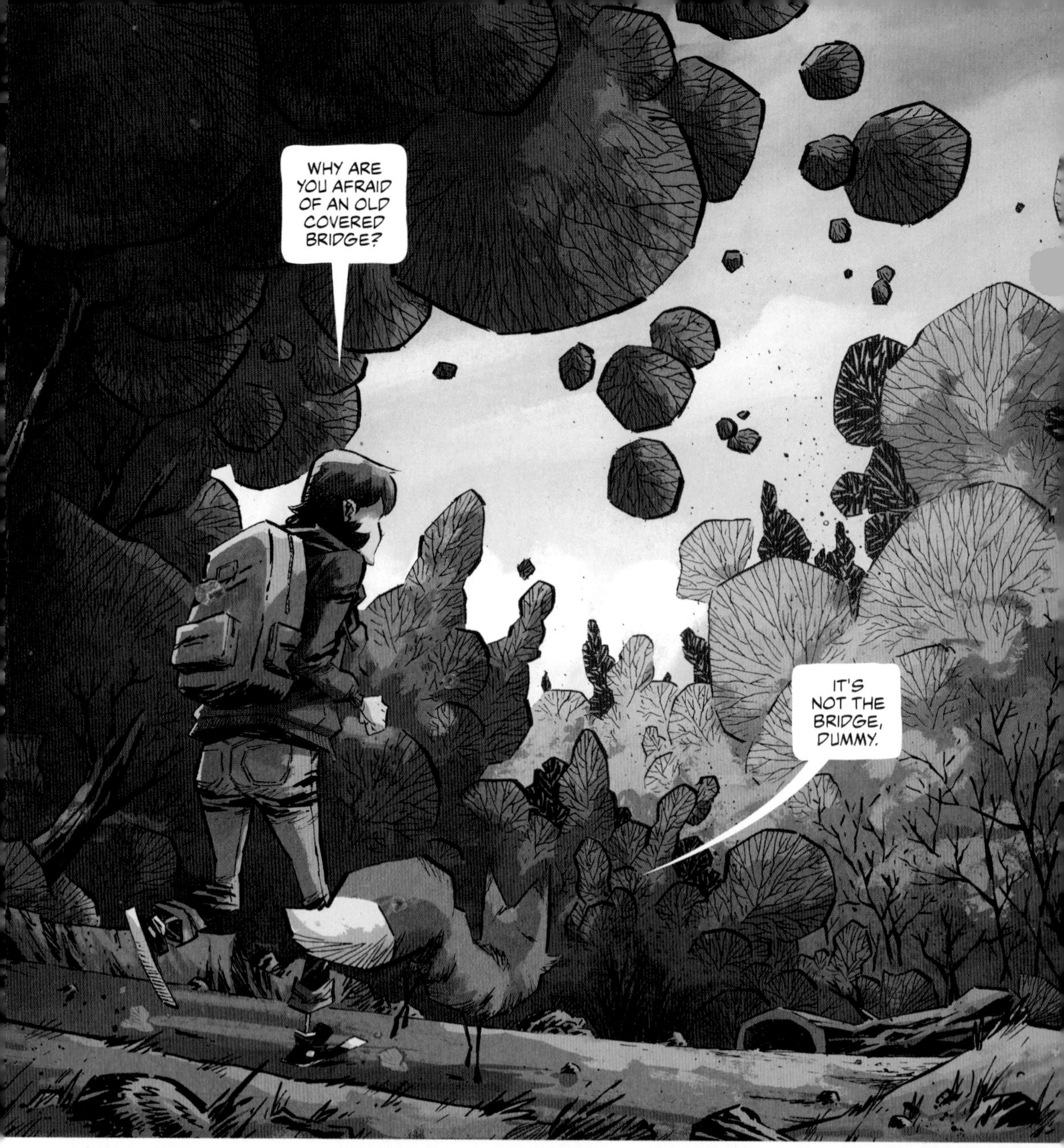
WHY ARE YOU AFRAID OF AN OLD COVERED BRIDGE?
IT'S NOT THE BRIDGE, DUMMY.

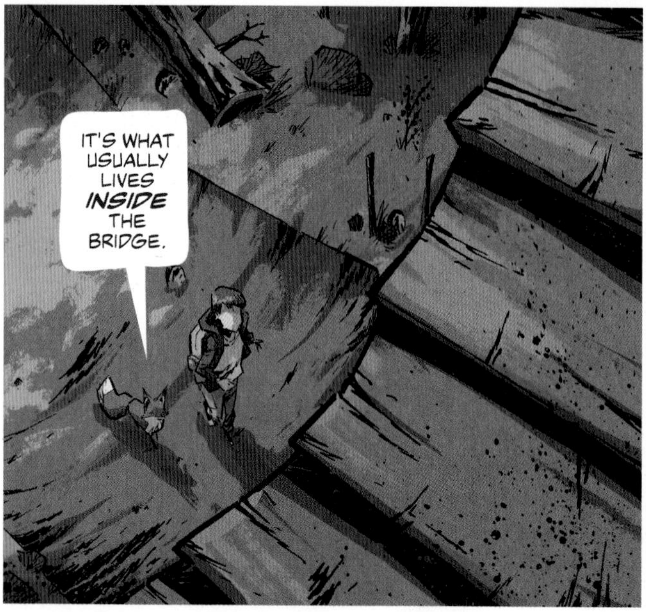
IT'S WHAT USUALLY LIVES **INSIDE** THE BRIDGE.

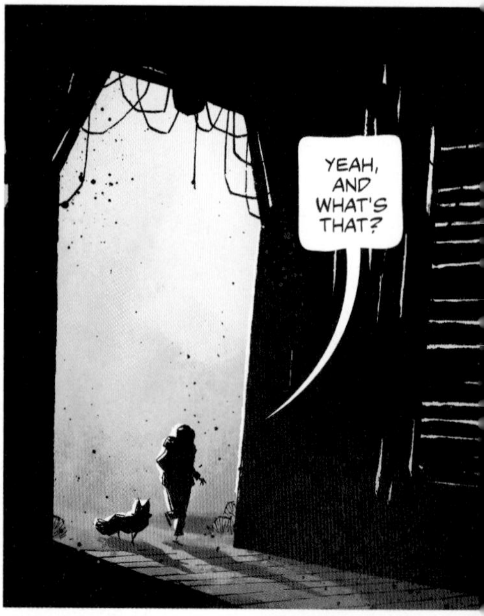
YEAH, AND WHAT'S THAT?

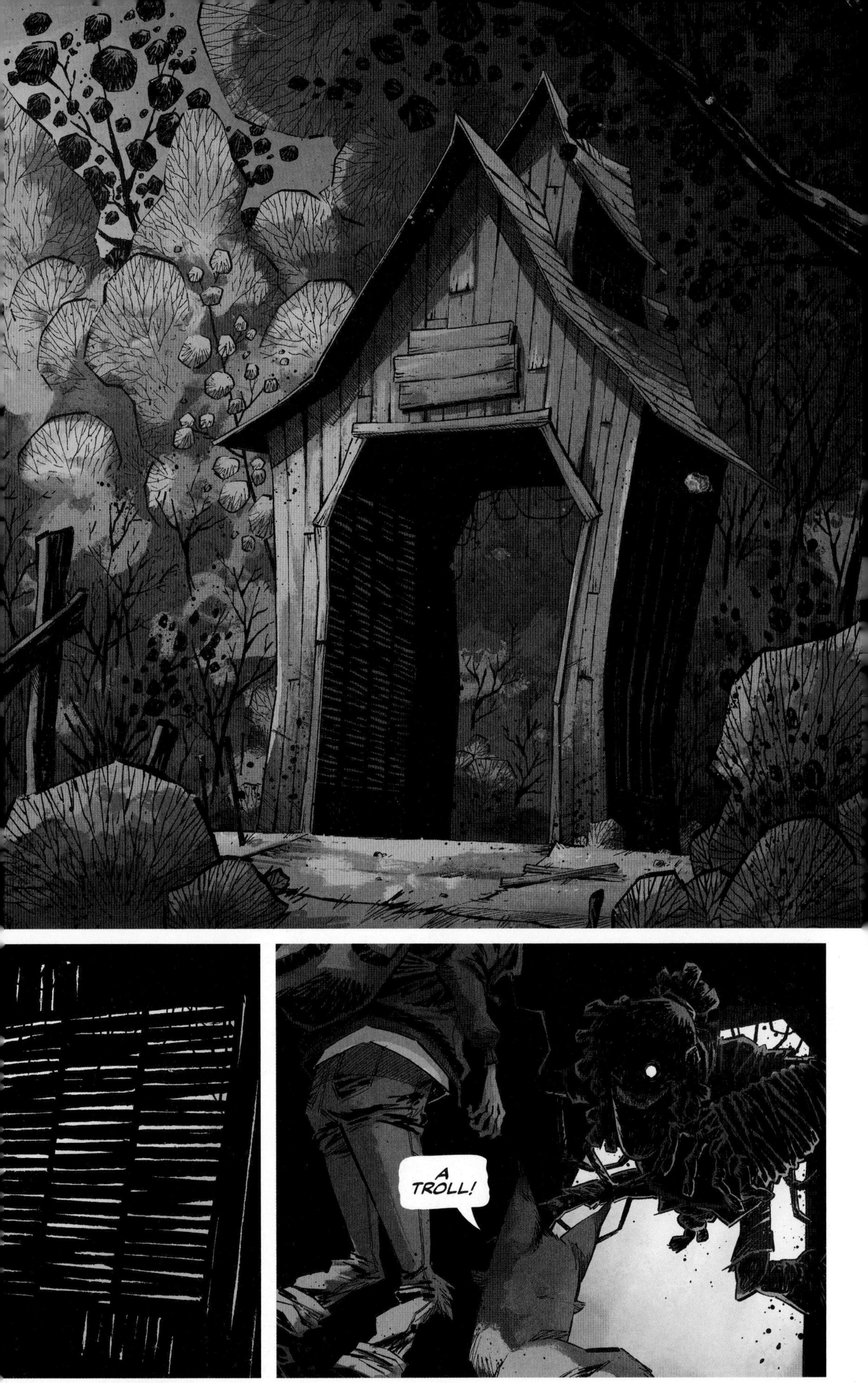
A TROLL!

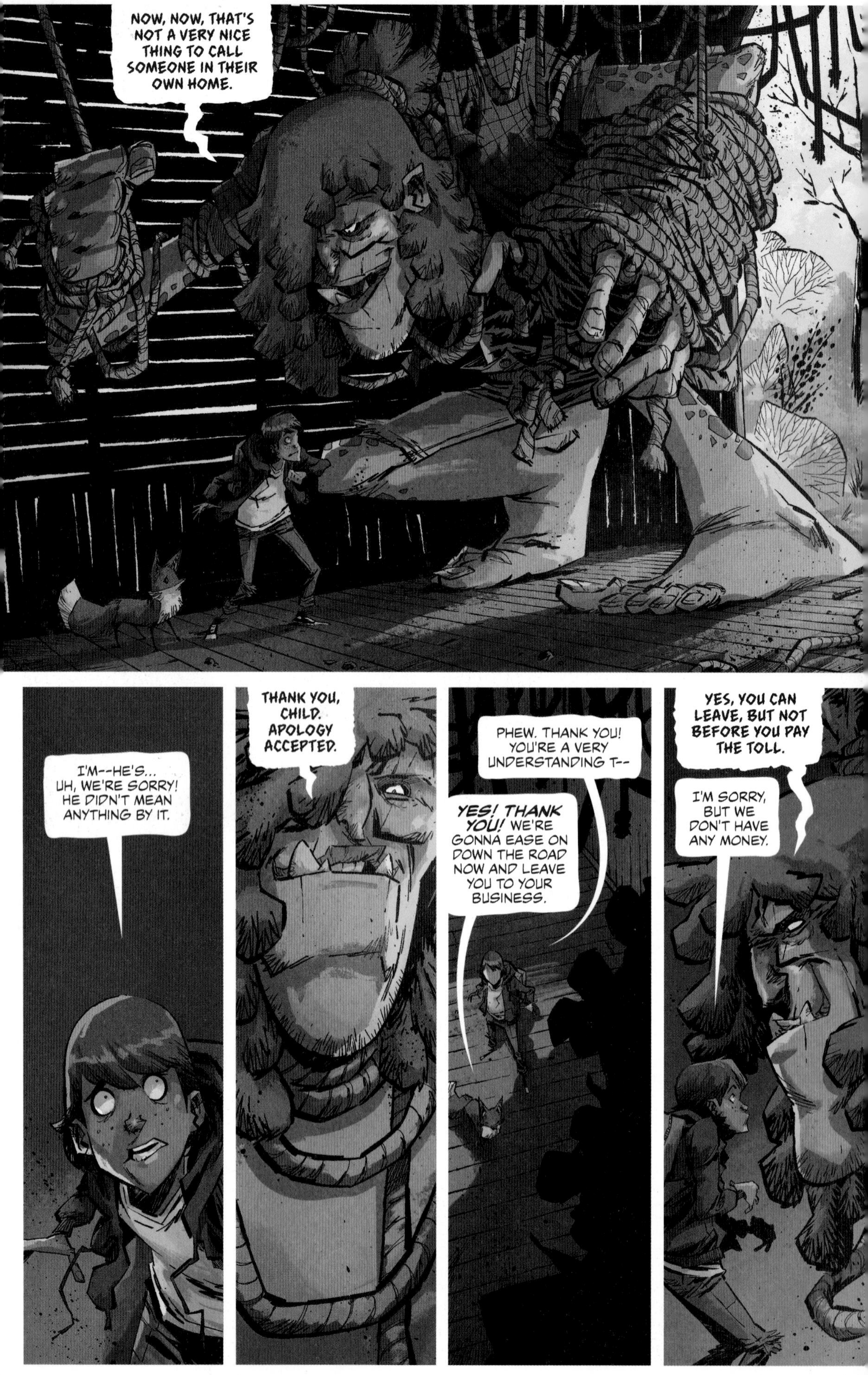
NOW, NOW, THAT'S NOT A VERY NICE THING TO CALL SOMEONE IN THEIR OWN HOME.
I'M--HE'S... UH, WE'RE SORRY! HE DIDN'T MEAN ANYTHING BY IT.
THANK YOU, CHILD. APOLOGY ACCEPTED.
PHEW. THANK YOU! YOU'RE A VERY UNDERSTANDING T--
YES! THANK YOU! WE'RE GONNA EASE ON DOWN THE ROAD NOW AND LEAVE YOU TO YOUR BUSINESS.
YES, YOU CAN LEAVE, BUT NOT BEFORE YOU PAY THE TOLL.
I'M SORRY, BUT WE DON'T HAVE ANY MONEY.

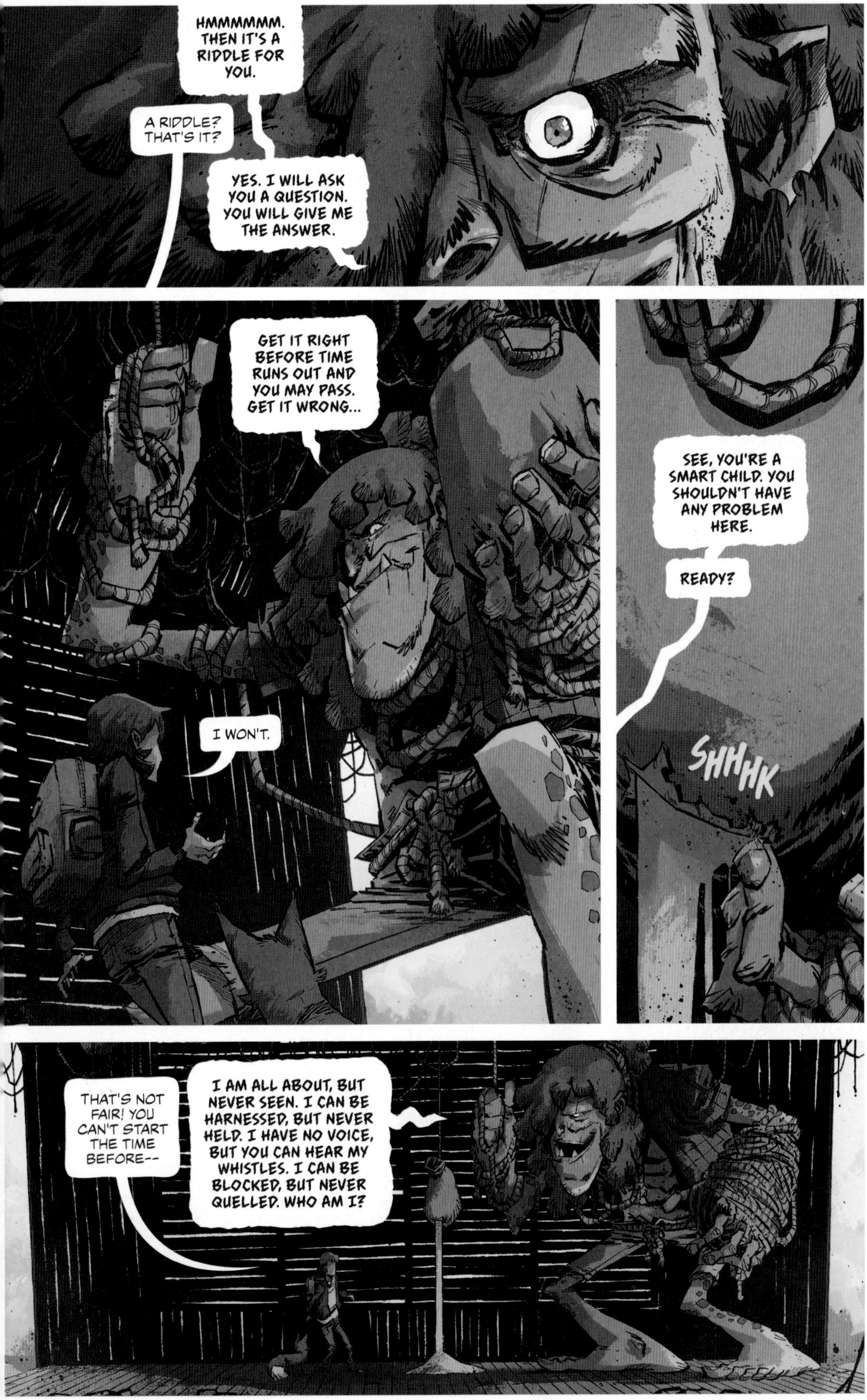
HMMMMMM. THEN IT'S A RIDDLE FOR YOU.
A RIDDLE? THAT'S IT?
YES. I WILL ASK YOU A QUESTION. YOU WILL GIVE ME THE ANSWER.
GET IT RIGHT BEFORE TIME RUNS OUT AND YOU MAY PASS. GET IT WRONG...
I WON'T.
SEE, YOU'RE A SMART CHILD. YOU SHOULDN'T HAVE ANY PROBLEM HERE.
READY?
SHHHK
I AM ALL ABOUT, BUT NEVER SEEN. I CAN BE HARNESSED, BUT NEVER HELD. I HAVE NO VOICE, BUT YOU CAN HEAR MY WHISTLES. I CAN BE BLOCKED, BUT NEVER QUELLED. WHO AM I?
THAT'S NOT FAIR! YOU CAN'T START THE TIME BEFORE--

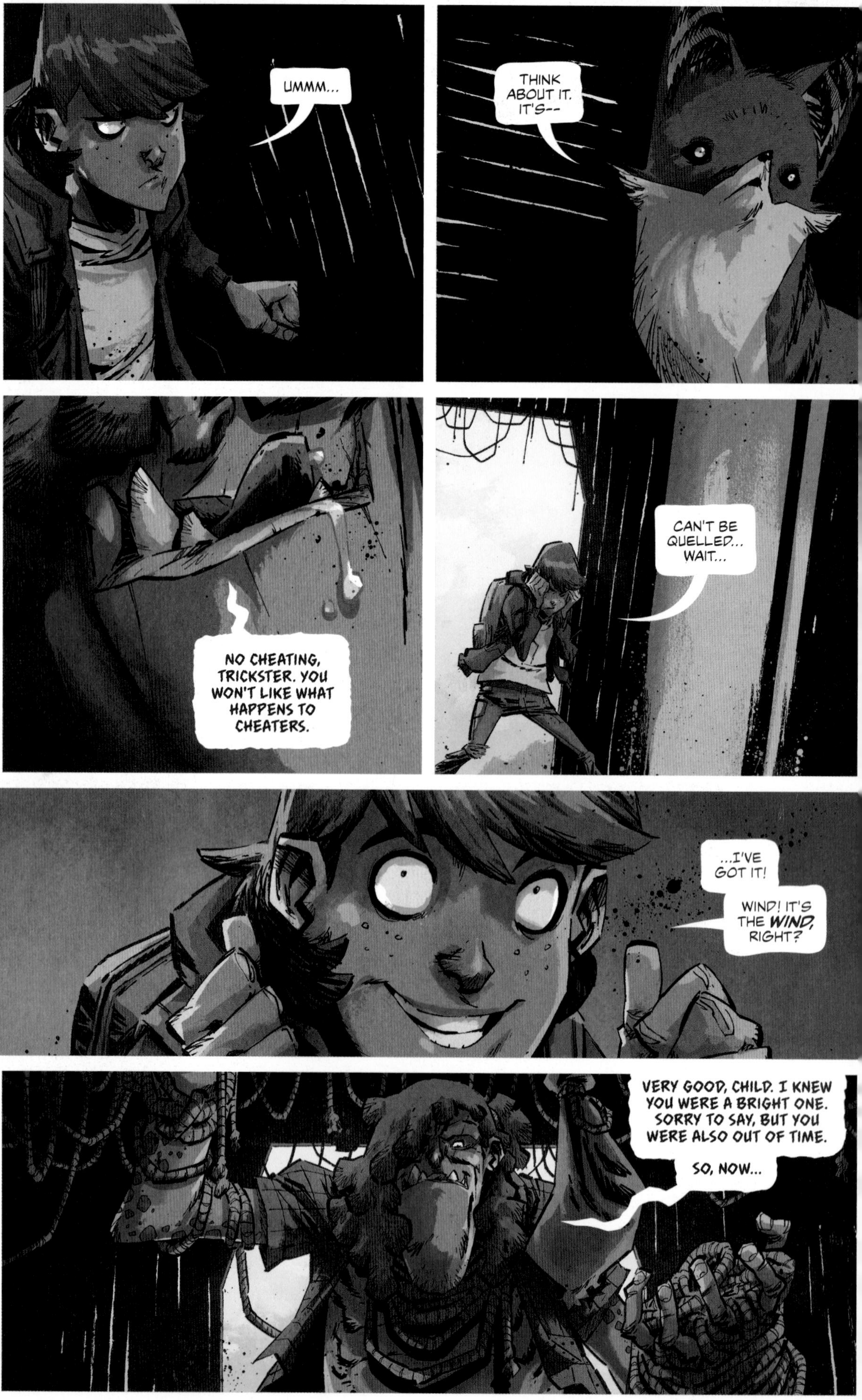
UMMM...
THINK ABOUT IT. IT'S--
NO CHEATING, TRICKSTER. YOU WON'T LIKE WHAT HAPPENS TO CHEATERS.
CAN'T BE QUELLED... WAIT...
...I'VE GOT IT!
WIND! IT'S THE *WIND,* RIGHT?
VERY GOOD, CHILD. I KNEW YOU WERE A BRIGHT ONE. SORRY TO SAY, BUT YOU WERE ALSO OUT OF TIME.
SO, NOW...

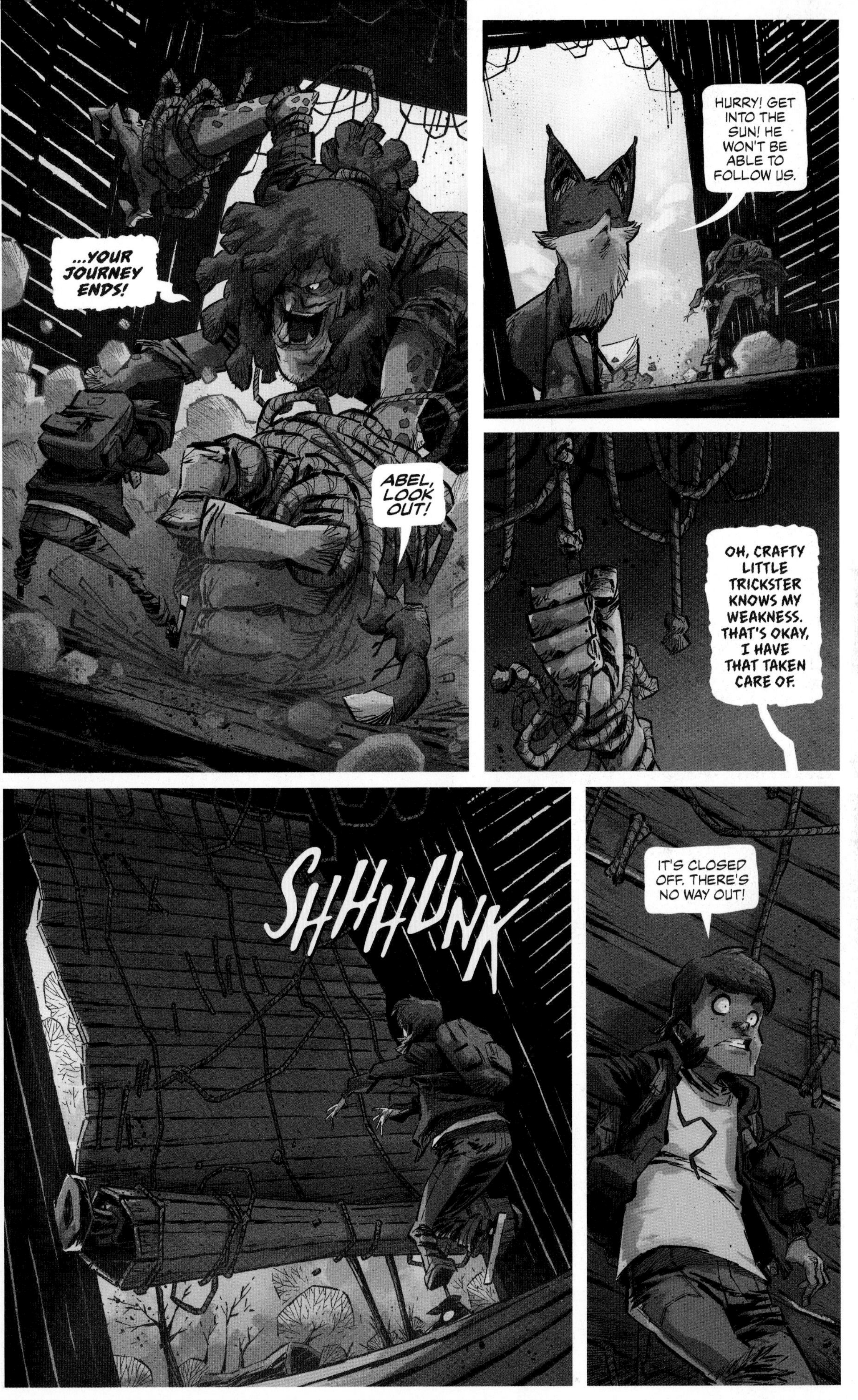
...YOUR JOURNEY ENDS!
ABEL, LOOK OUT!
HURRY! GET INTO THE SUN! HE WON'T BE ABLE TO FOLLOW US.
OH, CRAFTY LITTLE TRICKSTER KNOWS MY WEAKNESS. THAT'S OKAY, I HAVE THAT TAKEN CARE OF.
SHHHUNK
IT'S CLOSED OFF. THERE'S NO WAY OUT!

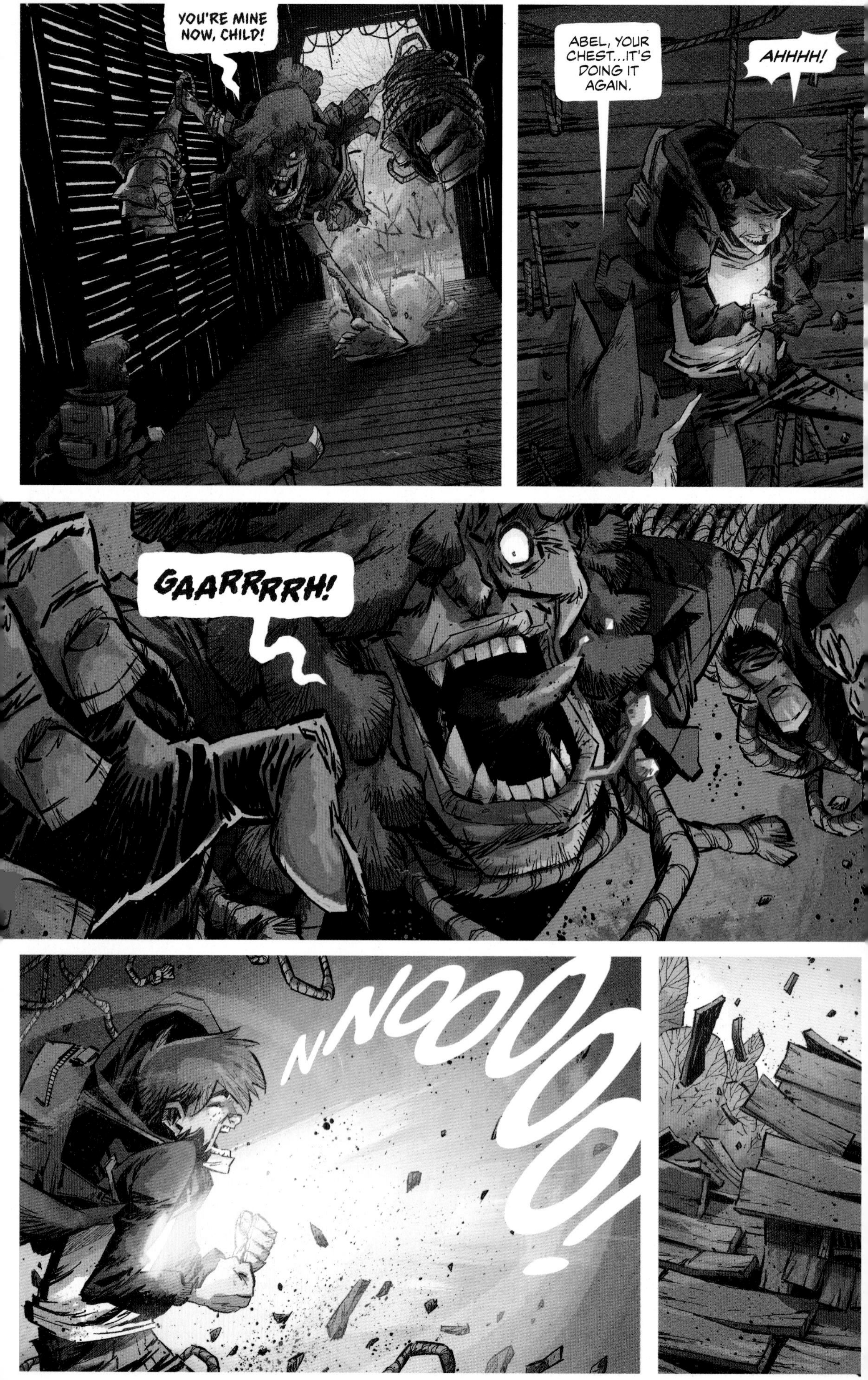
YOU'RE MINE NOW, CHILD!
ABEL, YOUR CHEST...IT'S DOING IT AGAIN.
AHHHH!
GAARRRRH!
NNOOOOOO!

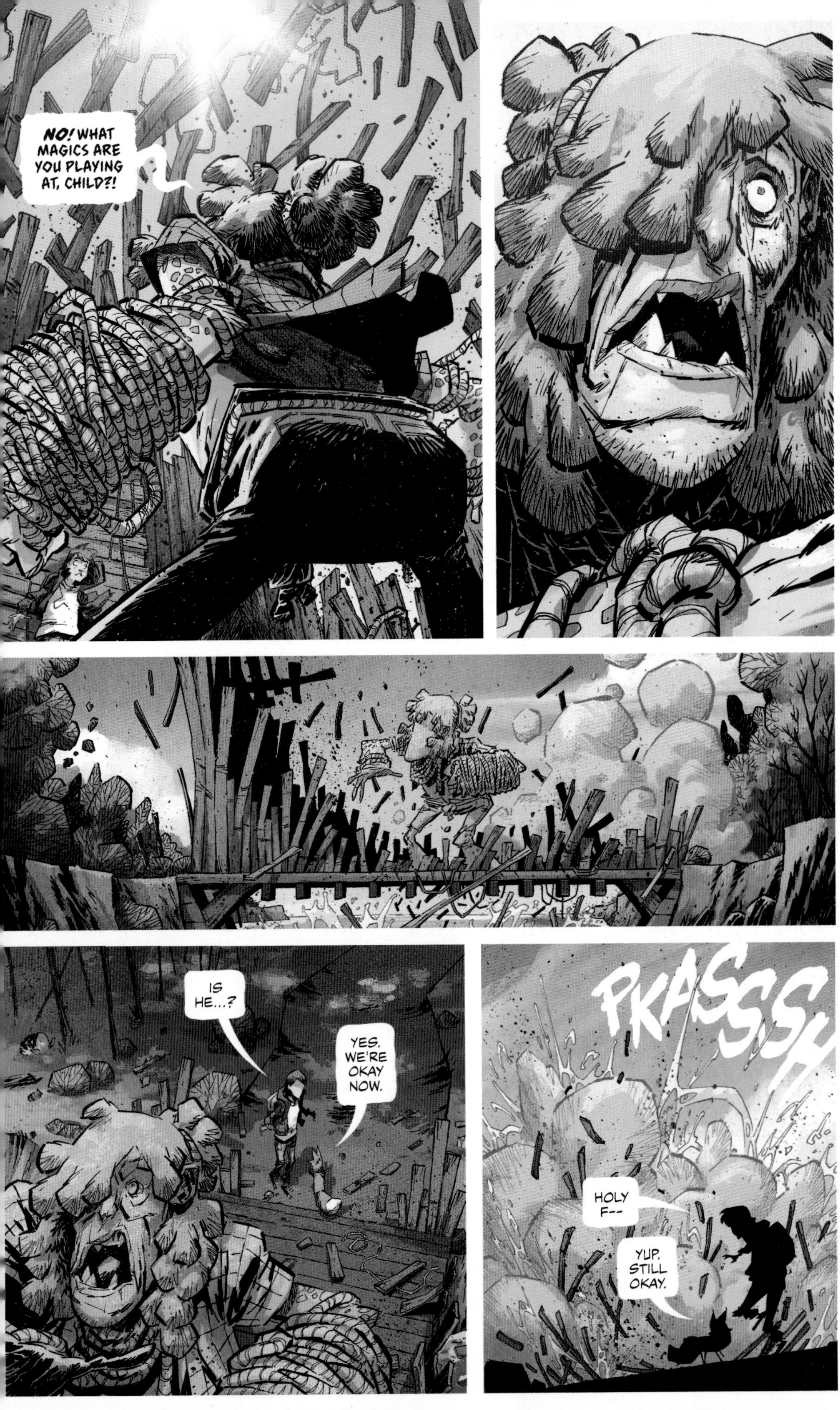
NO! WHAT MAGICS ARE YOU PLAYING AT, CHILD?!
IS HE...?
YES. WE'RE OKAY NOW.
PKASSSH
HOLY F--
YUP. STILL OKAY.

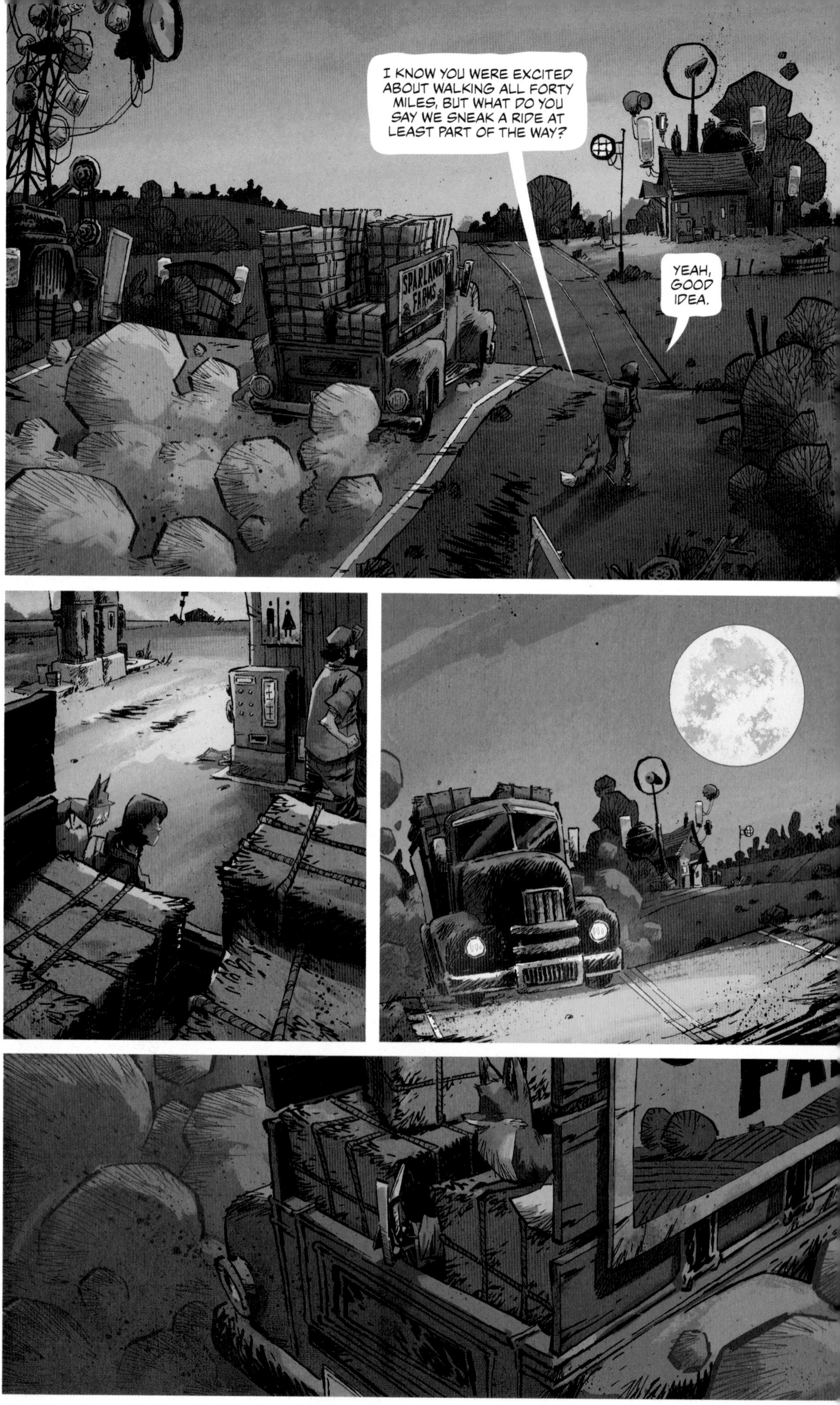
I KNOW YOU WERE EXCITED ABOUT WALKING ALL FORTY MILES, BUT WHAT DO YOU SAY WE SNEAK A RIDE AT LEAST PART OF THE WAY?
SPARLAND FARMS
YEAH, GOOD IDEA.

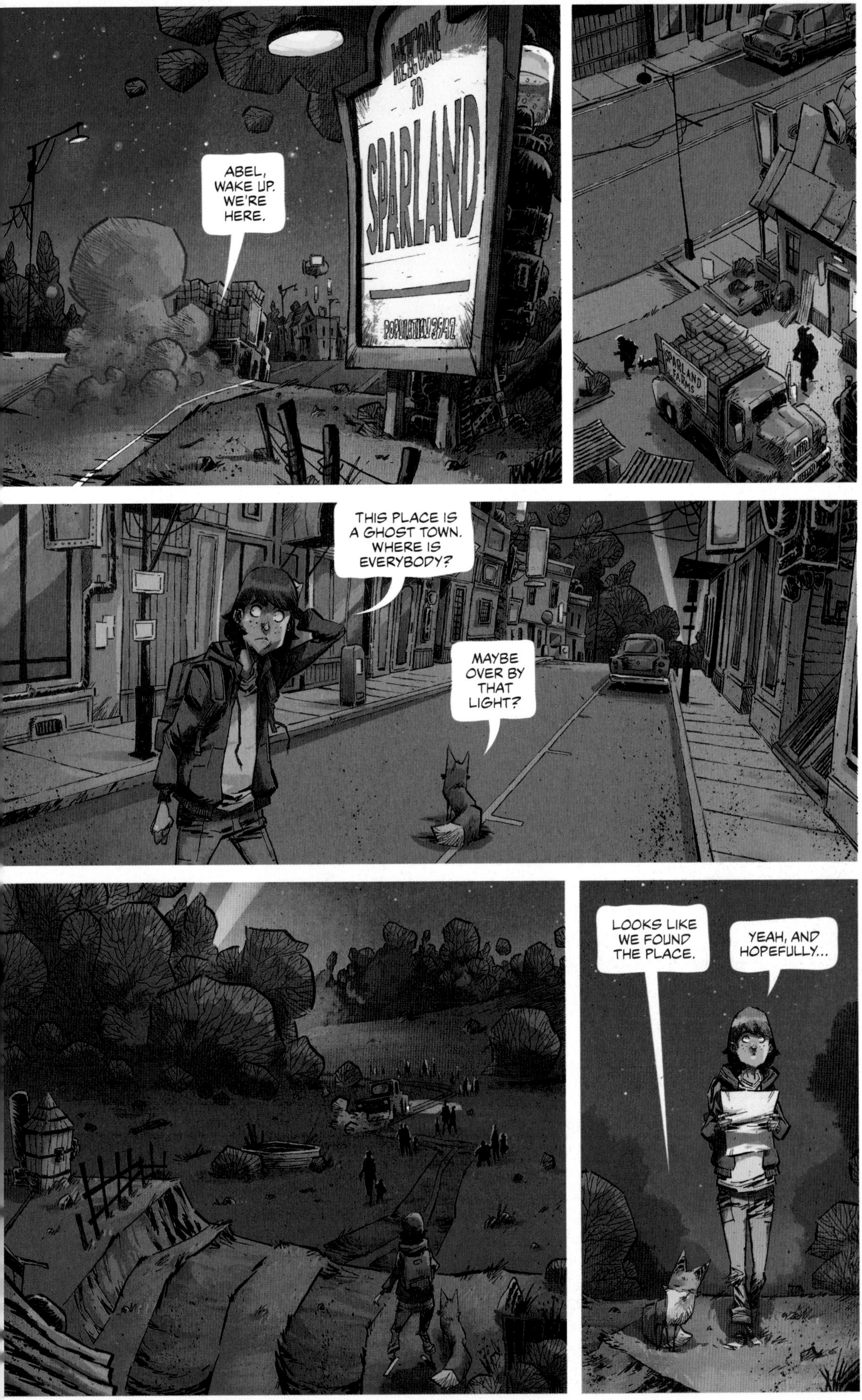
WELCOME TO
SPARLAND
ABEL, WAKE UP. WE'RE HERE.
SPARLAND FARMS
THIS PLACE IS A GHOST TOWN. WHERE IS EVERYBODY?
MAYBE OVER BY THAT LIGHT?
LOOKS LIKE WE FOUND THE PLACE.
YEAH, AND HOPEFULLY...

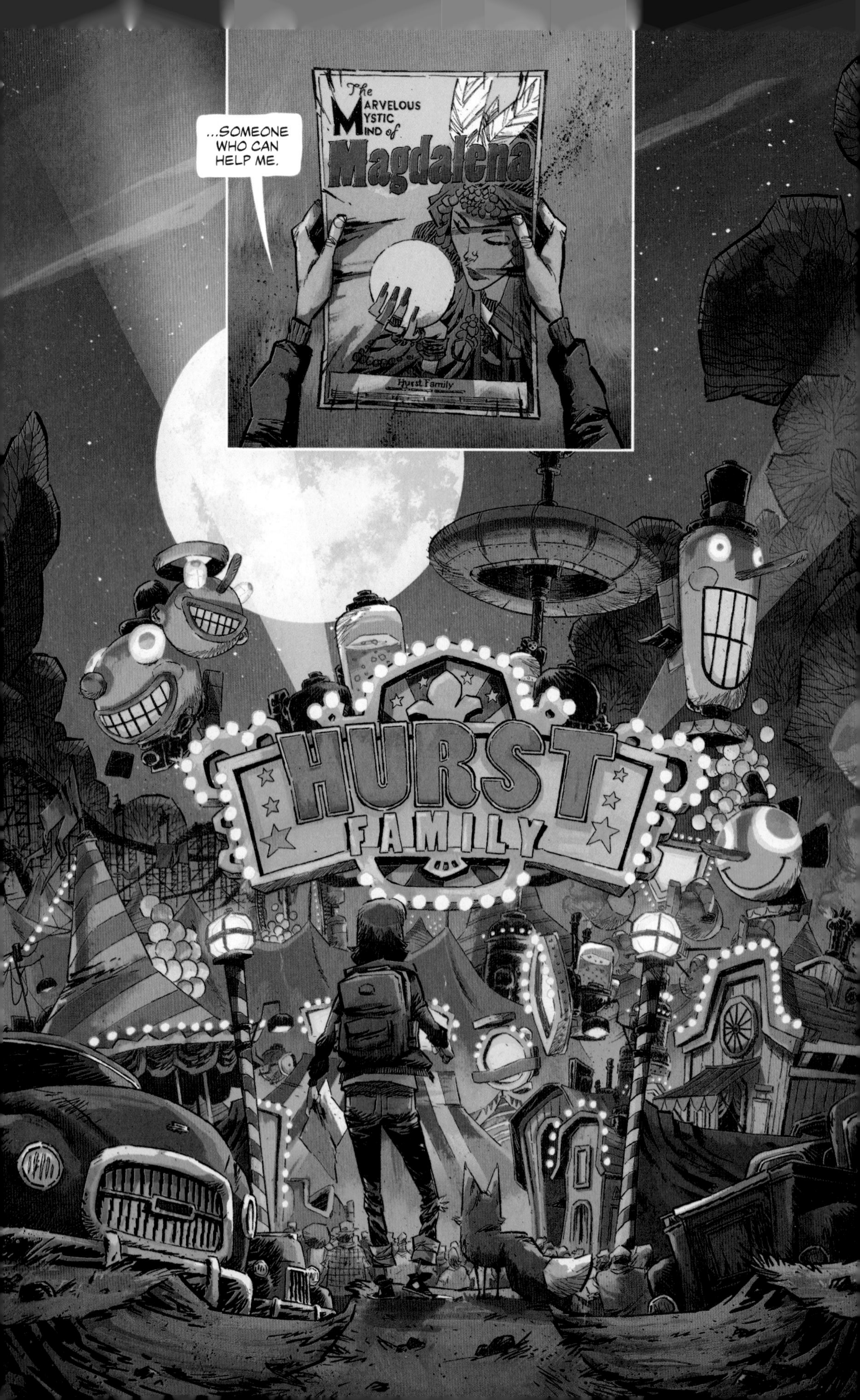
...SOMEONE WHO CAN HELP ME.
The Marvelous Mystic Mind of
Magdalena
Hurst Family
HURST
FAMILY

CHAPTER
FOUR

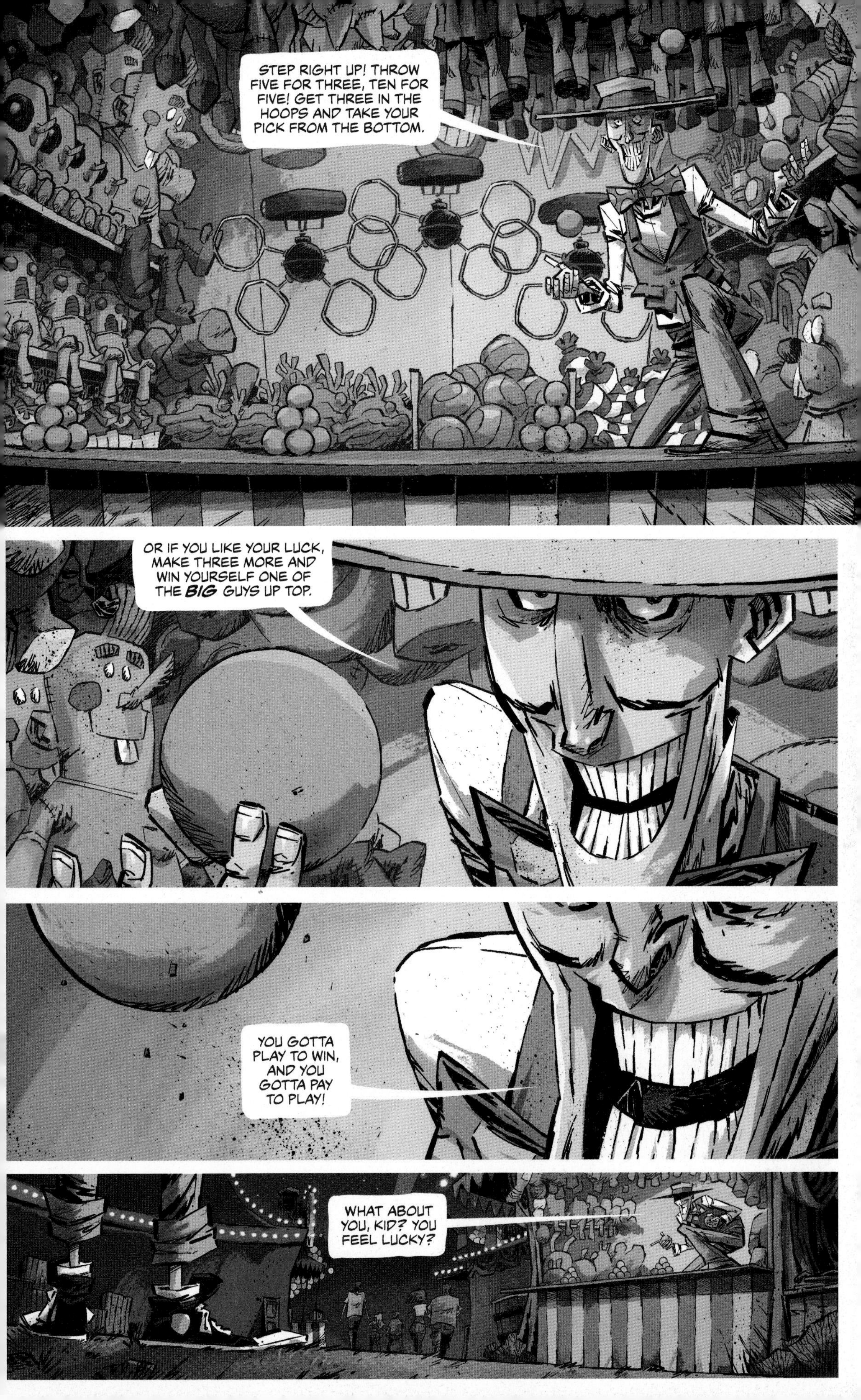
STEP RIGHT UP! THROW FIVE FOR THREE, TEN FOR FIVE! GET THREE IN THE HOOPS AND TAKE YOUR PICK FROM THE BOTTOM.
OR IF YOU LIKE YOUR LUCK, MAKE THREE MORE AND WIN YOURSELF ONE OF THE *BIG* GUYS UP TOP.
YOU GOTTA PLAY TO WIN, AND YOU GOTTA PAY TO PLAY!
WHAT ABOUT YOU, KID? YOU FEEL LUCKY?

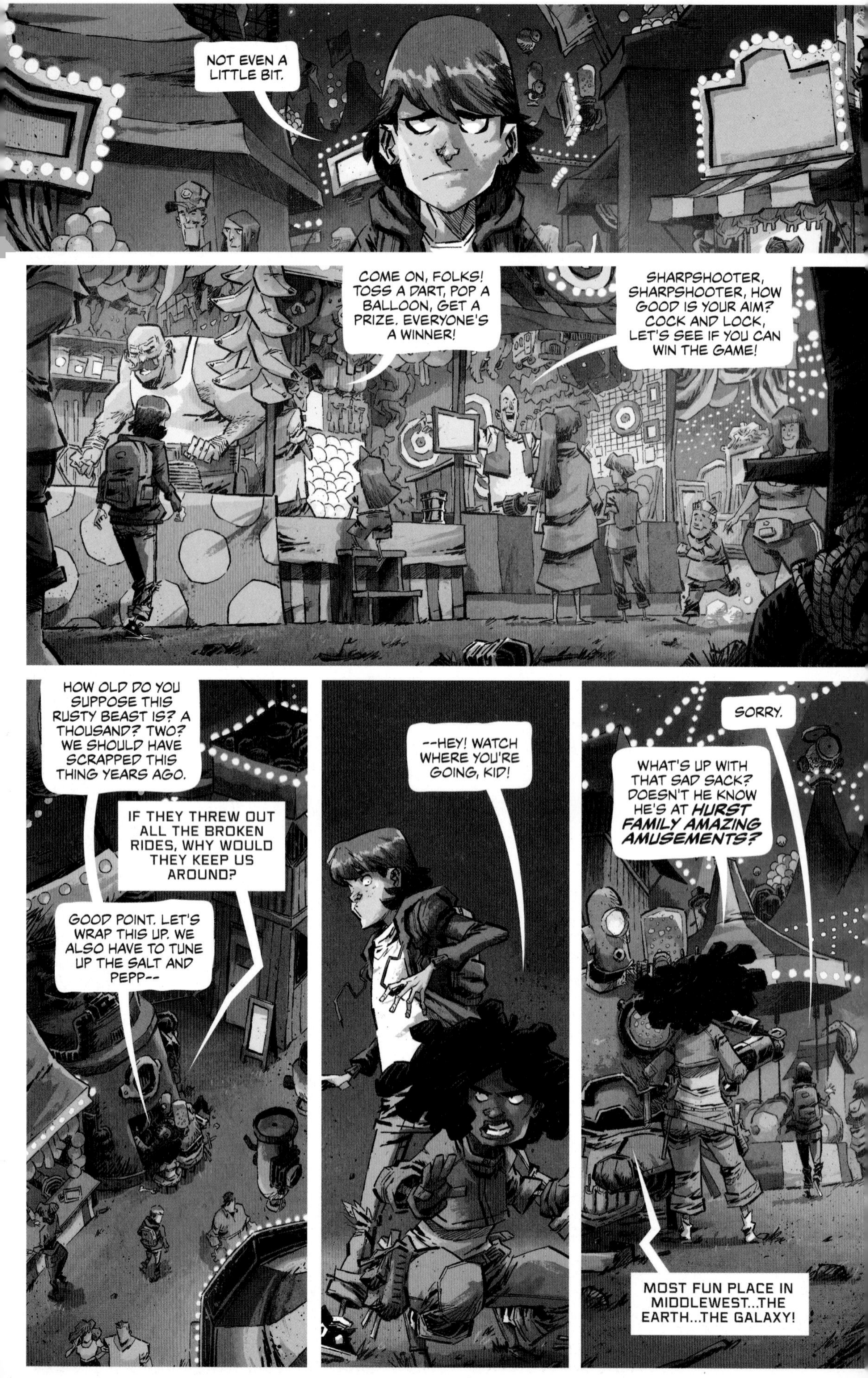
NOT EVEN A LITTLE BIT.
COME ON, FOLKS! TOSS A DART, POP A BALLOON, GET A PRIZE. EVERYONE'S A WINNER!
SHARPSHOOTER, SHARPSHOOTER, HOW GOOD IS YOUR AIM? COCK AND LOCK, LET'S SEE IF YOU CAN WIN THE GAME!
HOW OLD DO YOU SUPPOSE THIS RUSTY BEAST IS? A THOUSAND? TWO? WE SHOULD HAVE SCRAPPED THIS THING YEARS AGO.
IF THEY THREW OUT ALL THE BROKEN RIDES, WHY WOULD THEY KEEP US AROUND?
GOOD POINT. LET'S WRAP THIS UP. WE ALSO HAVE TO TUNE UP THE SALT AND PEPP--
--HEY! WATCH WHERE YOU'RE GOING, KID!
SORRY.
WHAT'S UP WITH THAT SAD SACK? DOESN'T HE KNOW HE'S AT HURST FAMILY AMAZING AMUSEMENTS?
MOST FUN PLACE IN MIDDLEWEST...THE EARTH...THE GALAXY!

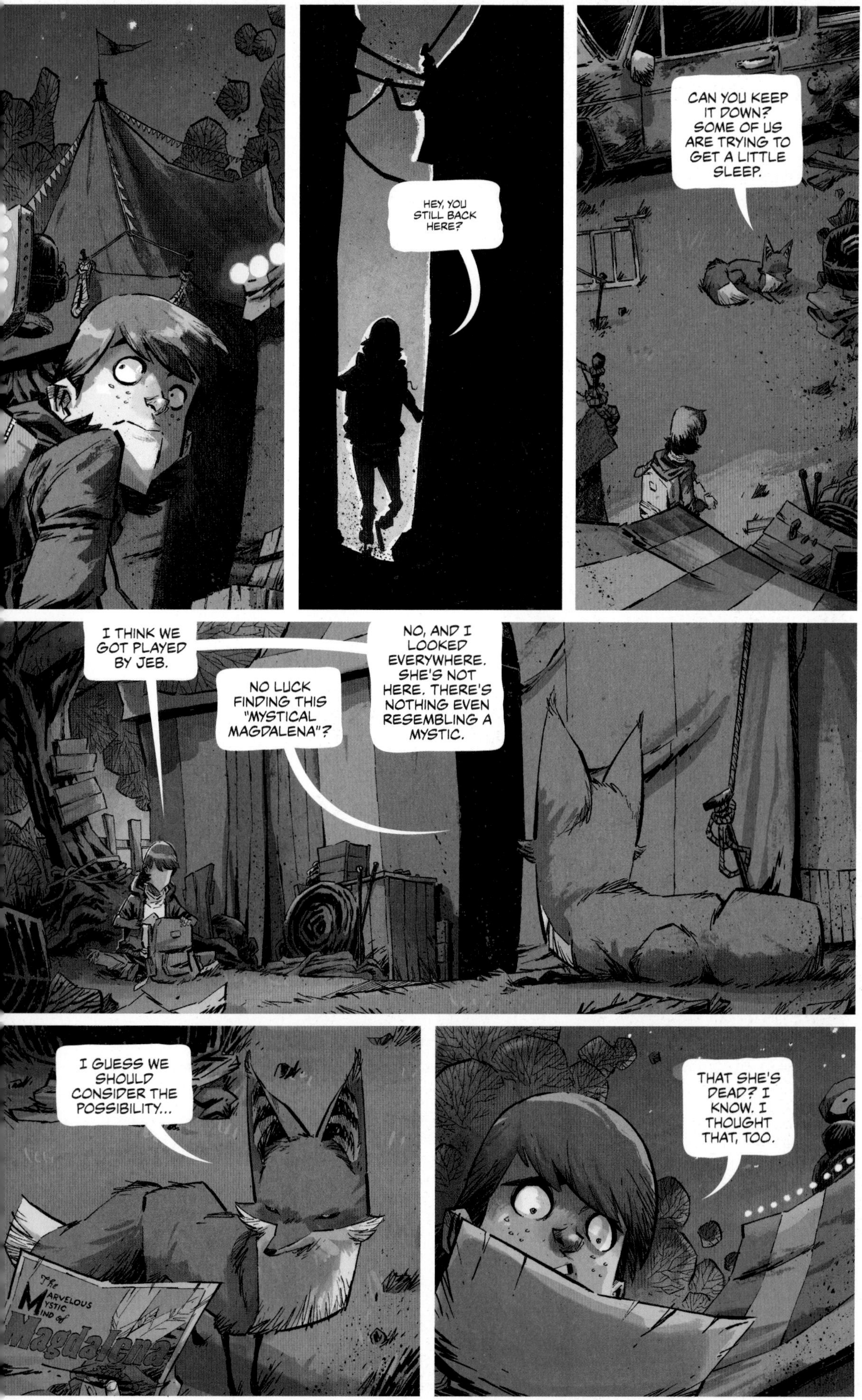
HEY, YOU STILL BACK HERE?
CAN YOU KEEP IT DOWN? SOME OF US ARE TRYING TO GET A LITTLE SLEEP.
I THINK WE GOT PLAYED BY JEB.
NO LUCK FINDING THIS "MYSTICAL MAGDALENA"?
NO, AND I LOOKED EVERYWHERE. SHE'S NOT HERE. THERE'S NOTHING EVEN RESEMBLING A MYSTIC.
I GUESS WE SHOULD CONSIDER THE POSSIBILITY...
The Marvelous Mystic Mind of Magdalena
THAT SHE'S DEAD? I KNOW. I THOUGHT THAT, TOO.

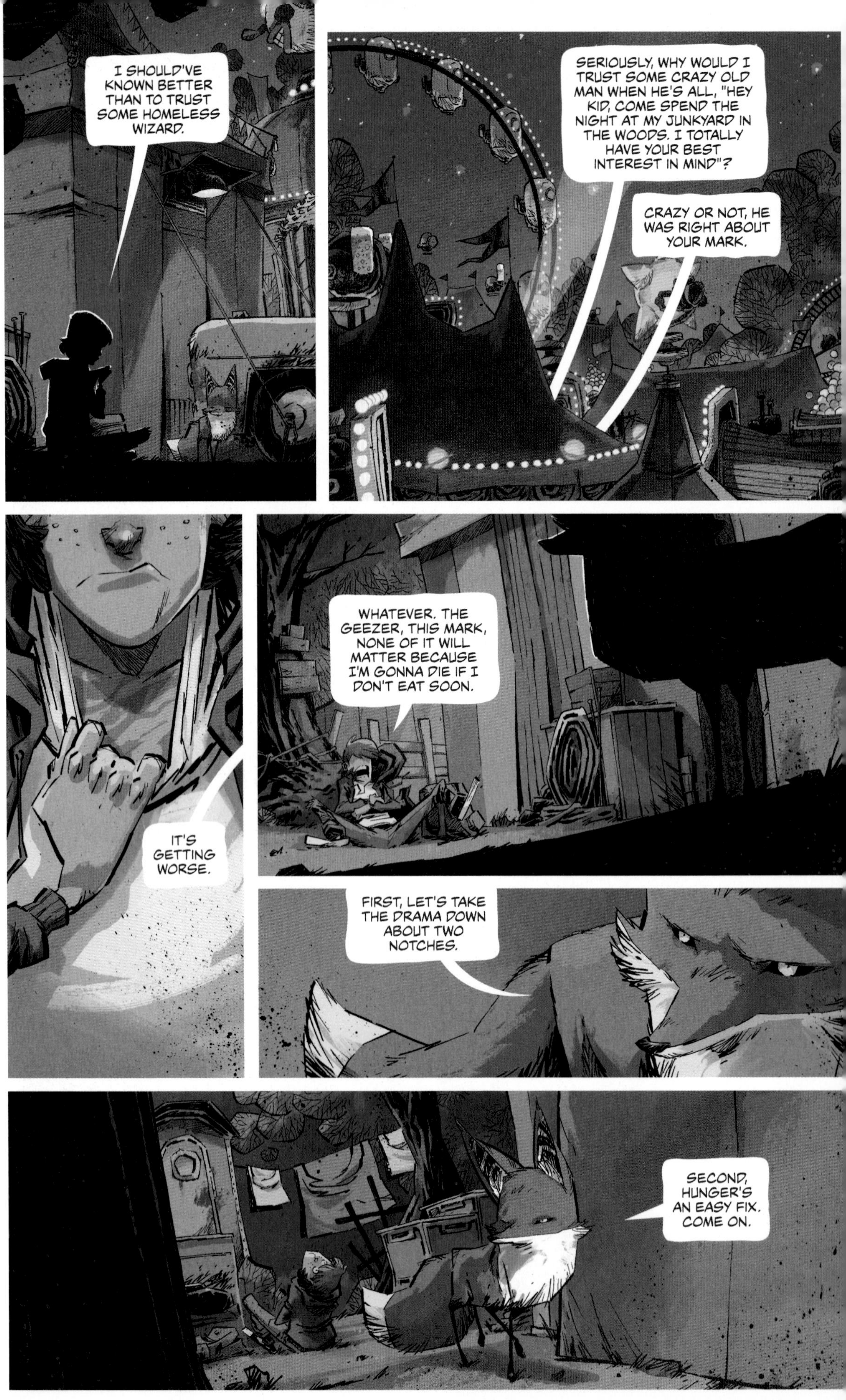
I SHOULD'VE KNOWN BETTER THAN TO TRUST SOME HOMELESS WIZARD.
SERIOUSLY, WHY WOULD I TRUST SOME CRAZY OLD MAN WHEN HE'S ALL, "HEY KID, COME SPEND THE NIGHT AT MY JUNKYARD IN THE WOODS. I TOTALLY HAVE YOUR BEST INTEREST IN MIND"?
CRAZY OR NOT, HE WAS RIGHT ABOUT YOUR MARK.
IT'S GETTING WORSE.
WHATEVER. THE GEEZER, THIS MARK, NONE OF IT WILL MATTER BECAUSE I'M GONNA DIE IF I DON'T EAT SOON.
FIRST, LET'S TAKE THE DRAMA DOWN ABOUT TWO NOTCHES.
SECOND, HUNGER'S AN EASY FIX. COME ON.

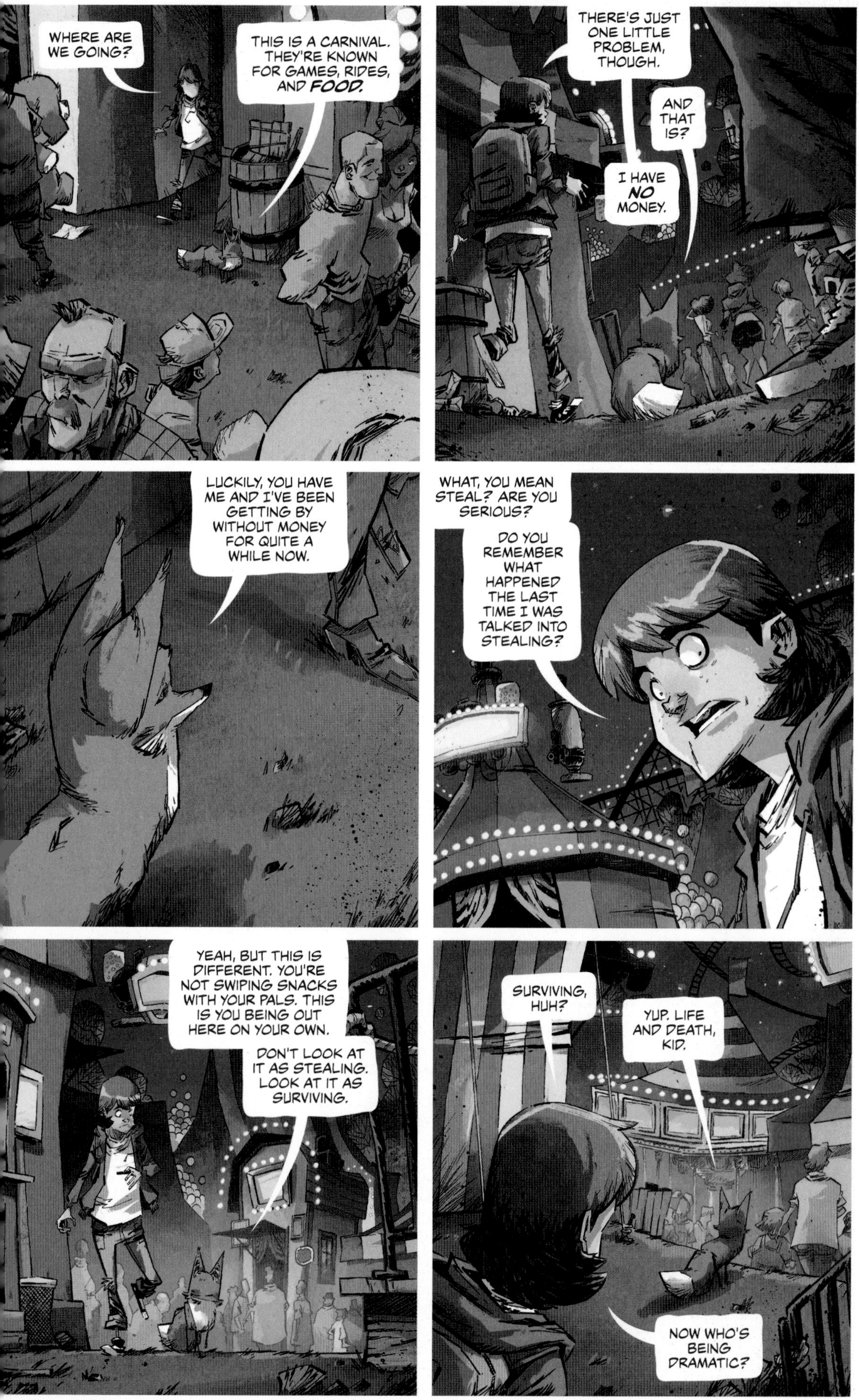
WHERE ARE WE GOING?
THIS IS A CARNIVAL. THEY'RE KNOWN FOR GAMES, RIDES, AND *FOOD.*
THERE'S JUST ONE LITTLE PROBLEM, THOUGH.
AND THAT IS?
I HAVE *NO* MONEY.
LUCKILY, YOU HAVE ME AND I'VE BEEN GETTING BY WITHOUT MONEY FOR QUITE A WHILE NOW.
WHAT, YOU MEAN STEAL? ARE YOU SERIOUS?
DO YOU REMEMBER WHAT HAPPENED THE LAST TIME I WAS TALKED INTO STEALING?
YEAH, BUT THIS IS DIFFERENT. YOU'RE NOT SWIPING SNACKS WITH YOUR PALS. THIS IS YOU BEING OUT HERE ON YOUR OWN.
DON'T LOOK AT IT AS STEALING. LOOK AT IT AS SURVIVING.
SURVIVING, HUH?
YUP. LIFE AND DEATH, KID.
NOW WHO'S BEING DRAMATIC?

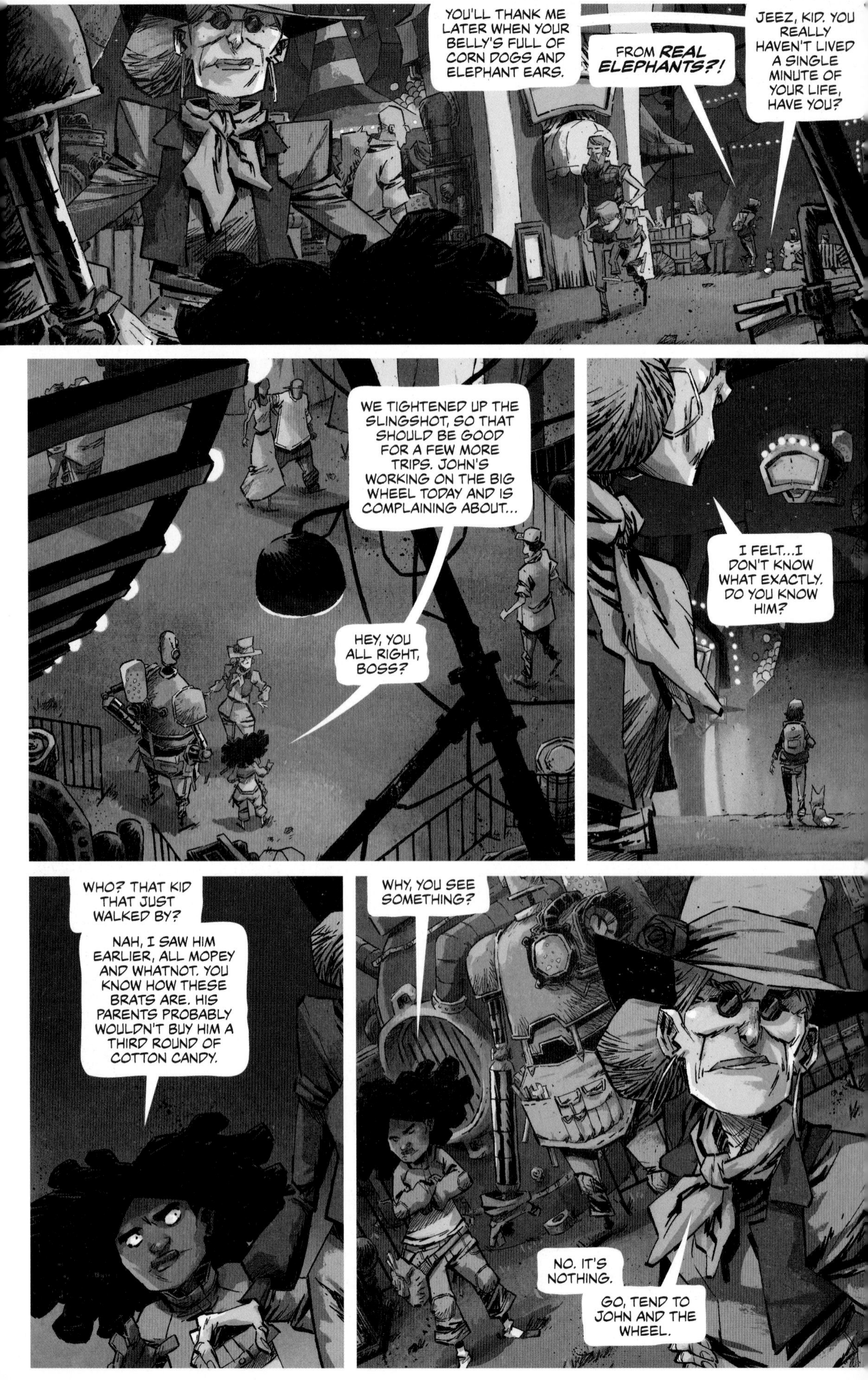
YOU'LL THANK ME LATER WHEN YOUR BELLY'S FULL OF CORN DOGS AND ELEPHANT EARS.
FROM REAL ELEPHANTS?!
JEEZ, KID. YOU REALLY HAVEN'T LIVED A SINGLE MINUTE OF YOUR LIFE, HAVE YOU?
WE TIGHTENED UP THE SLINGSHOT, SO THAT SHOULD BE GOOD FOR A FEW MORE TRIPS. JOHN'S WORKING ON THE BIG WHEEL TODAY AND IS COMPLAINING ABOUT...
HEY, YOU ALL RIGHT, BOSS?
I FELT...I DON'T KNOW WHAT EXACTLY. DO YOU KNOW HIM?
WHO? THAT KID THAT JUST WALKED BY?
NAH, I SAW HIM EARLIER, ALL MOPEY AND WHATNOT. YOU KNOW HOW THESE BRATS ARE. HIS PARENTS PROBABLY WOULDN'T BUY HIM A THIRD ROUND OF COTTON CANDY.
WHY, YOU SEE SOMETHING?
NO. IT'S NOTHING.
GO, TEND TO JOHN AND THE WHEEL.

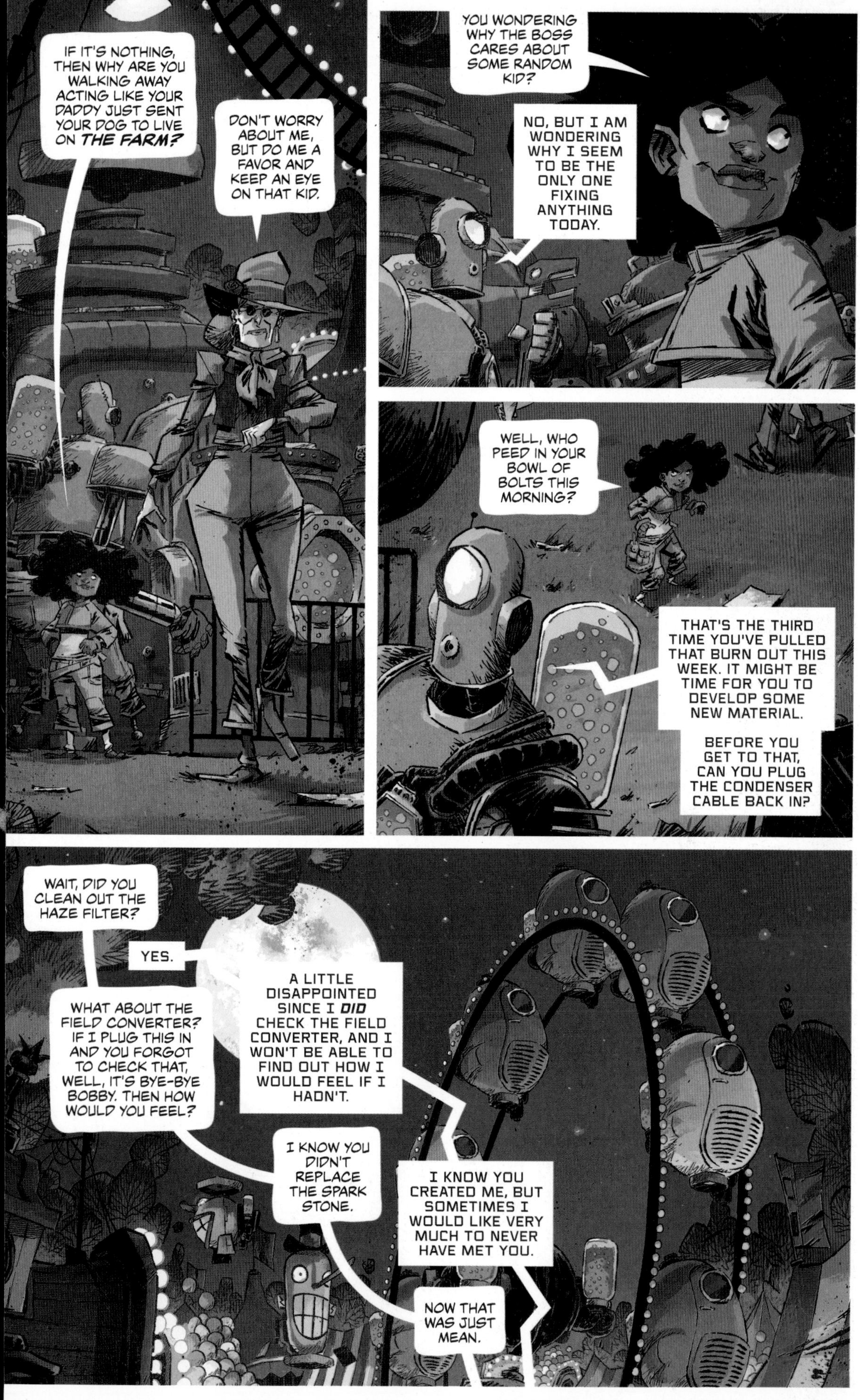

IF IT'S NOTHING, THEN WHY ARE YOU WALKING AWAY ACTING LIKE YOUR DADDY JUST SENT YOUR DOG TO LIVE ON *THE FARM?*
DON'T WORRY ABOUT ME, BUT DO ME A FAVOR AND KEEP AN EYE ON THAT KID.
YOU WONDERING WHY THE BOSS CARES ABOUT SOME RANDOM KID?
NO, BUT I AM WONDERING WHY I SEEM TO BE THE ONLY ONE FIXING ANYTHING TODAY.
WELL, WHO PEED IN YOUR BOWL OF BOLTS THIS MORNING?
THAT'S THE THIRD TIME YOU'VE PULLED THAT BURN OUT THIS WEEK. IT MIGHT BE TIME FOR YOU TO DEVELOP SOME NEW MATERIAL.
BEFORE YOU GET TO THAT, CAN YOU PLUG THE CONDENSER CABLE BACK IN?
WAIT, DID YOU CLEAN OUT THE HAZE FILTER?
YES.
WHAT ABOUT THE FIELD CONVERTER? IF I PLUG THIS IN AND YOU FORGOT TO CHECK THAT, WELL, IT'S BYE-BYE BOBBY. THEN HOW WOULD YOU FEEL?
A LITTLE DISAPPOINTED SINCE I *DID* CHECK THE FIELD CONVERTER, AND I WON'T BE ABLE TO FIND OUT HOW I WOULD FEEL IF I HADN'T.
I KNOW YOU DIDN'T REPLACE THE SPARK STONE.
I KNOW YOU CREATED ME, BUT SOMETIMES I WOULD LIKE VERY MUCH TO NEVER HAVE MET YOU.
NOW THAT WAS JUST MEAN.

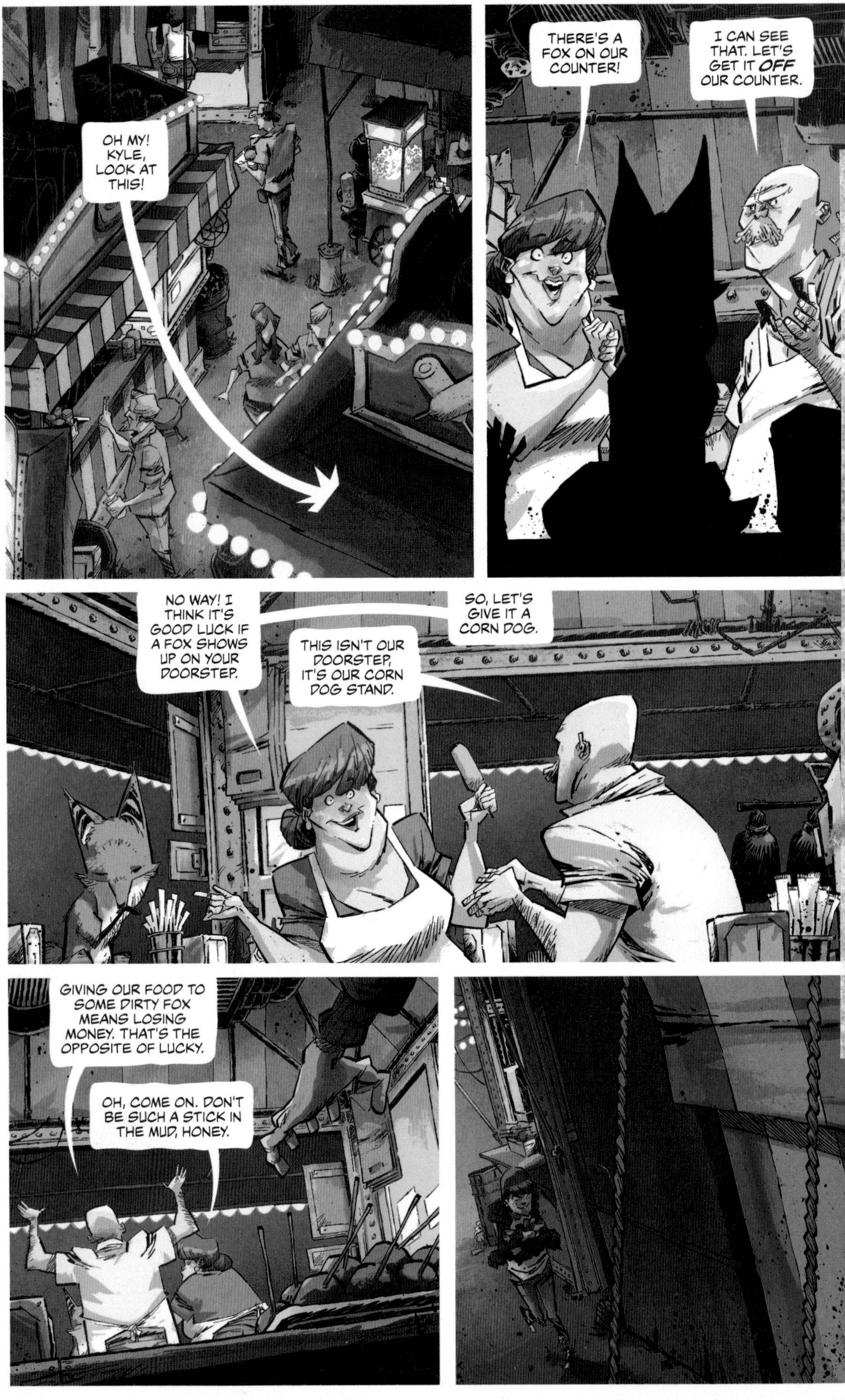
OH MY! KYLE, LOOK AT THIS!
THERE'S A FOX ON OUR COUNTER!
I CAN SEE THAT. LET'S GET IT OFF OUR COUNTER.
NO WAY! I THINK IT'S GOOD LUCK IF A FOX SHOWS UP ON YOUR DOORSTEP.
SO, LET'S GIVE IT A CORN DOG.
THIS ISN'T OUR DOORSTEP, IT'S OUR CORN DOG STAND.
GIVING OUR FOOD TO SOME DIRTY FOX MEANS LOSING MONEY. THAT'S THE OPPOSITE OF LUCKY.
OH, COME ON. DON'T BE SUCH A STICK IN THE MUD, HONEY.

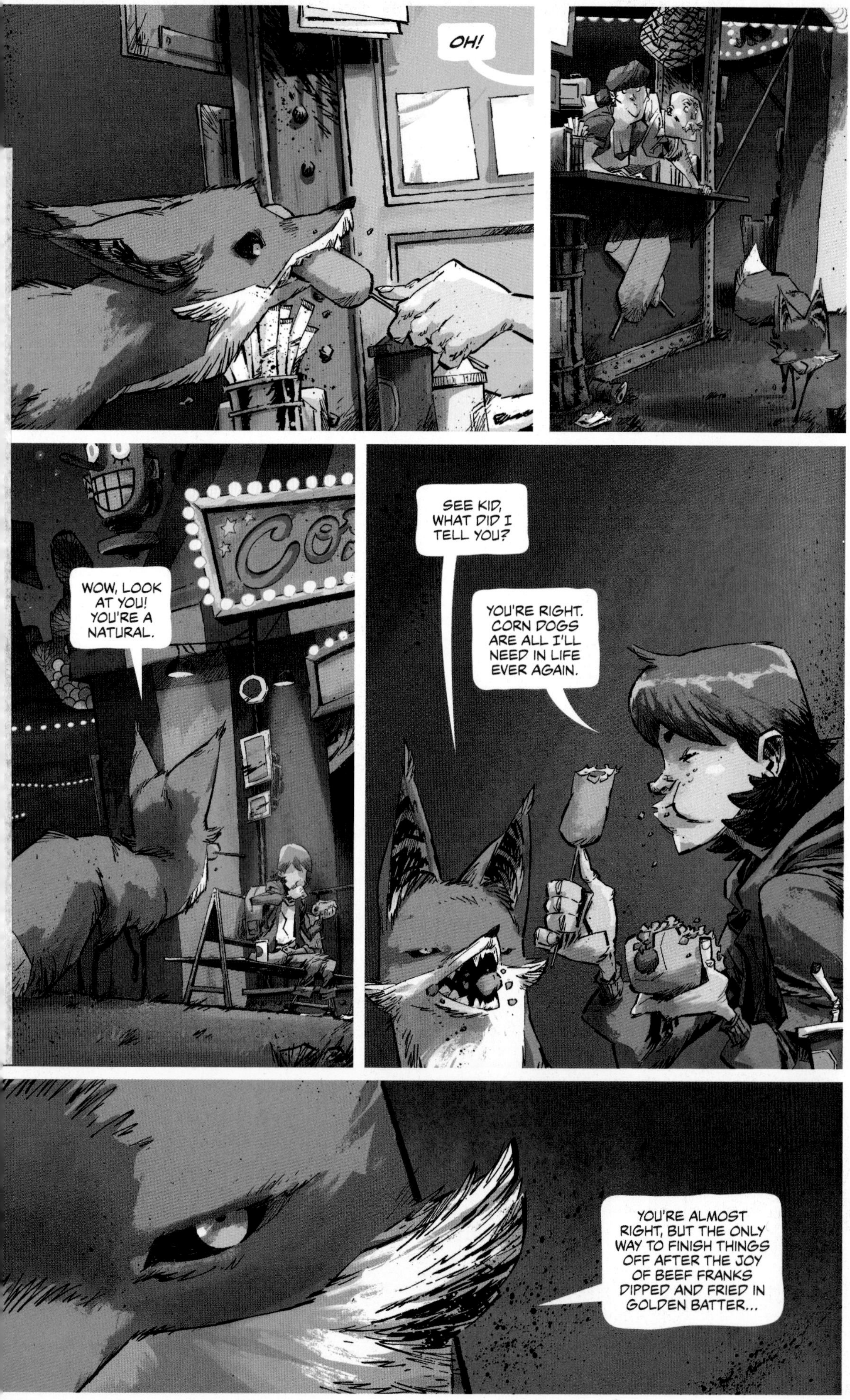
OH!
WOW, LOOK AT YOU! YOU'RE A NATURAL.
SEE KID, WHAT DID I TELL YOU?
YOU'RE RIGHT. CORN DOGS ARE ALL I'LL NEED IN LIFE EVER AGAIN.
YOU'RE ALMOST RIGHT, BUT THE ONLY WAY TO FINISH THINGS OFF AFTER THE JOY OF BEEF FRANKS DIPPED AND FRIED IN GOLDEN BATTER...

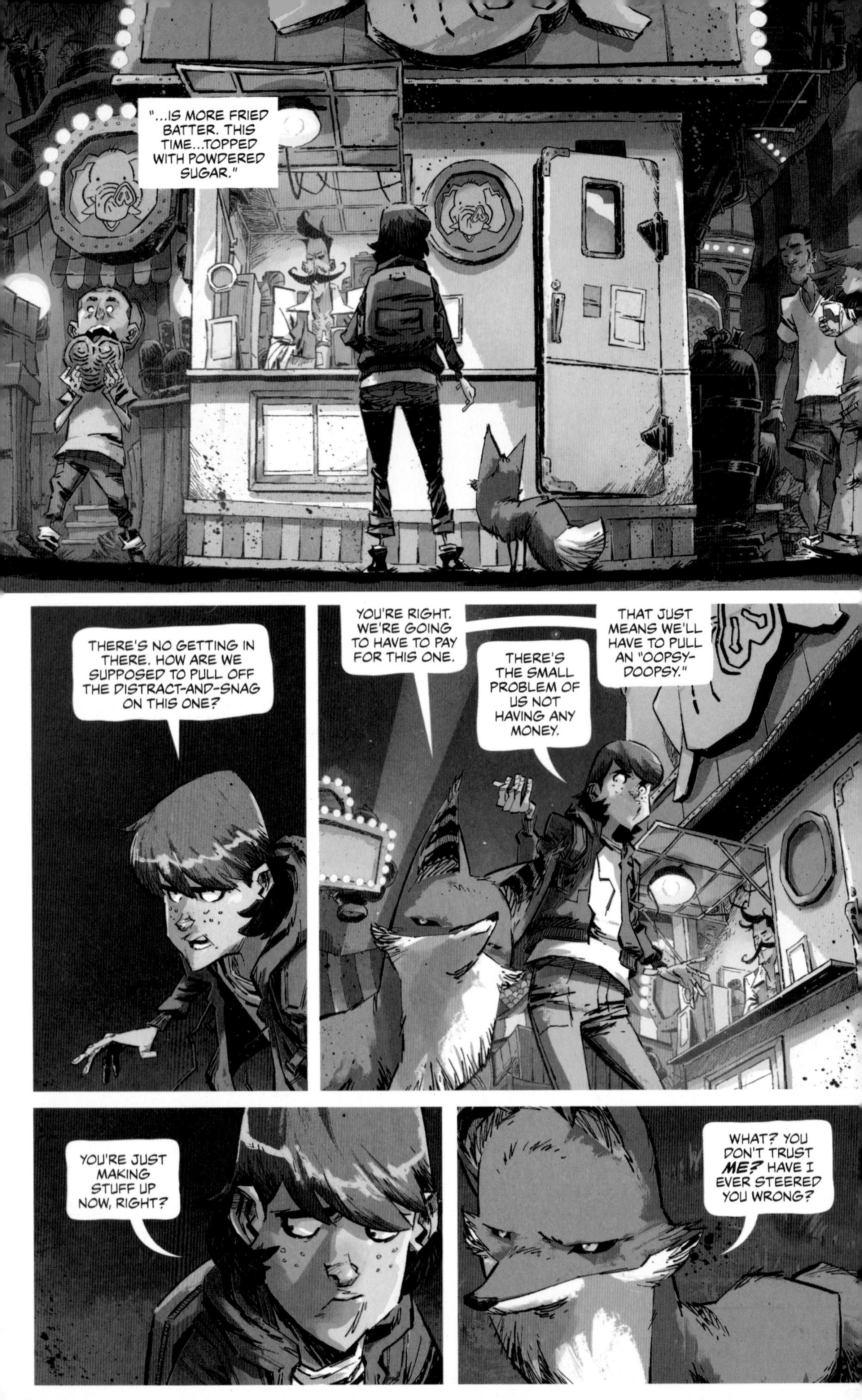
"...IS MORE FRIED BATTER. THIS TIME...TOPPED WITH POWDERED SUGAR."
THERE'S NO GETTING IN THERE. HOW ARE WE SUPPOSED TO PULL OFF THE DISTRACT-AND-SNAG ON THIS ONE?
YOU'RE RIGHT. WE'RE GOING TO HAVE TO PAY FOR THIS ONE.
THERE'S THE SMALL PROBLEM OF US NOT HAVING ANY MONEY.
THAT JUST MEANS WE'LL HAVE TO PULL AN "OOPSY-DOOPSY."
YOU'RE JUST MAKING STUFF UP NOW, RIGHT?
WHAT? YOU DON'T TRUST ME? HAVE I EVER STEERED YOU WRONG?

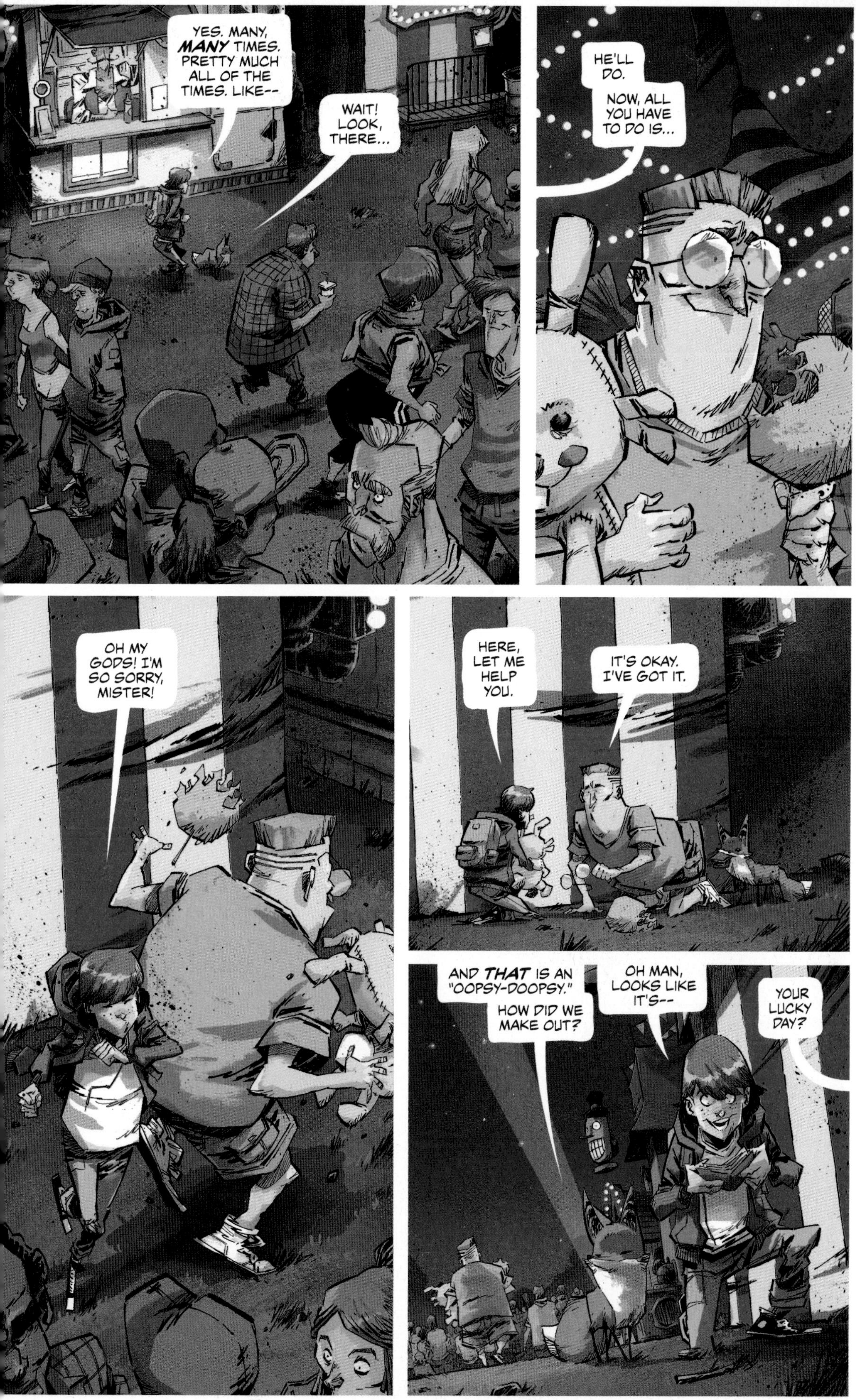
YES. MANY, *MANY* TIMES. PRETTY MUCH ALL OF THE TIMES. LIKE--
WAIT! LOOK, THERE...
HE'LL DO.
NOW, ALL YOU HAVE TO DO IS...
OH MY GODS! I'M SO SORRY, MISTER!
HERE, LET ME HELP YOU.
IT'S OKAY. I'VE GOT IT.
AND *THAT* IS AN "OOPSY-DOOPSY."
HOW DID WE MAKE OUT?
OH MAN, LOOKS LIKE IT'S--
YOUR LUCKY DAY?

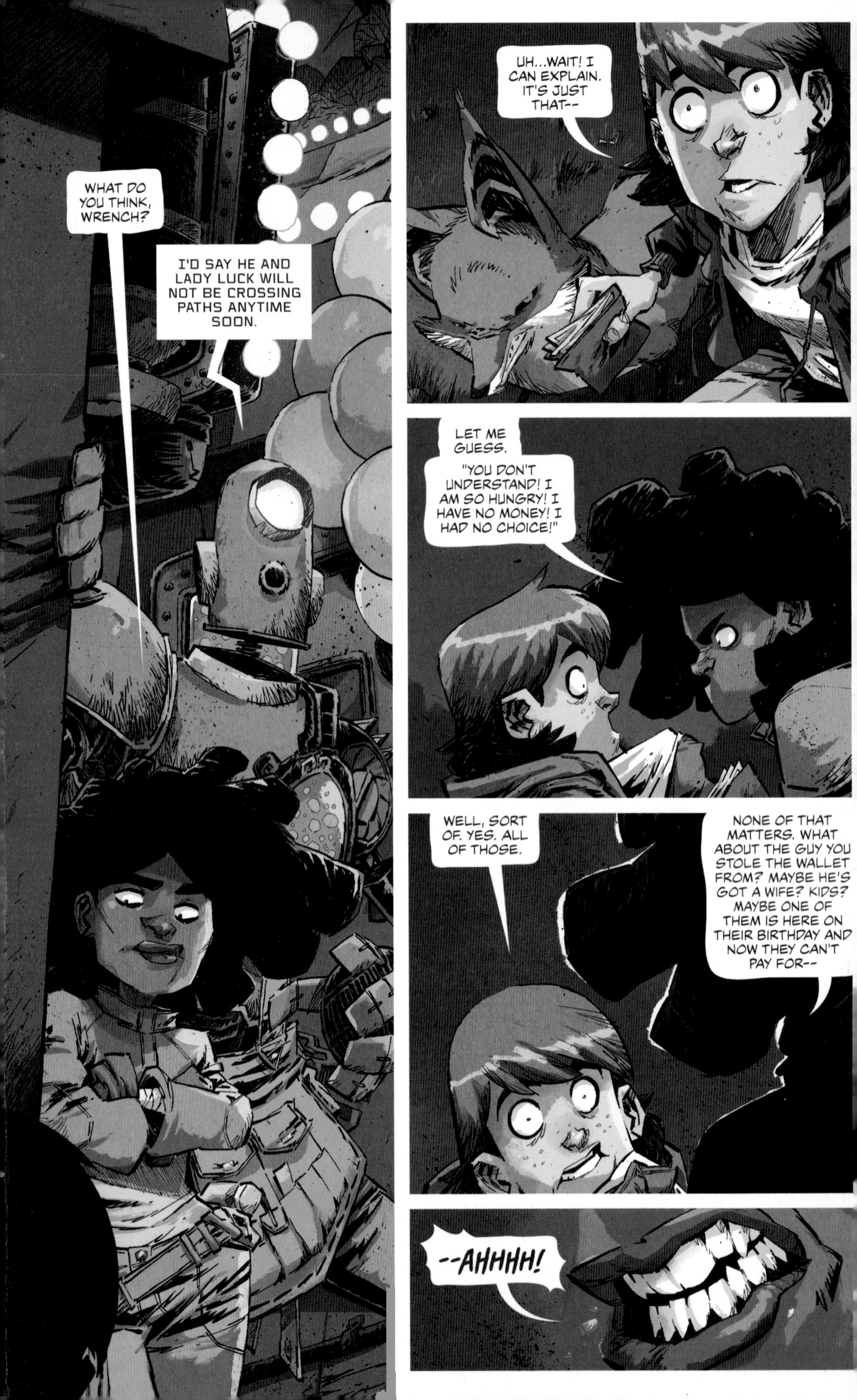
WHAT DO YOU THINK, WRENCH?
I'D SAY HE AND LADY LUCK WILL NOT BE CROSSING PATHS ANYTIME SOON.
UH...WAIT! I CAN EXPLAIN. IT'S JUST THAT--
LET ME GUESS.
"YOU DON'T UNDERSTAND! I AM SO HUNGRY! I HAVE NO MONEY! I HAD NO CHOICE!"
WELL, SORT OF. YES. ALL OF THOSE.
NONE OF THAT MATTERS. WHAT ABOUT THE GUY YOU STOLE THE WALLET FROM? MAYBE HE'S GOT A WIFE? KIDS? MAYBE ONE OF THEM IS HERE ON THEIR BIRTHDAY AND NOW THEY CAN'T PAY FOR--
--AHHHH!

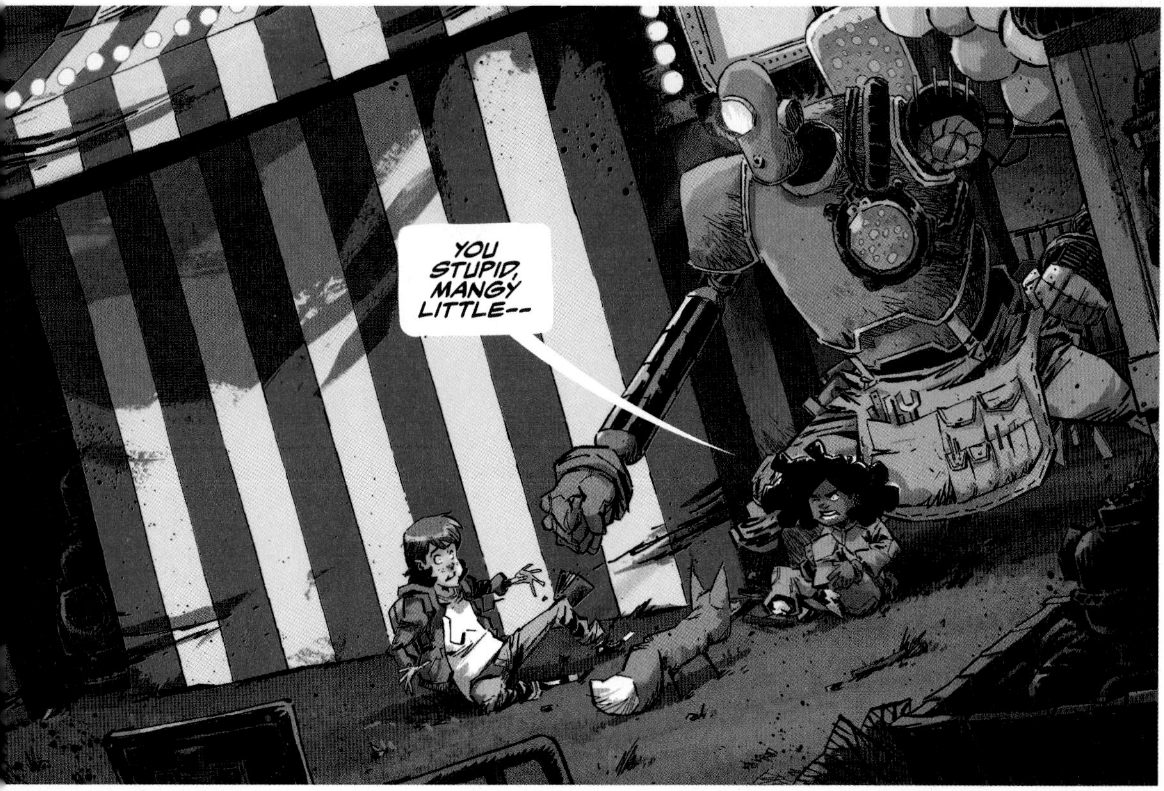
YOU STUPID, MANGY LITTLE--

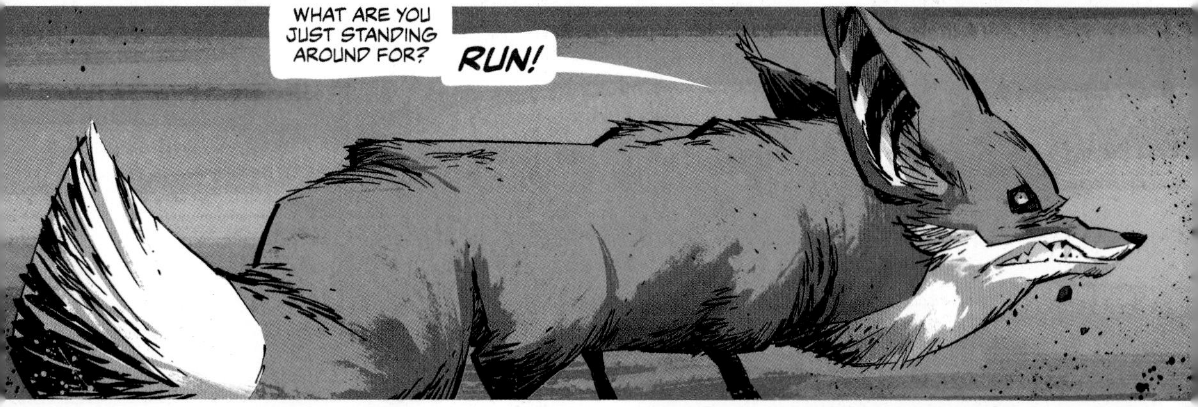
WHAT ARE YOU JUST STANDING AROUND FOR?
RUN!

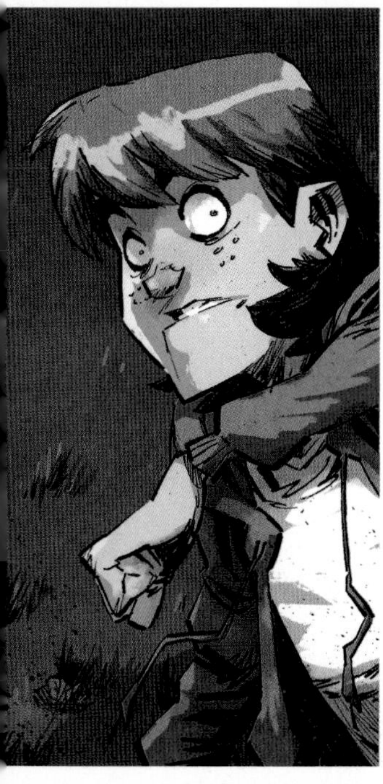

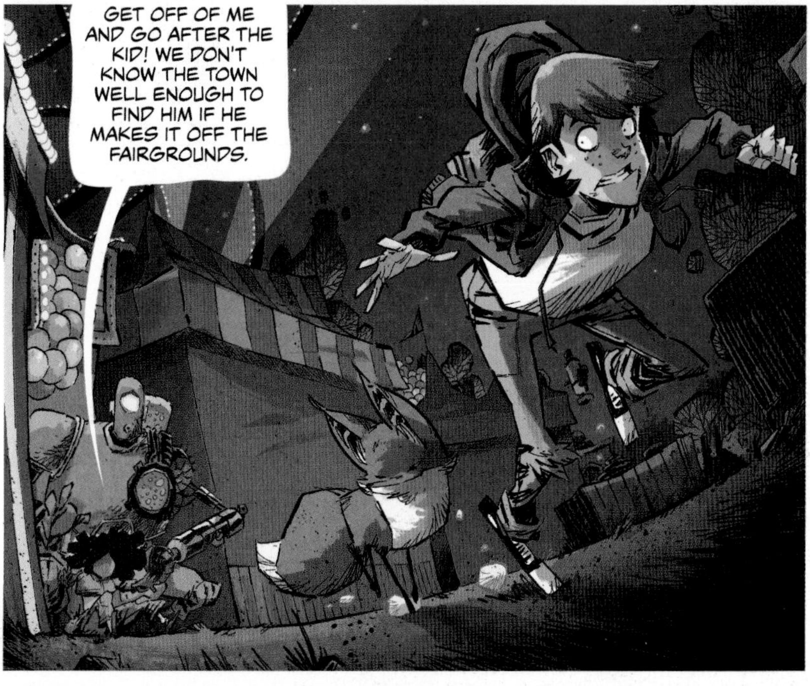
GET OFF OF ME AND GO AFTER THE KID! WE DON'T KNOW THE TOWN WELL ENOUGH TO FIND HIM IF HE MAKES IT OFF THE FAIRGROUNDS.

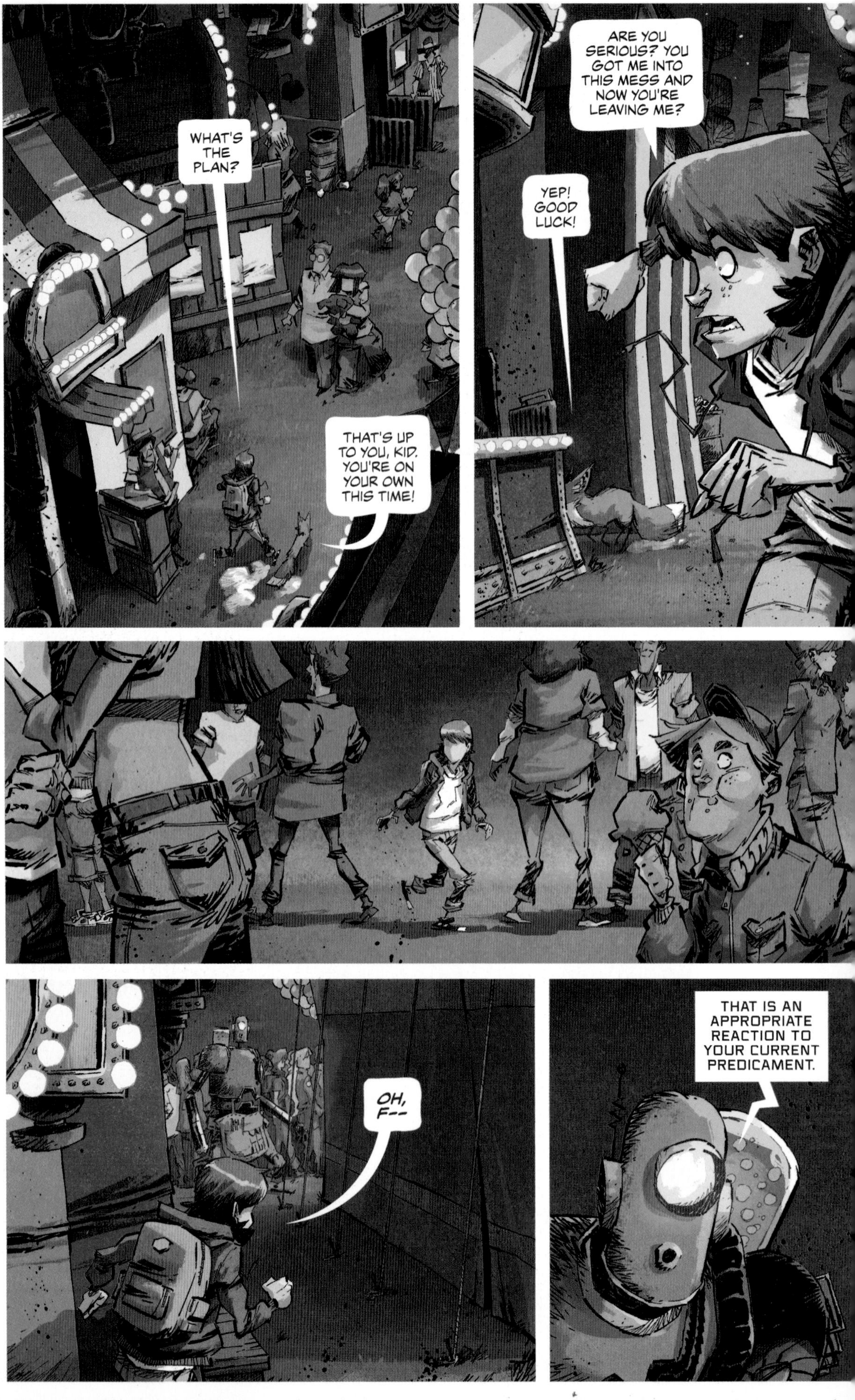
WHAT'S THE PLAN?
THAT'S UP TO YOU, KID. YOU'RE ON YOUR OWN THIS TIME!
ARE YOU SERIOUS? YOU GOT ME INTO THIS MESS AND NOW YOU'RE LEAVING ME?
YEP! GOOD LUCK!
OH, F--
THAT IS AN APPROPRIATE REACTION TO YOUR CURRENT PREDICAMENT.

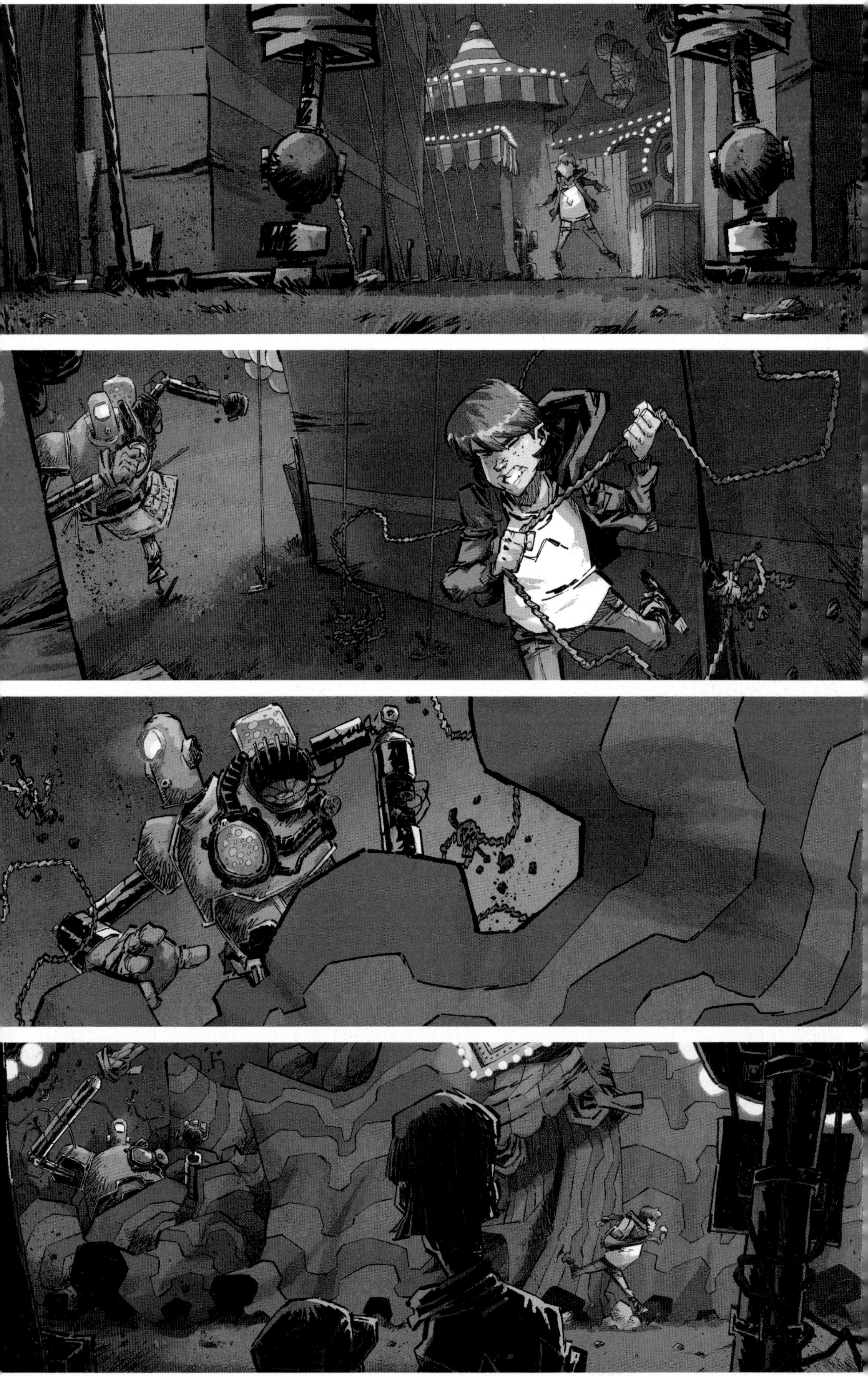

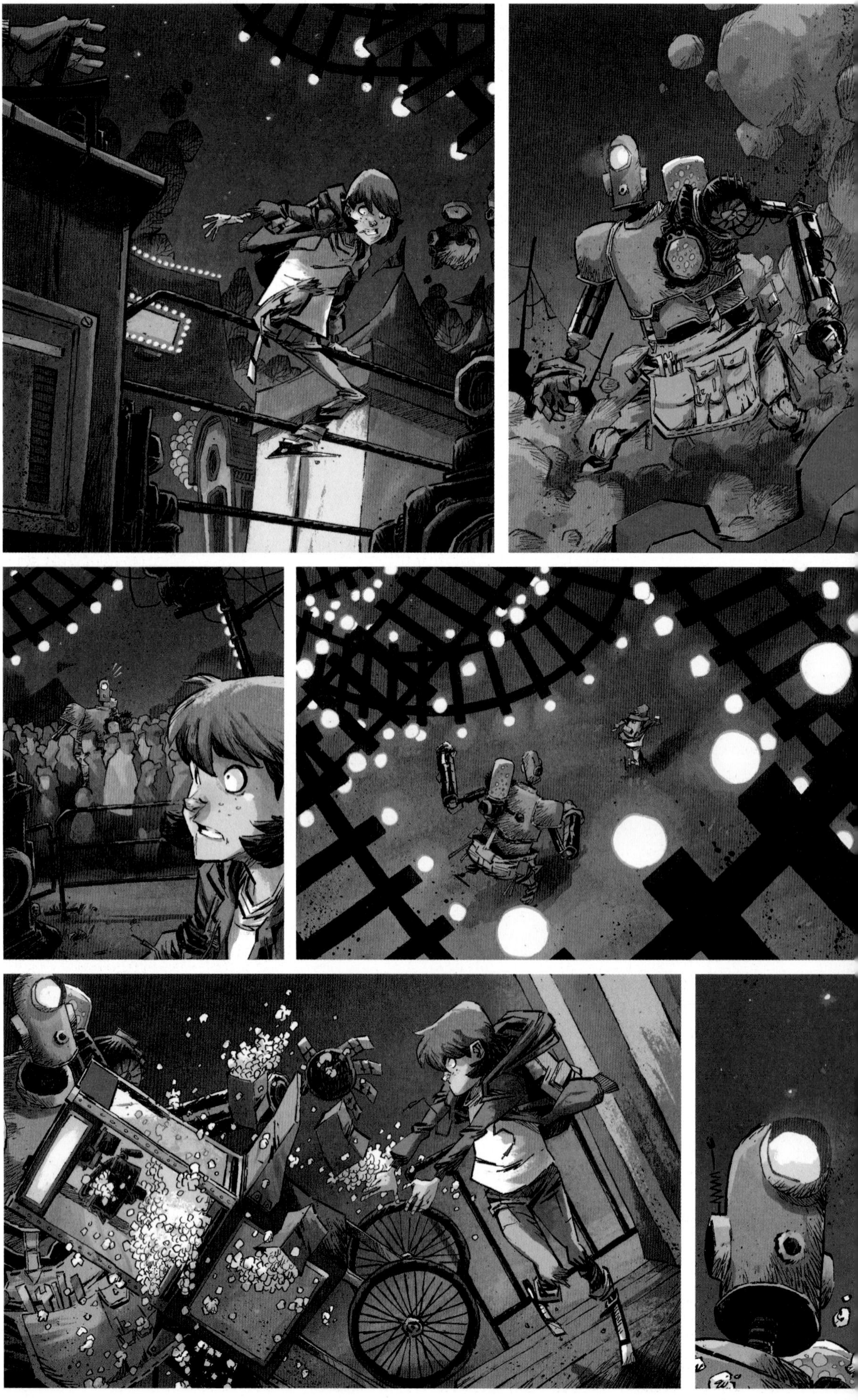

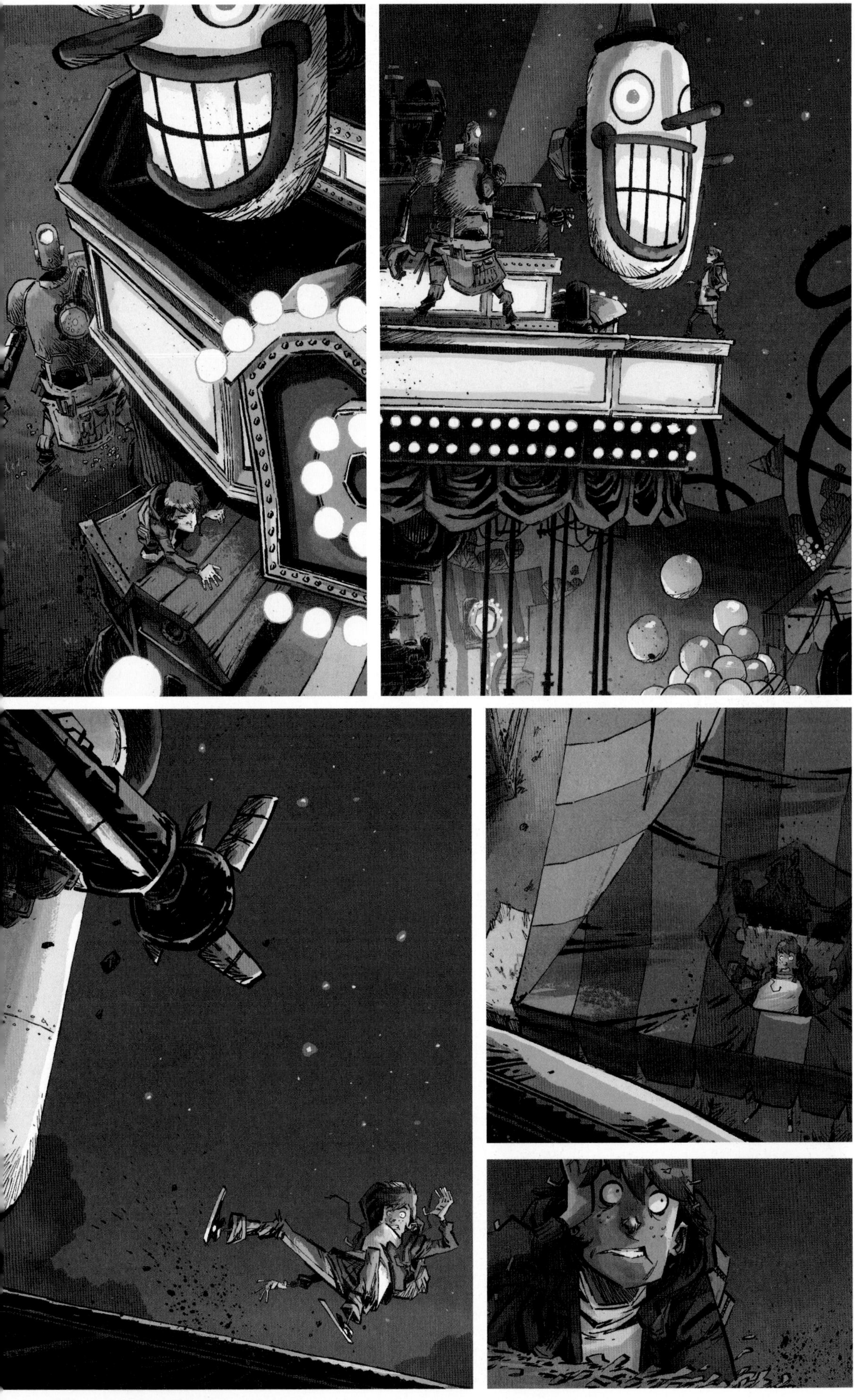

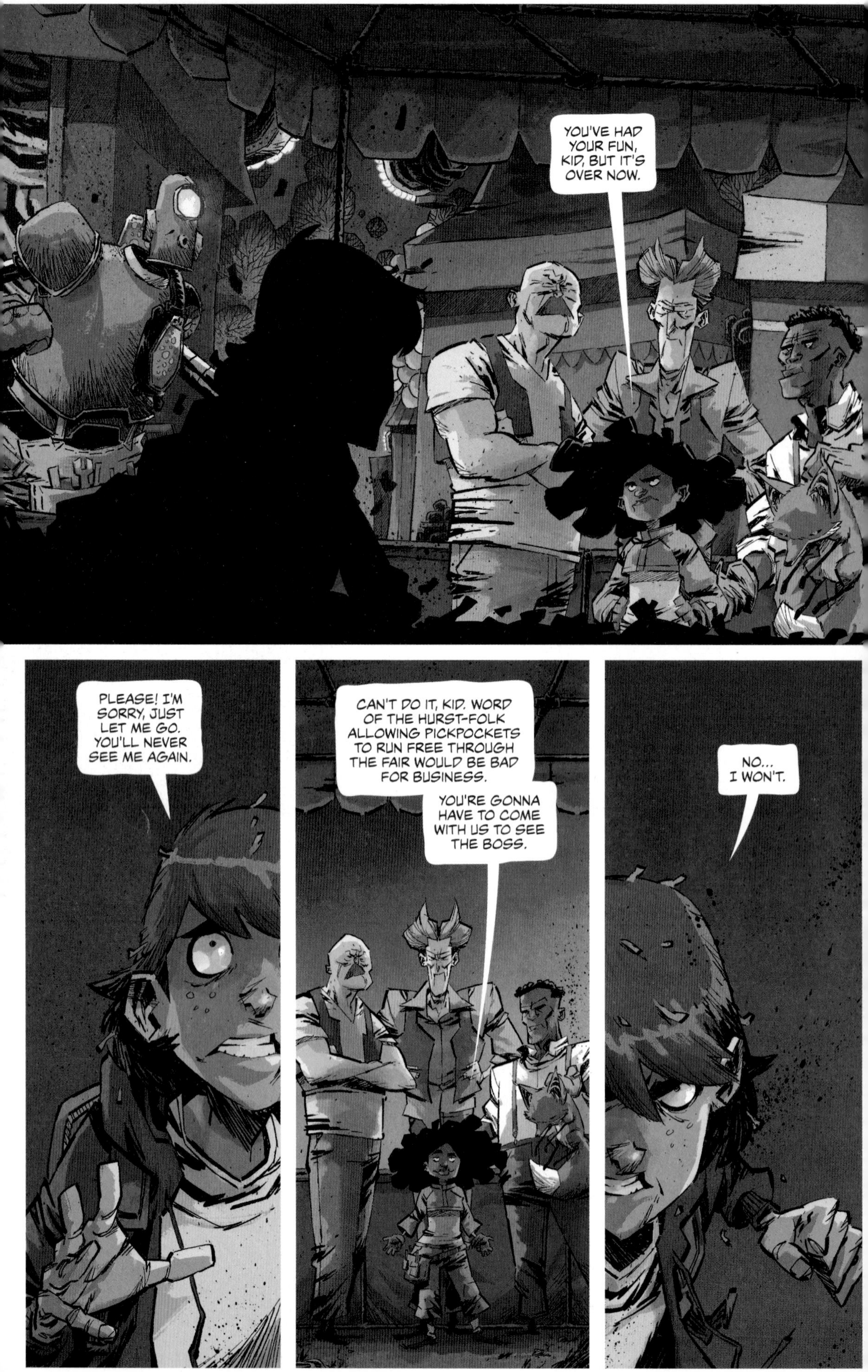
YOU'VE HAD YOUR FUN, KID, BUT IT'S OVER NOW.
PLEASE! I'M SORRY, JUST LET ME GO. YOU'LL NEVER SEE ME AGAIN.
CAN'T DO IT, KID. WORD OF THE HURST-FOLK ALLOWING PICKPOCKETS TO RUN FREE THROUGH THE FAIR WOULD BE BAD FOR BUSINESS.
YOU'RE GONNA HAVE TO COME WITH US TO SEE THE BOSS.
NO... I WON'T.

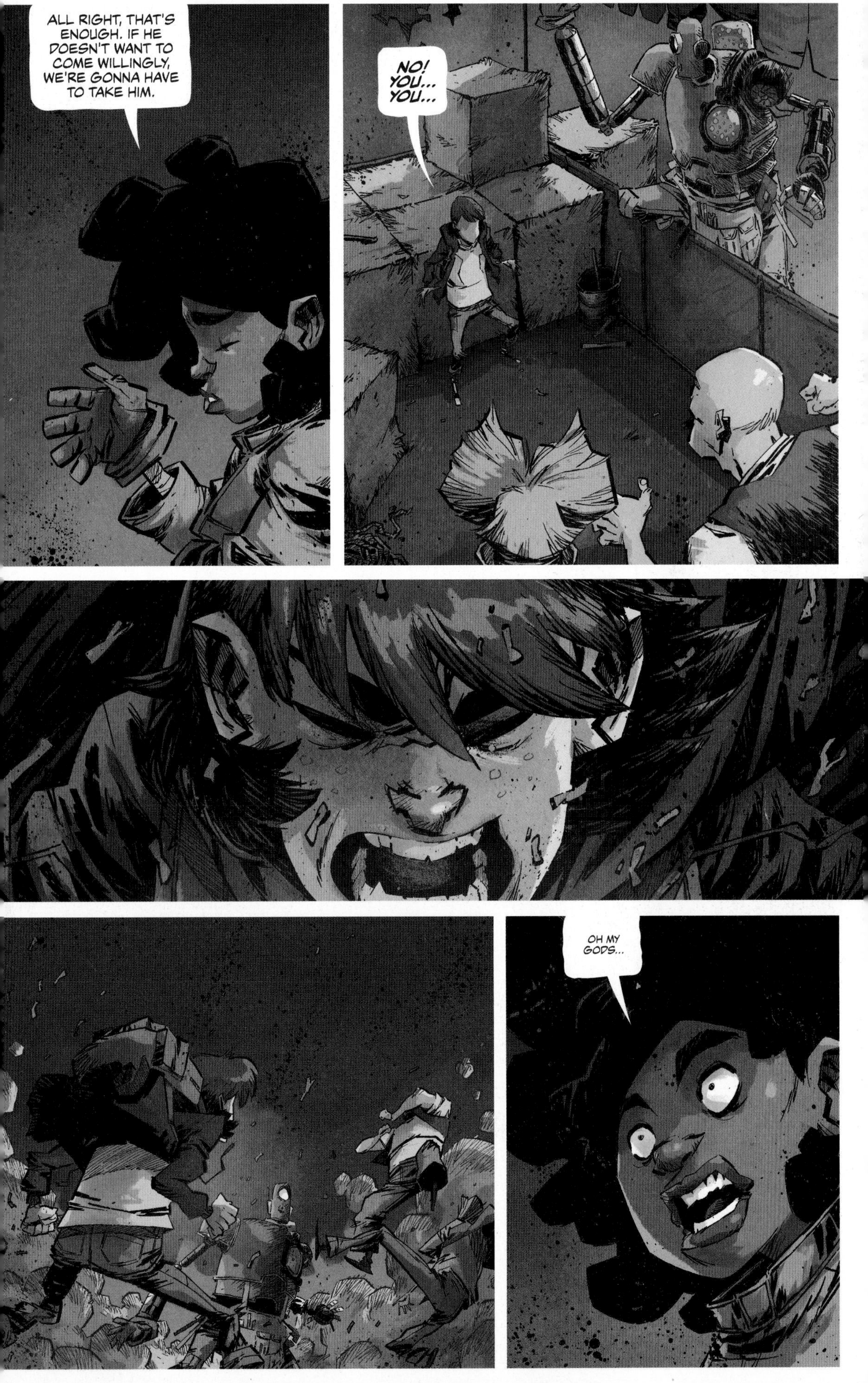
ALL RIGHT, THAT'S ENOUGH. IF HE DOESN'T WANT TO COME WILLINGLY, WE'RE GONNA HAVE TO TAKE HIM.
NO! YOU... YOU...
OH MY GODS...

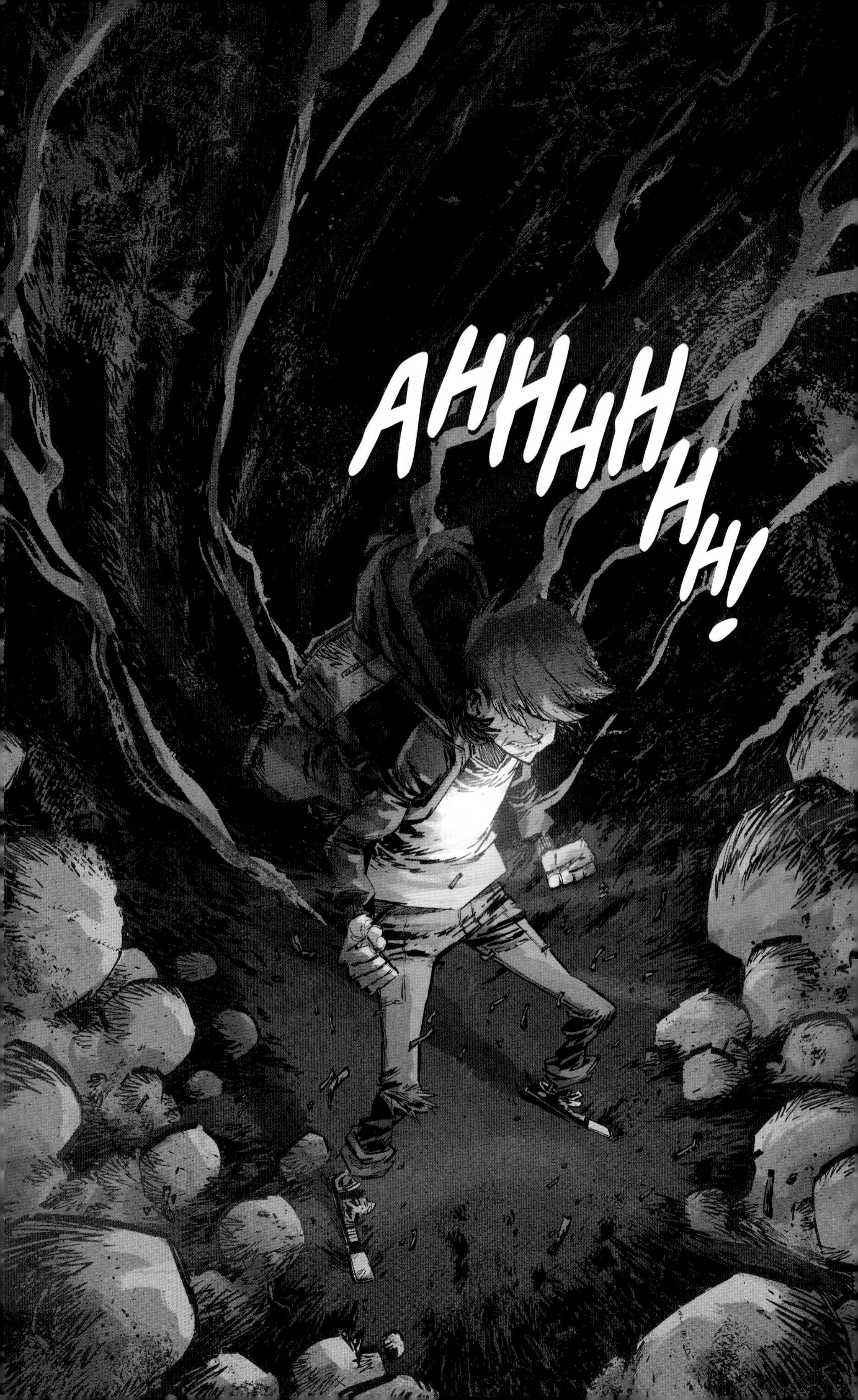
AHHHHHH!

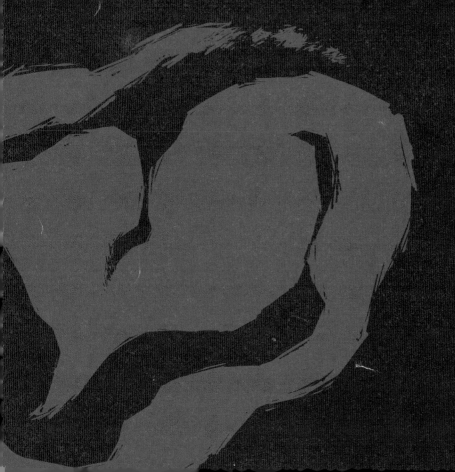

CHAPTER
FIVE

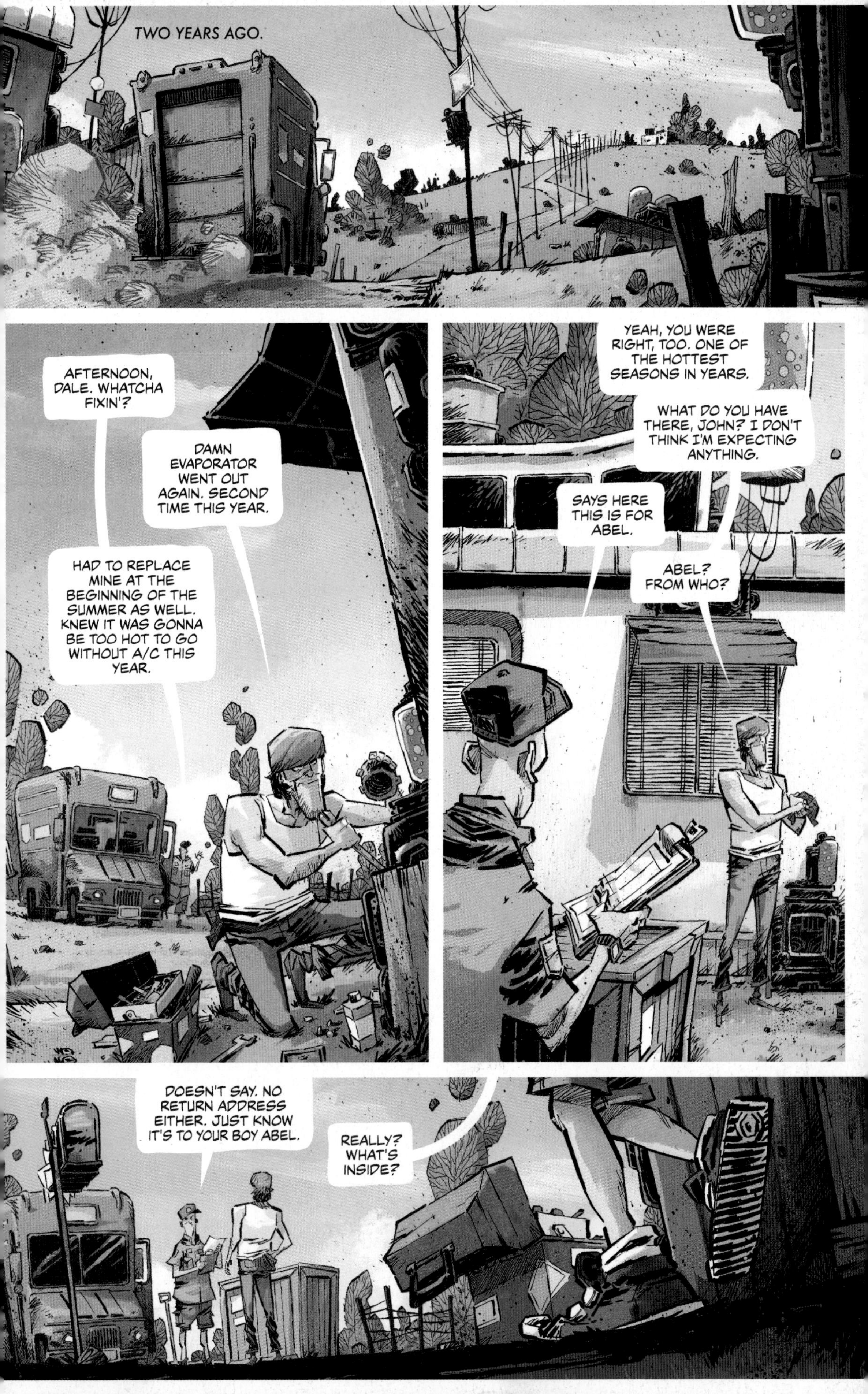
TWO YEARS AGO.
AFTERNOON, DALE. WHATCHA FIXIN'?
DAMN EVAPORATOR WENT OUT AGAIN. SECOND TIME THIS YEAR.
HAD TO REPLACE MINE AT THE BEGINNING OF THE SUMMER AS WELL. KNEW IT WAS GONNA BE TOO HOT TO GO WITHOUT A/C THIS YEAR.
YEAH, YOU WERE RIGHT, TOO. ONE OF THE HOTTEST SEASONS IN YEARS.
WHAT DO YOU HAVE THERE, JOHN? I DON'T THINK I'M EXPECTING ANYTHING.
SAYS HERE THIS IS FOR ABEL.
ABEL? FROM WHO?
DOESN'T SAY. NO RETURN ADDRESS EITHER. JUST KNOW IT'S TO YOUR BOY ABEL.
REALLY? WHAT'S INSIDE?

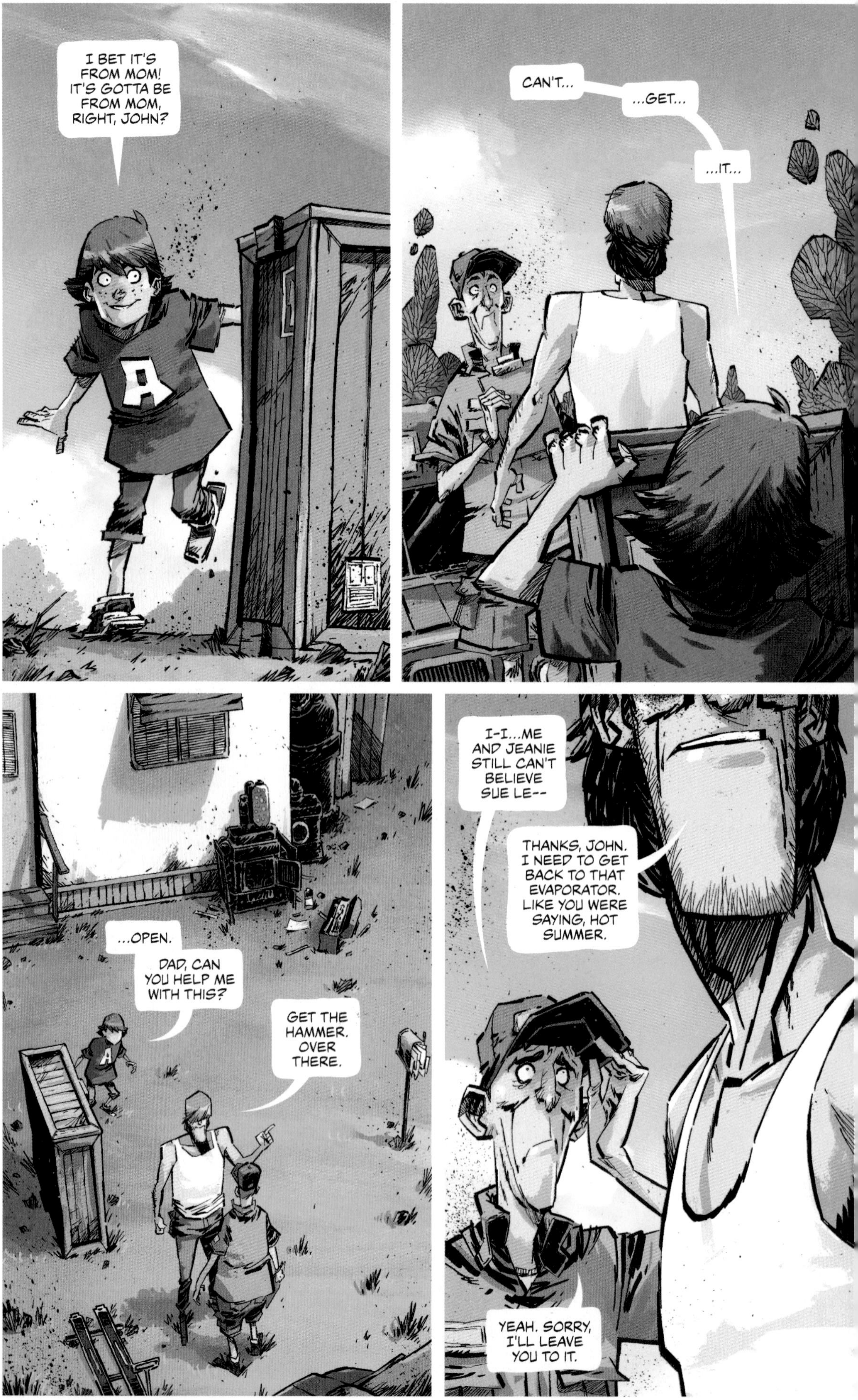
I BET IT'S FROM MOM! IT'S GOTTA BE FROM MOM, RIGHT, JOHN?
CAN'T...
...GET...
...IT...
...OPEN.
DAD, CAN YOU HELP ME WITH THIS?
GET THE HAMMER. OVER THERE.
I-I...ME AND JEANIE STILL CAN'T BELIEVE SUE LE--
THANKS, JOHN. I NEED TO GET BACK TO THAT EVAPORATOR. LIKE YOU WERE SAYING, HOT SUMMER.
YEAH. SORRY, I'LL LEAVE YOU TO IT.

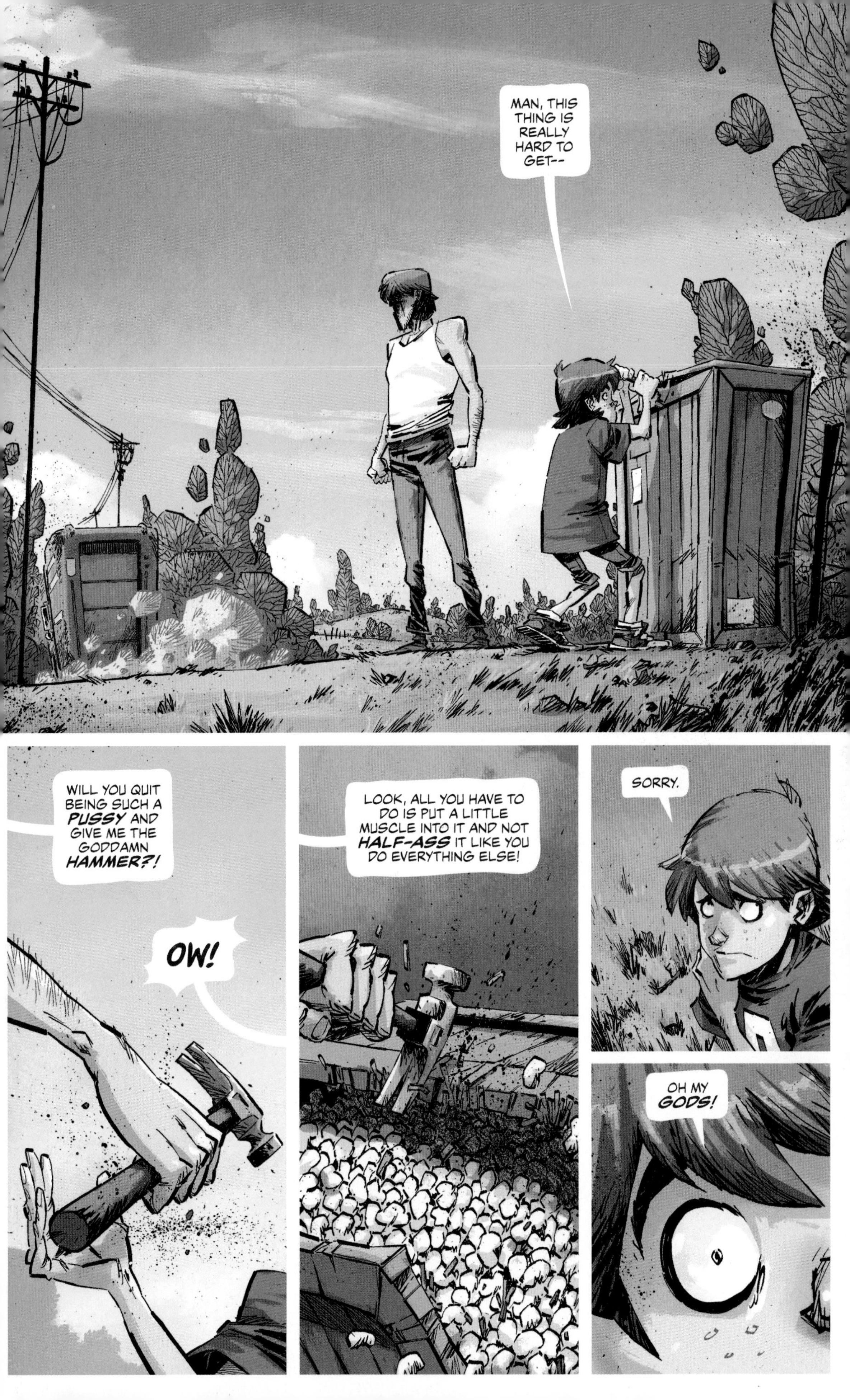
MAN, THIS THING IS REALLY HARD TO GET--
WILL YOU QUIT BEING SUCH A PUSSY AND GIVE ME THE GODDAMN HAMMER?!
OW!
LOOK, ALL YOU HAVE TO DO IS PUT A LITTLE MUSCLE INTO IT AND NOT HALF-ASS IT LIKE YOU DO EVERYTHING ELSE!
SORRY.
OH MY GODS!

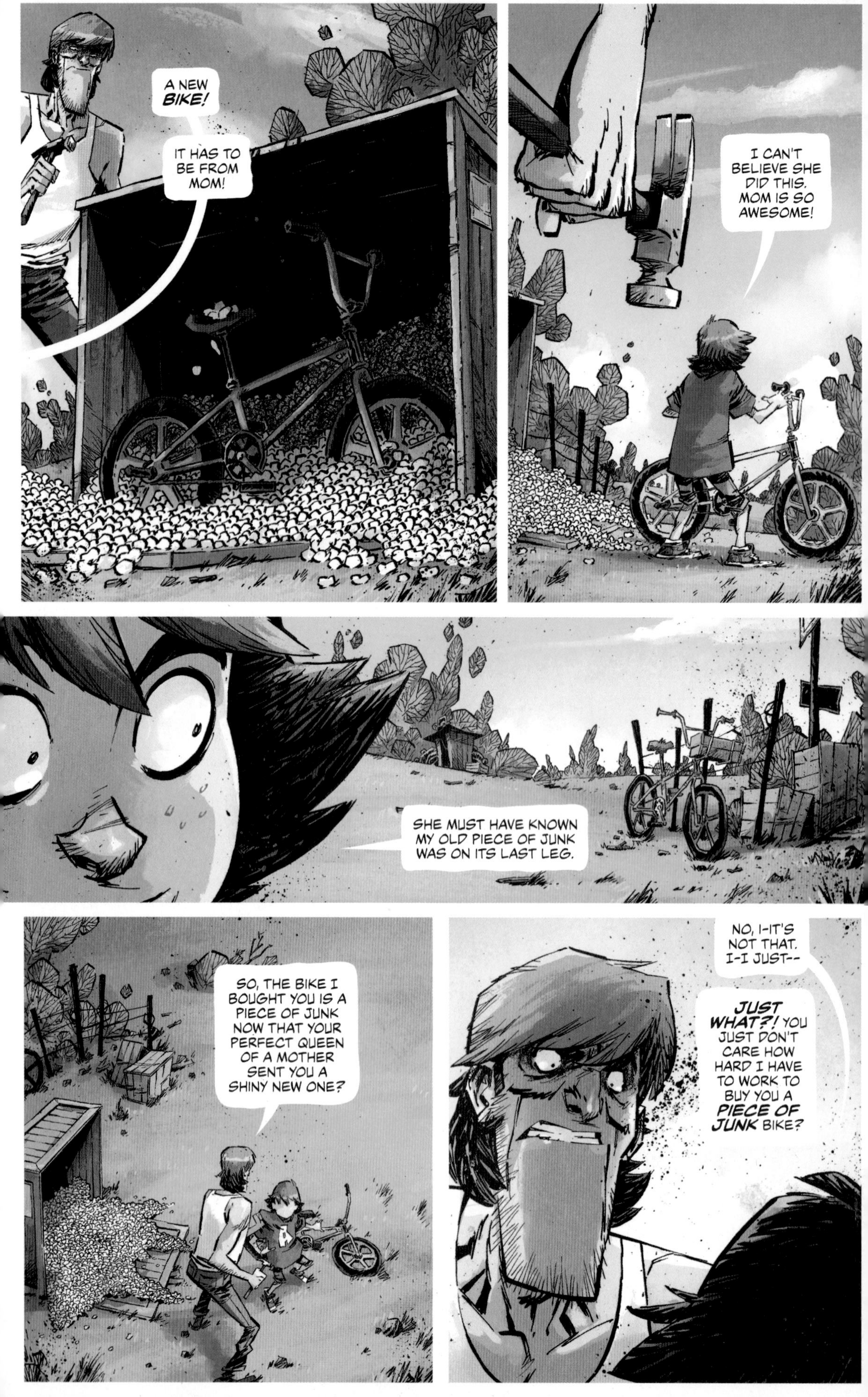
A NEW BIKE!
IT HAS TO BE FROM MOM!
I CAN'T BELIEVE SHE DID THIS. MOM IS SO AWESOME!
SHE MUST HAVE KNOWN MY OLD PIECE OF JUNK WAS ON ITS LAST LEG.
SO, THE BIKE I BOUGHT YOU IS A PIECE OF JUNK NOW THAT YOUR PERFECT QUEEN OF A MOTHER SENT YOU A SHINY NEW ONE?
NO, I-IT'S NOT THAT. I-I JUST--
JUST WHAT?! YOU JUST DON'T CARE HOW HARD I HAVE TO WORK TO BUY YOU A PIECE OF JUNK BIKE?

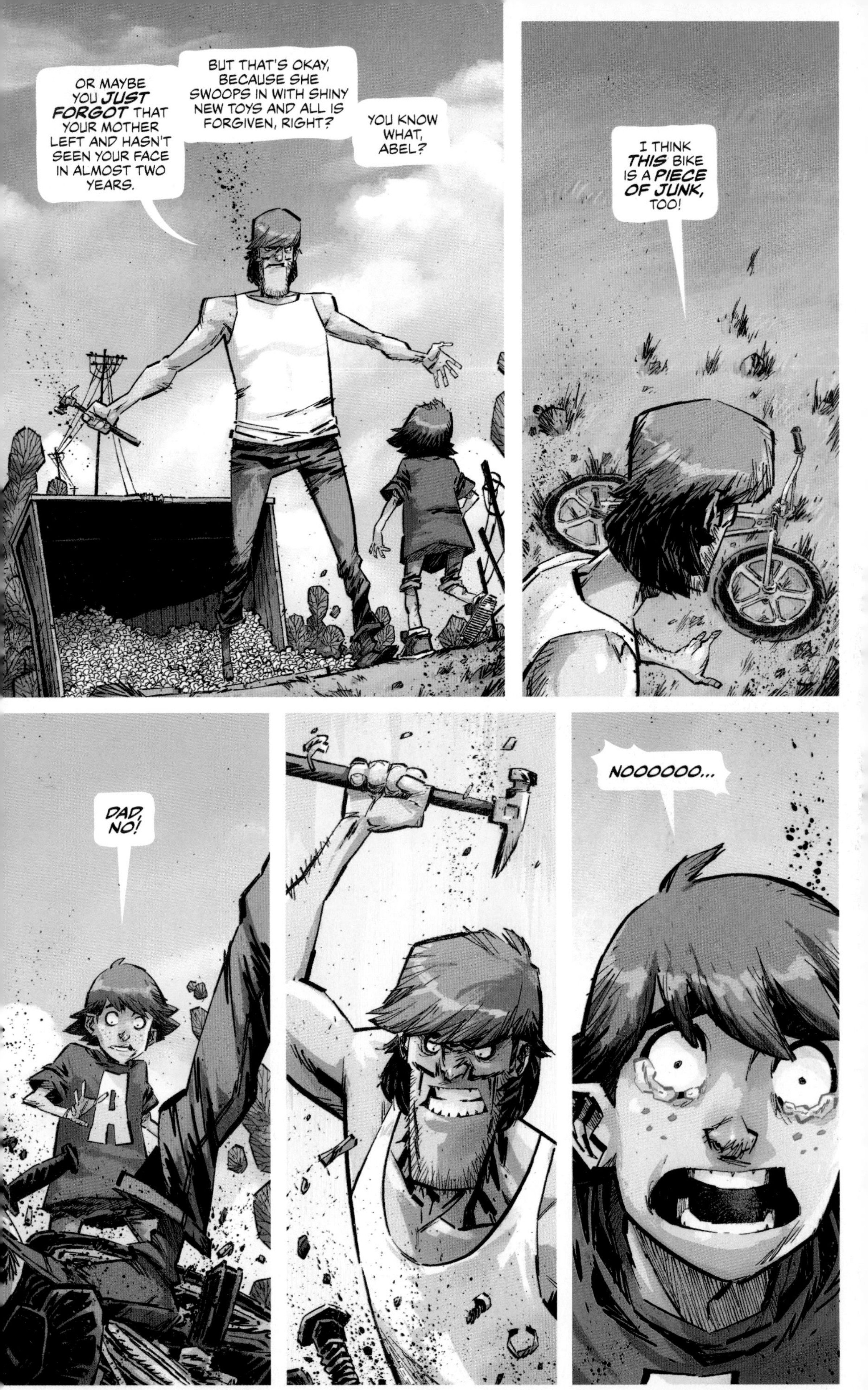

OR MAYBE YOU JUST FORGOT THAT YOUR MOTHER LEFT AND HASN'T SEEN YOUR FACE IN ALMOST TWO YEARS.
BUT THAT'S OKAY, BECAUSE SHE SWOOPS IN WITH SHINY NEW TOYS AND ALL IS FORGIVEN, RIGHT?
YOU KNOW WHAT, ABEL?
I THINK THIS BIKE IS A PIECE OF JUNK, TOO!
DAD, NO!
NOOOOOO...

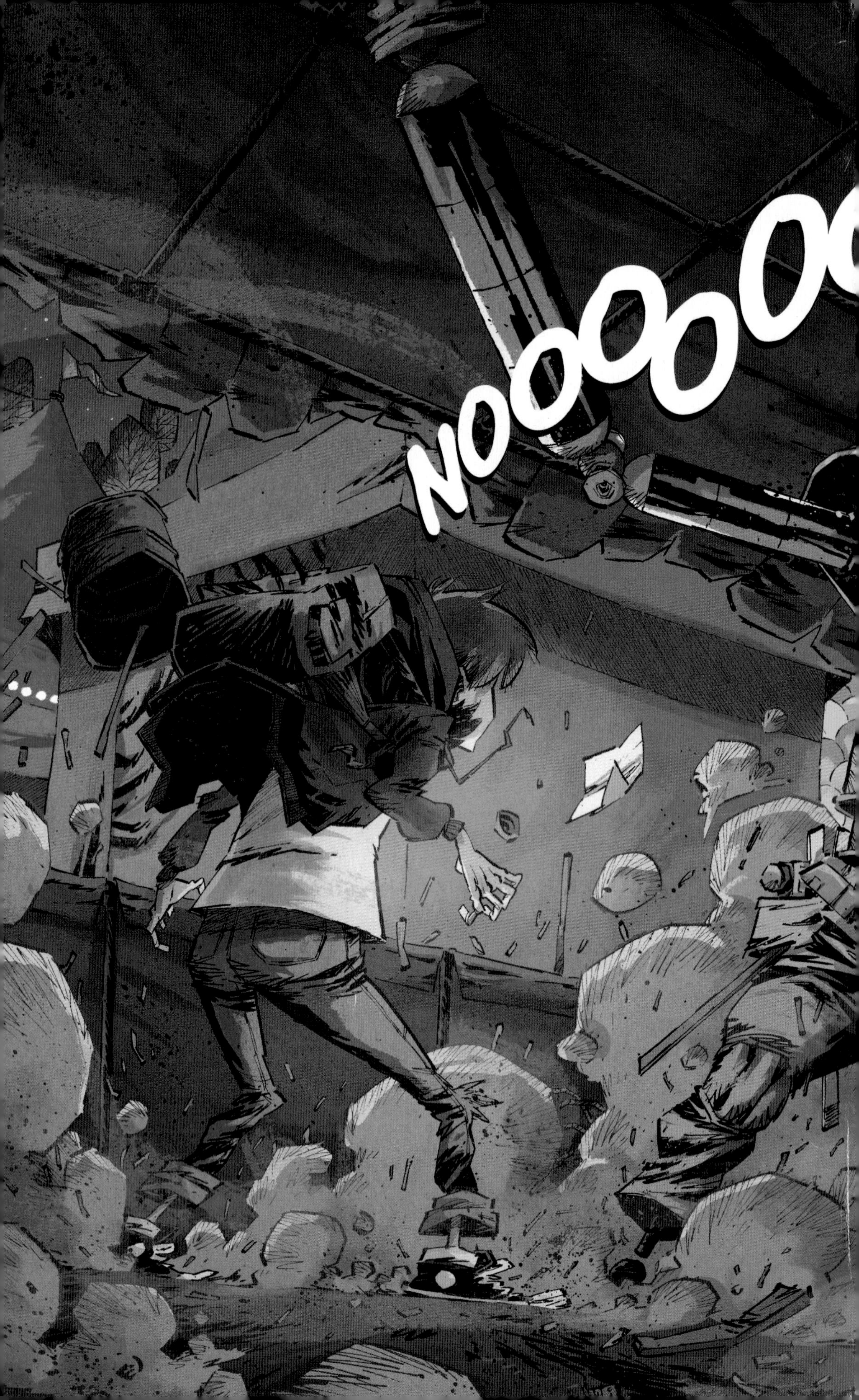
NOOOOOOO

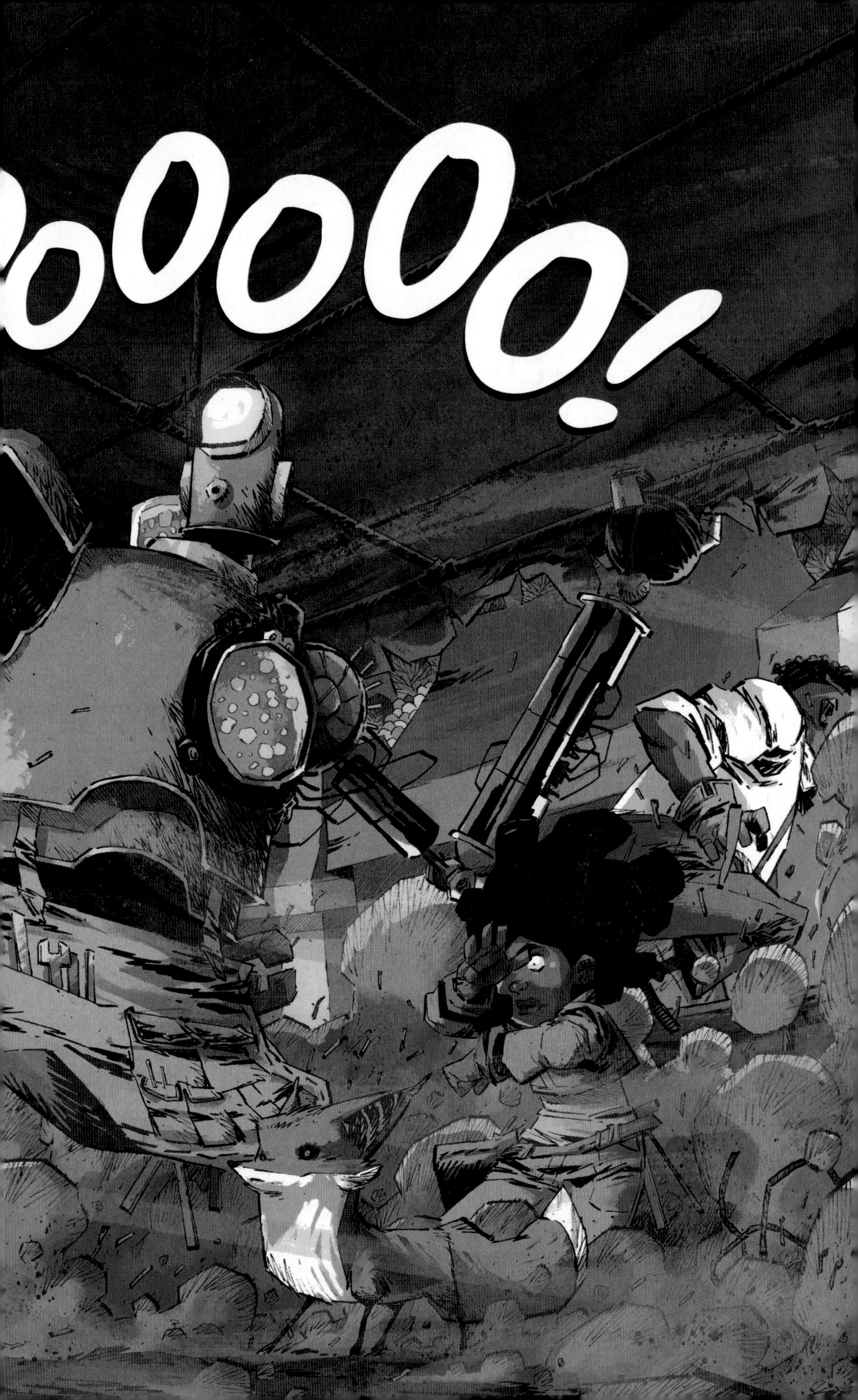
OOOOOO!

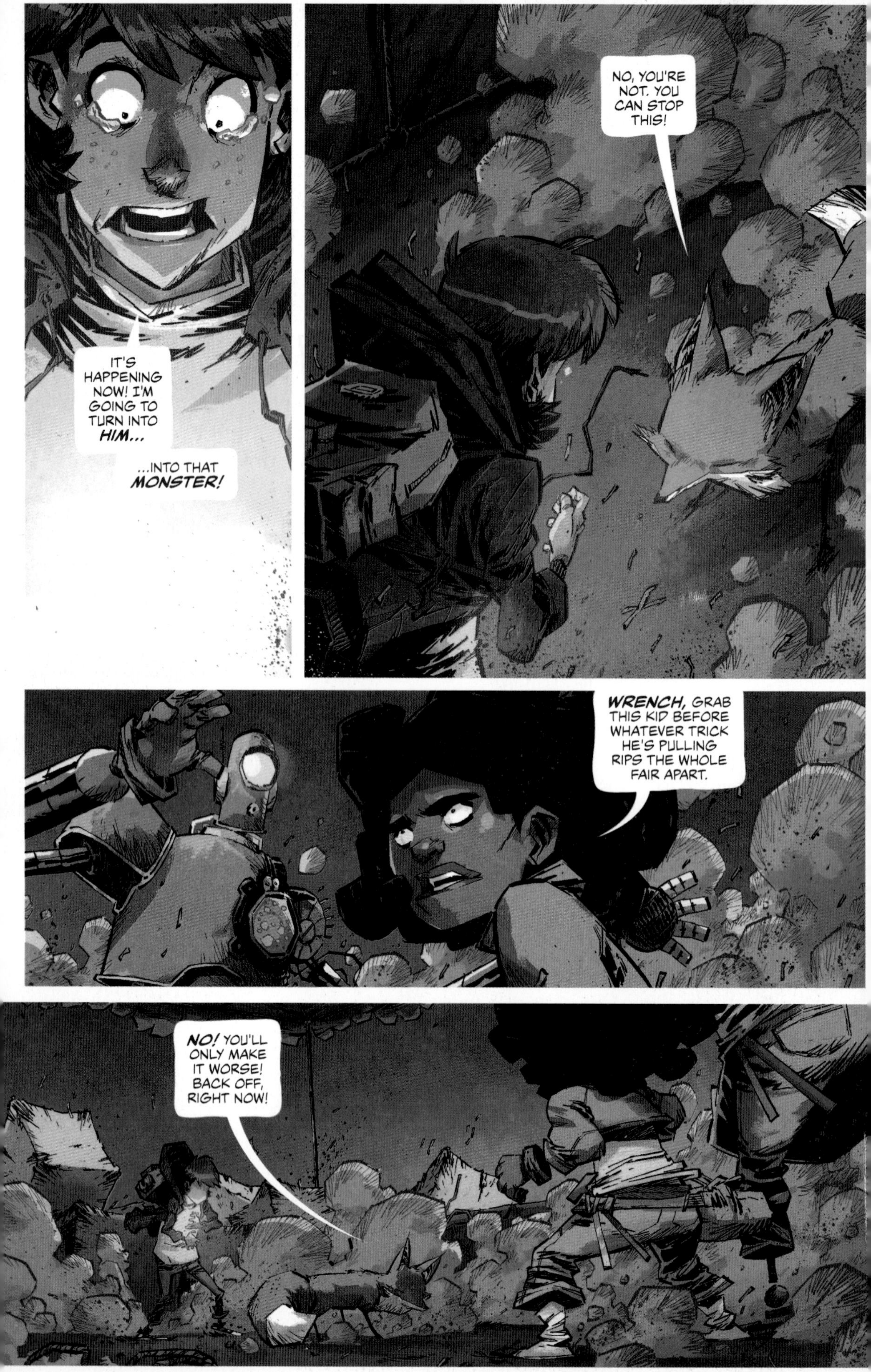
IT'S HAPPENING NOW! I'M GOING TO TURN INTO *HIM...*
...INTO THAT *MONSTER!*
NO, YOU'RE NOT. YOU CAN STOP THIS!
WRENCH, GRAB THIS KID BEFORE WHATEVER TRICK HE'S PULLING RIPS THE WHOLE FAIR APART.
NO! YOU'LL ONLY MAKE IT WORSE! BACK OFF, RIGHT NOW!

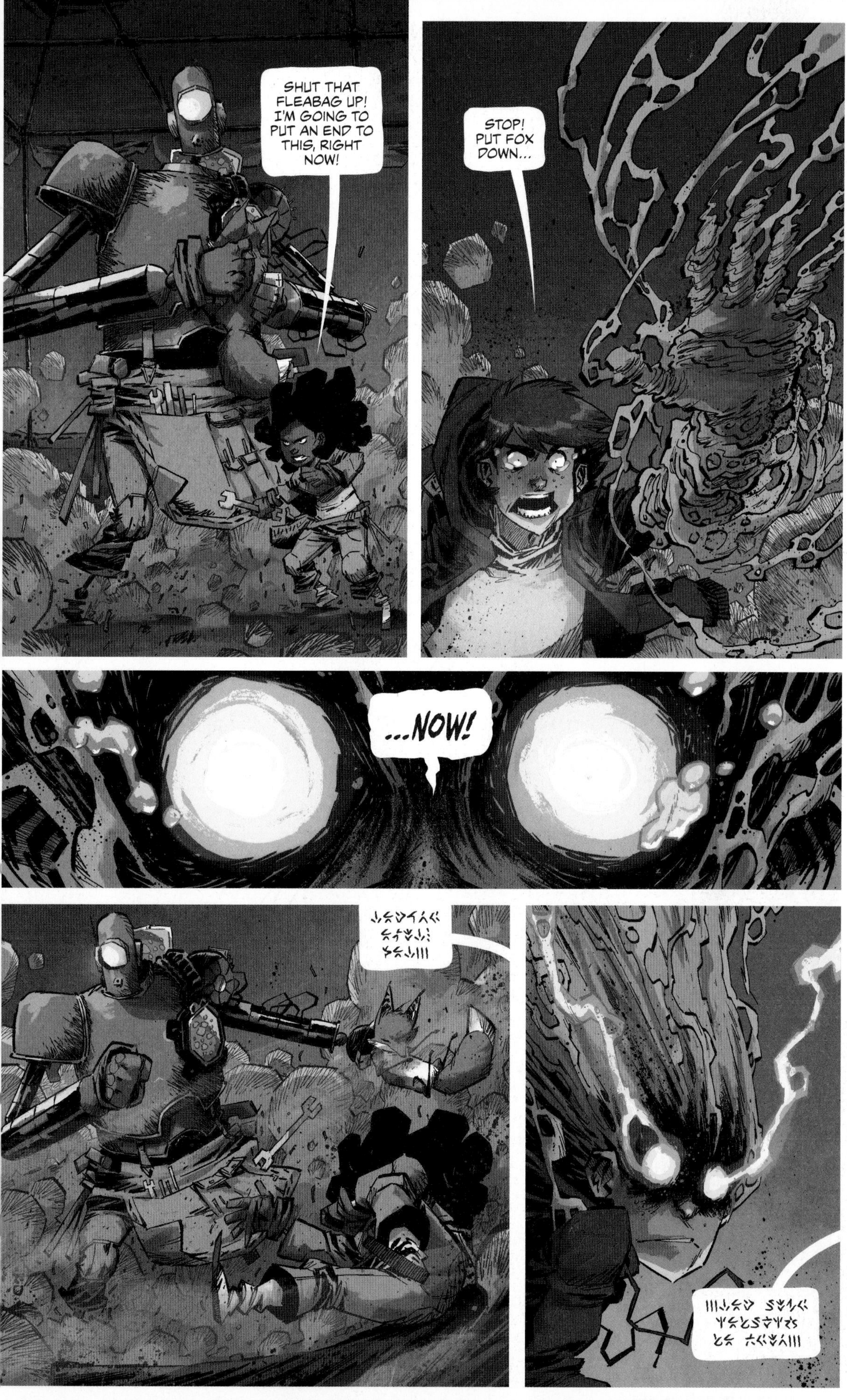
SHUT THAT FLEABAG UP! I'M GOING TO PUT AN END TO THIS, RIGHT NOW!
STOP! PUT FOX DOWN...
...NOW!

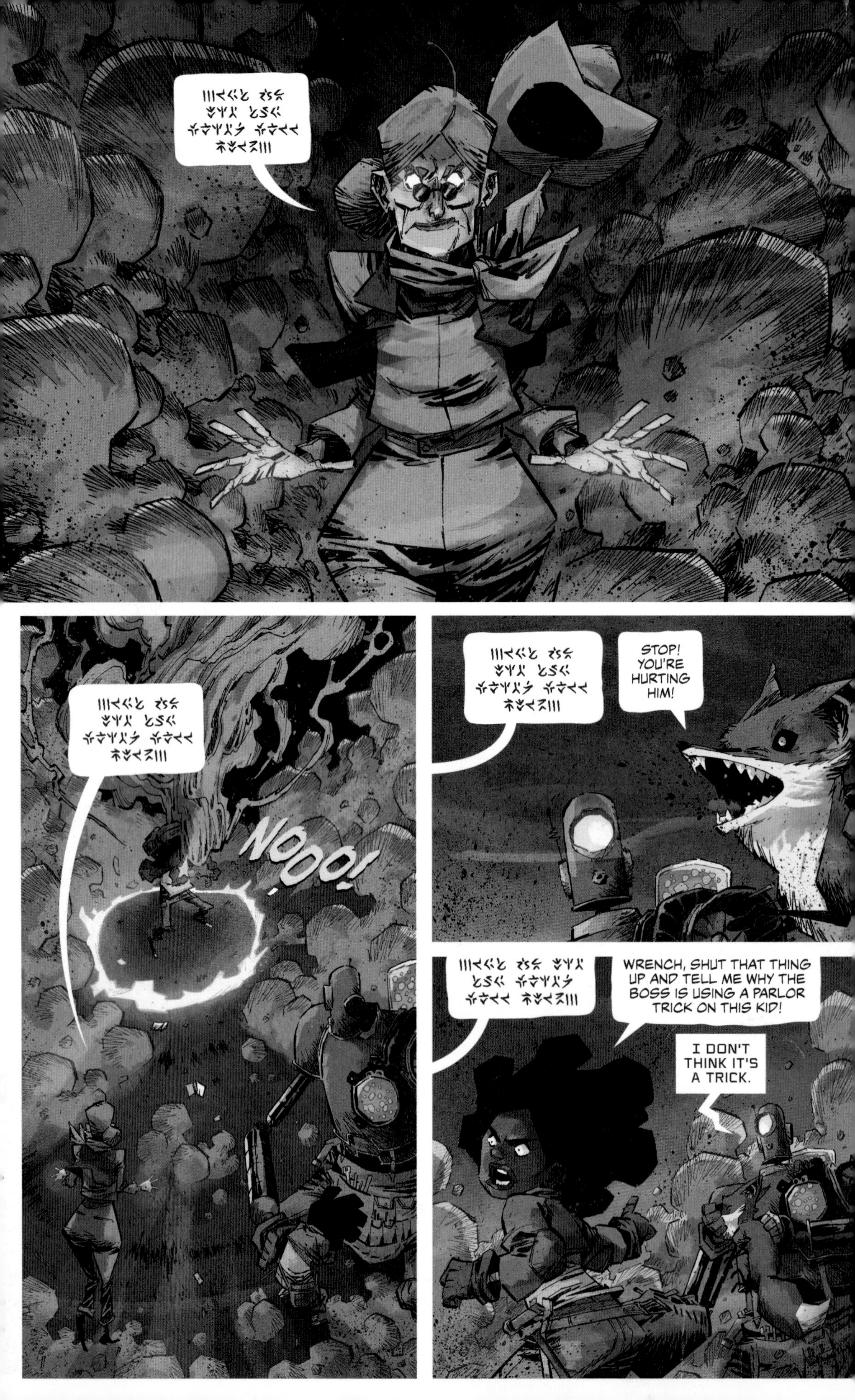
NOOO!
STOP! YOU'RE HURTING HIM!
WRENCH, SHUT THAT THING UP AND TELL ME WHY THE BOSS IS USING A PARLOR TRICK ON THIS KID!
I DON'T THINK IT'S A TRICK.

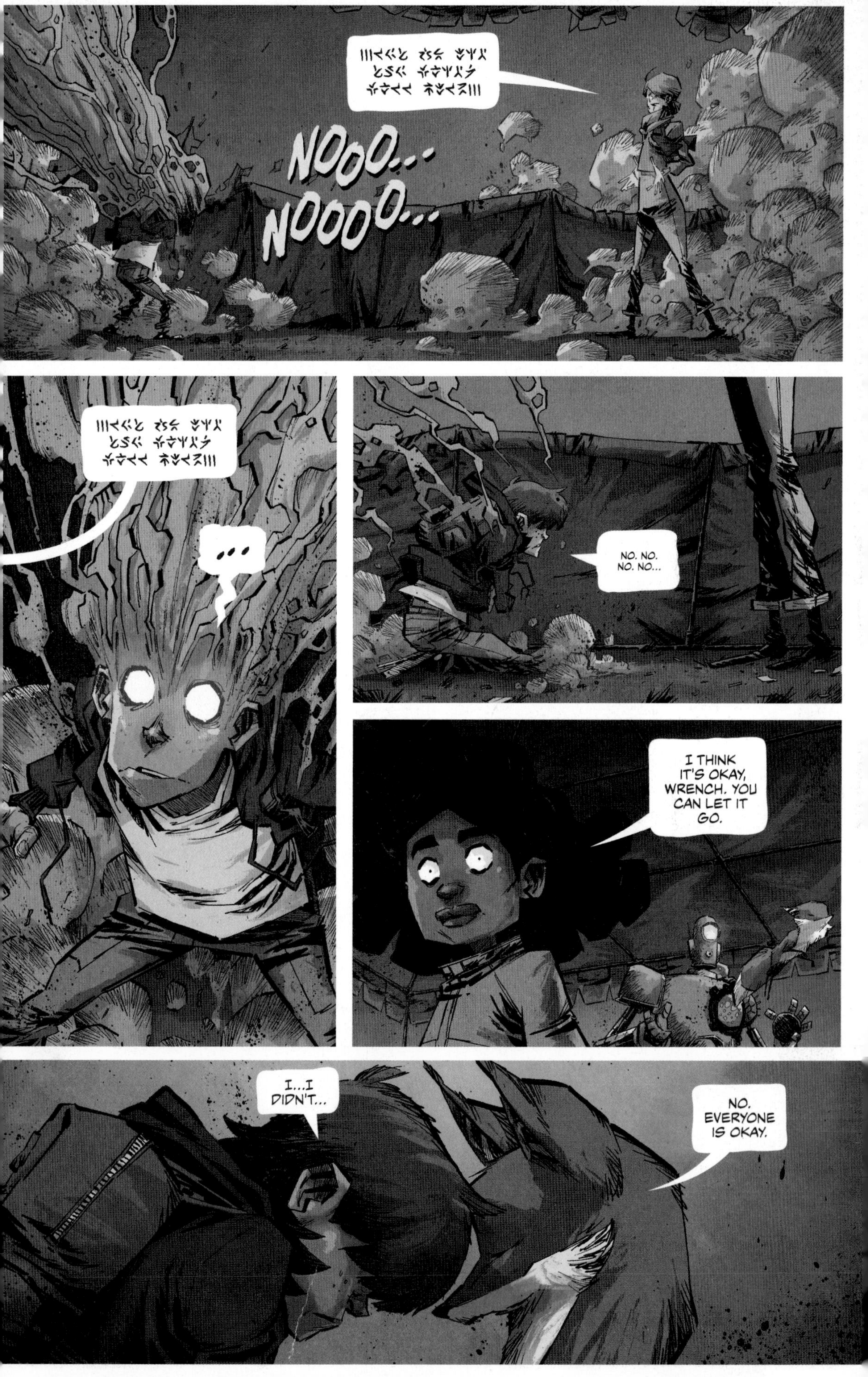
NOOO...
NOOOO...
...
NO. NO. NO. NO...
I THINK IT'S OKAY, WRENCH. YOU CAN LET IT GO.
I...I DIDN'T...
NO. EVERYONE IS OKAY.

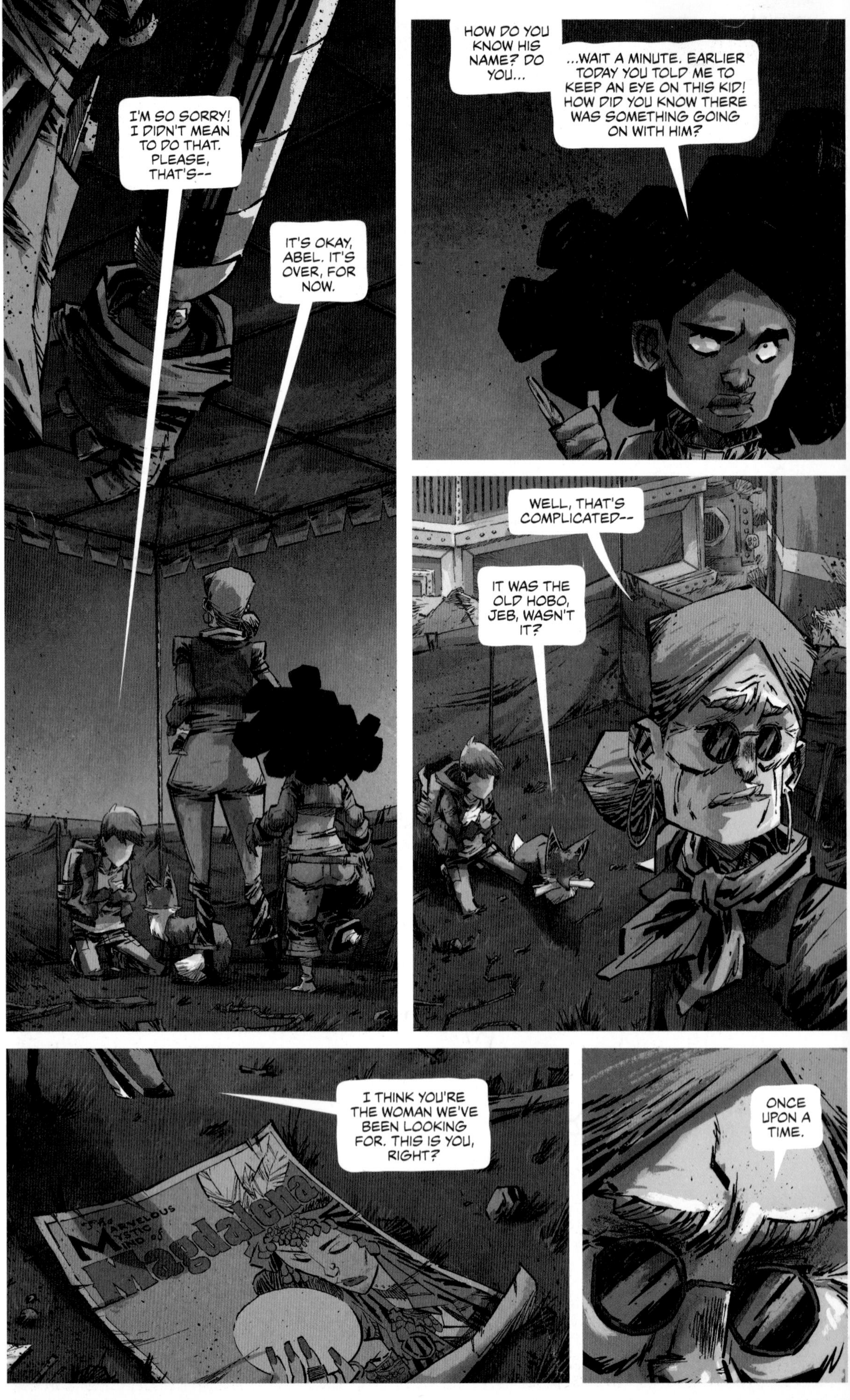
I'M SO SORRY! I DIDN'T MEAN TO DO THAT. PLEASE, THAT'S--
IT'S OKAY, ABEL. IT'S OVER, FOR NOW.
HOW DO YOU KNOW HIS NAME? DO YOU...
...WAIT A MINUTE. EARLIER TODAY YOU TOLD ME TO KEEP AN EYE ON THIS KID! HOW DID YOU KNOW THERE WAS SOMETHING GOING ON WITH HIM?
WELL, THAT'S COMPLICATED--
IT WAS THE OLD HOBO, JEB, WASN'T IT?
I THINK YOU'RE THE WOMAN WE'VE BEEN LOOKING FOR. THIS IS YOU, RIGHT?
ONCE UPON A TIME.

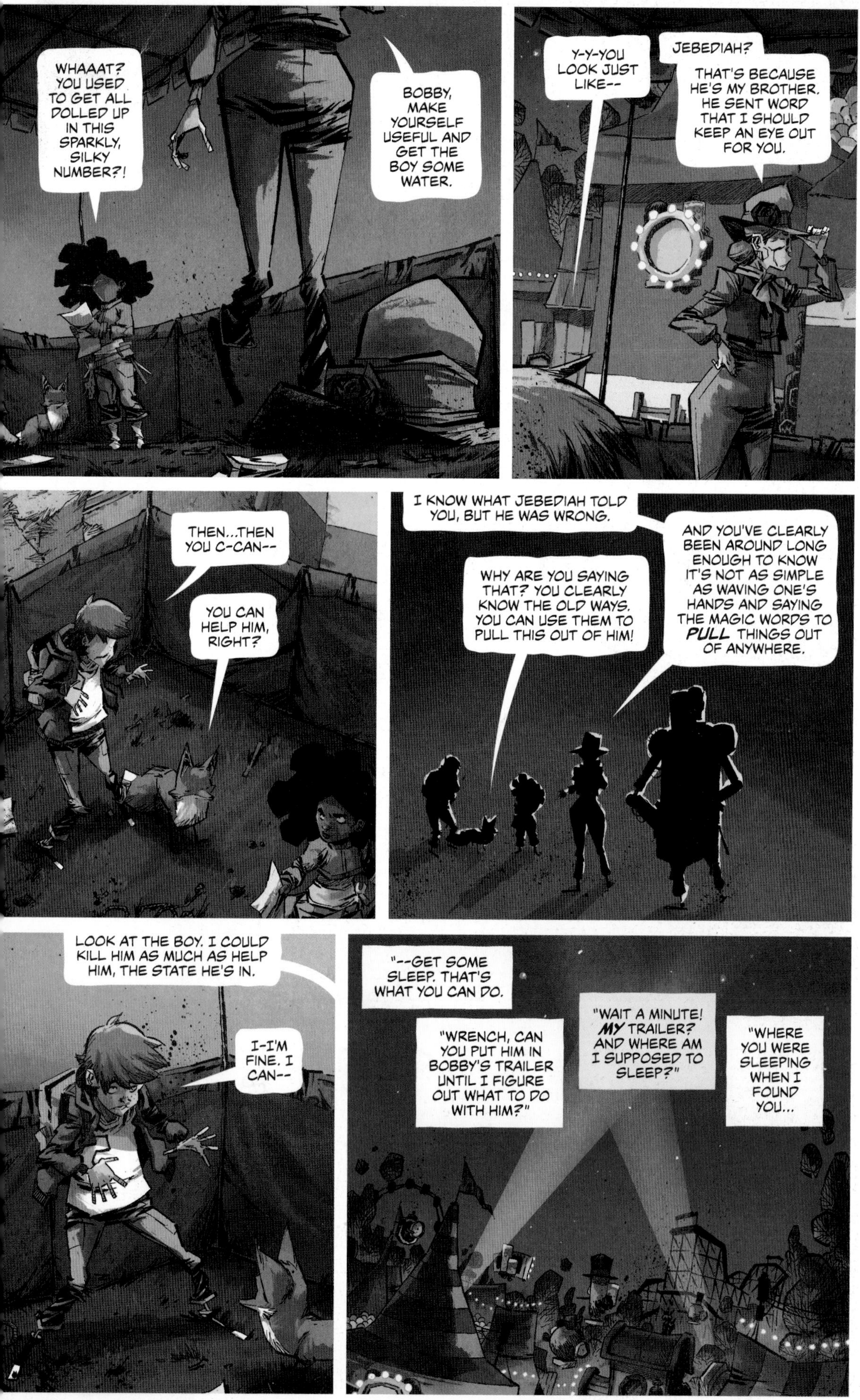
WHAAAT? YOU USED TO GET ALL DOLLED UP IN THIS SPARKLY, SILKY NUMBER?!
BOBBY, MAKE YOURSELF USEFUL AND GET THE BOY SOME WATER.
Y-Y-YOU LOOK JUST LIKE--
JEBEDIAH?
THAT'S BECAUSE HE'S MY BROTHER. HE SENT WORD THAT I SHOULD KEEP AN EYE OUT FOR YOU.
THEN...THEN YOU C-CAN--
YOU CAN HELP HIM, RIGHT?
I KNOW WHAT JEBEDIAH TOLD YOU, BUT HE WAS WRONG.
WHY ARE YOU SAYING THAT? YOU CLEARLY KNOW THE OLD WAYS. YOU CAN USE THEM TO PULL THIS OUT OF HIM!
AND YOU'VE CLEARLY BEEN AROUND LONG ENOUGH TO KNOW IT'S NOT AS SIMPLE AS WAVING ONE'S HANDS AND SAYING THE MAGIC WORDS TO PULL THINGS OUT OF ANYWHERE.
LOOK AT THE BOY. I COULD KILL HIM AS MUCH AS HELP HIM, THE STATE HE'S IN.
I-I'M FINE. I CAN--
"--GET SOME SLEEP. THAT'S WHAT YOU CAN DO.
"WRENCH, CAN YOU PUT HIM IN BOBBY'S TRAILER UNTIL I FIGURE OUT WHAT TO DO WITH HIM?"
"WAIT A MINUTE! MY TRAILER? AND WHERE AM I SUPPOSED TO SLEEP?"
"WHERE YOU WERE SLEEPING WHEN I FOUND YOU...

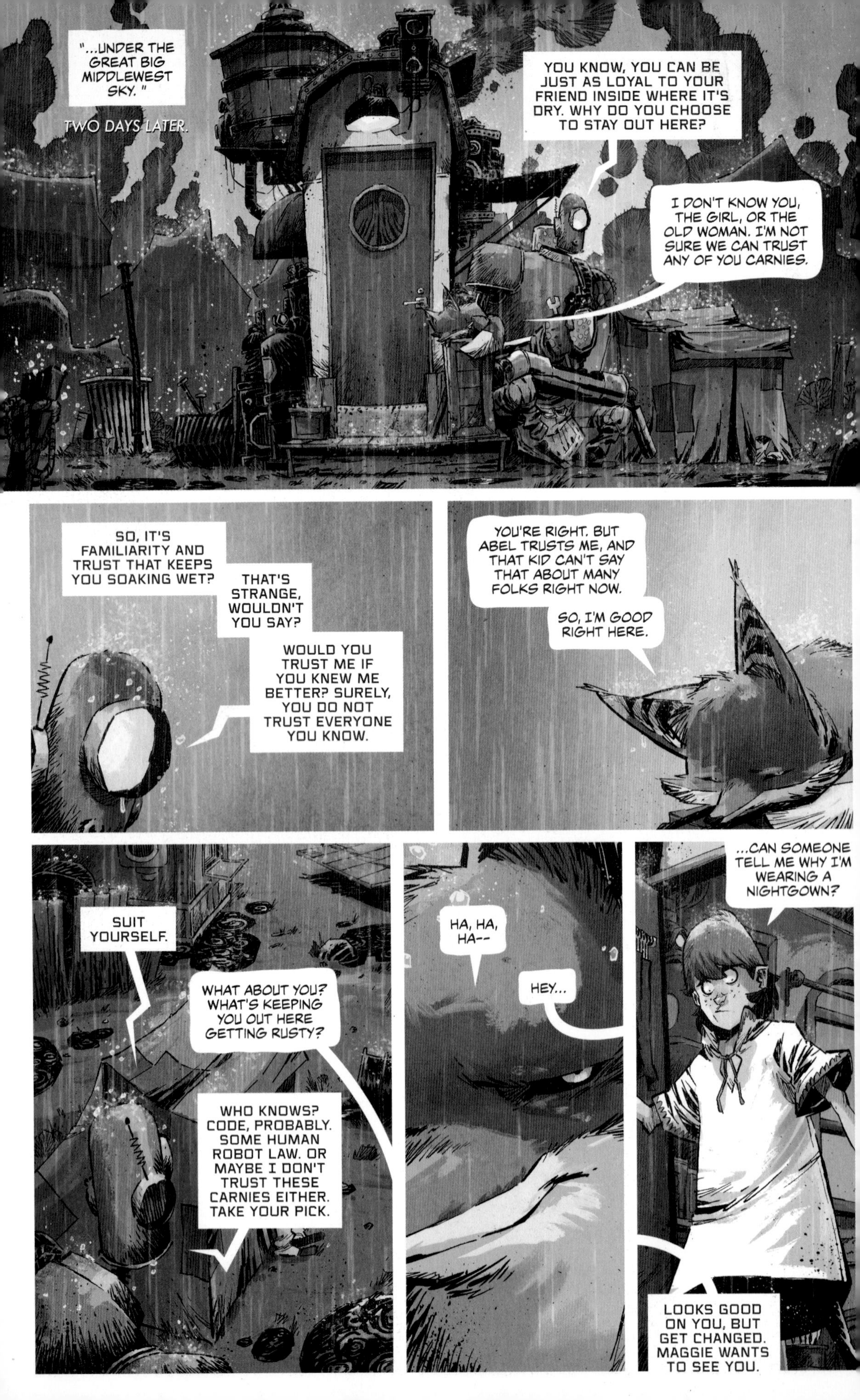
"...UNDER THE GREAT BIG MIDDLEWEST SKY."
TWO DAYS LATER.
YOU KNOW, YOU CAN BE JUST AS LOYAL TO YOUR FRIEND INSIDE WHERE IT'S DRY. WHY DO YOU CHOOSE TO STAY OUT HERE?
I DON'T KNOW YOU, THE GIRL, OR THE OLD WOMAN. I'M NOT SURE WE CAN TRUST ANY OF YOU CARNIES.
SO, IT'S FAMILIARITY AND TRUST THAT KEEPS YOU SOAKING WET?
THAT'S STRANGE, WOULDN'T YOU SAY?
WOULD YOU TRUST ME IF YOU KNEW ME BETTER? SURELY, YOU DO NOT TRUST EVERYONE YOU KNOW.
YOU'RE RIGHT. BUT ABEL TRUSTS ME, AND THAT KID CAN'T SAY THAT ABOUT MANY FOLKS RIGHT NOW.
SO, I'M GOOD RIGHT HERE.
SUIT YOURSELF.
WHAT ABOUT YOU? WHAT'S KEEPING YOU OUT HERE GETTING RUSTY?
WHO KNOWS? CODE, PROBABLY. SOME HUMAN ROBOT LAW. OR MAYBE I DON'T TRUST THESE CARNIES EITHER. TAKE YOUR PICK.
HA, HA, HA--
HEY...
...CAN SOMEONE TELL ME WHY I'M WEARING A NIGHTGOWN?
LOOKS GOOD ON YOU, BUT GET CHANGED. MAGGIE WANTS TO SEE YOU.

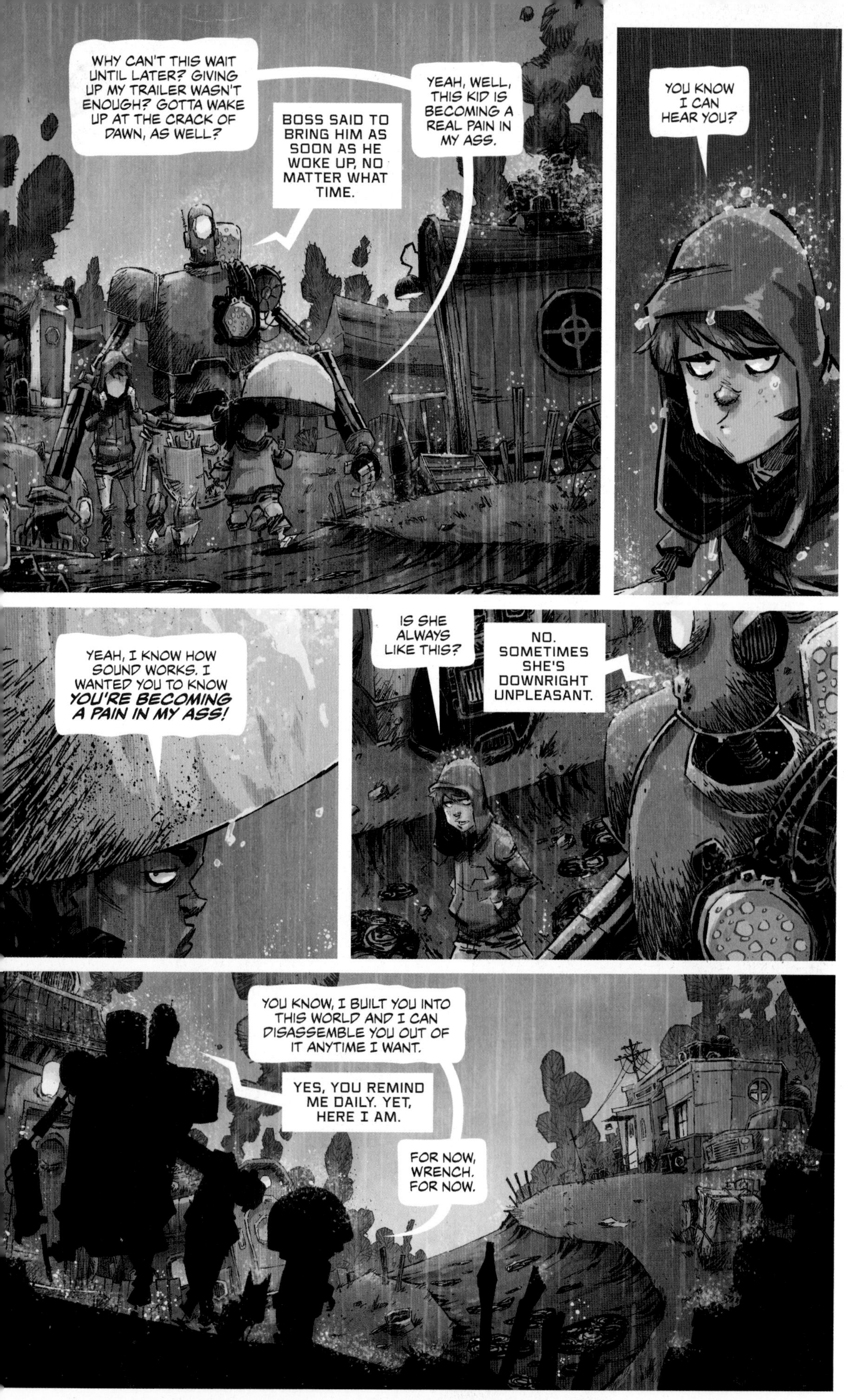
WHY CAN'T THIS WAIT UNTIL LATER? GIVING UP MY TRAILER WASN'T ENOUGH? GOTTA WAKE UP AT THE CRACK OF DAWN, AS WELL?
BOSS SAID TO BRING HIM AS SOON AS HE WOKE UP, NO MATTER WHAT TIME.
YEAH, WELL, THIS KID IS BECOMING A REAL PAIN IN MY ASS.
YOU KNOW I CAN HEAR YOU?
YEAH, I KNOW HOW SOUND WORKS. I WANTED YOU TO KNOW *YOU'RE BECOMING A PAIN IN MY ASS!*
IS SHE ALWAYS LIKE THIS?
NO. SOMETIMES SHE'S DOWNRIGHT UNPLEASANT.
YOU KNOW, I BUILT YOU INTO THIS WORLD AND I CAN DISASSEMBLE YOU OUT OF IT ANYTIME I WANT.
YES, YOU REMIND ME DAILY. YET, HERE I AM.
FOR NOW, WRENCH. FOR NOW.

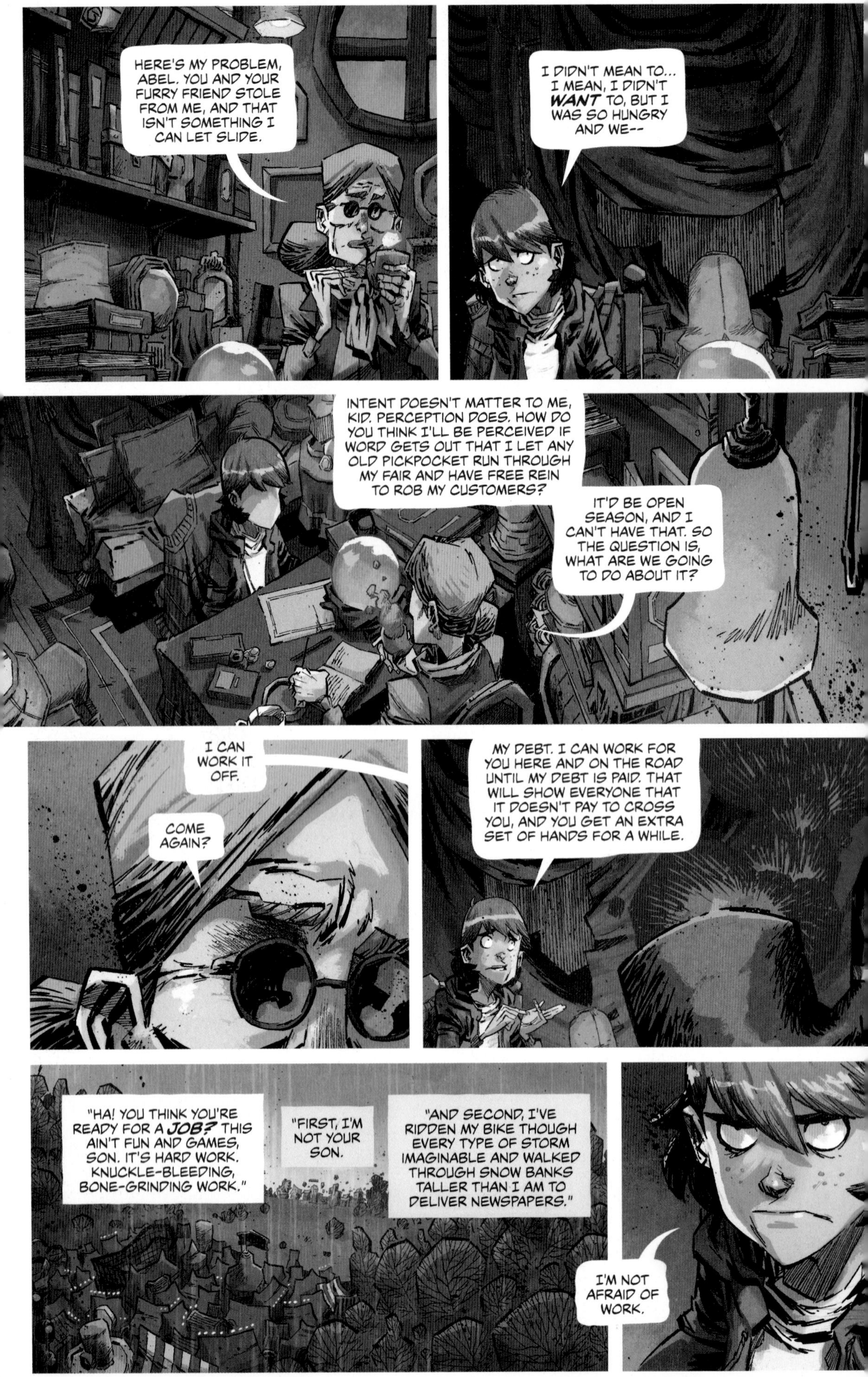
HERE'S MY PROBLEM, ABEL. YOU AND YOUR FURRY FRIEND STOLE FROM ME, AND THAT ISN'T SOMETHING I CAN LET SLIDE.
I DIDN'T MEAN TO... I MEAN, I DIDN'T WANT TO, BUT I WAS SO HUNGRY AND WE--
INTENT DOESN'T MATTER TO ME, KID. PERCEPTION DOES. HOW DO YOU THINK I'LL BE PERCEIVED IF WORD GETS OUT THAT I LET ANY OLD PICKPOCKET RUN THROUGH MY FAIR AND HAVE FREE REIN TO ROB MY CUSTOMERS?
IT'D BE OPEN SEASON, AND I CAN'T HAVE THAT. SO THE QUESTION IS, WHAT ARE WE GOING TO DO ABOUT IT?
I CAN WORK IT OFF.
COME AGAIN?
MY DEBT. I CAN WORK FOR YOU HERE AND ON THE ROAD UNTIL MY DEBT IS PAID. THAT WILL SHOW EVERYONE THAT IT DOESN'T PAY TO CROSS YOU, AND YOU GET AN EXTRA SET OF HANDS FOR A WHILE.
"HA! YOU THINK YOU'RE READY FOR A JOB? THIS AIN'T FUN AND GAMES, SON. IT'S HARD WORK. KNUCKLE-BLEEDING, BONE-GRINDING WORK."
"FIRST, I'M NOT YOUR SON.
"AND SECOND, I'VE RIDDEN MY BIKE THOUGH EVERY TYPE OF STORM IMAGINABLE AND WALKED THROUGH SNOW BANKS TALLER THAN I AM TO DELIVER NEWSPAPERS."
I'M NOT AFRAID OF WORK.

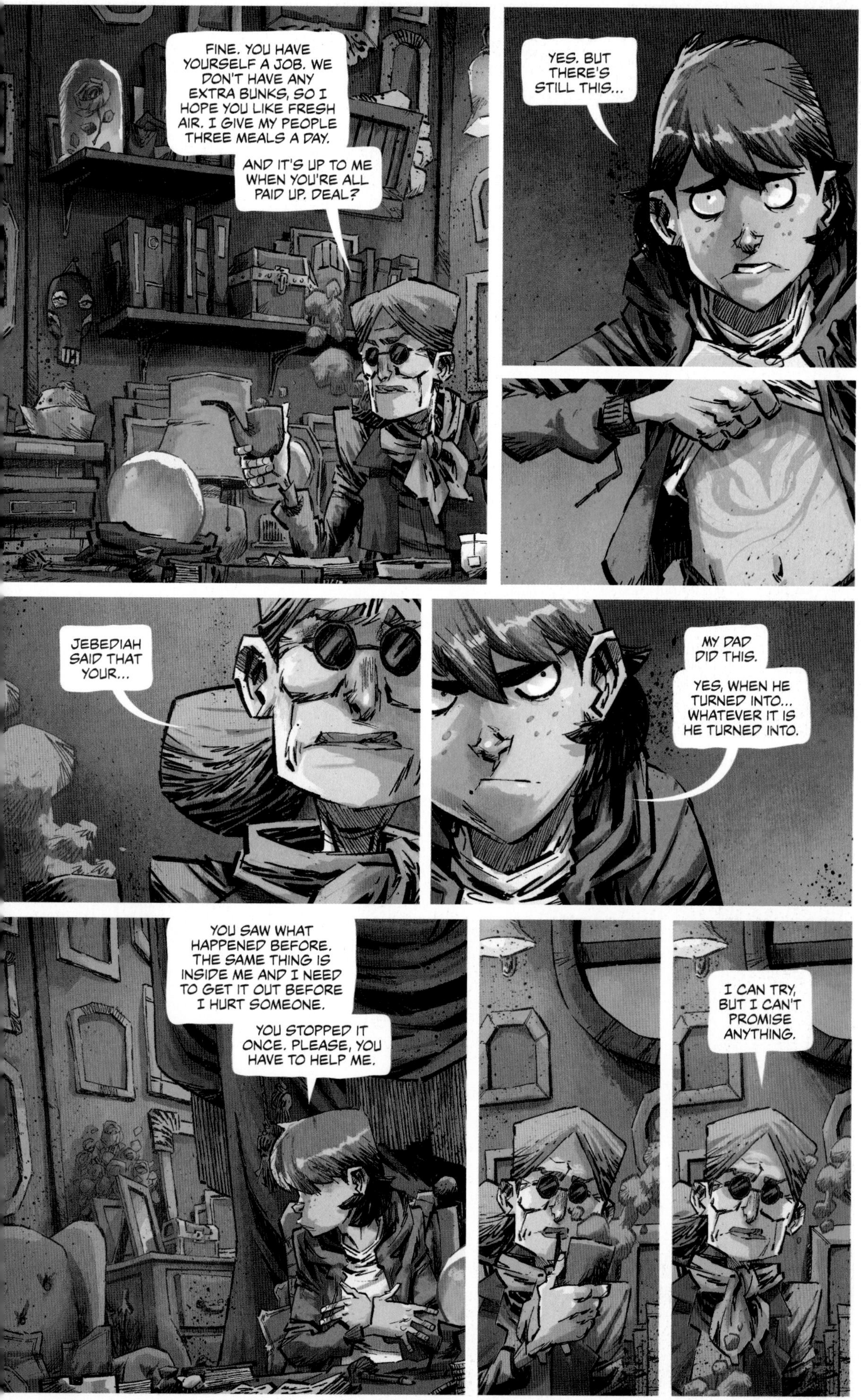

FINE. YOU HAVE YOURSELF A JOB. WE DON'T HAVE ANY EXTRA BUNKS, SO I HOPE YOU LIKE FRESH AIR. I GIVE MY PEOPLE THREE MEALS A DAY.
AND IT'S UP TO ME WHEN YOU'RE ALL PAID UP. DEAL?
YES. BUT THERE'S STILL THIS...
JEBEDIAH SAID THAT YOUR...
MY DAD DID THIS.
YES, WHEN HE TURNED INTO... WHATEVER IT IS HE TURNED INTO.
YOU SAW WHAT HAPPENED BEFORE. THE SAME THING IS INSIDE ME AND I NEED TO GET IT OUT BEFORE I HURT SOMEONE.
YOU STOPPED IT ONCE. PLEASE, YOU HAVE TO HELP ME.
I CAN TRY, BUT I CAN'T PROMISE ANYTHING.

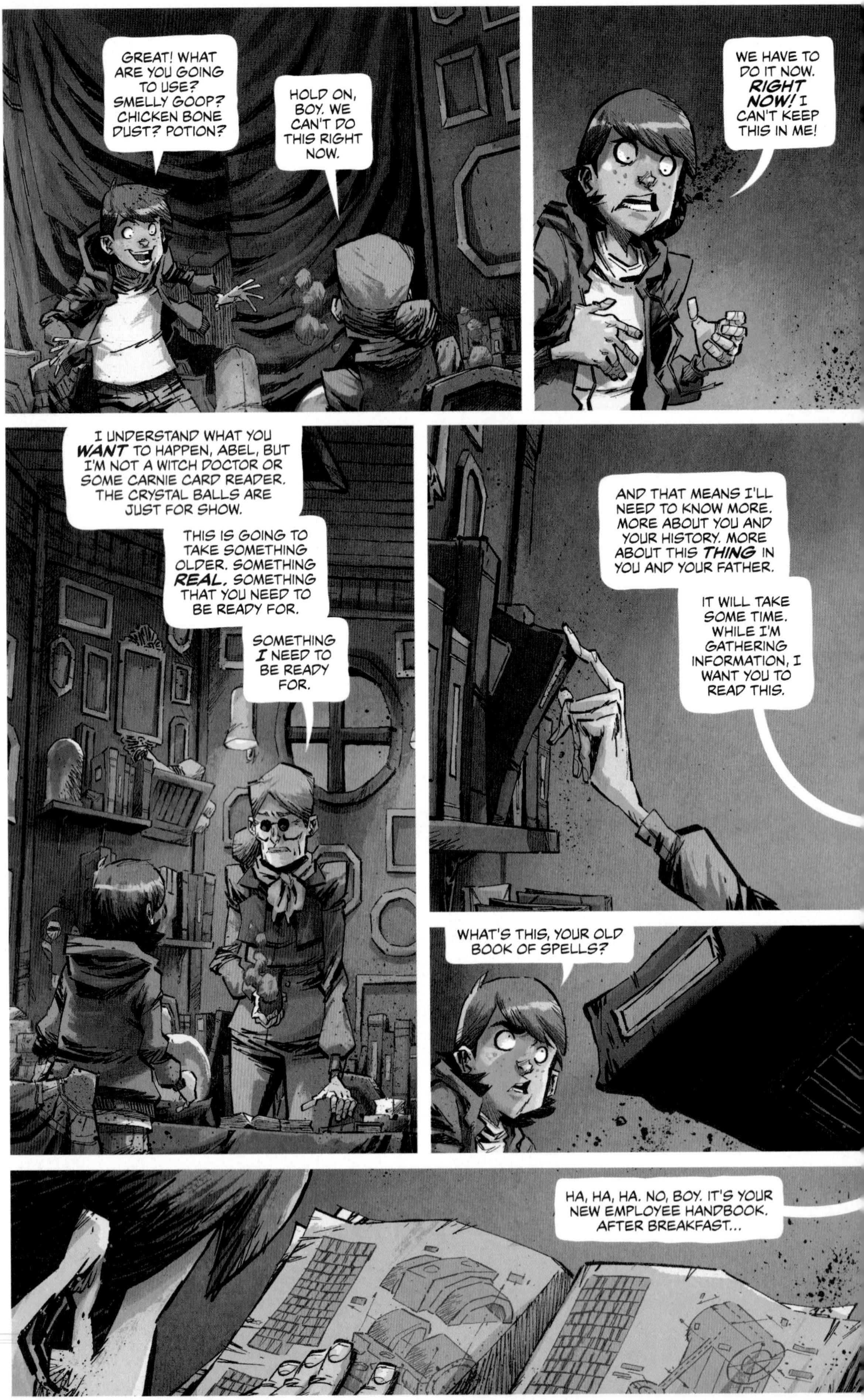
GREAT! WHAT ARE YOU GOING TO USE? SMELLY GOOP? CHICKEN BONE DUST? POTION?
HOLD ON, BOY. WE CAN'T DO THIS RIGHT NOW.
WE HAVE TO DO IT NOW. RIGHT NOW! I CAN'T KEEP THIS IN ME!
I UNDERSTAND WHAT YOU WANT TO HAPPEN, ABEL, BUT I'M NOT A WITCH DOCTOR OR SOME CARNIE CARD READER. THE CRYSTAL BALLS ARE JUST FOR SHOW.
THIS IS GOING TO TAKE SOMETHING OLDER. SOMETHING REAL. SOMETHING THAT YOU NEED TO BE READY FOR.
SOMETHING I NEED TO BE READY FOR.
AND THAT MEANS I'LL NEED TO KNOW MORE. MORE ABOUT YOU AND YOUR HISTORY. MORE ABOUT THIS THING IN YOU AND YOUR FATHER.
IT WILL TAKE SOME TIME. WHILE I'M GATHERING INFORMATION, I WANT YOU TO READ THIS.
WHAT'S THIS, YOUR OLD BOOK OF SPELLS?
HA, HA, HA. NO, BOY. IT'S YOUR NEW EMPLOYEE HANDBOOK. AFTER BREAKFAST...

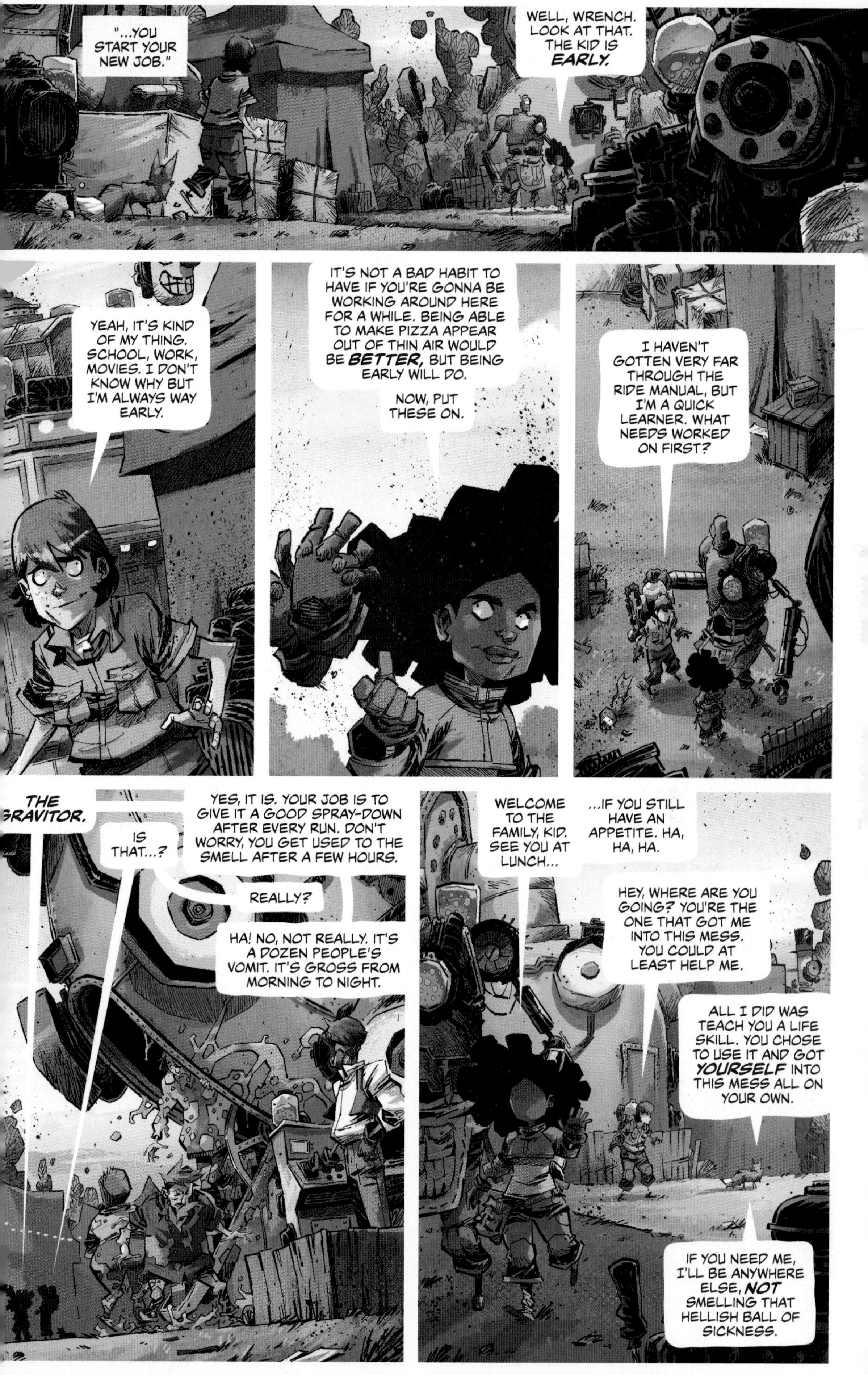
"...YOU START YOUR NEW JOB."
WELL, WRENCH. LOOK AT THAT. THE KID IS *EARLY.*
YEAH, IT'S KIND OF MY THING. SCHOOL, WORK, MOVIES. I DON'T KNOW WHY BUT I'M ALWAYS WAY EARLY.
IT'S NOT A BAD HABIT TO HAVE IF YOU'RE GONNA BE WORKING AROUND HERE FOR A WHILE. BEING ABLE TO MAKE PIZZA APPEAR OUT OF THIN AIR WOULD BE ***BETTER,*** BUT BEING EARLY WILL DO.
NOW, PUT THESE ON.
I HAVEN'T GOTTEN VERY FAR THROUGH THE RIDE MANUAL, BUT I'M A QUICK LEARNER. WHAT NEEDS WORKED ON FIRST?
THE GRAVITOR.
IS THAT...?
YES, IT IS. YOUR JOB IS TO GIVE IT A GOOD SPRAY-DOWN AFTER EVERY RUN. DON'T WORRY, YOU GET USED TO THE SMELL AFTER A FEW HOURS.
REALLY?
HA! NO, NOT REALLY. IT'S A DOZEN PEOPLE'S VOMIT. IT'S GROSS FROM MORNING TO NIGHT.
WELCOME TO THE FAMILY, KID. SEE YOU AT LUNCH...
...IF YOU STILL HAVE AN APPETITE. HA, HA, HA.
HEY, WHERE ARE YOU GOING? YOU'RE THE ONE THAT GOT ME INTO THIS MESS. YOU COULD AT LEAST HELP ME.
ALL I DID WAS TEACH YOU A LIFE SKILL. YOU CHOSE TO USE IT AND GOT ***YOURSELF*** INTO THIS MESS ALL ON YOUR OWN.
IF YOU NEED ME, I'LL BE ANYWHERE ELSE, ***NOT*** SMELLING THAT HELLISH BALL OF SICKNESS.

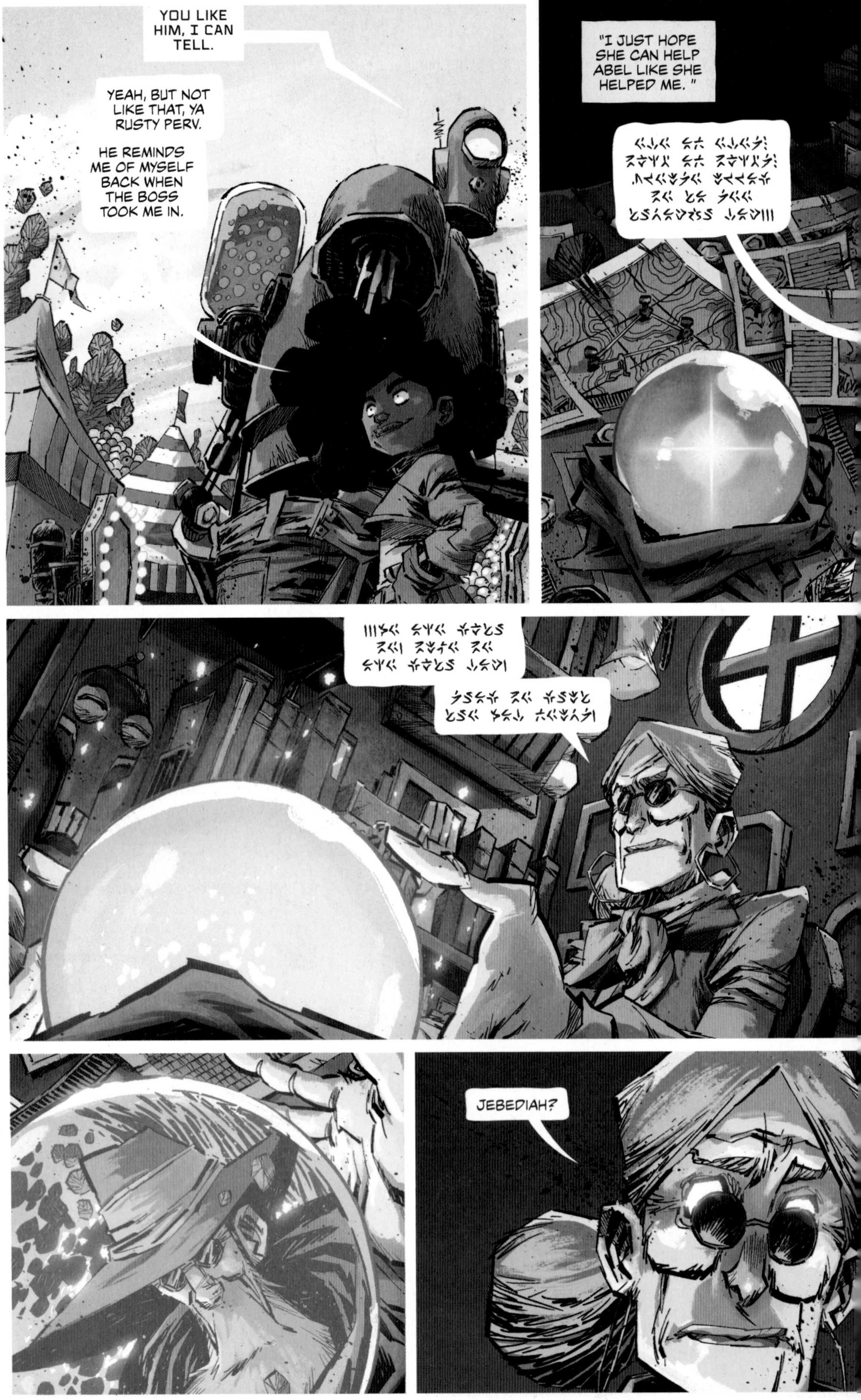
YOU LIKE HIM, I CAN TELL.
YEAH, BUT NOT LIKE THAT, YA RUSTY PERV.
HE REMINDS ME OF MYSELF BACK WHEN THE BOSS TOOK ME IN.
"I JUST HOPE SHE CAN HELP ABEL LIKE SHE HELPED ME."
JEBEDIAH?

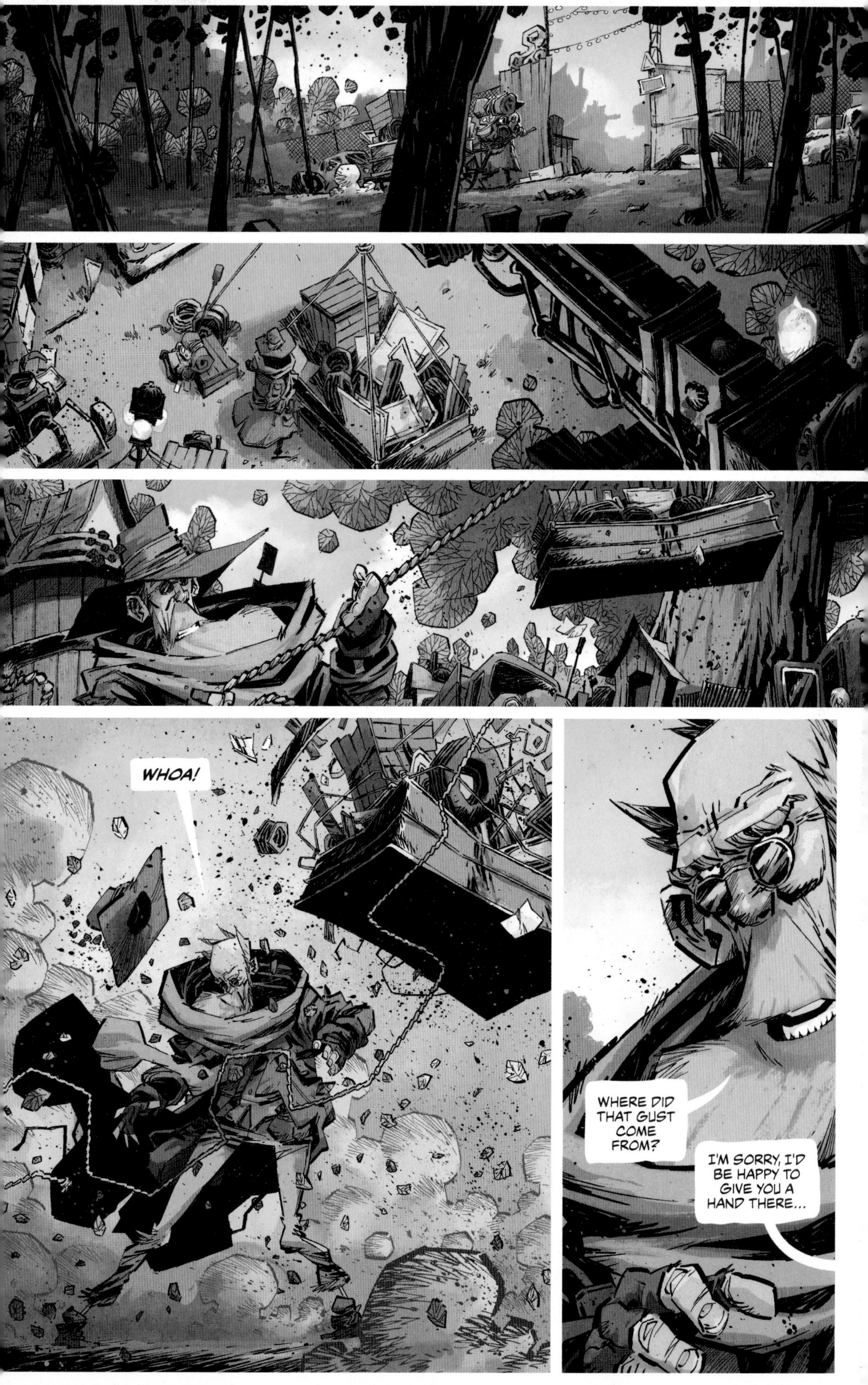
WHOA!
WHERE DID THAT GUST COME FROM?
I'M SORRY, I'D BE HAPPY TO GIVE YOU A HAND THERE...

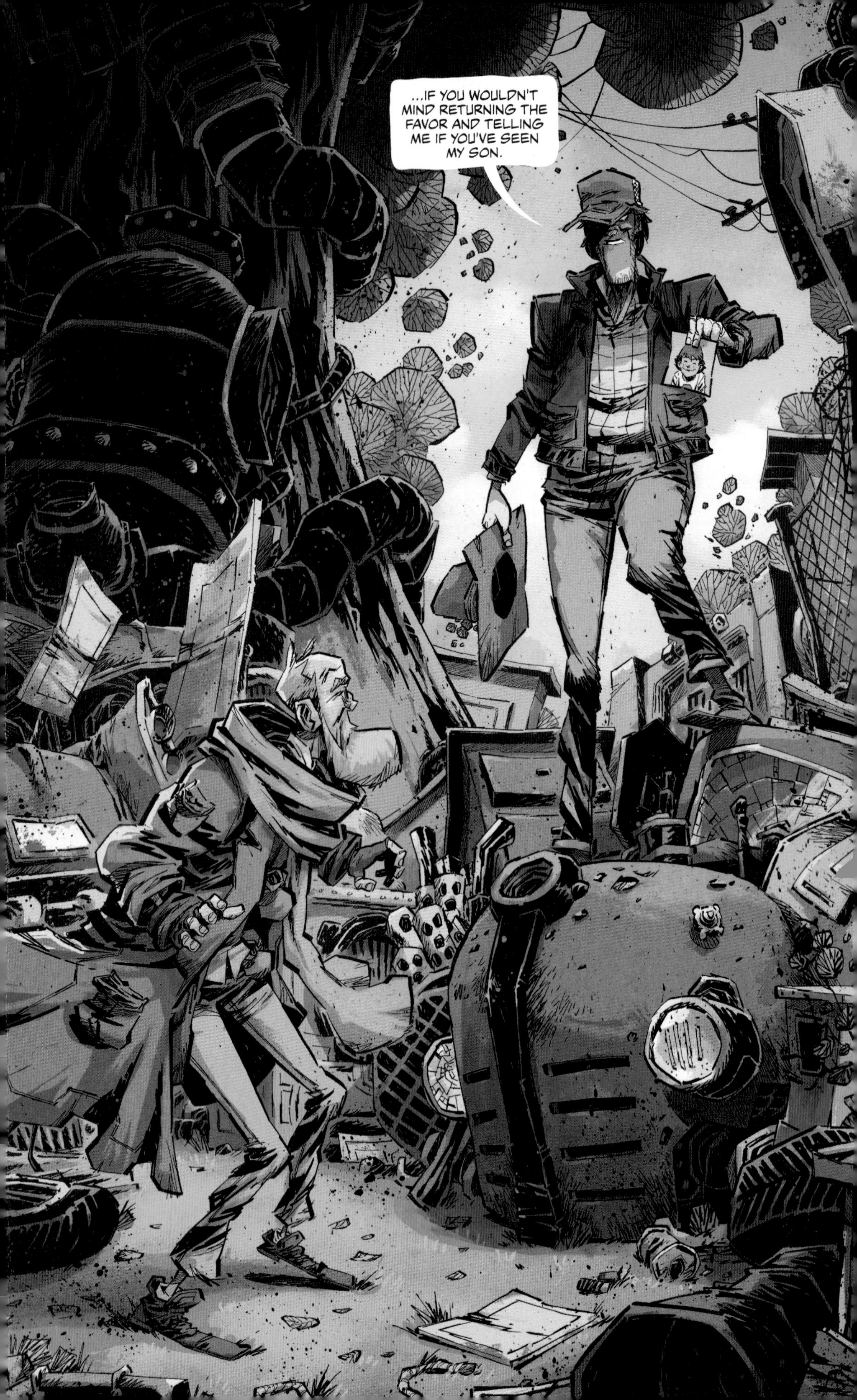
...IF YOU WOULDN'T MIND RETURNING THE FAVOR AND TELLING ME IF YOU'VE SEEN MY SON.

CHAPTER
SIX

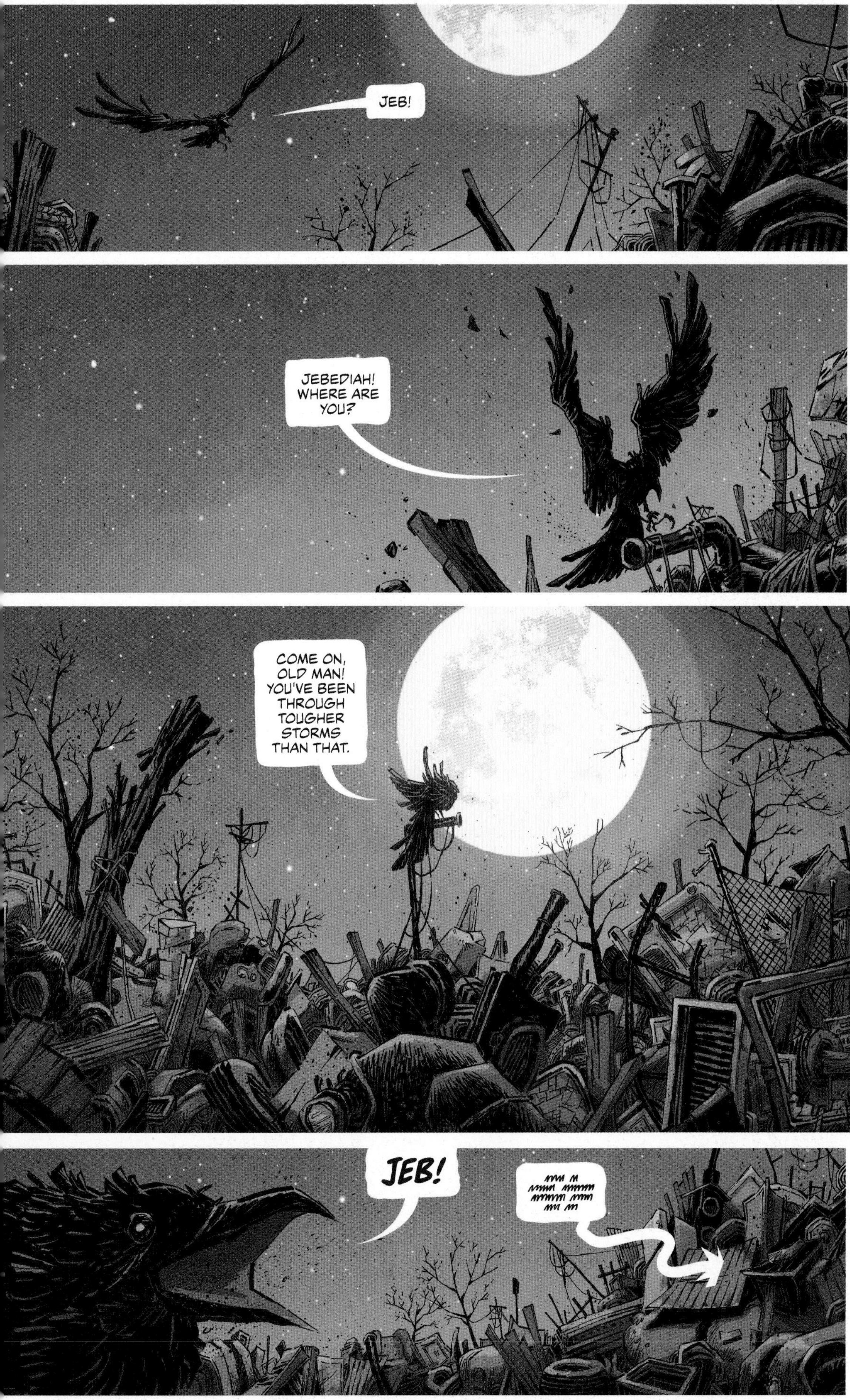
JEB!
JEBEDIAH! WHERE ARE YOU?
COME ON, OLD MAN! YOU'VE BEEN THROUGH TOUGHER STORMS THAN THAT.
JEB!

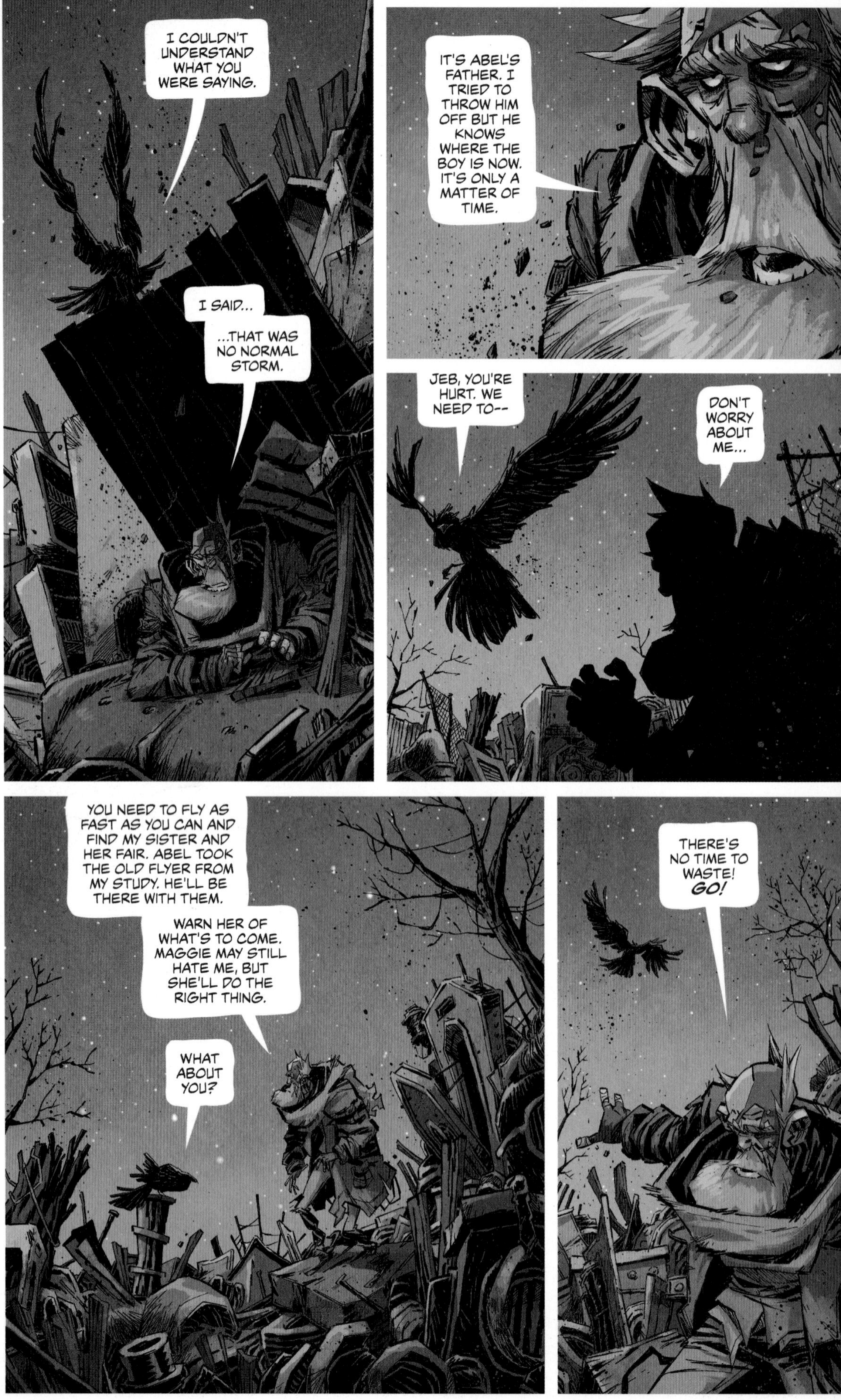
I COULDN'T UNDERSTAND WHAT YOU WERE SAYING.
I SAID...
...THAT WAS NO NORMAL STORM.
IT'S ABEL'S FATHER. I TRIED TO THROW HIM OFF BUT HE KNOWS WHERE THE BOY IS NOW. IT'S ONLY A MATTER OF TIME.
JEB, YOU'RE HURT. WE NEED TO--
DON'T WORRY ABOUT ME...
YOU NEED TO FLY AS FAST AS YOU CAN AND FIND MY SISTER AND HER FAIR. ABEL TOOK THE OLD FLYER FROM MY STUDY. HE'LL BE THERE WITH THEM.
WARN HER OF WHAT'S TO COME. MAGGIE MAY STILL HATE ME, BUT SHE'LL DO THE RIGHT THING.
WHAT ABOUT YOU?
THERE'S NO TIME TO WASTE! GO!

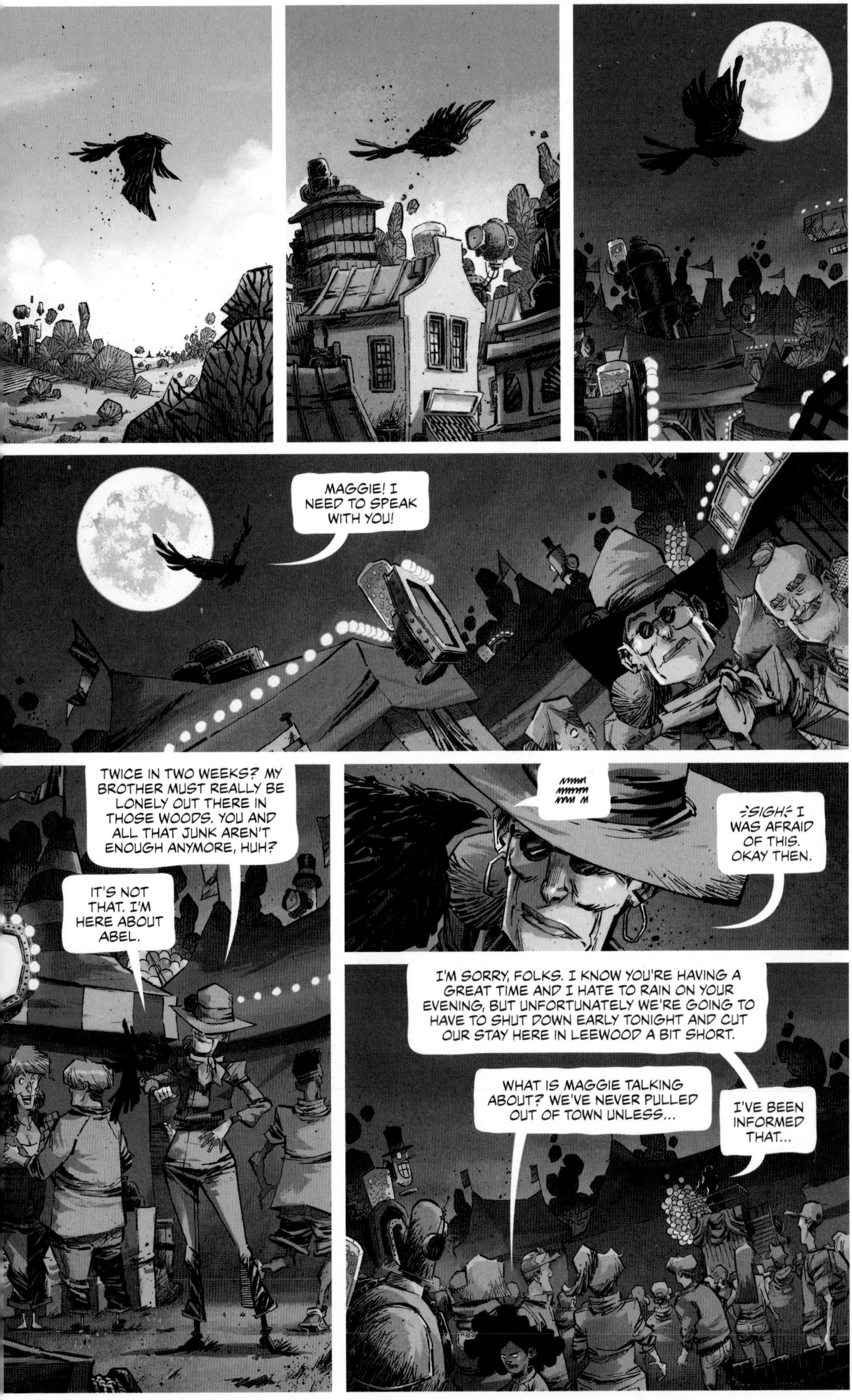
MAGGIE! I NEED TO SPEAK WITH YOU!
TWICE IN TWO WEEKS? MY BROTHER MUST REALLY BE LONELY OUT THERE IN THOSE WOODS. YOU AND ALL THAT JUNK AREN'T ENOUGH ANYMORE, HUH?
IT'S NOT THAT. I'M HERE ABOUT ABEL.
SIGH I WAS AFRAID OF THIS. OKAY THEN.
I'M SORRY, FOLKS. I KNOW YOU'RE HAVING A GREAT TIME AND I HATE TO RAIN ON YOUR EVENING, BUT UNFORTUNATELY WE'RE GOING TO HAVE TO SHUT DOWN EARLY TONIGHT AND CUT OUR STAY HERE IN LEEWOOD A BIT SHORT.
WHAT IS MAGGIE TALKING ABOUT? WE'VE NEVER PULLED OUT OF TOWN UNLESS...
I'VE BEEN INFORMED THAT...

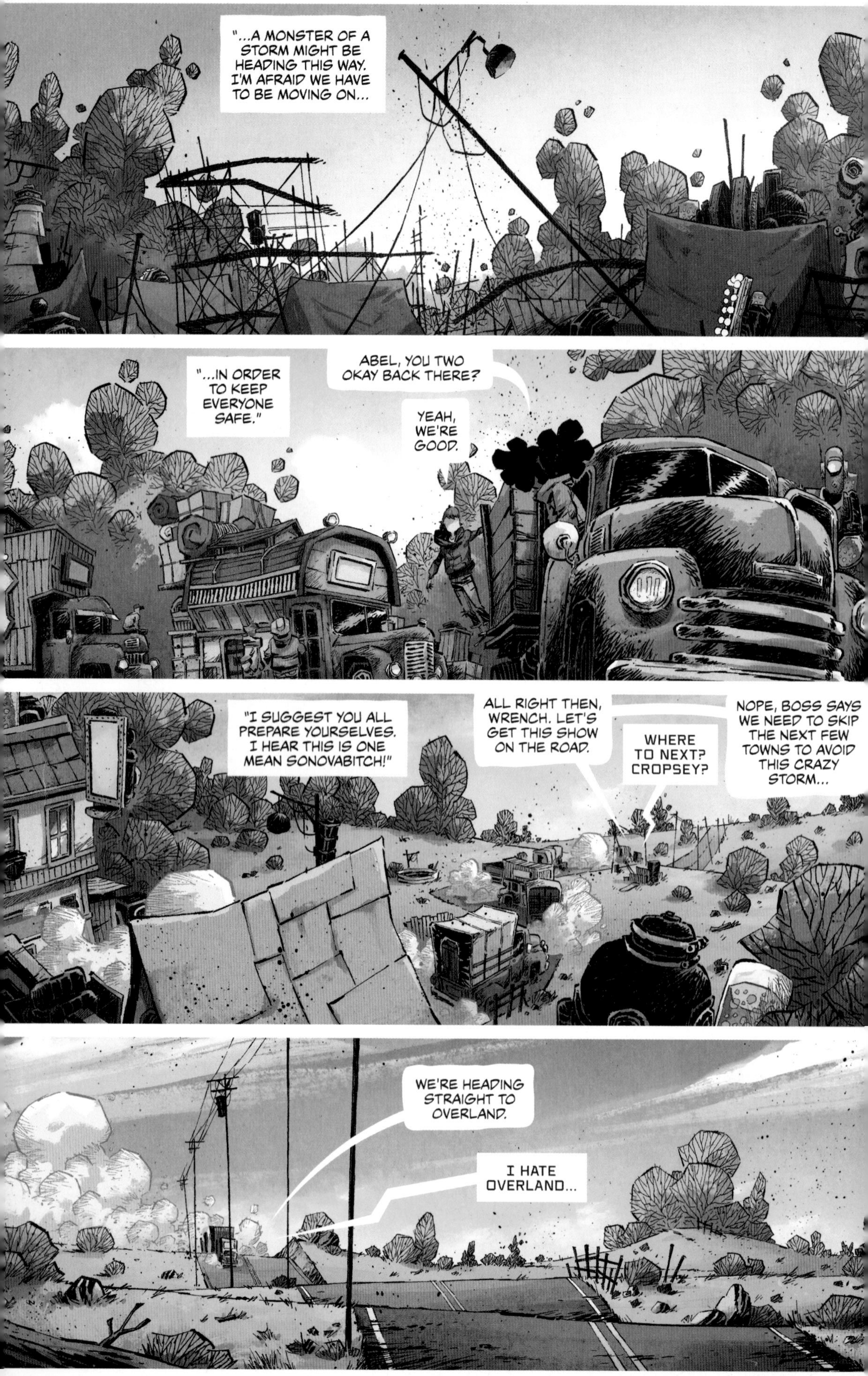
"...A MONSTER OF A STORM MIGHT BE HEADING THIS WAY. I'M AFRAID WE HAVE TO BE MOVING ON...
"...IN ORDER TO KEEP EVERYONE SAFE."
ABEL, YOU TWO OKAY BACK THERE?
YEAH, WE'RE GOOD.
"I SUGGEST YOU ALL PREPARE YOURSELVES. I HEAR THIS IS ONE MEAN SONOVABITCH!"
ALL RIGHT THEN, WRENCH. LET'S GET THIS SHOW ON THE ROAD.
WHERE TO NEXT? CROPSEY?
NOPE, BOSS SAYS WE NEED TO SKIP THE NEXT FEW TOWNS TO AVOID THIS CRAZY STORM...
WE'RE HEADING STRAIGHT TO OVERLAND.
I HATE OVERLAND...

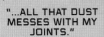

"...ALL THAT DUST MESSES WITH MY JOINTS."

WELCOME TO OVERLAND

THIS THING DOESN'T WANT TO GO IN. MAYBE YOU GAVE ME THE WRONG BULB.

LOOKS LIKE THE KID IS FITTING IN WELL. SEEMS LIKE A HARD WORKER.

FOX, DID YOU NOT TEACH YOUR FRIEND HERE ABOUT *RIGHTY-TIGHTY, LEFTY-LOOSEY?*

SURE...

AHHHH! THERE IT GOES! THANKS!

...BUT MAYBE NOT THE BRIGHTEST ONE.

GIVE HIM A BREAK, BOBBY. HE'S GOT A LOT OF THINGS GOING ON INSIDE HIM. FIGHTING AGAINST SOMETHING TOO BIG FOR A KID.

HELL, TOO BIG FOR ANYONE.

HE'S WHY WE SKIPPED OUR LAST FEW TOWNS, ISN'T HE?

IT'S COMPLICATED.

COMPLICATED AIN'T THE WORD, MAGS. THAT KID WAS... WAS...I DON'T EVEN KNOW WHAT THAT WAS, BUT--

BUT IT'S NOT FOR ME TO SHARE, BOBBY. NOW GET TO WORK BEFORE THAT *KID* STARTS TO OUTWORK YOU.

YOU'RE HILARIOUS! LAUGH A MINUTE. MAYBE WE ADD YOU TO THE COMEDY TENT THIS WEEKEND.

YEAH, YEAH, YEAH. I'LL KEEP THAT IN MIND.

GUYS, YOU KNOW YOU'RE PUTTING THE WRONG BULBS IN THERE, RIGHT? GREEN AND ORANGE GO ON THE WITCH'S WHEEL, NOT YELLOW AND BLUE.

WHAT?!

DON'T LISTEN TO HER. SHE'S JUST BUSTING YOUR BOLTS.

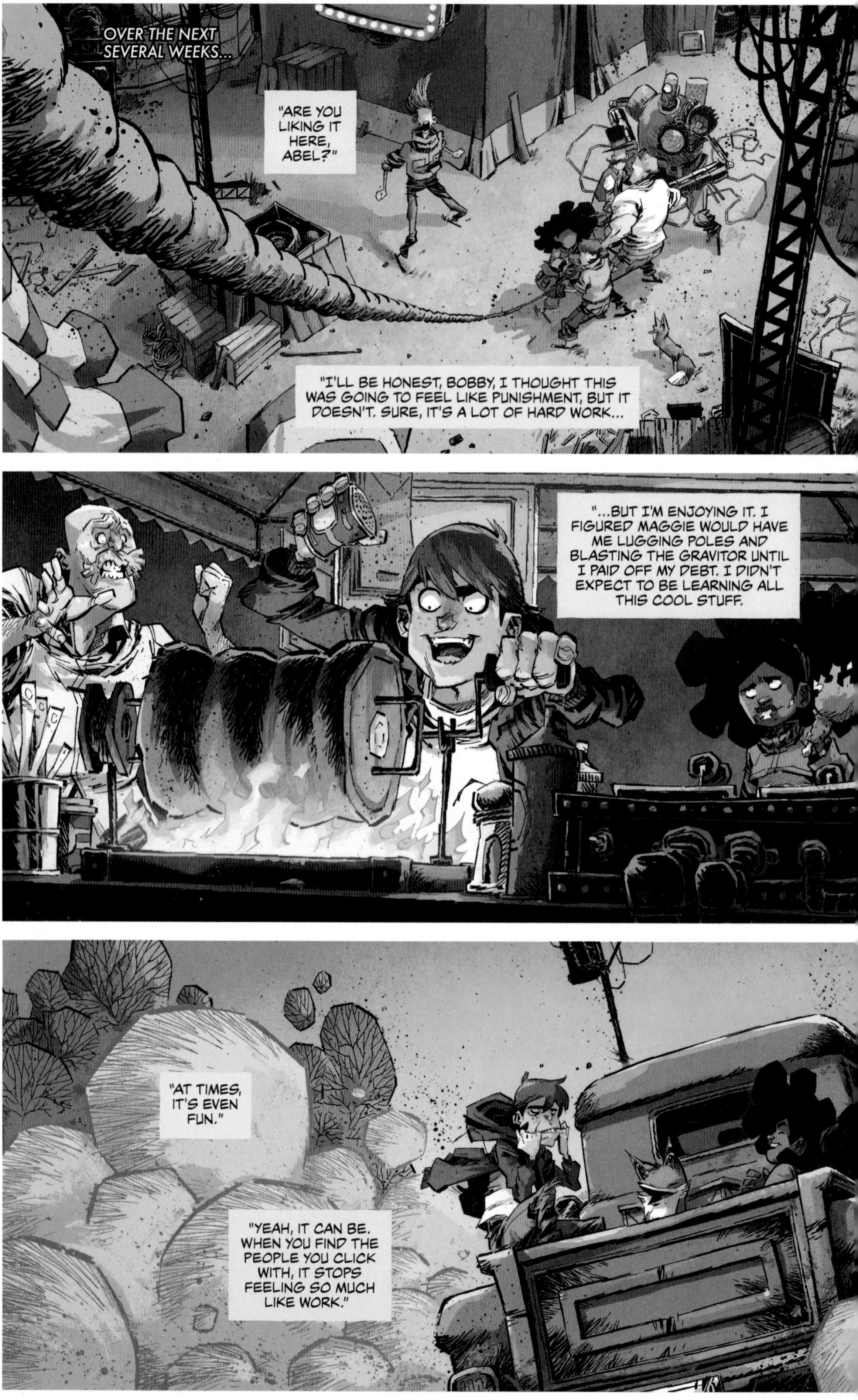
OVER THE NEXT SEVERAL WEEKS...
"ARE YOU LIKING IT HERE, ABEL?"
"I'LL BE HONEST, BOBBY, I THOUGHT THIS WAS GOING TO FEEL LIKE PUNISHMENT, BUT IT DOESN'T. SURE, IT'S A LOT OF HARD WORK...
"...BUT I'M ENJOYING IT. I FIGURED MAGGIE WOULD HAVE ME LUGGING POLES AND BLASTING THE GRAVITOR UNTIL I PAID OFF MY DEBT. I DIDN'T EXPECT TO BE LEARNING ALL THIS COOL STUFF.
"AT TIMES, IT'S EVEN FUN."
"YEAH, IT CAN BE. WHEN YOU FIND THE PEOPLE YOU CLICK WITH, IT STOPS FEELING SO MUCH LIKE WORK."

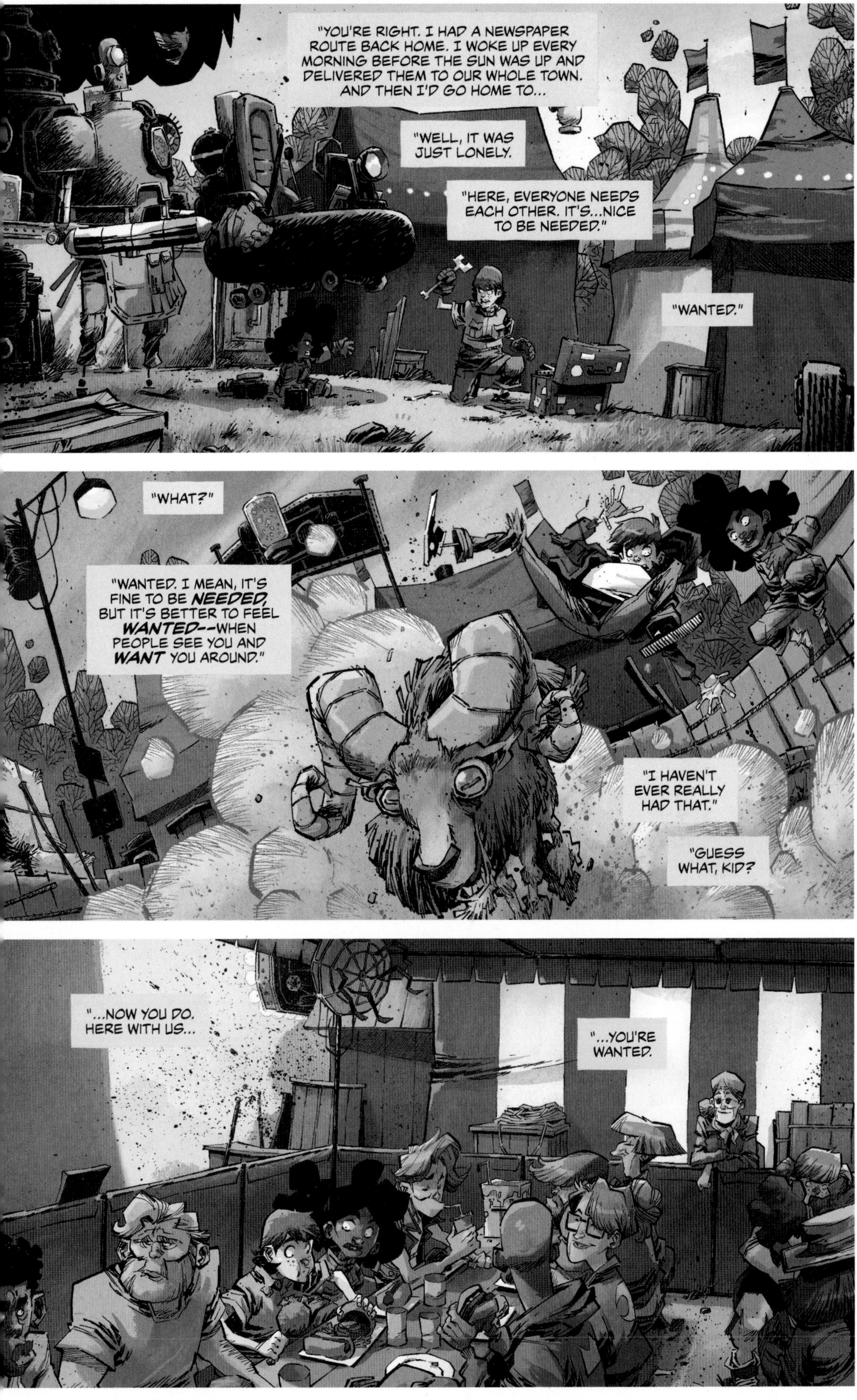
"YOU'RE RIGHT. I HAD A NEWSPAPER ROUTE BACK HOME. I WOKE UP EVERY MORNING BEFORE THE SUN WAS UP AND DELIVERED THEM TO OUR WHOLE TOWN. AND THEN I'D GO HOME TO...
"WELL, IT WAS JUST LONELY.
"HERE, EVERYONE NEEDS EACH OTHER. IT'S...NICE TO BE NEEDED."
"WANTED."
"WHAT?"
"WANTED. I MEAN, IT'S FINE TO BE ***NEEDED,*** BUT IT'S BETTER TO FEEL ***WANTED***--WHEN PEOPLE SEE YOU AND ***WANT*** YOU AROUND."
"I HAVEN'T EVER REALLY HAD THAT."
"GUESS WHAT, KID?
"...NOW YOU DO. HERE WITH US...
"...YOU'RE WANTED.

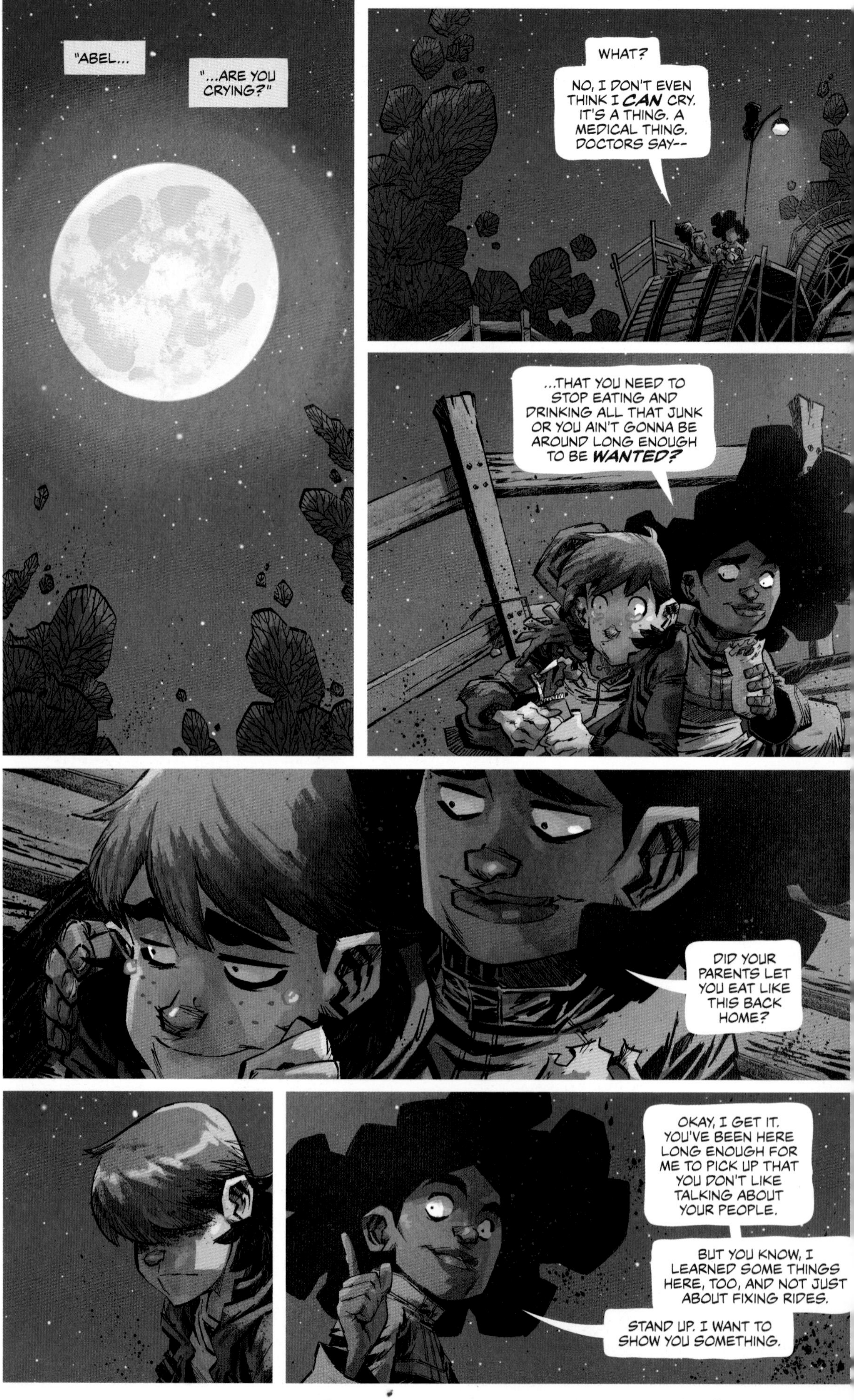
"ABEL...
"...ARE YOU CRYING?"
WHAT?
NO, I DON'T EVEN THINK I CAN CRY. IT'S A THING. A MEDICAL THING. DOCTORS SAY--
...THAT YOU NEED TO STOP EATING AND DRINKING ALL THAT JUNK OR YOU AIN'T GONNA BE AROUND LONG ENOUGH TO BE WANTED?
DID YOUR PARENTS LET YOU EAT LIKE THIS BACK HOME?
OKAY, I GET IT. YOU'VE BEEN HERE LONG ENOUGH FOR ME TO PICK UP THAT YOU DON'T LIKE TALKING ABOUT YOUR PEOPLE.
BUT YOU KNOW, I LEARNED SOME THINGS HERE, TOO, AND NOT JUST ABOUT FIXING RIDES.
STAND UP. I WANT TO SHOW YOU SOMETHING.

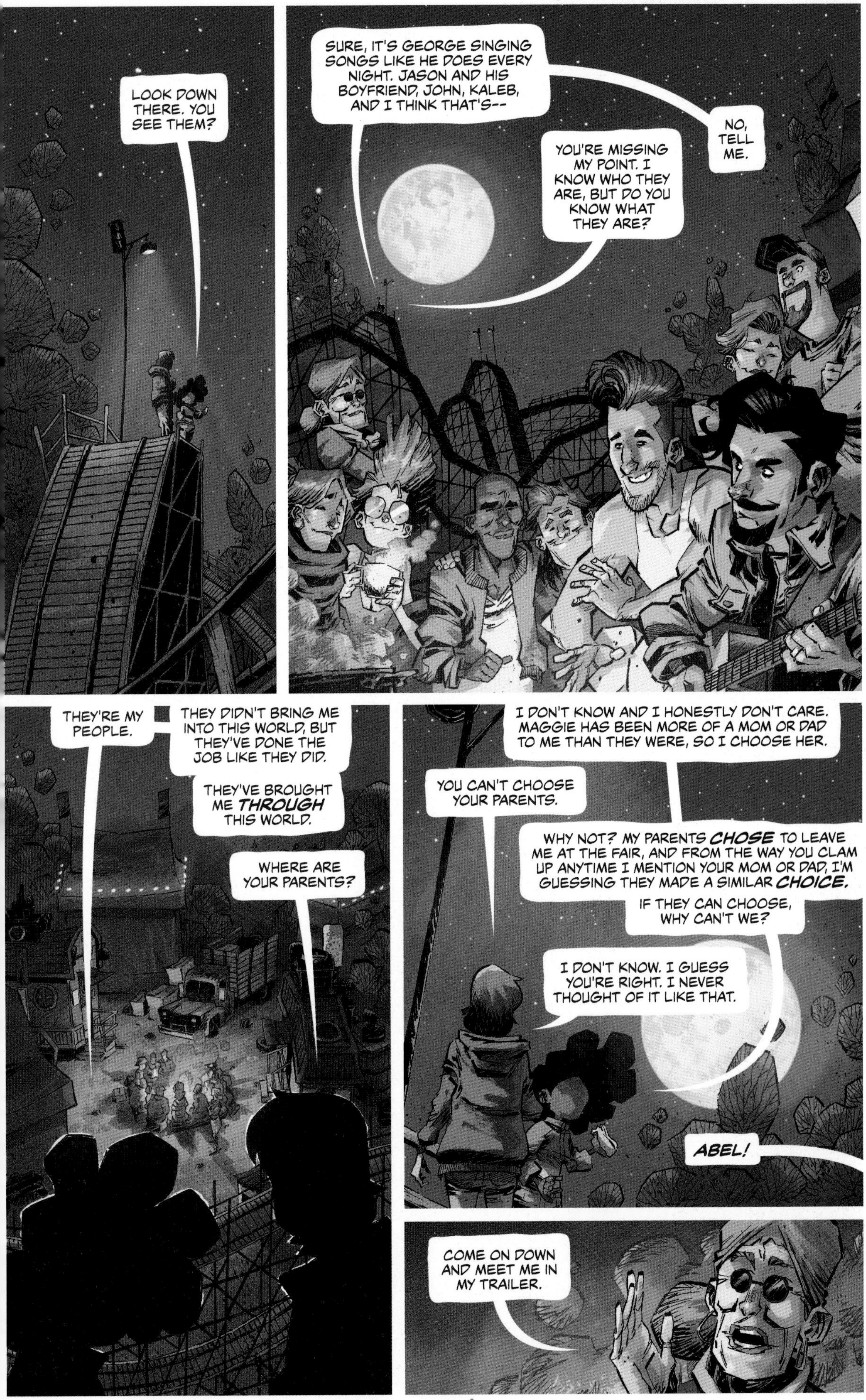
LOOK DOWN THERE. YOU SEE THEM?
SURE, IT'S GEORGE SINGING SONGS LIKE HE DOES EVERY NIGHT. JASON AND HIS BOYFRIEND, JOHN, KALEB, AND I THINK THAT'S--
NO, TELL ME.
YOU'RE MISSING MY POINT. I KNOW WHO THEY ARE, BUT DO YOU KNOW WHAT THEY ARE?
THEY'RE MY PEOPLE.
THEY DIDN'T BRING ME INTO THIS WORLD, BUT THEY'VE DONE THE JOB LIKE THEY DID.
THEY'VE BROUGHT ME THROUGH THIS WORLD.
WHERE ARE YOUR PARENTS?
I DON'T KNOW AND I HONESTLY DON'T CARE. MAGGIE HAS BEEN MORE OF A MOM OR DAD TO ME THAN THEY WERE, SO I CHOOSE HER.
YOU CAN'T CHOOSE YOUR PARENTS.
WHY NOT? MY PARENTS CHOSE TO LEAVE ME AT THE FAIR, AND FROM THE WAY YOU CLAM UP ANYTIME I MENTION YOUR MOM OR DAD, I'M GUESSING THEY MADE A SIMILAR CHOICE.
IF THEY CAN CHOOSE, WHY CAN'T WE?
I DON'T KNOW. I GUESS YOU'RE RIGHT. I NEVER THOUGHT OF IT LIKE THAT.
ABEL!
COME ON DOWN AND MEET ME IN MY TRAILER.

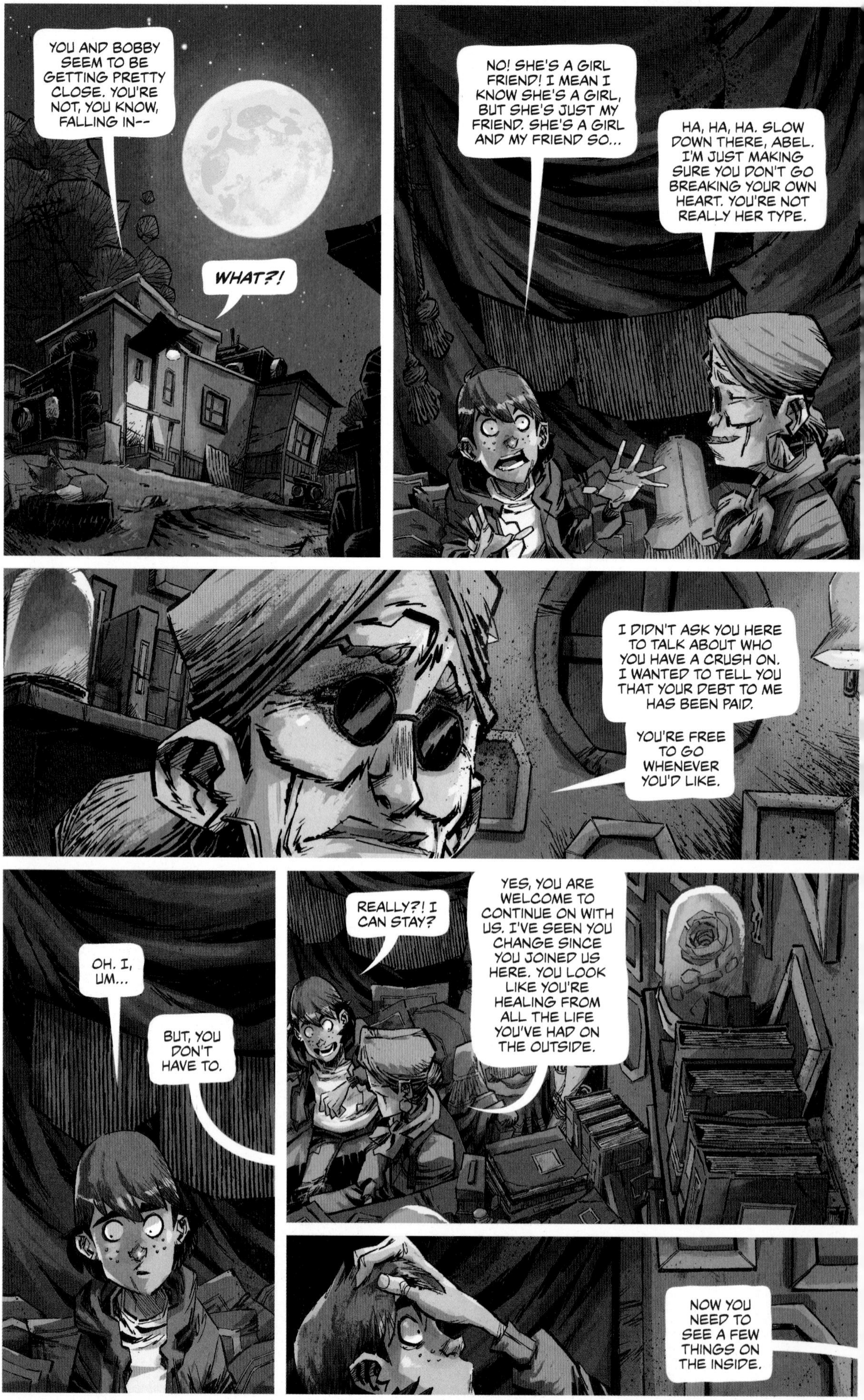
YOU AND BOBBY SEEM TO BE GETTING PRETTY CLOSE. YOU'RE NOT, YOU KNOW, FALLING IN--
WHAT?!
NO! SHE'S A GIRL FRIEND! I MEAN I KNOW SHE'S A GIRL, BUT SHE'S JUST MY FRIEND. SHE'S A GIRL AND MY FRIEND SO...
HA, HA, HA. SLOW DOWN THERE, ABEL. I'M JUST MAKING SURE YOU DON'T GO BREAKING YOUR OWN HEART. YOU'RE NOT REALLY HER TYPE.
I DIDN'T ASK YOU HERE TO TALK ABOUT WHO YOU HAVE A CRUSH ON. I WANTED TO TELL YOU THAT YOUR DEBT TO ME HAS BEEN PAID.
YOU'RE FREE TO GO WHENEVER YOU'D LIKE.
OH. I, UM...
BUT, YOU DON'T HAVE TO.
REALLY?! I CAN STAY?
YES, YOU ARE WELCOME TO CONTINUE ON WITH US. I'VE SEEN YOU CHANGE SINCE YOU JOINED US HERE. YOU LOOK LIKE YOU'RE HEALING FROM ALL THE LIFE YOU'VE HAD ON THE OUTSIDE.
NOW YOU NEED TO SEE A FEW THINGS ON THE INSIDE.

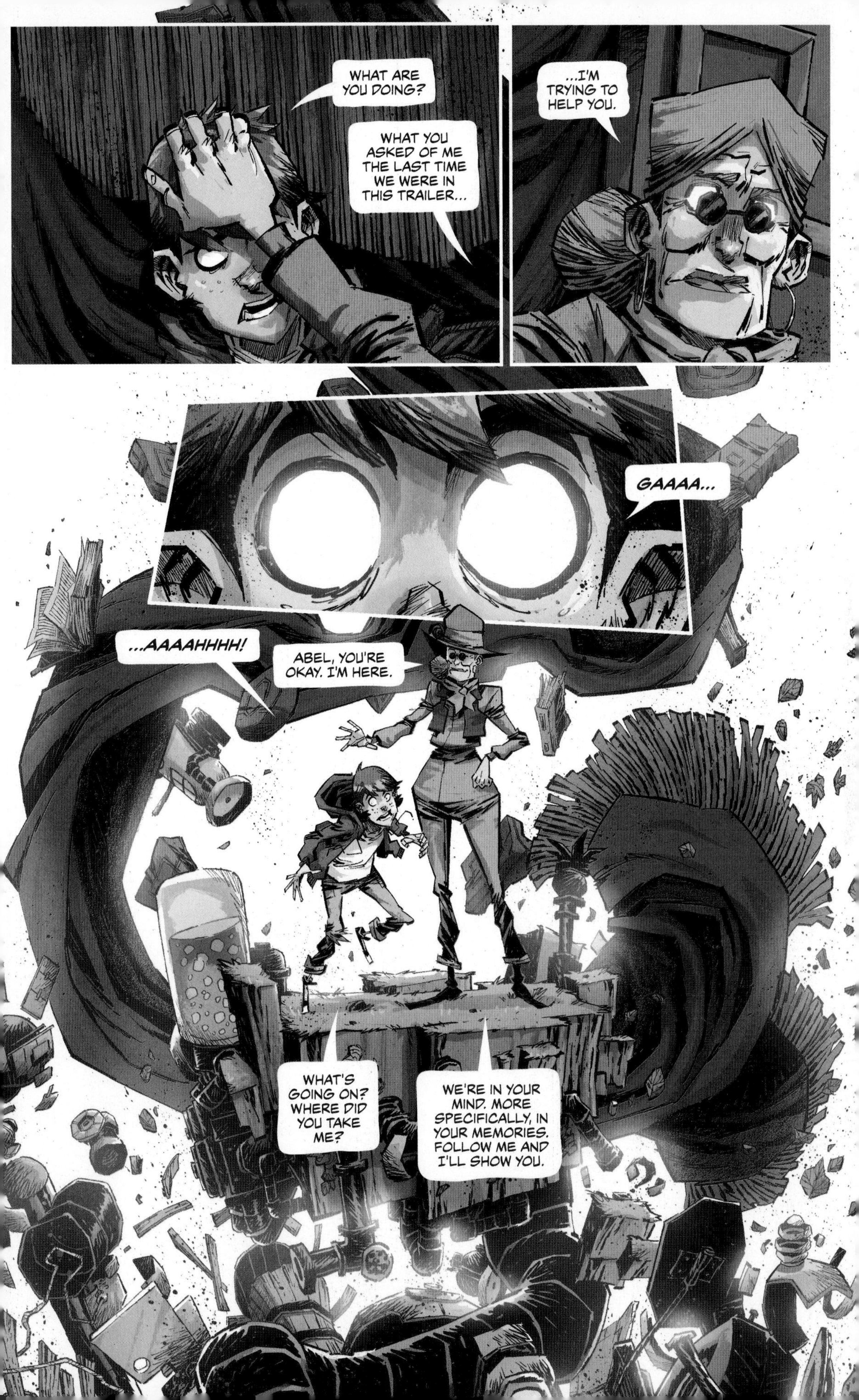
WHAT ARE YOU DOING?
WHAT YOU ASKED OF ME THE LAST TIME WE WERE IN THIS TRAILER...
...I'M TRYING TO HELP YOU.
GAAAA...
...AAAAHHHH!
ABEL, YOU'RE OKAY. I'M HERE.
WHAT'S GOING ON? WHERE DID YOU TAKE ME?
WE'RE IN YOUR MIND. MORE SPECIFICALLY, IN YOUR MEMORIES. FOLLOW ME AND I'LL SHOW YOU.

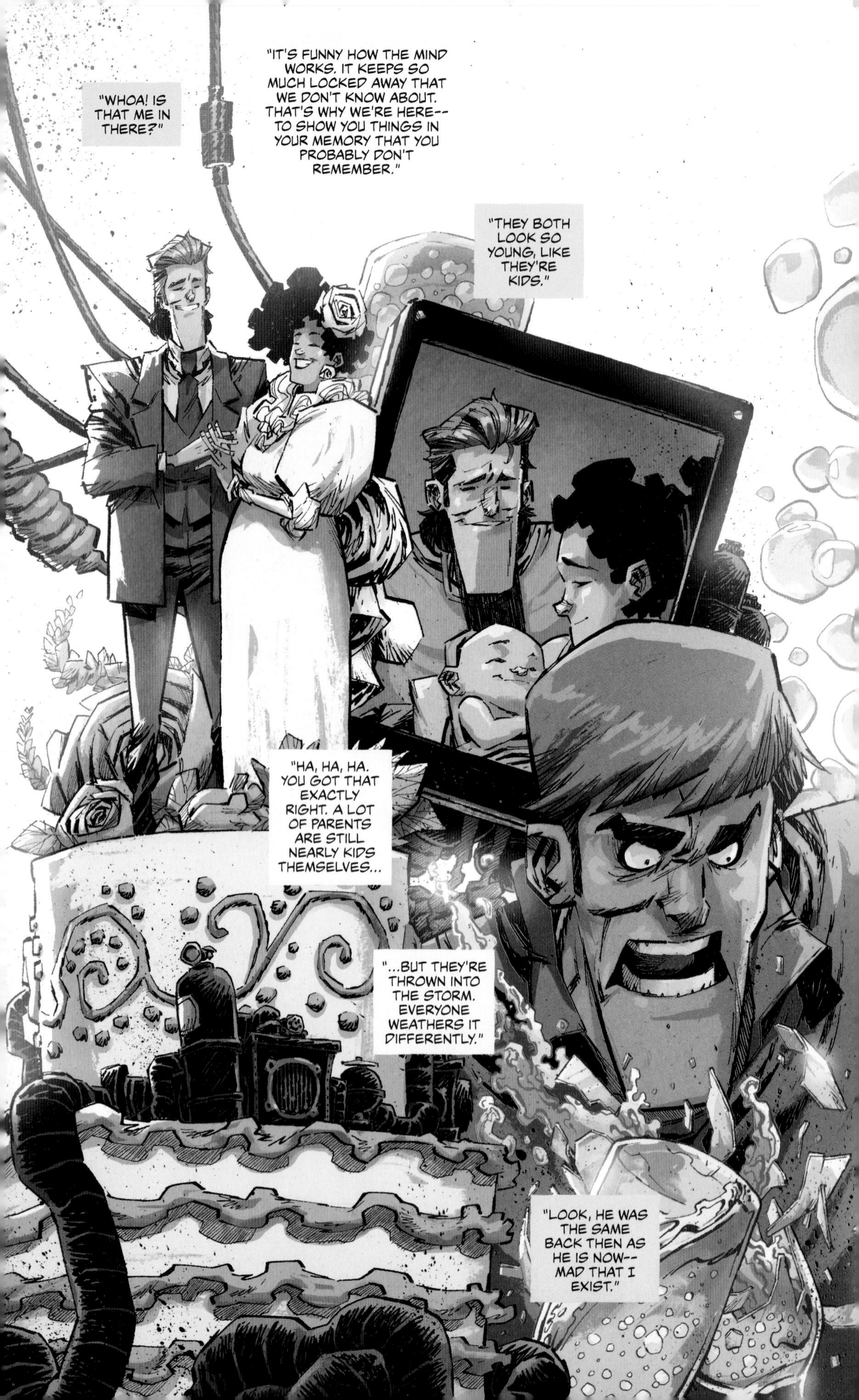
"WHOA! IS THAT ME IN THERE?"
"IT'S FUNNY HOW THE MIND WORKS. IT KEEPS SO MUCH LOCKED AWAY THAT WE DON'T KNOW ABOUT. THAT'S WHY WE'RE HERE--TO SHOW YOU THINGS IN YOUR MEMORY THAT YOU PROBABLY DON'T REMEMBER."
"THEY BOTH LOOK SO YOUNG, LIKE THEY'RE KIDS."
"HA, HA, HA. YOU GOT THAT EXACTLY RIGHT. A LOT OF PARENTS ARE STILL NEARLY KIDS THEMSELVES...
"...BUT THEY'RE THROWN INTO THE STORM. EVERYONE WEATHERS IT DIFFERENTLY."
"LOOK, HE WAS THE SAME BACK THEN AS HE IS NOW--MAD THAT I EXIST."

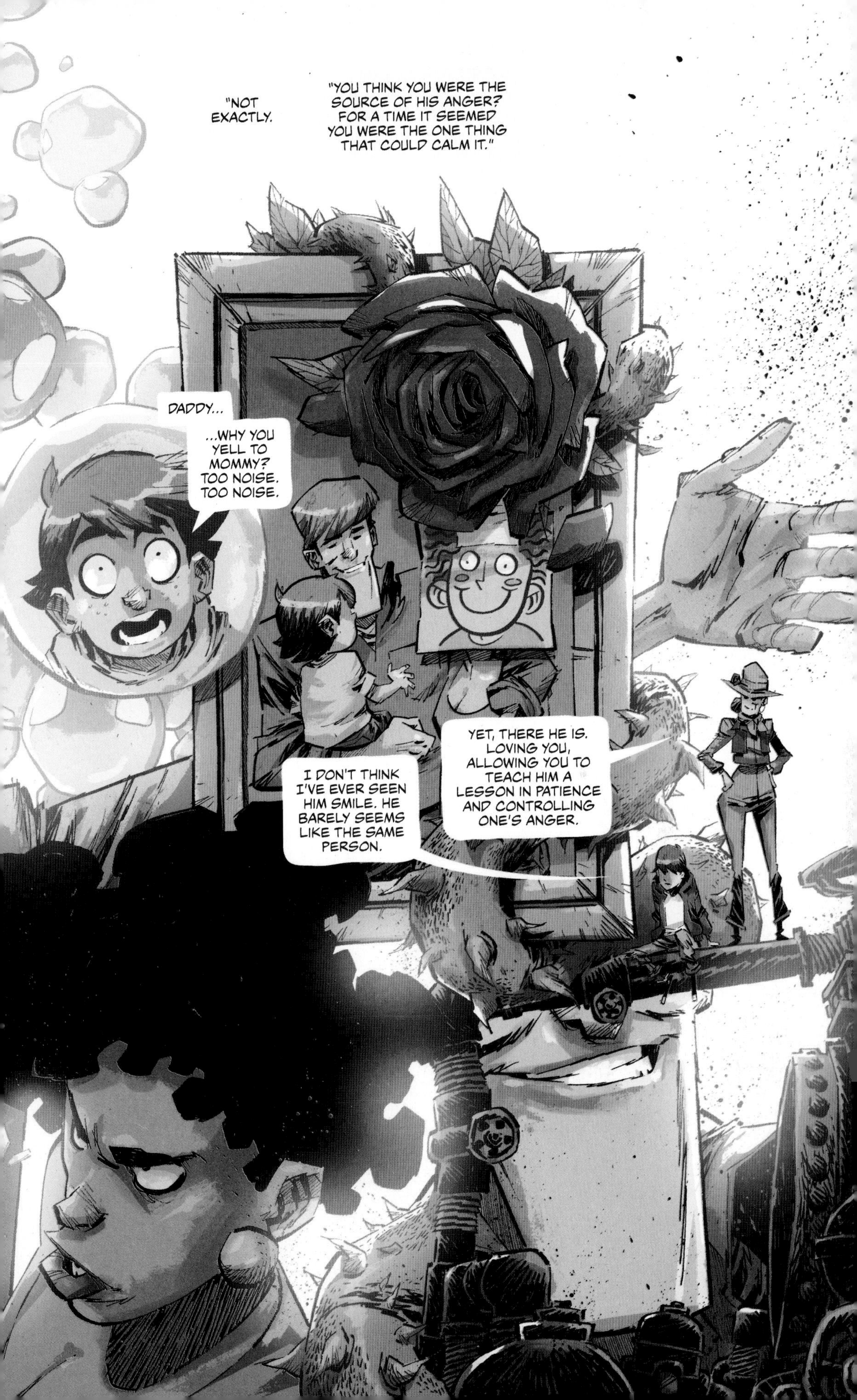
"NOT EXACTLY.
"YOU THINK YOU WERE THE SOURCE OF HIS ANGER? FOR A TIME IT SEEMED YOU WERE THE ONE THING THAT COULD CALM IT."
DADDY...
...WHY YOU YELL TO MOMMY? TOO NOISE. TOO NOISE.
YET, THERE HE IS. LOVING YOU, ALLOWING YOU TO TEACH HIM A LESSON IN PATIENCE AND CONTROLLING ONE'S ANGER.
I DON'T THINK I'VE EVER SEEN HIM SMILE. HE BARELY SEEMS LIKE THE SAME PERSON.

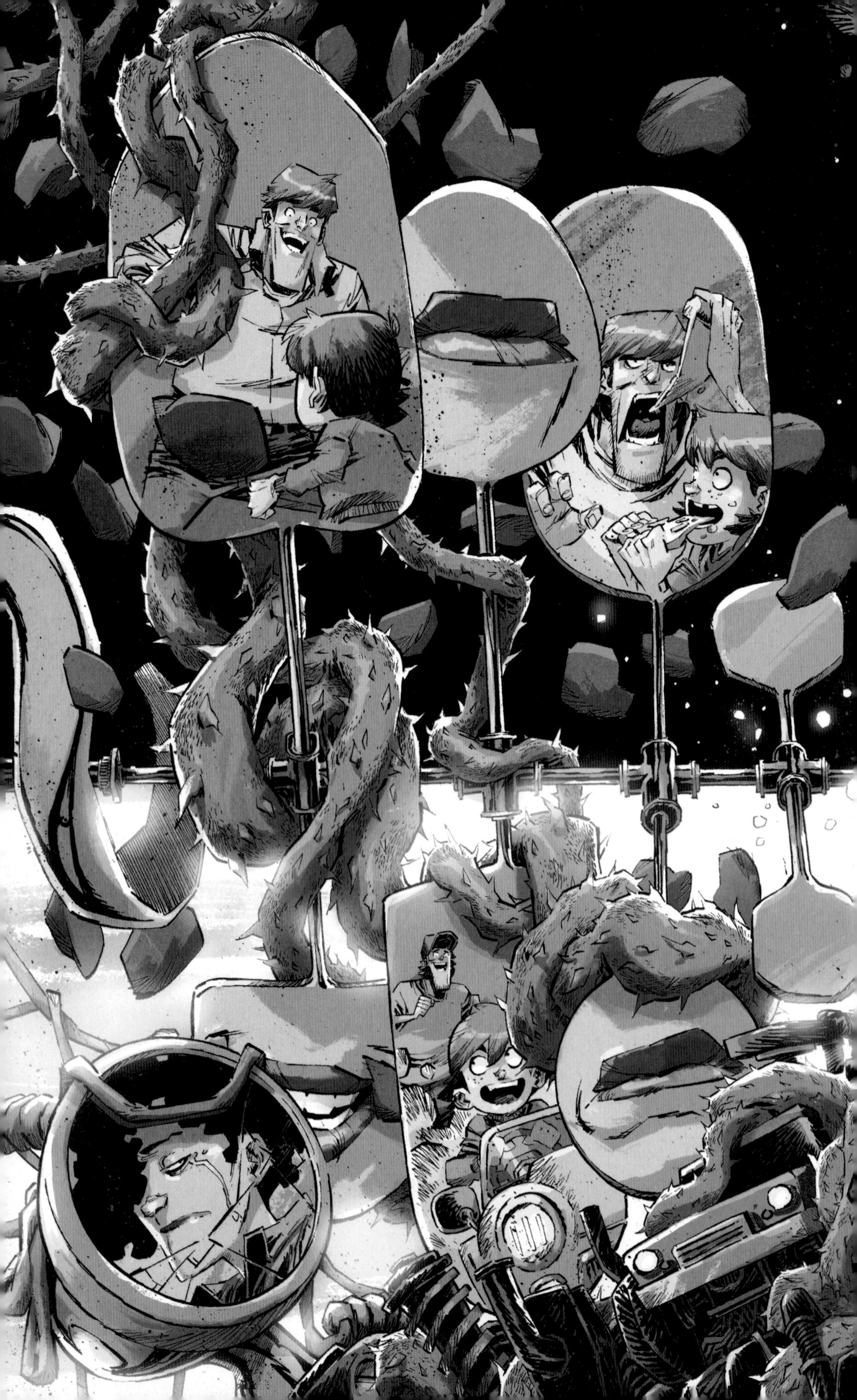

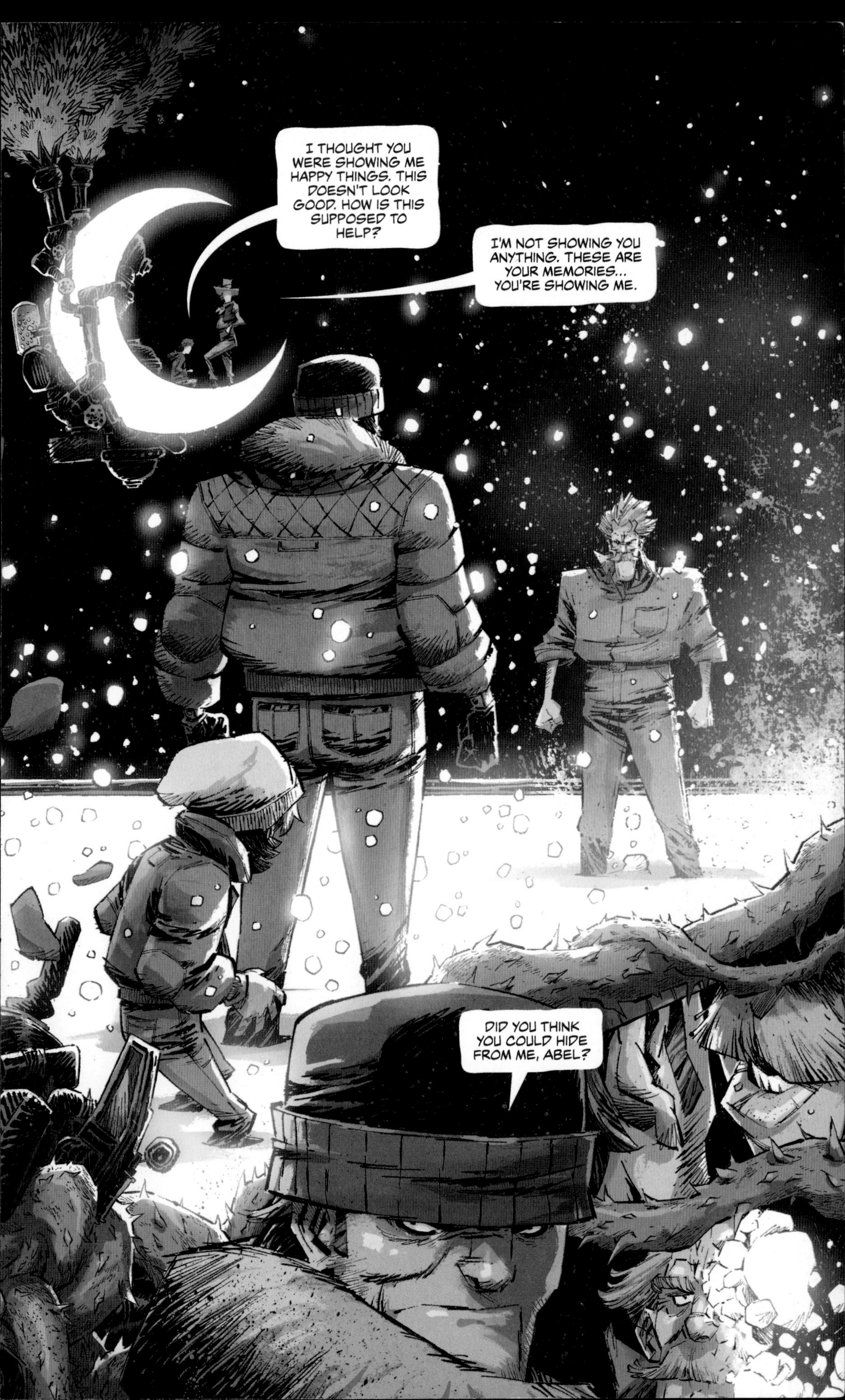
I THOUGHT YOU WERE SHOWING ME HAPPY THINGS. THIS DOESN'T LOOK GOOD. HOW IS THIS SUPPOSED TO HELP?
I'M NOT SHOWING YOU ANYTHING. THESE ARE YOUR MEMORIES... YOU'RE SHOWING ME.
DID YOU THINK YOU COULD HIDE FROM ME, ABEL?

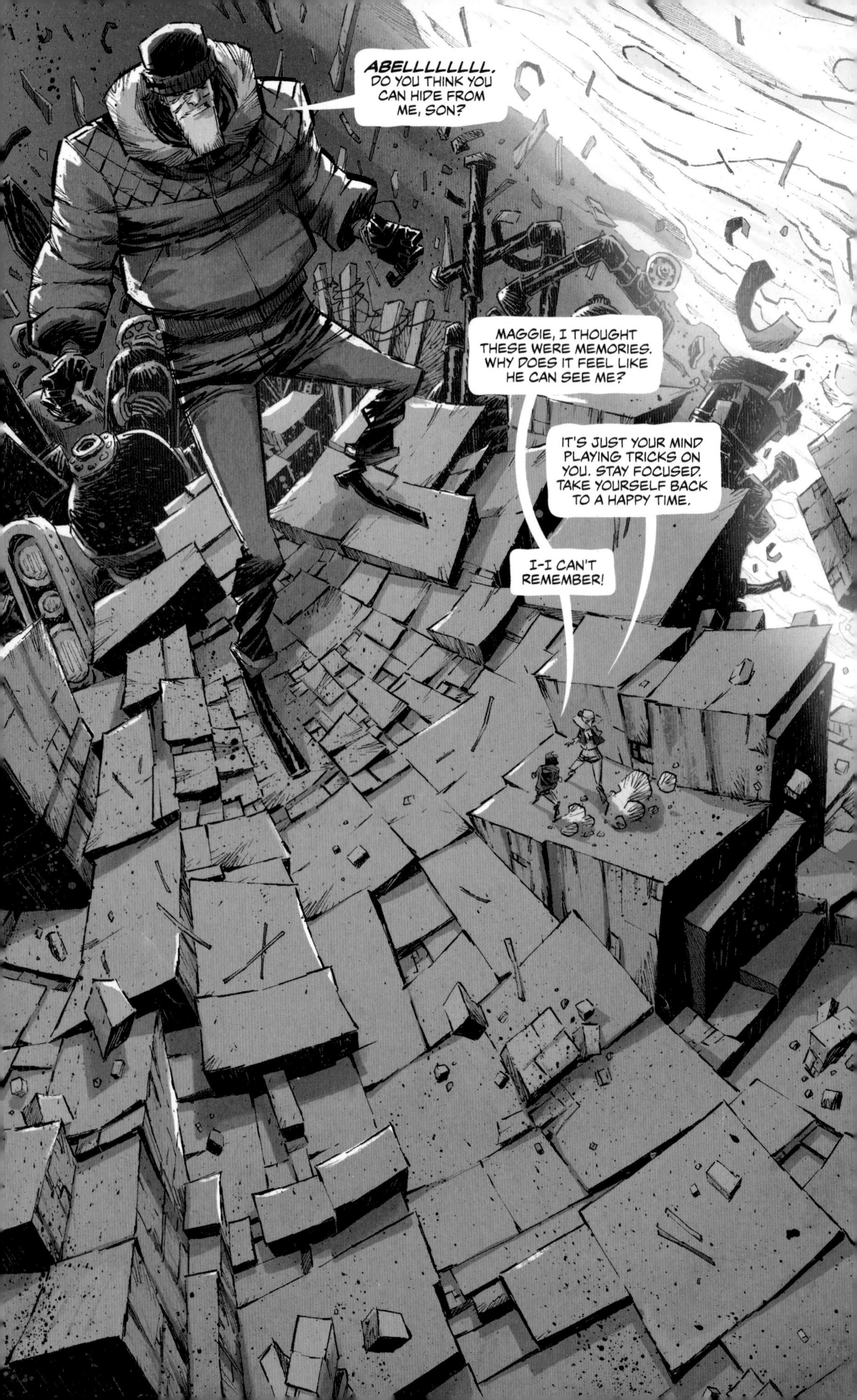
ABELLLLLLLL. DO YOU THINK YOU CAN HIDE FROM ME, SON?
MAGGIE, I THOUGHT THESE WERE MEMORIES. WHY DOES IT FEEL LIKE HE CAN SEE ME?
IT'S JUST YOUR MIND PLAYING TRICKS ON YOU. STAY FOCUSED. TAKE YOURSELF BACK TO A HAPPY TIME.
I-I CAN'T REMEMBER!

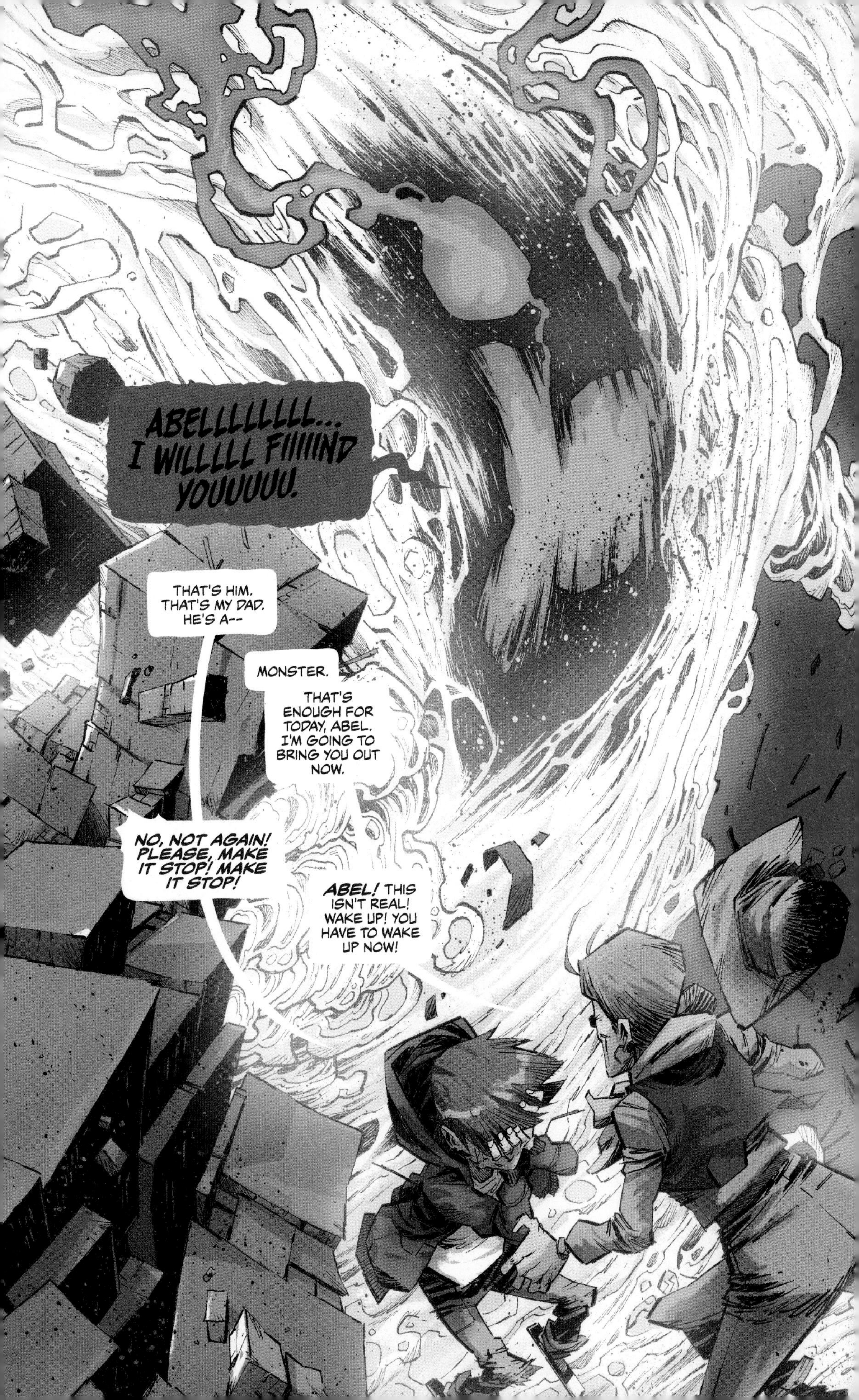
ABELLLLLLLL... I WILLLLL FIIIIIND YOUUUUU.
THAT'S HIM. THAT'S MY DAD. HE'S A--
MONSTER.
THAT'S ENOUGH FOR TODAY, ABEL. I'M GOING TO BRING YOU OUT NOW.
NO, NOT AGAIN! PLEASE, MAKE IT STOP! MAKE IT STOP!
ABEL! THIS ISN'T REAL! WAKE UP! YOU HAVE TO WAKE UP NOW!

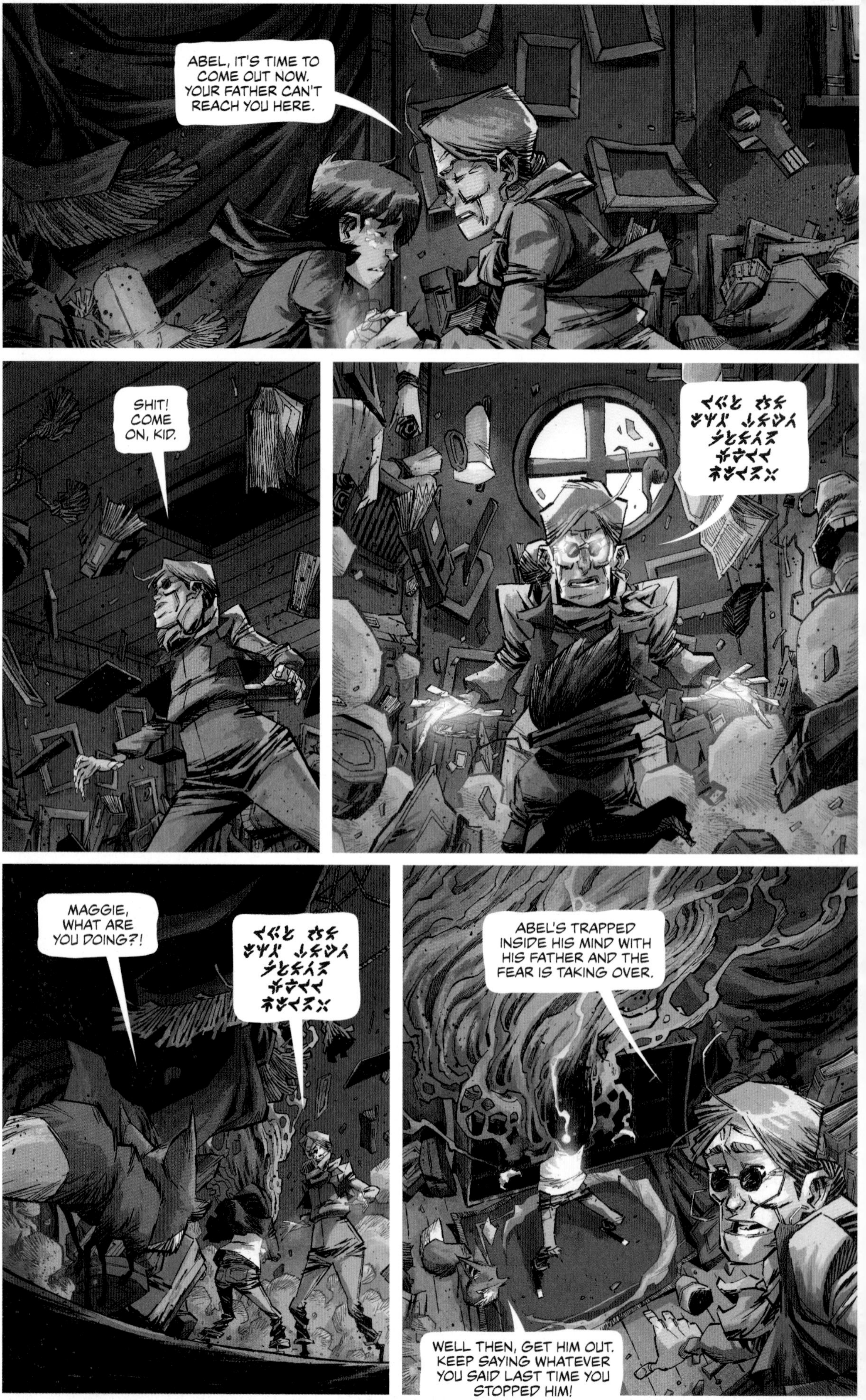
ABEL, IT'S TIME TO COME OUT NOW. YOUR FATHER CAN'T REACH YOU HERE.
SHIT! COME ON, KID.
MAGGIE, WHAT ARE YOU DOING?!
ABEL'S TRAPPED INSIDE HIS MIND WITH HIS FATHER AND THE FEAR IS TAKING OVER.
WELL THEN, GET HIM OUT. KEEP SAYING WHATEVER YOU SAID LAST TIME YOU STOPPED HIM!

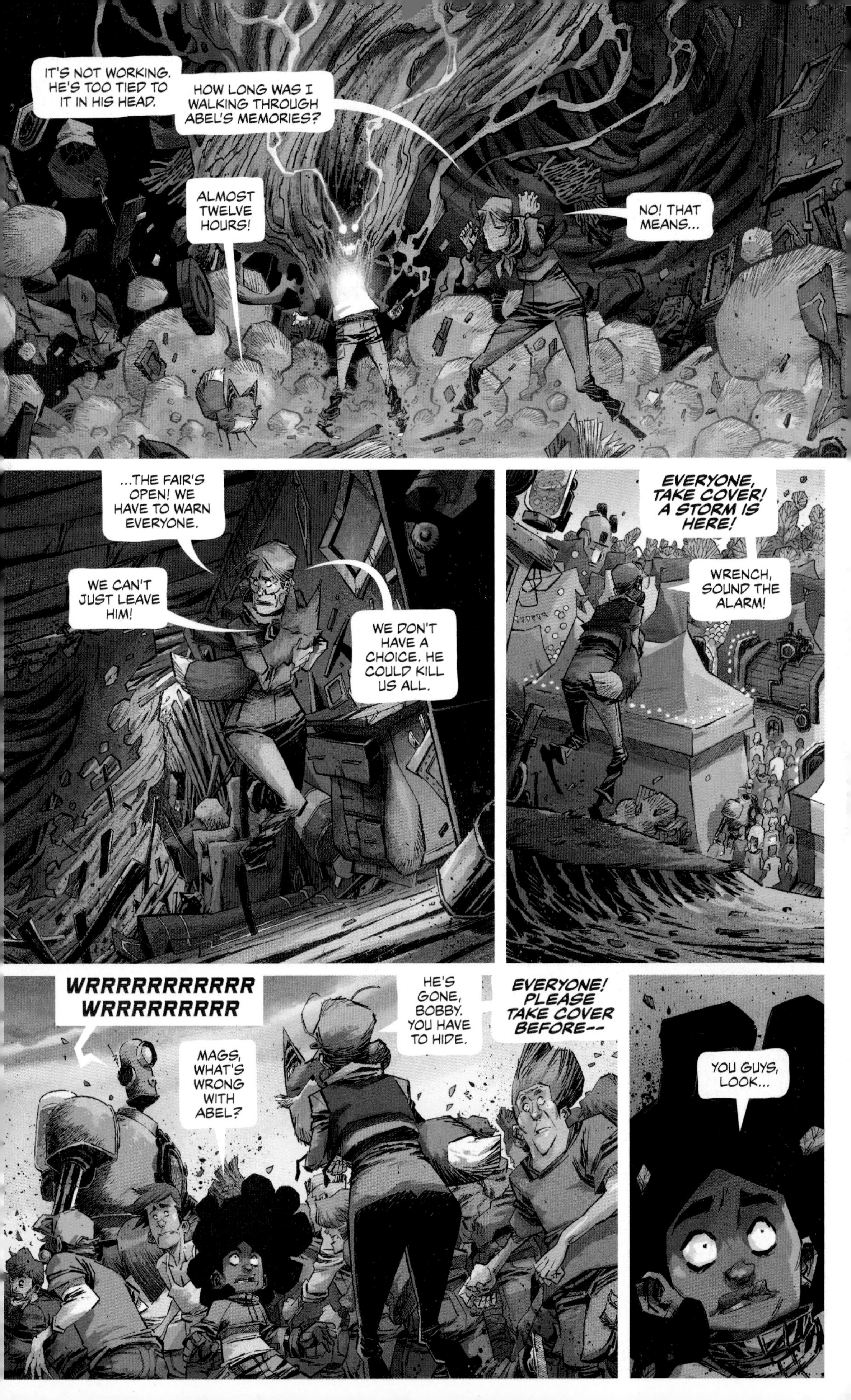
IT'S NOT WORKING. HE'S TOO TIED TO IT IN HIS HEAD.
HOW LONG WAS I WALKING THROUGH ABEL'S MEMORIES?
ALMOST TWELVE HOURS!
NO! THAT MEANS...
...THE FAIR'S OPEN! WE HAVE TO WARN EVERYONE.
WE CAN'T JUST LEAVE HIM!
WE DON'T HAVE A CHOICE. HE COULD KILL US ALL.
EVERYONE, TAKE COVER! A STORM IS HERE!
WRENCH, SOUND THE ALARM!
WRRRRRRRRRRR WRRRRRRRRR
MAGS, WHAT'S WRONG WITH ABEL?
HE'S GONE, BOBBY. YOU HAVE TO HIDE.
EVERYONE! PLEASE TAKE COVER BEFORE--
YOU GUYS, LOOK...

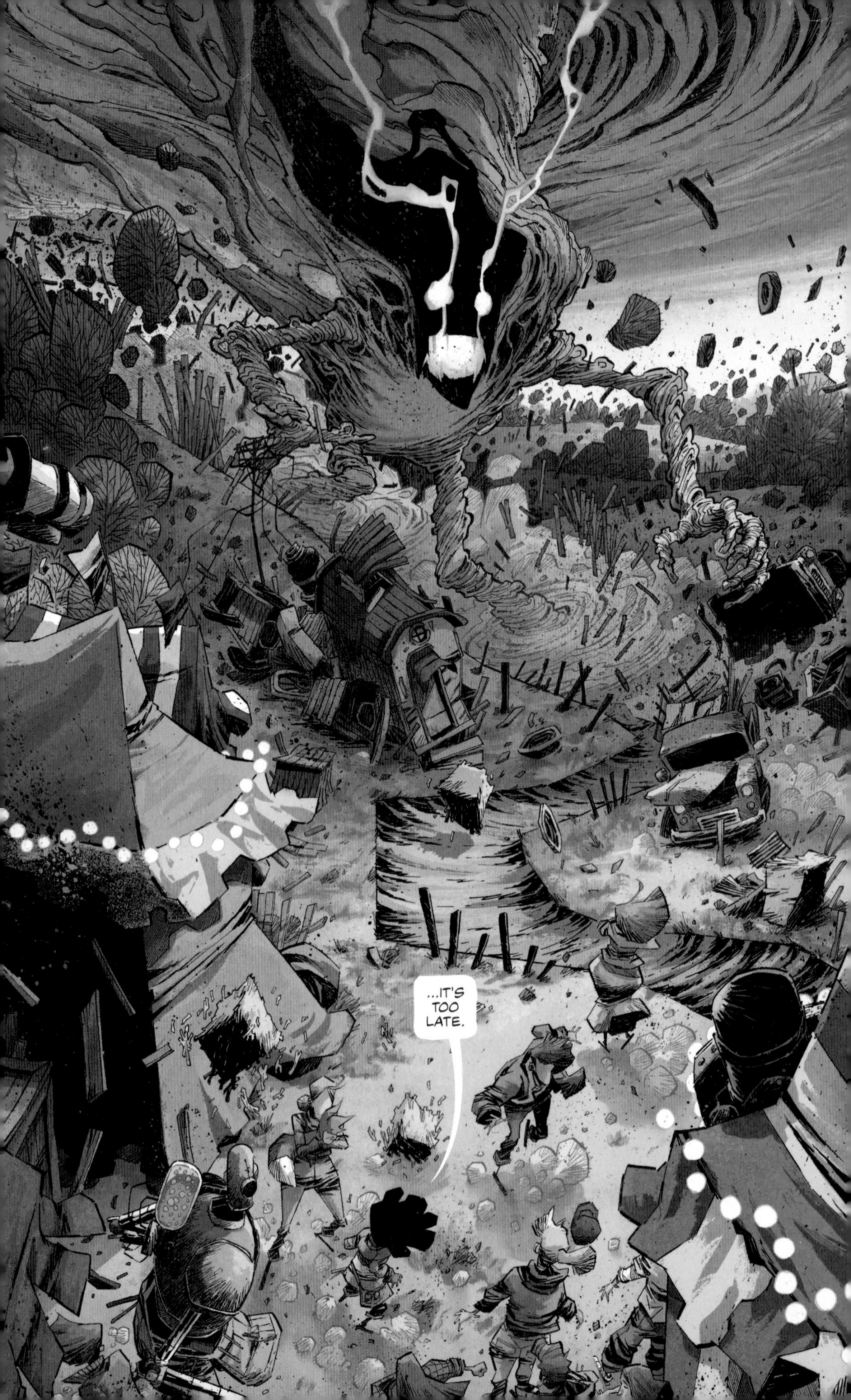
...IT'S TOO LATE.

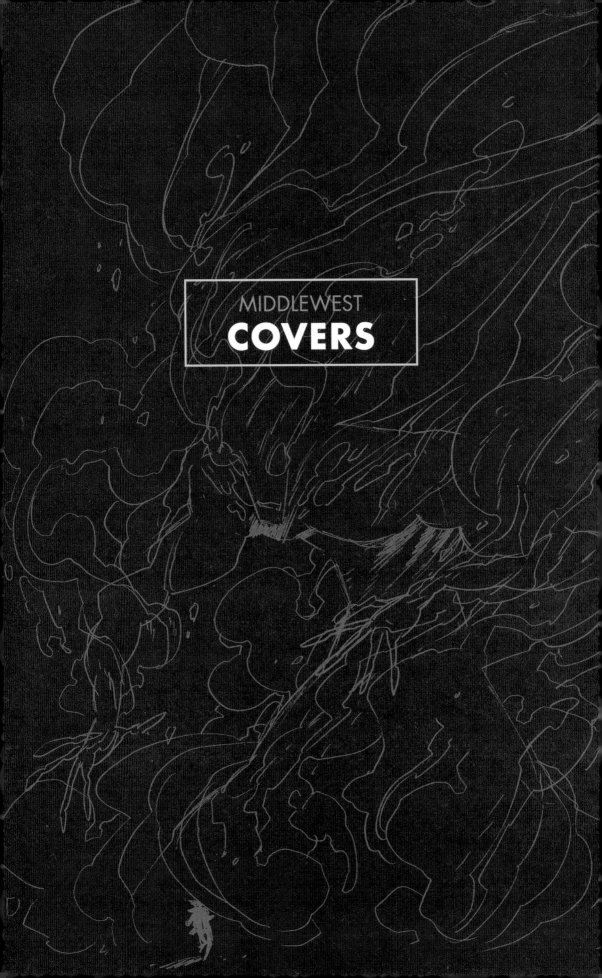

MIDDLEWEST
COVERS

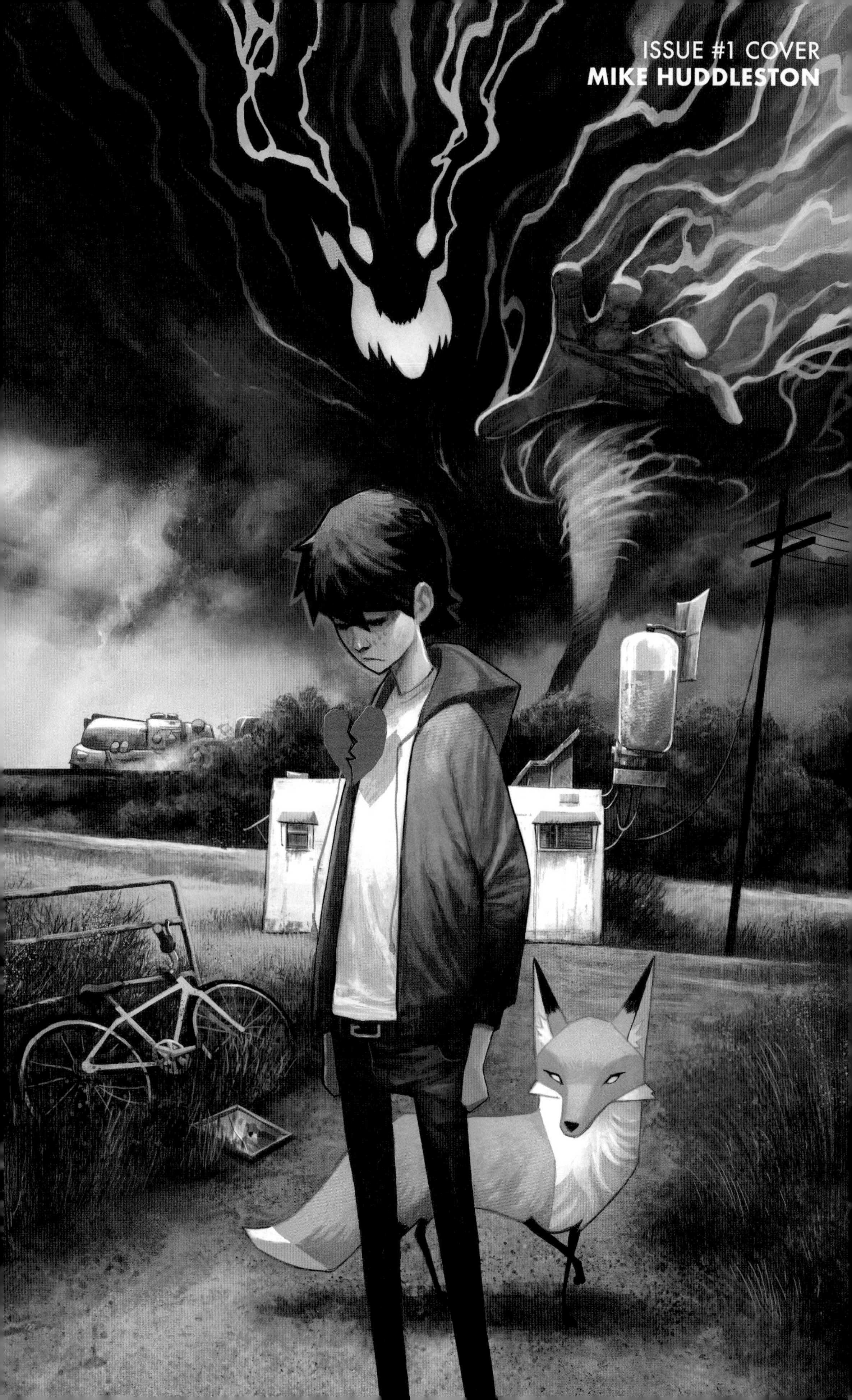

ISSUE #1 COVER
MIKE HUDDLESTON

ISSUE #2 COVER
MIKE HUDDLESTON

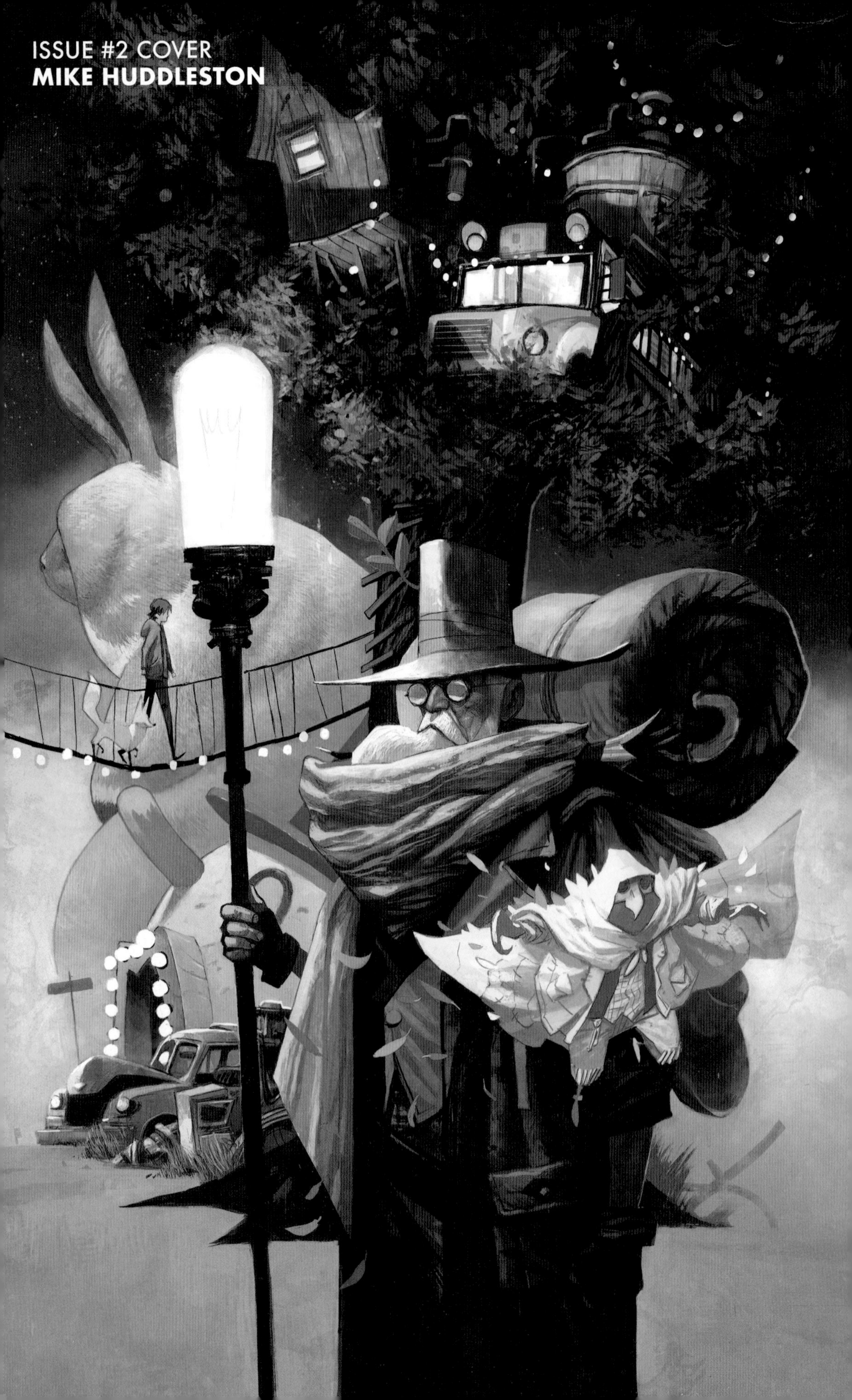

ISSUE #3 COVER
MIKE HUDDLESTON

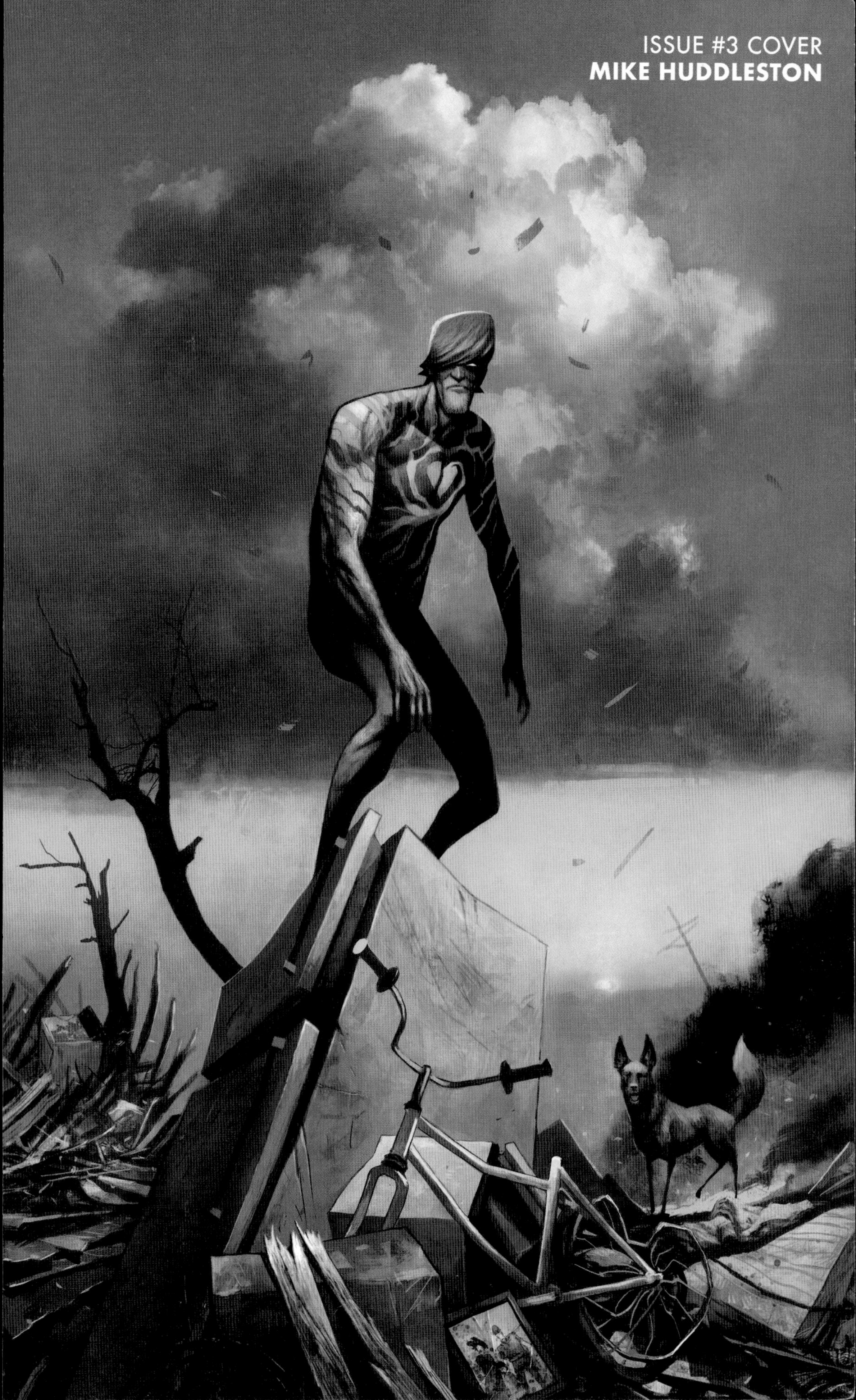

ISSUE #4 COVER
MIKE HUDDLESTON

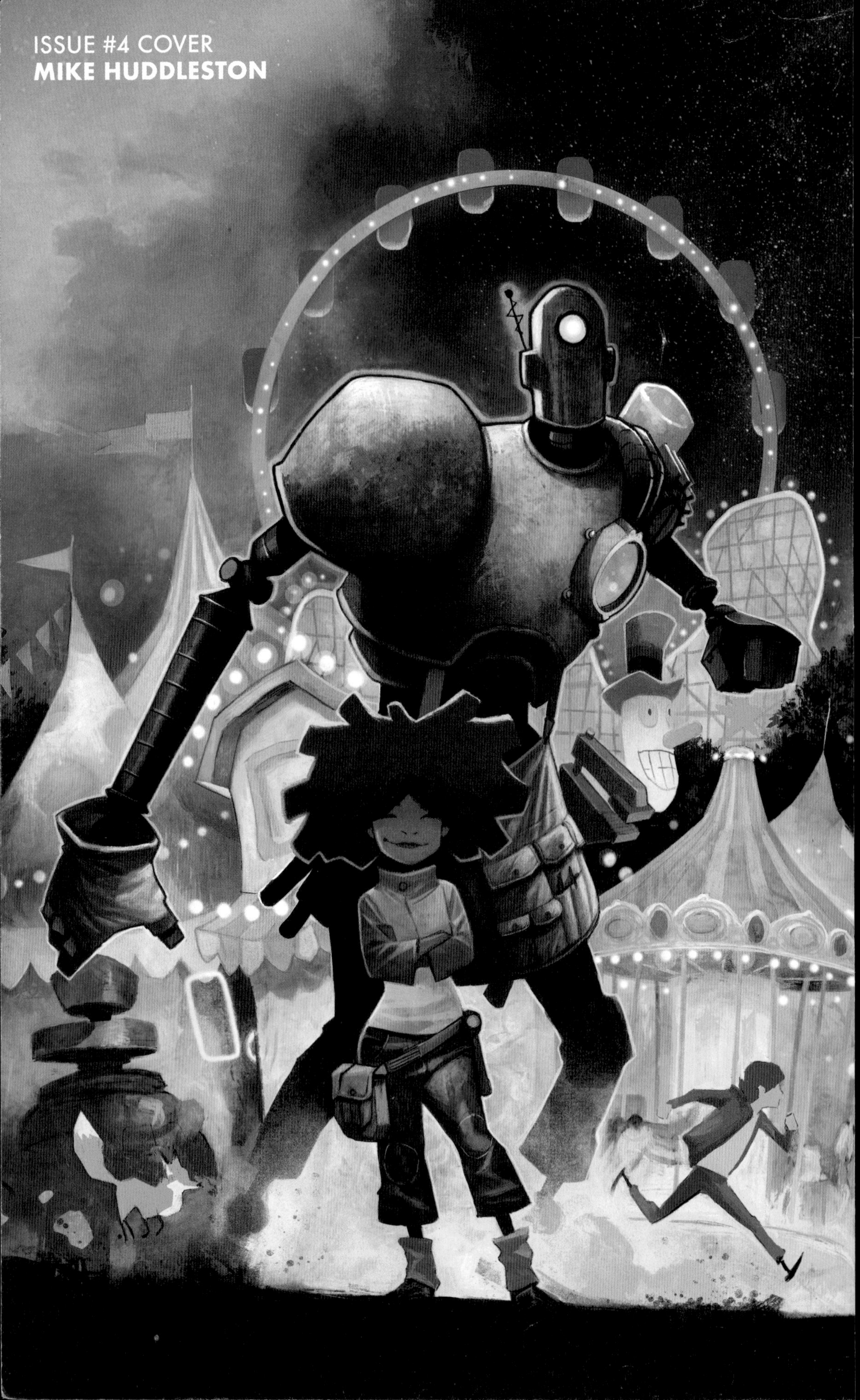

ISSUE #5 COVER
MIKE HUDDLESTON

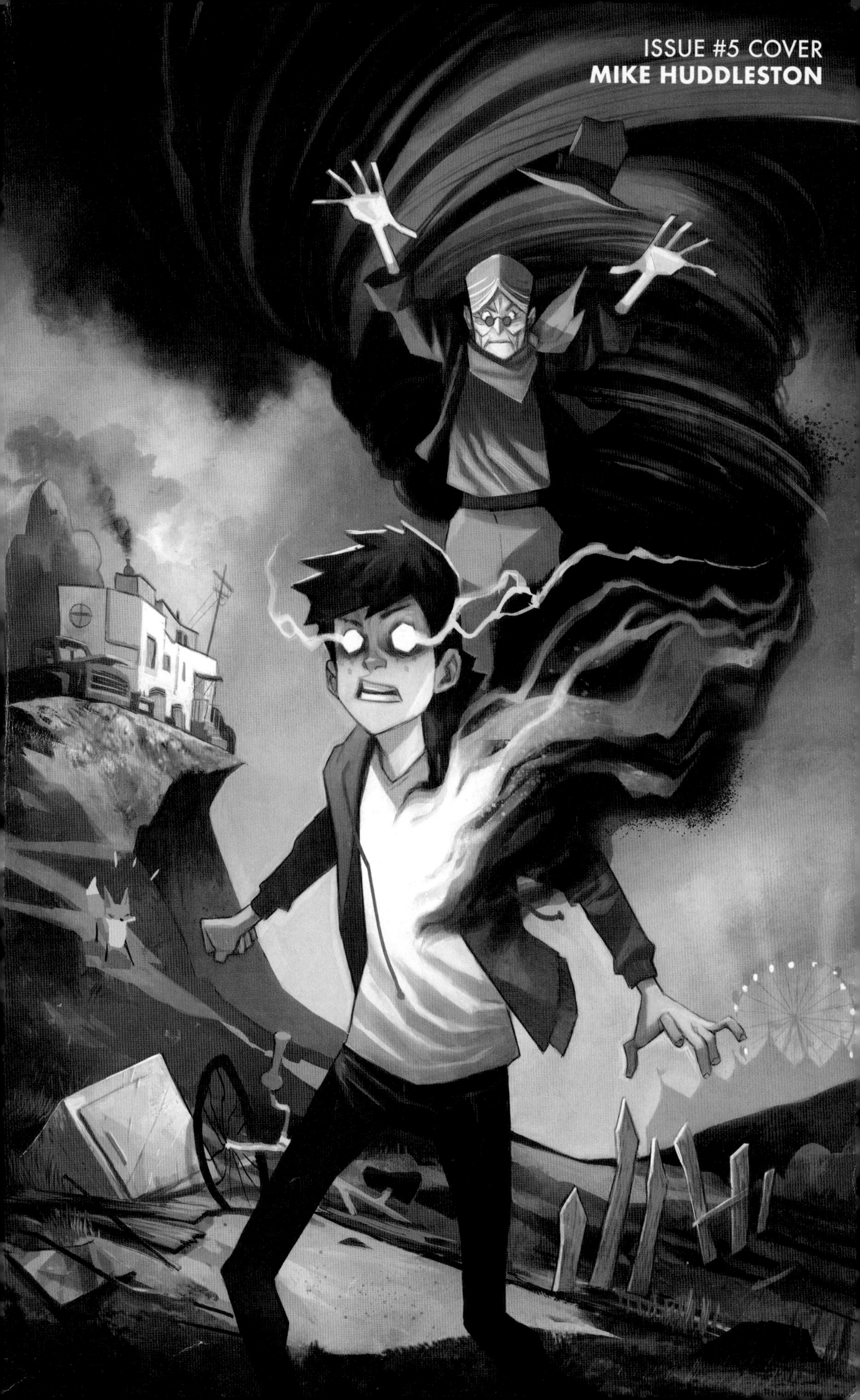

ISSUE #6 COVER
MIKE HUDDLESTON

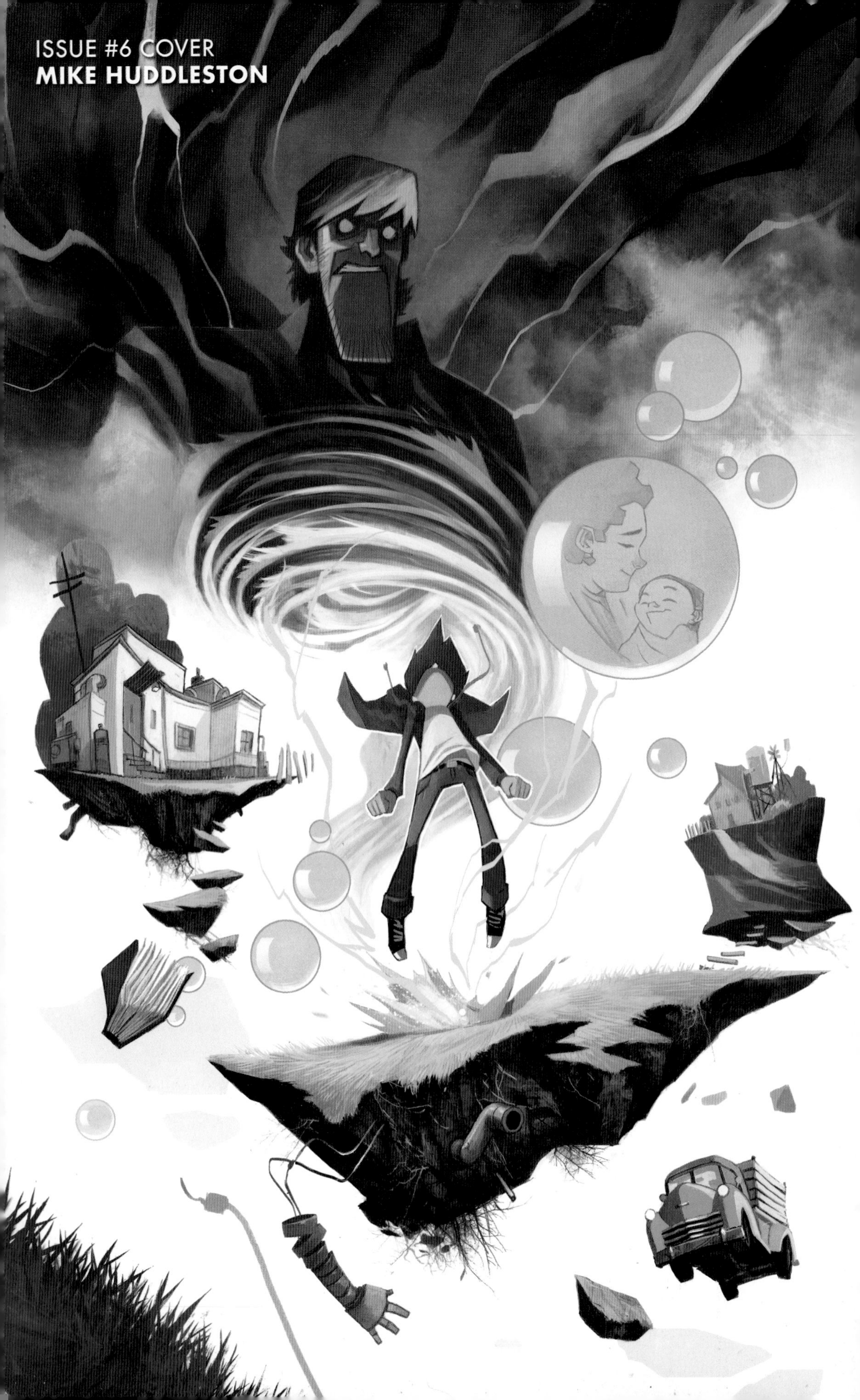